PRAISE FOR KENN[ETH JOHNSON'S]

FICTION

"Johnson takes a big gamble by telling such a complex tale [in *The Man of Legends*] invoking every genre imaginable while juggling distinct and deep characterizations. The bet pays off, resulting in a story that will be popular with book clubs and fun to discuss."

—Associated Press

"With *The Man of Legends* Kenneth Johnson has once again created a timeless tale that offers up adventure, suspense and romance all wrapped up tightly in a supernatural mystery."

—*Suspense Magazine*

"A century-spanning story of spirituality and the search for meaning in a very long life."

—*Kirkus Reviews*

"Johnson successfully draws the reader into the emotional turmoil that his characters experience. Indeed, one of the strengths of Johnson's writing is how much we come to care for the characters and their journeys . . . He is above all else a visually-oriented writer, and is intent on creating memorable visuals."

—Book Pleasures

"Johnson is especially effective . . . at introducing disparate, unrelated stories and slowly having them collide with one another throughout the course of the story."

—*The Pittsburgh Post-Gazette*

"Without question Kenneth Johnson is the closest our generation will come to the great Rod Serling. His understanding of the human mind has created some of the most developed and understood characters ever. When Kenneth Johnson puts something out, it is always quality."

—Scared Stiff Reviews

FILM

"The cerebral Kenneth Johnson, who created the [*Incredible Hulk*] series . . . went to great lengths to dramatize a cursed life—the kind chronicled in the novels of Victor Hugo, Robert Louis Stevenson and Mary Shelley."

—*The New York Times*

"*Alien Nation* is a bold move . . . Kenneth Johnson . . . creates a rich and fully invented world, and makes it pay off with well-developed characters and an interesting perspective on our own culture . . . It's innovative."

—*The Wall Street Journal*

"*Alien Nation* is first-rate entertainment. Most of the success probably has to do with the fact that it was written, produced and directed by Kenneth Johnson."

—*The Seattle Times*

"*V*—Victorious as sci-fi miniseries . . . Dazzling . . . An intelligent, imaginative, engrossing four-hour drama. *V* is a thought-provoking, sometimes shocking drama that keeps the viewer engaged."

—*The New York Daily News*

THE
DARWIN
VARIANT

ALSO BY KENNETH JOHNSON

The Man of Legends
V: The Second Generation
V: The Original Miniseries
An Affair of State

THE
DARWIN
VARIANT

KENNETH JOHNSON

"The force that through the green fuse drives the flower"
By Dylan Thomas, from THE POEMS OF DYLAN THOMAS, copyright ©1939 by New Directions Publishing Corp. Reprinted by permission of New Directions Publishing Corp. and by: David Higham Associates, Ltd., London.

Excerpts from ANIMAL FARM by George Orwell. Copyright 1946 by Sonia Brownell Orwell; Copyright ©renewed 1974 by Sonia Brownell Orwell. By permission of A M Heath & Co Ltd. Reprinted by permission of Houghton Mifflin Publishing Company. All rights reserved.

Imagine
Words and Music by John Lennon
©1971 (Renewed) LENONO MUSIC
All Rights Administered by DOWNTOWN DMP SONGS/DOWNTOWN MUSIC PUBLISHING LLC.
All Rights Reserved Used by Permission
Reprinted by Permission of Hal Leonard, LLC

Published by 47North, Seattle
www.apub.com

Amazon, the Amazon logo, and 47North are trademarks of Amazon.com, Inc., or its affiliates.

ISBN-13: 9781503954113 (hardcover)
ISBN-10: 1503954110 (hardcover)
ISBN-13: 9781503948884 (paperback)
ISBN-10: 1503948889 (paperback)

Cover design by Damon Freeman

Printed in the United States of America
First edition

For David and Barbara Welch
and the memories, laughter,
inspiration and love . . .

MISSION STATEMENT

It is an honor to have been chosen by the Smithsonian Institution to undertake this project as a documentarian. I have endeavored to create a thorough and detailed record of the eighteen months that quite likely will stand as the most startlingly brilliant, but also the most diabolically dangerous days in recorded human history.

This narrative has been assembled from personal diaries, depositions, court documents, material gathered and transcribed from security cameras, dash-cam and body-cam footage, cockpit cam, voice and flight data recorders and television broadcast archives, plus previously classified interagency communications including data, graphics, and text transmissions. Much information came from direct interviews with the principals, who were also encouraged to recall and express their personal feelings, emotions, and opinions. I've tried to faithfully transcribe their voices, dialects, and speech patterns exactly as I heard them. The original audio and video recordings, along with all other relevant materials, are archived at the Library of Congress.

I am indebted to NASA, its Planetary Defense Coordination Office and Jet Propulsion Laboratory, the Johns Hopkins University Applied Physics Laboratory, the State of Georgia and its police forces, the Federal Bureau of Investigation, and the US Departments of Justice and Defense for lending their full and honest cooperation. Also deserving at least honorable mention are the Central Intelligence and National Security Agencies, despite the many unhelpful redactions in material they supplied.

In particular I must express my extreme gratitude to research scientist Dr. Susan Perry of the Centers for Disease Control and Prevention in Atlanta, and Katharine McLane, a native of the small town of Ashton, Georgia, and only fourteen years old when the menace began. Their unique personal perspectives were vital and inform this narrative most deeply.

These events would never have been accurately recounted if those two incredibly courageous people—and a great many of their brave compatriots—had not valued the future of humanity over their own personal safety and their lives.

This work is respectfully dedicated to them and to the heroic souls who did not survive.

K.J.
Palo Alto, California

1

ANOMALY

The Documentarian...

Something was coming.

If it could have been observed from a vantage point out in the silent, primeval darkness beyond the planet Mars, it initially would have appeared to be just another star. But it would have grown steadily into a larger smudge of light, slowly taking on the distinctive, classical shape of a comet.

As it came closer the spectacle would have become monumental. The head of the comet was a Mount Everest–sized mass of space rock and ice, its surface sparkling, churning with cyclonic intensity, buffeted by the invisible solar wind that gusted particles out behind to form its radiant tail.

The teeming ice crystals, swirling furiously in the electromagnetic solar gale, would have seemed frantically animated, madly alive. If their primal molecular voices could have been heard in the vacuum of space, they might have sounded like a trillion dangerous insects buzzing in a cacophony of discord.

We know now that deep within the comet's rock and ice something was indeed living. Frozen solid in the near–absolute zero cold of inter-stellar space, it was nonetheless alive. And waiting.

The comet, with its gossamer tail trailing a thousand miles, would have been moving at astonishing speed: more than thirty-four kilometers per second. Forty-five times faster than a bullet. As the comet neared the inner solar system, the menace it represented was still unknown. But that was about to change.

Along with the course of human history.

Concetta Cordaro, PhD, 32, astrophysicist...

That November night I smiled as I looked up at the huge steel dome curving ninety feet over my head. As a ten-year-old in Cleveland, I'd clutched my thirty-dollar telescope, gazed deeply into the chilly night sky over Lake Erie, and fantasized about someday working at the great observatory atop California's Mount Palomar. I had no idea it would take twenty years and be such a difficult climb.

The world's most powerful telescopes, the "Big Eyes," were greatly coveted by the Boys. Climbing into the viewing capsule at Palomar or Mauna Kea was a measurement of machismo. We female astronomers laughingly referred to it as "penile enhancement of astronomical proportions." Even now at the end of the second decade of the twenty-first century, it was easier for a woman to become a toreador than to get time at Palomar. But after thirteen months on the waiting list, here I was. And the weather was perfect.

I smiled with pride and delight, sipping my Constant Comment. The tea's orangey fragrance was friendly, and the *Star Trek* mug was warm between my hands. I looked upward at the sixty-foot-long open-girder cylinder that cradled the magnificent two-hundred-inch mirror of the Hale reflecting telescope. The huge mechanism weighed five hundred tons but was so superbly balanced that only a one-twelfth horsepower motor was required to move it. My gaze traveled along the beautiful instrument, then across the gracious curve of the dome to the shutter, a ten-yard-wide vertical opening through which the telescope looked out toward the dark heavens beyond. For six nights that November, the Big

Eye at Palomar was mine. Every time I thought about it, a bubble of pure elation rose up in me. I was savoring every single moment.

Right outside the door to the Palomar control room was a poster of the Milky Way with a "You Are Here" arrow pointing at the tiny dot which humorously represented our sun, one of a hundred billion stars. I smiled as I passed it and entered the control center. In the cluttered, piecemeal laboratory, over the years new equipment had been sandwiched in and jerry-rigged to interface with the quaint, older equipment. Some of it dated all the way back to 1948, when the telescope first became operational. Cables stretched chaotically through open overhead racks from one console to another, as computers and other equipment had been added, layered in, upgraded, and supplemented over the years. I particularly liked how fellow astronomers had humanized the room with personal notes, Post-its, and cartoons.

I plugged in the old dented kettle to make some fresh tea, then peeled off the new red parka I'd rewarded myself with for finally achieving Palomar. Beneath it was my favorite MIT sweatshirt, well-worn proudly since my first year in the doctorate program.

The room hummed and breathed with the various small cooling fans built into the equipment. The steady, reliable sounds were comforting. And, excitingly, they connected me to the infinity of stars beyond.

I brushed my dark hair back as I settled in at a binocular viewing device. I was using it to compare a digital photograph I'd just exposed with another photo I'd taken the previous night. But looking through the viewer, I frowned immediately. Something felt wrong.

"Wait. What?" I whispered.

My view through the eyepieces showed a narrow field of stars. As I clicked from one plate to the other and back, the points of light all remained stationary. Except one. I'd expected that. For the last several days I'd been in the midst of doing a spectrographic analysis of DF Tau, an intriguing binary star system 140 parsecs distant in the constellation Taurus. I knew that Avery's Comet was due to pass through the foreground of my field of view, and had spotted it in my photos two days prior. But now it did not seem to be in the location where it should have been. I attached a tiny red locator arrow to it, whispering to the image, "I don't think you're supposed to be *there*."

I carefully logged in the coordinates of the comet's anomalous position and used Palomar's ultra-high-speed 200 Gbps connection to search the MIT computer. I found the baseline of Avery's well-documented orbit around our sun. Then I compared it to what I saw. The difference was disturbing. Unless I was mistaken, something was definitely wrong. The comet seemed outside its historic trajectory. I stared at the screen for a moment, then pushed a speed dial number, frowning. The man's voice was sleepy. "Yeah?"

"Gary? Hi, it's Connie up at Palomar. I'm on the Hale two-hundred-inch, and I've picked up an anomaly with Comet Avery. I mean, I can't believe it's right, but I'd like to jump on the JPL massive server and check some orbital dynamics projections."

"Hang on," he said, yawning. I heard him tapping a keyboard. "Hey, you still owe me another movie, Con." I was barely listening, preoccupied by the unsettling image on my viewer.

". . . What?"

"A movie."

"Soon as I get back, Gare." I was impatient. "Would you please—"

"Yep. Here y'go."

In an eyeblink a stream of figures and graphs from JPL's powerful mainframe suddenly wiped across my large screen. Then curving lines appeared, representing the orbits of the inner planets.

I carefully entered the coordinates of Avery's position yesterday and then today's set. The code set to work doing a UOD, updated orbit determination.

A new line began to creep across my screen, representing the trajectory that the out-of-place smudge on my photographic plate would likely follow. It arced from its present location in the vicinity beyond

Mars and slowly traced across my screen toward the inner solar system. I knew the potent JPL computer was taking into account all the various gravitational factors acting upon the comet as it crossed through space.

Then I slowly began to have a premonition of where it was headed, felt my blood getting chilly. ". . . No . . ." I whispered, "No, no, no . . ."

On the other end of the phone, Gary sensed my concern. "What's wrong? . . . Connie?"

But I was speechless as I watched the updating trajectory on my monitor continue its curving path inward. I stared at the screen, growing increasingly incredulous. Frightened.

Behind me the boiling teakettle began to scream.

The Documentarian...

Three days later an old Toyota pickup was barely holding together as it rumbled much too fast down the dusty backcountry road in Bangladesh. It ran between the rice paddies and thick, verdant, subtropical vegetation on either side. The truck's paint had long ago been replaced by rust, the back window had no glass, the fenders were badly battered, and the bald left front tire threatened to come off each time it slammed violently into yet another pothole on the sunbaked road.

The driver, Daruk, a wiry Bangladeshi wearing a white lace skullcap, leaned on the horn, beep beep beeping as he wheeled into the small village of old stucco houses with corrugated metal roofs on the northern outskirts of Kalaganj. He dodged between lines of elementary schoolchildren. Like the other village people, some were dressed colorfully; others were more ragged and emaciated. The speeding truck sent scrawny chickens flapping aside as Daruk drove toward the makeshift hospital set up in military-style tents on a field along one edge of the impoverished village.

Lying in the back of the truck was an unconscious, painfully thin seven-year-old Bangladeshi girl. A clear oxygen mask was affixed over her face. A thirty-three-year-old Caucasian woman knelt over her, administering urgent CPR compressions. The woman's T-shirt was soaked with sweat. From her ponytailed auburn hair to her faded jeans, she was grimy, covered with the dust of the road.

Dr. Susan Perry, 33, CDC epidemiologist...

I was pretty near exhausted. I paused the compressions on little Aniha to check quickly—and vainly—for a carotid pulse, then started cardiac massage again, pumping hard on her frail chest while I simultaneously scanned the compound ahead. I felt a touch of relief, seeing Lauren run out of the ramshackle field-hospital tents toward us. Dr. Lauren Fletcher was twenty years my senior and always reminded me of another vintage Lauren: Bacall. I was continually amazed how she managed to look imperiously blonde and attractive even in the jungle, even when she was near exhaustion, like I knew she was now. I shouted to her, "Cardiac arrest! The O₂ ran out a mile back. I was making one last pass through Tarali and—"

"You gave her CPR all the way from there to *here*!?"

"Me and the Bee Gees."

Lauren pulled herself up onto the truck. "The Bee Gees?"

I nodded, keeping up the compressions while gasping, "Pump, pump, pump, pump, '*Stay*-ing A-*live*.' The *per*-fect, *rhy*-thm, *per*-fect *song*."

Lauren pulled a syringe from her EM kit, tapping it to disperse the air bubbles. "Jesus, honey, you really *are* out to save the world!" She injected the comatose child's bone-thin arm, calling the dose, "One mil of epi." Then she shouted toward the open front of our field hospital, "Where's the damned O₂?!"

"Coming, Mum!" replied Kindur, a small native man who hurried from the tent toward us. I loved Kindur. His name meant "big and strong," but like so many of his chronically undernourished people, he was anything but. He more than made up for it, however, with his extreme dedication and hospitality. When I'd arrived three weeks earlier, he and his wife, Jasima, along with their preteens, Mayura and Dheeraj, had taken me into their very modest home and under their wing.

Like most Bangladeshis their clothing was an eclectic mix of Western Hemisphere and East Indian styles with many hand-me-down T-shirts, patched jeans, and colorful saris that had been lovingly maintained. Two of our local assistants followed right behind Kindur with a stretcher.

"Let's bag her," Lauren directed Kindur, and he handed up a fresh oxygen mask to her. Lauren clapped it over Aniha's narrow little face and began pumping the bag that forced O_2 into the girl's chest, saying, "Y'know, Susan, I was already up to my ears and then had to cover for you not being here."

I'd expected that and kept up my CPR. "Sorry."

"You shouldn't have gone off on your own like that . . . Again."

Okay, okay. I heard her the first time and knew she was right, but if I hadn't gone, this poor little kid would have died already. And I feared that she had anyway. I laid my ear on her little bony chest, whispering urgently, "Come on, Aniha."

"Let me try," Lauren said briskly as she slid into position opposite me, and Kindur took over pumping the O_2 bag. Lauren expertly assumed the CPR, asking with tired annoyance, "Why the hell didn't she get inoculated when we were up there?"

"Her father'd kept her back." I slumped momentarily against the hot metal inside the truck, trying to catch my breath. "He wanted to make sure boys in the area got treated first."

"Even if his daughter died," Lauren grumbled. "Sometimes I hate people."

Lauren continued the compressions as I leaned down closer to the fragile girl's narrow, dusty face, pressing my index and middle fingers on her carotid artery. "Still no pulse. Shit. Come on, Aniha. Please!"

The child suddenly shivered. "Oops. I think she heard you, Susan," Lauren said, easing up on the compressions as I monitored the throbbing artery.

"Feels steady . . . About sixty."

Lauren smiled, said lightly, "Guess she just needed the master's touch." I glanced at her as she gave me her patented wink, implying that she was just kidding. But I knew better. Lauren was always pleased whenever her personal involvement did the trick. Aniha coughed and gasped in a deep breath. I looked down at her as her dusty eyelids flickered open.

Aniha Banerjee, 7...

I am most clearly remembering that moment of awakening. It was bright, very bright, but most cloudy, hard to see. First I was thinking I had died and passed into the next world. Slowly I could better see a face close to mine that I had never seen before. I thought I must be looking at a goddess. Her face was most beautiful. Sunlight sparkled in her red hair. It seemed like magic light. Her eyes were the color of the blue sky. She touched my cheek gently, and her voice was most soft when she whispered, "Easy, Aniha, easy."

And then, most sweetly, she laughed. And I saw her eyes have tears come into them. I knew then that I was to be alive.

Dr. Susan Perry...

Aniha gazed into my eyes. Then smiled slightly. Seeing her revive made me laugh again spontaneously. I sniffed and wiped away my happy tears. Lauren condescended to gift me with her acerbic smile and a head-shake for my stubborn tenacity. I was just proud that we'd saved Aniha.

An ancient FIAT that had once been red sputtered into the compound. It had followed behind us. Aniha's mother jumped out. Seeing her daughter alive, she was overwhelmed. She shouted praises to the gods. Kindur and the assistants eased the little girl onto the stretcher. I gave Aniha a final squeeze of encouragement as Lauren instructed Kindur to get her on a Lactated Ringer's drip; we'd sort out later what other meds she might need. Aniha's mother grasped my hand and pressed it to her bowed forehead with utmost gratitude. The best reward for any doctor.

Lauren hopped off the back of the old truck as I painfully unbent my own knees that were on fire with cramps.

Lauren helped me get my feet to the ground. "You realize she'll have to name her first daughter after us."

"Not bad," I smiled. "Susan Lauren Banerjee."

Lauren cocked an eyebrow. "Well, I was thinking more like, Lauren Susan." We exchanged smiles and a genteel high-five as we walked through the dust toward the brown military tents of the Doctors Without Borders field hospital. Lauren continued, "Been checking the stats. Looks like we've broken the back of this cholera."

"I hope so. God, I must've inoculated a thousand kids yesterday."

"Eight hundred thirty-two, actually. I did nine hundred and eighty."

I glanced wryly at my trim superior. "But who's counting, huh?"

"You're closing in on me, kid."

"What can I say? You're a great role model. But a tough act to follow."

Lauren smiled, as though she appreciated the compliment. And its accuracy.

At our home base, the Centers for Disease Control and Prevention in Atlanta, Dr. Lauren Fletcher was the preeminent research scientist. Dr. Ernest Levering was the actual head of the CDC, but was more administrator than scientist. Within the medical and scientific communities, Lauren was regarded as the top of the CDC pyramid. She rarely went into the field, but did so occasionally to keep her own skills honed. And keep her subordinates like me on our toes.

During our time together in Bangladesh, I'd picked up more details about Lauren's history. She was born the third child of five in a pious lower-middle-class family, but when she was sixteen, her revered older brother died of typhoid fever, and her religious beliefs evaporated. They were replaced by a burning anger. Lauren developed a fierce determination to fight back: she was driven to medicine not so much by a desire to save the lives of patients as she was by a desire to conquer diseases. She felt proud that she hadn't wasted a moment in her life, but achieved an intense focus while still a teenager and had never wavered. Her single-mindedness made her something of a loner and supported her ambition to ascend to the top of the medical profession.

With her excelling intellect Lauren had graduated first in her class at Columbia premed then at Harvard Medical. Even during residency she had done pioneering epidemiological research that led to substantial breakthroughs and caught the attention of many prominent physicians. She was courted by the CDC, and after joining it, her efficient, no-nonsense field research made her particularly effective. She moved swiftly up through the ranks. When a tuberculosis outbreak threatened Chicago in 2004, Lauren headed the team that contained it, and her face was soon familiar to millions watching TV network news as the CDC's on-the-scene spokesperson.

Thereafter Lauren became the go-to expert whenever the media had a question regarding medicine and particularly her specialty, viral disease. Her ability to explain complex concepts clearly and succinctly, plus her elegant attractiveness, made Dr. Lauren Fletcher a much sought-after interviewee. She also handled press conferences and mass conference calls to alert the media about outbreaks. Though she often dismissed such appearances as inconsequential, I sensed that Lauren privately enjoyed the limelight, even cultivated it with the same great care and political manipulation she brought to her scientific career. Like others who worked closest to Dr. Fletcher and who recognized this thread of egoism weaving through all her efforts, I accepted it as common and permissible among those with Lauren's obvious talents, knowledge, and skill at handling people. During epidemiological emergencies she was masterful at guiding officials and the public through dangerous, even lethal, situations.

I learned firsthand that Dr. Fletcher did not suffer fools, myself sometimes included. She was also very open about the fact that both of her brief marriages had ended in divorce. Lauren joked that she couldn't blame her exes' departures, saying she was just too opinionated for anyone to live with on a full-time basis.

At fifty-three Lauren was at the top of her game and her profession. But at the same time she always kept a close eye on young upstarts rising beneath her. A couple of our colleagues had quietly told me that Lauren recognized in me a talent approaching her own. I was flattered, but doubted Lauren thought that. I did recognize, however, that sincere personal warmth and empathy never seemed to be among Lauren's strong suits or qualities she prized. There were numerous times when she needled me about being "too touchy-feely"—as she put it—to become the ideal physician-scientist I might have were I more reserved, clinical, and objective. Also, like many shrewd and successful people, Lauren never took anyone at face value, but rather she expected others to be equally as sly as she could be to achieve her ends.

As we followed the others into the triage tent in the Bangladesh emergency camp that morning, Kindur waved his lean hand urgently to get our attention. "Dr. Lauren, Dr. Susan, look, look!" He was pointing to an antiquated, thick first-generation flat-screen TV sitting precariously on some medicine crates. Kindur's expression was greatly agitated.

On the screen, CNN International was showing views of Palomar Observatory, orbital charts, and then a live press conference room crammed with international reporters and camera crews. We caught a CNN reporter midsentence saying, "And increasing speculation across the internet about some astronomical discovery that's been made in the last two or three days, but NASA, JPL, and others have remained closedmouthed, noting only that they have been reviewing and carefully examining all pertinent information. Moments ago WikiLeaks posted that a source characterized as 'unofficial but informed' said that 'if confirmed it would likely not be good news.'"

Lauren and I traded a glance as the reporter continued. "The White House has only said that the administration will have no comment until the exact situation has been verified and announced here at NASA. I'm speaking to you from the assembly room at NASA headquarters on E Street in Washington, DC. Reporters began gathering here some twenty-two hours ago. Several times we've been told to expect an announcement shortly, but it's now just past midnight eastern time and so far . . ." The reporter paused when there came the sound of activity in the background that caused him to turn and continue, "And now . . . someone is entering and—"

A woman about my age was being ushered into the crowded room along with several officials who guided her toward the small platform in front. They all had ID badges hanging around their necks. The reporter said, "I believe that the dark-haired woman entering may be Dr. Concetta Cordaro, the young astronomer who is rumored to have made the discovery. She's being shepherded by several NASA personnel."

A bespectacled gray-haired gentleman in a white shirt with sleeves rolled up stepped onto the platform and up to the cluster of microphones on the podium. Watching the old TV in Bangladesh, I noted his expression was somber. "Thanks for your patience. If we could all just . . ." The shuffling and movement of the gathering settled. "Yes . . . Thank you very much. I'm Robert LaPorta, an associate administrator here at NASA. One of our respected colleagues, Dr. Concetta Cordaro,"—he nodded in the direction of the dark-haired young woman, and there was a flutter of clicking camera shutters and strobe flashes—"working under the auspices of her alma mater, the Massachusetts Institute of Technology, was doing spectrographic research at the Palomar Mountain observatory three days ago when she unexpectedly made a startling discovery." LaPorta paused. For a moment it seemed that he was unclear about how exactly to continue. Finally he said, "I think it's best to let Dr. Cordaro explain . . ." He looked again in her direction, and the camera panned to focus on her close-up. She looked like someone facing her own execution.

Concetta Cordaro...

The room was a blur. I hadn't had more than a few minutes of sleep in three days. Now the heat from the TV lights and the humid mass of people crowded into the room was suffocating. I felt like I was sleepwalking through a nightmare.

Dr. Susan Perry...

Lauren said, "My God, she looks blitzed." Kindur and our other Bangladeshi aides who were gathered beside us nodded agreement as we watched the staticky image carefully. The close-up of the young astronomer revealed dark circles beneath her eyes. She appeared completely bedraggled; her dark brown hair was clumped back into a loose bun. She had that sleep-deprived look I knew very well, I'd seen it in the mirror myself when I'd been surviving solely on double-shot caffeine injections. Her veneer seemed paper thin. I empathized with her, having faced my share of press conferences where I'd been completely strung out and exhausted yet had to deliver terrible news about deadly viral outbreaks. I read from Dr. Cordaro's expression that whatever information she was about to reveal was dire.

She set her laptop on the podium, looked down at the screen, then took a breath, trying to control her nerves. "First let me say that I am deeply indebted to all my learned colleagues here at NASA, at MIT, JPL, Cambridge, the Applied Physics Lab of Johns Hopkins, and the many other universities with whom we've been in touch. I'm also grateful to the dozens of my fellow astronomers and astrophysicists across America and around the world who have spent the last seventy-two hours in constant communication and teleconferencing with us. Their combined, exhaustive, and extraordinary efforts in checking and rechecking my initial computations have confirmed my initial calculations are—"

"Calculations about *what*?" an impatient reporter shouted.

Dr. Cordaro remained collected. "Avery's Comet is about ten kilometers in diameter, roughly the size of Mount Everest. Like other comets it's composed of rock or iron and ice. It's been tracked by astronomers for over four hundred years, and its orbital dynamics and trajectory are extremely well documented."

"But now the bad news?" Lauren muttered grimly. I glanced over and saw her dark eyes riveted on the screen. When I looked back at the TV, Concetta Cordaro was taking a breath.

"I was doing a spectrographic analysis of DF Tau, a binary star system in the constellation Taurus, the bull, which is on the ecliptic. That's the center of a band we call the zodiac where the sun, moon, planets, and most comets are always seen to move. Though Avery's Comet had no bearing on my research, I knew that it would pass through my field of view, and it did. Let me illustrate this for you."

She tapped her laptop, and an image appeared on the large video screen behind her. It was a photo in which a dozen stars of varying brightness appeared against the blackness of space. "These are stars in the middle of Taurus. The brightest is DF Tau, the binary I'm studying. It's four hundred fifty-seven light-years from Earth." A small yellow box appeared on the screen labeling it. "And this smudge above it is a foreground object which is very much closer. It is Comet Avery."

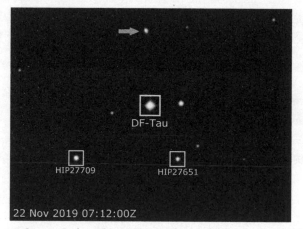

Courtesy Concetta Cordaro, PhD, MIT; Uday Shankar & Justin Atchison, JHUAPL

With a click she attached a pointer arrow to the smudge. "In this shot, it is at a distance of forty-one million miles. It's moving at a speed of roughly thirty-four kilometers per second, or about seventy-six thousand miles per hour. This is the first of three photos taken one night apart, beginning six days ago. Now here's the second photo."

Courtesy Concetta Cordaro, PhD, MIT; Uday Shankar & Justin Atchison, JHUAPL

It appeared as she continued, "You can see all the dots of light are in the same place except one. The comet." She clicked back and forth between the photos, and the comet "smudge" jumped slightly from one position to another. "And now here is the *third* photo taken twenty-four hours later, showing the comet's progress."

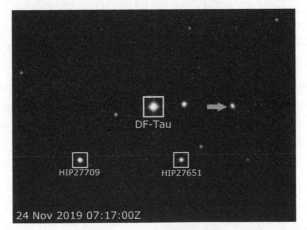

Courtesy Concetta Cordaro, PhD, MIT; Uday Shankar & Justin Atchison, JHUAPL

"Cut to the chase, honey," Lauren said, sniffing with characteristic impatience.

Concetta continued, "Now *this* image is an overlay of all three dots connected by the line that represents current trajectory." The new image appeared.

"And finally, here is a broken line that shows what Avery's *normal* trajectory should be." The new line was somewhat above the first one.

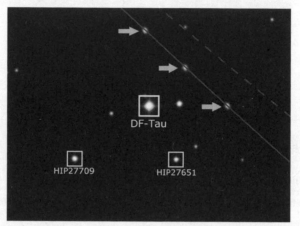

Courtesy Concetta Cordaro, PhD, MIT; Uday Shankar & Justin Atchison, JHUAPL

"As you can see there is a slight, but clearly noticeable, discrepancy. Apparently on the comet's last outward journey, somewhere far beyond our planetary system, it must have encountered some large gravitational mass. Or it might have had an actual collision with an asteroid or some kind of debris that altered the comet's elliptical orbit very slightly. But that small variation has been amplified by the trillions of miles the comet travels. Calculations made in conjunction with all my colleagues are now indicating that . . ." Concetta paused, clearly feeling an enormous weight and knowing the apparent impact of what she was about to say. She drew a breath. ". . . that Comet Avery is now on a course that will bring it very close to Earth."

We heard shouts from multiple reporters of, "What's 'close'? How close!?"

"It could be perilously close." Then she added quickly, "But let me emphasize that at this distance, we cannot be conclusive. We've had barely

18

seventy-two hours. There will be outgassing that will change the comet's mass as it approaches the sun, and there still may be subtle gravitational variations that may improve the situation, improve the odds. But—"

"What *are* the odds?" several shouted.

"At this point . . ." Concetta's mouth had gone dry. "With all the computer models we've run . . . we're estimating about a sixty-seven percent probability of a collision with Earth."

A gasp came from the off-camera reporters as well as all of us in the makeshift field hospital. The news reporters all began shouting at once, "Do you have an exact—" "If it's so far away, how can you—" "Do you know when it—?!"

I could see that poor Concetta felt overwhelmed by the tumult, and I greatly sympathized with the beleaguered young scientist. But she steeled herself, firmly held out both hands for silence, and waited until the gathering complied. Then she said, "Let me give you an overview. Earth moves at roughly seventy thousand miles per hour in its orbit." She brought up a graphic that visualized her description.

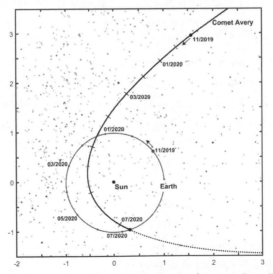

Courtesy Concetta Cordaro, PhD, MIT; Uday Shankar & Justin Atchison, JHUAPL

"Think of Earth's orbit as a clock. On this diagram, Earth right now, today, is currently at approximately the two o'clock position, labeled '11/2019.'" A blue-green disk representing Earth appeared on the upper right of its orbit line. "Avery's Comet will be approaching from way off on the upper right side." A red disk appeared at the extreme upper right edge of the screen, also labeled '11/2019.' "So right now Earth is moving toward the comet." The blue-green Earth disk began moving counterclockwise toward twelve o'clock, then down toward eleven o'clock. "At about ten o'clock, roughly mid-March, next year, Earth begins moving away from Avery. But as we continue on around the sun, passing six o'clock, in mid-May next year, and Earth begins curving up toward five o'clock"—the earth's symbol moved accordingly—"the oncoming comet will pass its perihelion, where it's closest to the sun, and slightly decrease its speed because of the sun's gravity as it closes in on Earth from behind."

There were overlapping shouts of, "How long will it—?" "What speed will it—?" "Do you have a date when—?"

Dr. LaPorta stepped up beside the young astronomer and held his hands out to quell the reporters. "Please. *Please*. Give Dr. Cordaro a chance."

She drew another deep breath and leaned closer to the microphones, speaking more quietly. Lauren, our Bangladeshi aides, and I also leaned closer to hear her words. "Again let me emphasize that our calculations and models are based on the most accurate data currently available. The situation may improve, it may remain the same, or it may deteriorate. Whichever happens we estimate that the comet's speed toward us will be in excess of twenty-eight kilometers per second, that's over sixty-three thousand seven hundred miles per hour, by the time it intercepts our Earth." Concetta paused, inhaling with her lips tightly together, then she said, "And that will take place in seven months and thirteen days. On the tenth of next July."

2

DEFENSE

Concetta Cordaro...

Naturally there were skeptics, particularly among the governments of Russia and China, who instantly scoffed. They doubted the declaration, particularly one originated by "a junior-level, publicity-seeking, potentially hysterical female astronomer."

Wow. Thanks for the vote of confidence, gentlemen. They also raised suspicions of it being merely political subterfuge giving the US an excuse to enhance our nuclear arsenal. They presented scientists of their own, many who dismissed our predictions in their entirety. Other scientists in those countries, if admitting the remotest possibility, argued that our calculations were simply wrong. That it would be a near miss, certainly close enough to be frightening, but nonetheless a miss. They argued that at most there was only a 40 or 50 percent chance of actual impact.

But for the US government, NASA, and ESA (the European Space Agency) those odds were more than strong enough to call for defensive action. They began scrambling to make immediate preparations to try to prevent such an irreversible catastrophe. Research had been ongoing for several years about dealing with such an incoming object by somehow creating an explosive shockwave nearby to alter its path, but as yet we had neither the technology nor the time to pursue that course. So a direct confrontation was the only choice.

The basic game plan they put forth sounded relatively simple and achievable: launch a number of rockets armed with nuclear warheads to intercept and explode the incoming comet before it could strike Earth. Many thought that was a good idea. We certainly had many intercontinental ballistic missiles sitting around at our disposal.

Or did we?

TELCOM UNIDIR0686118;
Transmit Date & Time: 12/12/19 17:09:32 GMT

Sender: UNIDIR

Recipient(s): POTUS, SECDOD, NASA, ESA, USAF Centcom, USN Centcom,

NSA, NRC, UNSG

Re: Project on Transparency & Accountability in Nuclear Disarmament

In response to numerous interdepartmental and interagency inquiries regarding the number of USA ICBMs currently armed with nuclear devices and ready to deploy, the most recent UNIDIR assessment (Blk # E76634, File doc UNADIR-7117693625) estimates 557. This includes both land-based and submarine-based missiles.

>>> USAF Centcom, USN Centcom, SECDOD please confirm.

VERIFY RECEIPT - TELCOM UNIDIR 0686118

END TRANSMISSION

Courtesy UNIDIR Information Office

The Documentarian...

The number of missiles was actually correct. But there was a major problem.

—ɯ—

From: Benjamin.Lancaster@OfcChiefAdmin.NASA.gov
To: POTUS, ESA, USAF Centcom, USN Centcom,
SECDOD, NSA, NRC, UNSG
Date: 12/14/19 13:22:56 ZULU
Subject: Defense against Comet Avery

Mr. President et al.,

It must be immediately understood that all the ICBMs described in UNIDIR**6118 had never been designed for, nor are they capable of, penetration deeply enough into space to accomplish the extraordinary mission at hand. None of them have the size or thrust necessary to do the job.

They are therefore <u>all</u> <u>useless</u> for this mission. Instead, essentially starting from scratch, an <u>entirely</u> <u>different</u> <u>fleet</u> will have to be created and deployed. What is needed is a number of <u>multistage</u> rockets with <u>heavy-lift</u> thrust capabilities such as carry payloads into orbital insertion. And not merely into low Earth orbits (LEO) of 200+/- mile altitudes where the International Space Station operates and many shuttles have flown.

This special mission requires much more powerful rockets such as (at a minimum) those used for lifting payloads into geosynchronous transfer orbits (GTO) some 26,000 miles above the earth.

These would include specially modified versions of the Delta IV Heavy, Vulcan two-stage, or SpaceX Falcon 9 heavy-lift vehicles.

Between NASA, the US military, SpaceX, and ESA (Elliot Kinsmore-Smythe please confirm) there are at this moment only perhaps four such launch vehicles that are even close to being ready for fitting with nuclear warheads and deployed against the comet.

Benjamin Lancaster
Chief Administrator

Courtesy NASA

Concetta Cordaro...

So the obvious, but seemingly impossible, challenge was to create as many more of these massive 240-foot-tall launch vehicles as possible. I was kept closely in the loop while I led the team that continued to refine the comet's orbital assessments. There were seven active launch complexes at the Kennedy Space Center (KSC), but never had more than two such rockets been launched anywhere near simultaneously. Even assuming that the necessary number of rockets could be constructed, transported, and readied, the launch of seven at once would require an enormous, probably impossible, expansion of KSC's ground facilities and Houston's Mission Control to accommodate the necessary command and control hardware plus all the personnel.

Vandenberg Air Force Base on California's coast could host three, perhaps four, of the SpaceX Falcon launches. ESA's facility, Guiana

Space Centre near Kourou on the Atlantic Coast of French Guiana, could handle two of the Ariane 5 variety and also had the ability to launch Russian Soyuz-class rockets.

Taken together it might be possible, though infinitely difficult, to launch from those three facilities as many as twelve or thirteen rockets targeting the comet; however, the odds were outrageously long that all the rockets could be constructed in time, readied for launch, and also perform reliably. NASA's chief administrator, Dr. Benjamin Lancaster, put the probability of all vehicles reaching the target at 62 percent. Major General Maxwell Kent, US Air Force chief of staff, wasn't as optimistic. His prediction of successful missions was only 48 percent.

Nonetheless the wheels began moving on the unprecedented project that was given the combined mission name Operation Home Run. About ten days into the undertaking, my colleagues and I used new data to refine our calculations, and MIT released the statement that the probability of collision had risen from 67 percent to 71 percent.

Later that same week 107 concerned Russian scientists under the leadership of Nobel astrophysics laureate and president of the Russian Academy of Sciences, Dr. Dimitri Kutuzov, descendant of Prince Mikhail Kutuzov who had defeated Napoleon, petitioned Moscow to accept that the Americans' dire predictions were correct. Three days thereafter the Kremlin announced that they would join the mission. They made it sound as though they had actually been working on it internally not just since the initial finding but perhaps they had discovered the oncoming calamity *before* the United States had. They were preparing two Soyuz- and two Progress-class rockets for launch from their Baikonur Cosmodrome, the Russian spaceport in the steppes of Kazakhstan. Additionally, they would transport another Soyuz to ESA's launch facility in French Guiana.

It took two more weeks for the Chinese to see the light, but finally they committed to launching two Chang Zheng 7 (CZ-7 or Long March 7, comparable to the US Delta IV) missiles from Jiuquan

Dongfeng Space City north of Beijing. They would also endeavor to prepare and launch two others from their newest facilities on Hainan Island, which lies north of Vietnam on the South China Sea.

The USA, China, and Russia all surprised each other by how quickly each was able to mount such a massive offensive and get such heavy-lift rockets in the production line to face the challenge. It was clear that some secrets about their capabilities had been closely guarded all along until the very survival of the entire planet was in question. Hopes were held that there might possibly be a total of twenty-one rockets. But only in a perfect world.

Unfortunately the world was imperfect. Despite everyone's best efforts there were international bureaucratic tangles, miscommunications, systems incompatibilities, unforeseen complications, industrial accidents, including some that cost lives. Ultimately far fewer rockets would ever reach a launch pad. But all the scientists, technicians, and everyday workers involved dusted themselves off from each grave disappointment and redoubled their efforts.

Signs and bumper stickers appeared in many languages around the world, expressing the same sentiment: "We All Need a Home Run."

Meanwhile I pictured Avery's Comet in the vast blackness of space, relentlessly torpedoing toward its rendezvous with the third planet.

Lisa McLane, 17...

A few days before we heard about the comet, my eleventh-grade English teacher, Ms. Banakowski, told me to stay after class. I was totally freaked because I'd like never been the world's greatest student. Always had to struggle for just a 3.0. My friend Stephanie and some others always made it seem effortless. I have to admit I was a little jealous of them. So it surprised me when Ms. Banakowski said the short story I'd just written was very good. That I had "extremely interesting insights and excellent possibilities as a writer."

She suggested I start keeping a diary where I could like "carefully document my observations of people and places" and train myself to select the words that described them "most evocatively." She said it would also be a great way to like explore my innermost thoughts and stuff and "find my voice." Then see what stories might come out. I got excited thinking about it. How cool would it be if I turned into a famous novelist? Made lots of money. Fat chance, I knew. But still . . . Anyway, here's how my diary began:

I, Lisa Anne McLane, entered this world in Ashton, Georgia, seventeen years ago, and I still abide there, the daughter of Eileen and Jason McLane who were unpleasantly separated eighteen months ago. My father has chosen to live in Atlanta with his GF, and I only see him occasionally. My mother still misses him dreadfully, and deeply yearns for them to be reunited.

It has been said that I am not unattractive, though I often feel inferior to several of my friends. I have but one sibling, Katharine (Katie) who is fourteen, though she seems younger and prefers remaining a tomboy rather than maturing.

Naturally the first person I want to write more deeply about in this diary should be Charley Flinn. He would so be like such a good, big-hearted character in a book. Charley and I grew up together in Ashton, which is one of those small American towns like you see in old movies. He'd been my best friend since we were tiny children. We were like Velcroed at the hip. We were playmates and confidants, like fond siblings. Except that Charley and I never had disagreements. Our parents called us Chip 'n Dale, a nickname we later bequeathed to my younger sister Katie and her own best friend, Darren Green. Charley was my age, with a hardy, Irish American, farm-boy freckly face and thick sandy hair. He was a good, honest person. When other elementary school boys teased him about his best friend being a girl, Charley ignored them and stuck by me. He was only an average student like myself, but he always tried hard in school. Now in our junior year he was like totally determined to finally make first-string quarterback on the football team next fall. I cheered him on, although I privately feared that the odds would not be ever in his favor.

When dating age came upon us, we each went out with others, but Charley and I remained the very closest and most faithful friends. When Charley told me he'd gotten a crush on one of my best girlfriends, Jenna, I was worried Charley might not stay such a close friend to me if they developed a serious relationship, but they didn't. Charley and I remained steadfast, truest friends to each other. We continued sharing our private jokes, multitudinous laughs, glorious dreams, and endless confidences.

Until mid-November of this, our eleventh-grade year, when Charley suddenly became shy around me, not conversing like we used to, even going out of his way to avoid me. My calls or texts often went unanswered. I was confused, then hurt, then worried. Finally on one quiet winter evening, I caught up with him walking home beneath the moonlit maple trees that stood as proud, leafless sentinels along our street. "Charley?" I caught the maroon wool sleeve of his varsity jacket and cautiously inquired, "What's wrong?" He slowed to a stop. I intuited from his uneasy frown and unusual awkwardness that something was indeed troubling him deeply. He couldn't look me in the eye. He shifted from one foot to the other. Had I done something wrong? He shook his head negatively, causing one lock of his sandy hair to drop *tres* adorably across his forehead. With his eyes downcast and a very small voice, Charley confessed to me how he had chanced to glimpse a young woman silhouetted by the playground lights outside our old brick gym after the dance last month. He had known in that moment that she was the love of his life.

I was apprehensive, barely able to breathe, whispering, "Who . . . who is she, Charley?" He said nothing. Then slowly he shyly raised his head until his liquid, warm brown eyes were looking into mine. I stopped breathing altogether.

Suddenly I understood. I felt a wave of surprising warmth well up within my throbbing heart. I'll forever remember Charley gazing at me with the moonlight bathing his sweet befreckled face. We stood there silently for an eternal moment. Then from his varsity jacket he withdrew a slightly wrinkled piece of three-ring notebook paper. I perceived that his young but strong hand was shaking slightly as he held it out to me. Unfolding it, I recognized his charmingly boyish handwriting. He had composed a poem about the girl he'd seen that homecoming night: she was I.

His poem was uneven, even slightly awkward, but the lines mostly rhymed, and it flattered my "lithe form" and "lovely face." Happy, balmy tears welled in my eyes. And also in Charley's. It was a magical, mystical moment. That comprehension of first true love opening up my heart. A love that had been there all along, waiting to be discovered and that matched his equally.

Our lives had forever changed.

And they changed again drastically the very next day when we learned about the comet.

Jimmy-Joe Hartman, 19, unemployed...

It wuz gettin' on toward April, 'bout four months since we heard that astrologer woman tellin' 'bout the comet comin'. I wuz on the front porch of the old frame house we'd always lived in down on Sylvan, south of the railroad tracks. Shit, our old rundown 'hood wuz south of 'bout ever'thing in Atlanta.

I wuz talkin' to my bud Scooter. He's a little half-pint who says he's a white dude like me, but I think back in his gramma's day, maybe somebody picked up a little bit of some other color. It's all good, though, 'cause Scooter's sharp. Got hisself a sweet little home garden. Raisin' him some first-class, dee-lectable weed. He gimme lotsa free samples. That day he wuz after me 'bout helpin' him move new TVs that he said "fell offa truck." Way he was grinnin' kinda sideways, I knew he'd boosted 'em. He done it before. Sometimes I helped him out fer a cut. He appreciated it 'cause I had 'bout twenty pounds on him, and he didn't have no muscle.

It wuz gettin' toward sundown, so I told Scooter to come off the porch. My sister, Claire'd, be home soon from her shift at county hospital. She didn' like Scooter none, and I didn' want her gettin' in his face. Or mine.

Sure 'nough I seen her gettin' off the bus up the corner right then, so I hustled Scooter round the side. It always 'mazed me how Claire's nurse scrubs still looked all sky blue and fresh as a daisy even after her twelve-hour shift. Then I seen Poppa off in the distance, drivin' home in his old Ford sedan. That damn car wuz older than me. But that's the sorta man Poppa wuz. Ol' Joseph Hartman never spent a penny on anything he didn' ab-so-lutely need to. Wore the same damn wire-rimmed glasses twenty years. "Ain't nothin' wrong with 'em, James boy. Don't need to get me no new ones." All his janitor uniforms wuz years old, too. At work they called him a "custodian," but a janitor's a janitor, know what I'm sayin'? My poppa, Joseph, was a janitor. But he worked hard, I give him that. And he taked good care of his clothes. Poppa said he liked the routine of washin' and ironin' 'em. He'd always shared the housework with Momma, then taked it all over in the nine years since she'd died o' that mellynoma cancer shit.

Poppa'd lived in this same house for most of his fifty-seven years; since he wuz a kid hisself. Always talkin' 'bout how he'd watched the neighborhood tryin' hard to hold its own 'gainst the poverty and violence. Poppa always said how there wuz too much graffiti, too many drug deals, not enough love. He worked hard to "increase the peace" round here. Said he wuz like some dude called Sissypuss: he kept pushin' this king-size rock toward the top of the hill, prayin' that this time it might stay up there. Poppa felt it just might, if he had hisself enough faith.

Churchy stuff always been the big thang in Poppa's life. "My cornerstone and my anchor," he'd say. Me? I bailed on all that "God is good" crap after Momma died. If God's so goddamn good, how come he taked Momma away when I just turned ten? Made me spittin' mad. But Poppa kep' holdin' on. Just like most bad thangs ever happened in his life, he figured this big-ass comet comin' wuz some kinda Bible deal. He warn't the only one. Lotsa folks sayin' that, since them news people kept on blabbin' how the damage to Earth'd be cat-ass-trophic. Gonna be "global, biblical per-portions." If ya could believe that shit. Which I didn'.

But Poppa did. He called it Ar-mag-geddon. On the news you'd see them in-your-face videos 'bout it. The comet wuz big as that mountain Everest. They said a bullet goes less than two thousand miles an hour, but this sucker's gonna hit the atmosphere at almost *sixty-four thousand*! It wuz gonna "impact 'gainst the planet with an ex-plosive force of a hun'erd million megatons of TNT." Which wuz obviously a shitload.

And that wuz gonna make this damn shock wave that'd flatten ever'thing inside of two hundred miles, and "wreak untold diz-aster beyond that." Like *vaporize* stone that'd blast a hole right up through the atmosphere. Then them vaporized rocks'd get cool and turn back into zillions of tiny ones, which'd burn up when they come fallin' back down as meaty-o-rites, heatin' the air up till it glowed pink. It'd be so goddamn hot that steam'd come boiling out of green leaves, and buildings all gonna burst into flame. And the gasses in the air'd mix up together to make rain like battery acid.

But that warn't all. They talked about this here plume of dust and ashes that'd wrap around the world like a thick blanket, makin' it real dark all the time and which'd ramp up global warmin', melt them polar caps so the oceans'd rise up and sweep a thousand miles inland.

Shee-it. But I mean, c'mon. Sound to me like some crazy-ass superhero movie. Too gi-normous to believe. 'Cept they said shit like this happened bunches of times before there wuz people. Said last time

Earth got hit by somethin' like this wuz sixty million years ago. Said that's what created the Gulf o'Mexico, killed off the dinosaurs. The scientists said ol' Earth'd survive. But "unfortunately civilization would not." Our ass wuz gonna be grass.

Poppa, Claire, an' me'd seen lotsa stuff on the news, like when the U-nited Nations had them 'mergency sessions? We knew they wuz all gettin' together to build some big-ass rockets to shoot down the comet with nukes before it smacked into us.

Claire, she wuz five years older'n me and always a goody-goody. She thought they might just be able to do it. She wuz usually right 'bout science stuff. But Poppa wuz different. He said he wuz just gonna keep his faith placed way higher than the U-nited Nations. He wuz a soft-spoke' man from old-school *Jaw-juh*. Sometimes when I wuz a kid, and him and me wuz drivin' someplace late—like home from seein' Momma at the hospital—he'd think I wuz asleep, but I'd hear him whisperin', havin' these heart-to-hearts with Jesus. He always had hisself a little plastic Jesus on the dashboard. He didn't push religion on most people, though. Other than me. Particularly after I turned thirteen and started gettin' busted for different shit. Lotsa times he called me his prodigal son. Said he had faith in me finally findin' my path, seein' the light. Gotta admit, even when I wuz the world's biggest asshole, Poppa wuz patient, sweet to me. But Claire? Woo-eee. She wuz just a bantamweight, little brunette, but I mean to tell ya, she's a tough chick. Always bustin' my balls, peckin' at me in her snooty, nursey way, sayin I was showin' all the promise of becomin' white trash. She 'bout chewed me a new asshole when I dropped outta school. But I hated it there. Ain't never been back.

With only a few months t'go before the comet hit, Poppa's talk wuz mostly 'bout the book of Rev-e-lations. Seemed like his only big hope wuz if nothing else, my "wayward heart might be turned round to embrace and accept Jesus 'fore the 'Pocalypse come down on us."

That day I heard Claire callin' out to him as he drived up. "Poppa, come here. Got something to show you." She was fishin' in that ol' carpetbag purse o'hers. I told Scooter he best buzz off. I'd pop down to his place later to get the de-tails 'bout them TVs. He did, and I watched Poppa get outta the car.

He wuz pushin' sixty, but could work harder and longer than men half his age. Hair wuz gettin' thinner, though, and grayer. Ever since we heard 'bout the comet. Claire give him a hug. She wuz always doin' that, even if she wuz just goin' down the street a minute.

I watched from round side the house as Poppa leaned down toward the left front tire and sniffed, sayin', "Think we might be needin' some new pads. Brakes feel kinda mushy."

Claire shaked her head. "World may be coming to an end, and that's what you're worried about?"

Poppa gave a little sigh. "That and your brother." Then he seed somethin' in her hand. "Whatcha got there, missy?"

"Binoculars. Dr. Bleifer loaned 'em to me. Come here, and I'll show you." Claire pulled him round the magnolia tree to where they could get a view o'the sky over Atlanta. It wuz gettin' twilighty. She looked through them binoculars a second and said, "Okay. There it is." She passed 'em to him. "Take a look, Poppa. Right over the Hendersen's chimney there. Then up a pinch above the buildings downtown." He lookd through 'em out at the sky.

"What am I lookin' for, honey?" Poppa axed.

"Faint little smudge of light."

"Okay . . . oh, yeah. I see it. And that's it?" Poppa said, curious-like.

Claire took her a long slow breath. "Yes, Poppa . . . that is it."

"Why, honey, it looks like it's pointin' sideways, not comin' at us!" He got real hopeful. "Praise Jesus! You gonna tell me it done changed direction or—!?"

"No, Poppa"—I'd heard her 'splain it to him before—"the tail always points away from the sun, remember? But it's still coming right at us."

Poppa kept lookin' at it while Claire looked at him. I seen she wuz hurtin', like she hated the thought o'them losin' each other. Then she glanced at the house and caught me watchin'. I made like I wuz just seein' 'em and bopped on over. "Yo, y'all."

Claire blew out that sour puff of hers. I knowed it real good. She told me more'n once 'bout her nurse trainin' sayin' how humans wuz 90 percent water, but she always said I wuz 90 percent *attitude*. She didn't get that I wuz proud of that. Got my high-tops with the laces untied, got my baggy black jeans barely hangin' on my hips, got me a dope collection of cool in-your-face T-shirts, got my wraparound sunglasses, my blond hair spiked up slick. Man, I wuz all style and 'tude, and I liked it. Shit, I wuz free, white, and *nineteen*, know what I'm sayin'? But Claire just didn't get it. And I loved to needle her. "S'up, my peeps?"

She shaked her head. "Got a long way to go with your white-boy impression of black gangsta rap, James Joseph."

"Jimmy-Joe to you." I grinned at her, then axed, "What y'all lookin at?"

Claire nodded toward the skyline. "The comet. They said we'd be able to really see it about now, and there it is."

Poppa handed them binoculars to me. I looked and then I seen it, too. Kinda made me freeze up a mite. 'Course I seen lotsa photos of it on the TV, but seeing it for real with my own eyes that first time . . . I dunno . . . kinda creeped me out. I looked over at Poppa. He wuz still gazin' out toward where it was, kinda half whisperin', "Sweet Jesus . . . Is this gonna be your Last Judgment?"

I smirked. "Aw, Pop. Ain't no damn Judgment. Lotsa folks sayin' it probably won't even come near us. Just more scientist crap like that climate change horseshit."

Claire looked her daggers at me. "What if it's *not*, James Joseph?"

I just chuckled. "They gonna send up them rockets. Blow it all to hell!"

Claire started gittin' in my face. "And what happens if the rockets don't do the job, *Jimmy-Joe*?" She made my name sound like so much dog shit.

So I threw it right back at her. "Then you just better put your head 'tween your legs and kiss your ass goodbye." I chortled at her.

But Claire's eyes wuz drillin' right into me. "What *happens*, James?"

I jus' stared right back at her. And heard Poppa sayin' real quiet, "And he said that the next time the world gonna end in fire." Poppa wuz still starin' off at the sky, then looked kinda sideways at me. "I'm tellin' ya true, Jimmy: you better get yourself right with God."

"Yeah, yeah. Okay." I give him a little fist pop on the shoulder as I started t'go. "I'll check in with him." I didn't look at Claire, but I felt them hazel eyes of hers borin' into my back. So I just stretched a little, casual-like, like it didn' make no nevermind, and headed off t'Scooter's.

But when I got down round the corner where they couldn't see me, I did sneak me another look up at the sky. It wuz gettin' darker. I couldn't see that sucker with just my eyes.

But I knew it wuz out there. Headin' this way. And I couldn't git it outta my head.

Concetta Cordaro…

As I worked every day in my cramped office at MIT, I'd glance out at the Harvard Bridge, at the people and traffic moving back and forth over the Charles River. All those people. All their personal stories. All their lives hanging in the balance.

Every astrophysicist I knew personally, and thousands more, were continually revising the calculations when we got any new shred of data. One of the more peculiar discoveries was that Avery's mass was *larger* than it had been on its previous appearance sixty-five years ago. The comet had actually grown slightly in size by nearly a kilometer while out in deep space. That suggested its orbit had been altered by an actual collision with an asteroid. Or another comet.

Or something unknown.

And a portion of that something had essentially melded into Avery and become part of it, made it an even larger projectile coming at us.

By April the probability of collision had risen to 82 percent. Avery had passed the halfway point from where it was when I first saw it, and its velocity was increasing slightly more than expected.

I found myself constantly imagining what it looked like out there. I knew that as it gained proximity to the sun, its tail had grown thousands of miles longer from the increasing intensity of the solar wind. The ice crystals close to the surface of the comet's mountainous head would be sublimating more fiercely and chaotically, like some hellish cauldron.

From where the comet was now, the earth would no longer appear to be just another point of light in the starry universe. Earth would already be discernible as what the great astronomer Carl Sagan had poetically called "a pale blue dot," tiny and vulnerable among the stars.

—⁂—

From: Benjamin.Lancaster@OfcChiefAdmin.NASA.gov
To: Ronald.Schwartz@HomeRun.NASA.gov
Date: 04/22/20 17:42:23 ZULU
Subject: REVISED Draft Press Statement for UN Gen Assembly Presentation

Ron—
See my attached notes, **bolded, underlined, and incorporated** into your draft.
Be sure to make all indicated changes. I will need to review the final before you go with it.
BL
Chief Administrator, NASA
300 E St. SW, Washington, DC 20546
(202) 358-0000

—⁂—

From: Ronald.Schwartz@HomeRun.NASA.gov
To: Benjamin.Lancaster@OfcChiefAdmin.NASA.gov
Date: 04/22/20 15:06:51 ZULU

Subject: Draft Press Statement for UN Gen Assembly
Presentation

Dear Ben . . .
Attached is the draft press release I'm suggesting
to accompany your presentation at the UN day after
tomorrow. Please give me any notes, additions, or
changes—**bolded and underlined**—you want to
make ASAP so we can have it ready.
Thnx.

NASA Office of Information—Statement from UN Home Run Session 2 (Abstract)

For Immediate Release

Today Dr. Benjamin Lancaster of the US National Aeronautics and Space Administration's Planetary Defense Coordination Office again addressed the United Nations General Assembly in New York City. Dr. Lancaster updated the member nations about the scope and complexity of Operation Home Run, the international effort ~~underway being spearheaded by NASA~~ to destroy or deflect Comet Avery before it can impact Earth in two months and ~~seventeen~~ **sixteen** days. Dr. Lancaster prepared his remarks with the assistance of [list to be finalized and included].

Dr. Lancaster introduced and thanked the other scientists from the US, the UK, the EU, Russia, and China who were seated nearby. He said they represented **tens of** thousands of their fellow scientists and technicians who had all been working tirelessly since the discovery of the impending disaster.

He then reiterated how the launch facilities at Kennedy Space Center, Vandenberg Air Force Base, the Russian Baikonur Cosmodrome, the Jiuquan Space City **and Hainan Island** complex**es** in China, and the European Space Agency's French Guiana launch area were working 24/7 to prepare for launching missiles equipped with nuclear warheads. He announced that the original total of 21 missiles had been reduced to ~~20~~ **17** due to production or subcontractor difficulties, but that smaller number ~~would~~ **should** not affect the outcome of the mission. He expressed **great** confidence that the mission ~~would~~ **should** indeed be a home run.

One of the principal issues that had been ~~hotly debated~~ **under discussion** was the most advantageous sequence of missile launches. For example: Should the missiles be launched in separate waves so that if the first assault failed there could be a second **and perhaps third** attempt? That would seem ~~wisely conservative~~ **wise** and was clearly the favorite approach of many ~~military~~ advisors involved with the mission. But there were two problems: 1) Given the incoming speed of the comet, the **window of** opportunity for a successful strike was extremely short—literally only a few seconds; and 2) Any nuclear explosion from a first-wave missile could damage or ~~incapacitate~~ **destroy** any second-wave missile that was right behind it. (**The Fratricide Problem**.)

Dr. Lancaster reminded the gathering that the comet's head was mountainous. He said that many of his colleagues ~~himself included~~ felt strongly that all the missiles should reach the ~~targets~~ **comet's** head simultaneously to have the maximum possible explosive power. Finally, it had been ~~unanimously~~ agreed that this was the best approach.

Dr. Lancaster projected several images onto a viewing screen to explain how launching the missile fleet was a ~~nearly impossible~~ **very complex** mathematical challenge. Each missile was designated for a slightly different section of the comet which is five miles across. The rockets must all converge simultaneously, intercept the comet at exactly the same ~~location~~ **astronomical coordinates**, and detonate at precisely the same moment.

But the rockets are not all the same type. Some will be faster than others. And they will be launched from six **very** different places on the planet. Not only are some launch sites halfway around the world from each other, they were also at different ~~latitudes~~ **distances** **north** **of** **the** **equator**.

That is a factor because for maximum efficiency rockets heading into space are generally launched ~~to the east~~ **in** **an** **easterly** **direction** to get an extra boost from the speed of Earth's eastward rotation. But Earth's rotation speed varies depending upon location: it is ~~faster~~ **fastest** at the equator, spinning at 1,037 miles per hour. Farther north at the Kennedy Space Center, situated at 28.5 degrees North Latitude, the rotation speed is only 916 miles per hour. And the Baikonur Cosmodrome, at 46 degrees, could provide a boost of only 720 miles per hour.

Dr. Lancaster concluded his remarks by saying, "The world's top astrophysicists and most powerful computers are laboring to compute the precise instant that each rocket must be launched from each location to achieve the required success. I again express my appreciation to them and to the **tens of** thousands of men and women around the world for the collaborative manner in which they are all working so ~~desperately~~ **diligently** to save our world."

END OF ABSTRACT

For full transcript and digital image files contact Info@HomeRun.NASA.gov

Courtesy NASA

Clarence Frederick, 49, Everett Biochemical plant manager...

It was about two weeks after that second UN announcement. I had just taken another Prilosec, trying to get my gastroesophageal reflux to calm down. Seemed like my stomach was *always* queasy now. I was definitely more nervous every single day as we counted down. I knew so many people must be feeling the same or worse. But not my wife, Simone. Through the lacy curtains in our front window, I saw her standing in our front yard, enjoying the balmy May evening. Like me, she was middle-aged. But she carried her age much better than I and certainly seemed much younger. She was looking through her tortoise-shell bifocals up into the evening sky over our West Atlanta neighborhood. It was a nice area, with sidewalks, clean streets, and well-tended yards. It was inviting, comfortable, a fine place for kids to grow up. Such a tragic shame that it would soon be catastrophically incinerated. And us along with it.

Simone didn't believe that, of course. The sunny, yellow print dress she had on reflected her optimistic outlook toward life. She had a closetful of similar ones. She also favored them because she felt they drew attention away from what she perceived was her slightly thick midriff. No one else ever even noticed it, but Simone was constantly, and with a healthy dose of humor, at war with it.

Fortunately, Simone's personable humor extended to me. Her glass-is-half-full attitude was always a counterpoint to mine half-empty. I'd been an overanxious sort since childhood. I was always small for my age and barely taller than Simone. I exercised diligently on our low-impact elliptical, but it never seemed to help my physique. My black hair was trimmed to within an inch of my scalp and sprinkled with gray. Simone called it my powdered sugar. A lot more powder in the last six months.

"Hey, Clarence . . . honey . . ." She called to me from out front. "Come look."

I walked out, knowing what I was going to see would make me more uneasy. She glanced at me, joking lightly, "Oh, you're back at

40

that nail again." I was chewing on my left thumbnail, unconsciously as usual. "I swear, honey, you're gonna bite 'em all the way to your elbows. Or die of the fidgets."

I glanced up apprehensively at the darkening sky. "Don't think it's the fidgets that's going to kill me." The smudge of the comet was much more visible than it had been a week earlier.

Simone was studying it, like millions of others were. "It's *really* beginning to look like a comet now."

"It should, with only fifty-eight days left," I said, feeling my stomach roil again. "I'm telling you, we should get tickets for South America or—"

"Oh now, Clarence," Simone said with a patient smile, "they're still not sure exactly where the damn thing's gonna hit."

"Yeah. Northern Hemisphere."

"Only a few're saying that," she said. "And only if it really does hit."

"We should get tickets anyway."

Simone shook her head. "There're none left. Even through my office." Simone worked in the public affairs press office at the State Capitol. "Unless you go to a scalper. And we don't have twenty thousand dollars. A piece."

That startled me. "So you did check?" My pulse rate picked up. "You *are* worried."

"Of course I am, Clarence. My God, honey, who isn't? But there's nothing we can do. Even FEMA's acknowledged that."

I looked around, like maybe there was some answer nearby, maybe down our quiet middle-class street lined with trees that were only as old as the neighborhood, about twenty years. We'd moved in when it was new. The houses were similar yet with enough individual touches it never felt like a tract. Most were redbrick like ours, some were clapboard or even stone, and they were all nicely kept up. Folks in the neighborhood cared. For many like us it was their first real house. Good mix of folks, too. Some white, some black like us, some Hispanic, a few same-sex couples, too. Our overall mix was fine with everybody. Lot different from where I'd grown up down on the South Side. This was a good place to live.

But now we were all going to die. I was chewing my thumbnail again. I couldn't help it. I was deep into "dread time." That's what Simone called it whenever I worried about something ahead of me. Could be a dental appointment or my annual evaluation at the plant. Simone said I always spent so much time dreading upcoming things that I missed life while it was going by; said she had to be Pollyanna to my Eeyore. But this was different. This time we were staring at obliteration. And not exactly a peaceful, slipping-away-in-your-sleep kind of dying.

Our sixteen-year-old son, LeBron, came out of the house. Simone told me that most of the girls in LeBron's high school, and a couple of guys as well, went out of their way to get into his line of sight. LeBron's skin was a couple shades lighter than mine, like his mother's. His thick brown-black hair was straight and lately brushed with such casual-but-time-consuming precision that it made me chuckle. He had a swimmer's body: broad shoulders, narrow waist, his physique enhanced by endless laps for his high school's championship team. From some white slave-owner ancestors, he'd picked up striking green eyes. We knew he was aware of his good looks and the attention they brought him from his classmates. He'd told us offhandedly how several girls said he ought to be a fashion model. We worried that LeBron had begun to think he might be able to cruise through life by taking advantage of his looks instead of doing real work to earn a living. Not that any of that seemed to matter much, given what was coming. He handed Simone our binoculars.

"Thanks, honey." Simone smiled, then glanced at me. "And besides, if that thing hits *anywhere*, there's gonna be so much dust—"

"That *we're* gonna be dusted." LeBron laughed nervously. "Just like the damn dinosaurs."

Simone looked at him, then upward again through the binoculars. "I don't think that'll happen. I'm pretty sure the rockets'll get it."

LeBron arched one of his dark eyebrows. "You were pretty sure the Braves'd win the series, too, Mom."

Simone kept gazing at the damnable smudge in the sky as she drew a long breath. I could see that she was preparing to project a mother's confidence, and she didn't disappoint. "Well, maybe we'll all win this time."

LeBron and I traded a troubled glance. We were both far less certain.

3

STARFIRE

CLASSIFIED LEVEL THREE
From: Anita.Perez@NatSecAdv.WhiteHouse.gov
To: SECDOD, CSAF, CNO
Date: 05/02/20 06:48:15 ZULU
Subject: Starfire Deployment

To All—

Alexandra Willis, Chief of Combined Operations, Operation Home Run [NASA-HOUSTON-HR CCO] has urgently requested POTUS to make the **Starfire Optical Range** immediately available for deployment to assist and substantially improve the possibilities of success of Home Run.

Since we are advised that there may be serious natl sec issues regarding Operation Home Run's use of Starfire, POTUS wants full background on it along with plans for deployment.

Need **immediate**—repeat **immediate**—response
before action can be authorized. Please cc D/CIA, D/
NSA.

Standing by—AP

—⚡—

CLASSIFIED LEVEL THREE
From: Maj. Gen. G. Montgomery, CSAF
To: Anita.Perez@NatSecAdv.WhiteHouse.gov
CC: D/CIA@CIA.gov, D/NSA@NSA.gov
Date: 05/02/20 07:17:17 ZULU
Subject: Starfire Deployment

Dear Ms. Perez et al.,

Here is the essential USAF background information you
requested for POTUS regarding Starfire and HR CCO's
Request for Deployment. **Note**: this is a condensation
of the full, classified 278-page Starfire spec and mission
file attached.

The Starfire Optical Range (SOR) is located at a former
missile defense site which was reactivated in 2005 (cost
$27M) for the construction of the SOR at Kirtland AFB,
Albuquerque, NM. It sits atop North Oscura Peak, elevation 7,998. SOR is a Secure Lab Facility (SLAB) operated by USAF Space Command of the Directed Energy
Directorate (DED) of the AF Research Lab (AFRL).

It is housed inside a facility with a roof and circular walls
which retract to allow the equipment a horizon-to-horizon
view of the sky through its 1.5 and 3.5-meter telescopes.

They were specially designed for tracking and observing satellites in orbit. The scopes are paired with 1.0-meter laser beam director (referred to as LIDAR) which is a powerful high-intensity laser consisting of two solid state IR lasers, 1.064 & 1.319 microns, that are usually summed (combined). The laser beam light is orange, wavelength 590 nm.

(Note that on May 3, 2006, the NY Times reported, "Research is also being conducted at the base into how to use such ground-based lasers to disable satellites, i.e., as an anti-satellite weapon." That reportage has never been publicly confirmed nor denied by DOD, DED, or AFRL.)

It is in the public record that the LIDAR beam can put a laser pinpoint on an object at least to 29,357 miles into space. LIDAR is normally used to lase satellites so the telescopes can follow them. Currently there are over 1,300 total satellites which can be tracked. Classified specs note that LIDAR actually has considerably more power: it could be used to incapacitate or destroy certain satellites and can project a pinpoint of laser light on an object at least as far away as the moon (238,000 miles) with enough heat at that distance to start a fire if oxygen were available.

CURRENTLY: As part of Operation Home Run, NASA-Houston CCO, Alexandra Willis, has requested us to use the Starfire LIDAR to lase the head of the oncoming Comet Avery. This would allow the nuclear missiles to use the laser pinpoint as A SUPPLEMENTARY TARGETING COORDINATOR. This is similar to much smaller lasers used by drones to laser-target their air-to-ground missiles. The technique is called "painting" or "lighting up" the intended target by projecting the laser beam onto it. HR CCO stresses that this would definitely be an enormous potential aid in obtaining a successful Home Run mission.

THE PROBLEM: Avery's Comet is expected to make its final approach at a speed of 28.1 KPS or 62,856 MPH slanting in northwest bound passing over Nigeria on the western coast of Africa at 11.4 degrees East Longitude at an altitude of 46,300 miles. Interception of the comet and detonation of the missiles is to occur 1.17 seconds later at an altitude of 27,000 miles over the Cape Verde Islands in the southwestern Atlantic at 13.77 degrees West Longitude. If interception and destruction of the comet fails, then it will likely impact 1.01 seconds later in the southcentral USA vicinity east of the Mississippi River embayment.

HOME RUN CCO REQUEST: In order for Starfire's LIDAR to have the EARLIEST POSSIBLE ACQUISITION of and NECESSARY DIRECT LINE OF SIGHT to the comet in order to "paint" the incoming target, the LIDAR and its support equipment would need to be MOVED IMMEDIATELY from Starfire's current New Mexico location to the peak of Cerro de Punta 18.1725° N Latitude, 66.5918° W Longitude elevation 4,390 feet, in the Cordilla Central range, Zamas, Jayuya, Puerto Rico.

That is the reason why Home Run CCO has asked for immediate emergency authorization to move Starfire/ LIDAR to Puerto Rico. THE USAF TOTALLY SUPPORTS CCO WILLIS'S REQUEST AND IS STANDING BY.

IN ORDER TO HAVE STARFIRE READY IN TIME, WE CANNOT STRESS STRONGLY ENOUGH THE

NECESSITY OF US RECEIVING THIS AUTHORIZATION IMMEDIATELY.

Respectfully,
Maj. General Geraldine Montgomery,
Chief of Staff, USAF

—⁊⁊—

CLASSIFIED LEVEL THREE
From: Marion.Berger.D/CIA@CIA.gov
To: Anita.Perez@NatSecAdv.WhiteHouse.gov
CC: CSAF, D/NSA@NSA.gov
Date: 05/02/20 08:22:39 ZULU
Subject: Starfire Deployment

Ms. Perez—

With all due respect to Chief of Staff USAF, General Montgomery, because of the extremely close involvement of other nationals, particularly those of ▮▮▮▮ and ▮▮▮▮, in the Home Run mission, our agency **[CIA]** expresses considerable concern about exposing Starfire and ▮▮▮▮ to their scrutiny.

The new and ▮▮▮▮ technology of Starfire has shown that it could be a ▮▮▮▮ defensive tool in our arsenal with the potential to ▮▮▮▮ ▮▮▮▮ satellites such as might be utilized by ▮▮▮▮, and even ▮▮▮▮ against the United States or its allies in the event of hostilities.

The risks of exposure by transporting it from New Mexico to Puerto Rico and giving ▮▮▮▮ and ▮▮▮▮

or even ████████ access to its targeting capabilities could seriously compromise US interests in the future.

The CIA therefore urges POTUS to consider all other options available before authorizing the use of Starfire and ████████.

Marion Berger
Director, Central Intelligence Agency

—∿∿—

CLASSIFIED LEVEL THREE
From: D/NSA@NSA.gov
To: Anita.Perez@NatSecAdv.WhiteHouse.gov
CC: CSAF, D/NSA@NSA.gov
Date: 05/02/20 09:40:13 ZULU
Subject: Starfire Deployment

Ms. Perez—

The NSA is **shocked** that POTUS would even ████████ exposing the ████████████████ of ████████ and the ████████████████ to any foreign ████████ ████████ particularly those of ████████, ████████, ████████, and potentially others like ████████████, and ████.

The danger of ████████, ████████████, and ████████ ████████ falling into the hands of ████ ████████ could have ████████ consequences against our ████████ to ████████ in areas like ████ ████████████ and beyond.

49

Since our national security would definitely be severely compromised we absolutely RECOMMEND AGAINST involving Starfire or ████ ████████.

Lloyd Winchester
NSA

—⁓—

CLASSIFIED LEVEL THREE
From: Anita.Perez@NatSecAdv.WhiteHouse.gov
To: SECDOD, CSAF, CNO, D/CIA, D/NSA
Date: 05/02/20 10:32:01 ZULU
Subject: Starfire Deployment

Thank you all. POTUS appreciates your speedy counsel.

A presidential directive is being issued this morning **AUTHORIZING the use and immediate relocation of Starfire** to Puerto Rico while immediately supplying all pertinent scientific, technical, and targeting information to all nations involved in Home Run.

POTUS said that "national security won't amount to a hill of beans if we don't have a planet."

Courtesy the White House, USAF, AFRL, DED, CIA, NSA (Reclassified)

Dr. Susan Perry...

My home in Atlanta for the last several years had been a rented two-bedroom condo on the twenty-fourth floor of a nice high-rise called the Mayfair Renaissance. It was situated on Thirteenth Street off Juniper, in Atlanta's inviting Midtown area north of the city center. The CDC headquarters was just a short drive east. As the Mayfair brochure enthused: "It combines appealing urban living with restaurants, shops, leafy streets, and

Piedmont Park next door." I often jogged around the oval surrounding its baseball and soccer fields or all the way up to the botanical gardens. My sister, Lilly, three years older than me and now thirty-six, particularly liked walking through the Children's Garden up there.

Whenever I came back from fieldwork, such as in Bangladesh, I would immediately collect Lilly from the assisted care facility. They were excellent, caring people, but I always wanted Lilly near me as much as possible. She stayed there only whenever I had to be away from Atlanta for any more than a few days, which I'd avoided doing since discovery of the comet. People often remarked on our family resemblance. I knew they were being polite, however, when they said we were equally pretty. I didn't look too bad if I'd had a chance to put on some makeup, but Lilly wore none and never needed any. Her eyes were blue. She was fine featured and reminiscent of our French Canadian ancestors, although there was also a clear spark of our Irish grandmother, Lillian, reflected in Lilly's light freckles, pale skin, and hair even more auburn than mine. Her hair always made me smile. Despite my best efforts at keeping it neat, Lilly's always managed to be somewhat flyaway.

Whenever I brought her home, I would take her out onto our little balcony to look at the Atlanta skyline and let her get reoriented. I did that a lot after Bangladesh, after I'd heard about the comet. I found myself staring uneasily at the sky overhead, knowing what was out there, heading our way. But when I'd glance at Lilly, she would have already taken in the vista and was back into her standard mode: looking downward blankly at her iPad on which some lengthy text was scrolling way too fast for me to read. Anyone meeting her for the first time usually sensed, correctly, that there was something a little bit off about Lilly.

The blessing was Lilly's innocent unawareness of the impending danger. My sweet, dear sister stood there leaning gently against me, taking comfort from my arm around her. I took equal comfort from hers around me. We'd been through a great deal together, and I was not one to give up yet.

Since the news of possible disaster, some of our building's occupants began a weekly nondenominational prayer meeting. I didn't attend. I'd shied away from organized religion years ago. But I did harbor a trust in an overriding order within the cosmos. Like Einstein before me, I firmly believed that God didn't merely play dice with the universe. My fieldwork for the CDC and Doctors Without Borders brought me into hands-on involvement with people of so many nationalities, beliefs, and circumstances that it had given me a sense of optimism about our shared world.

The enormous satisfaction I'd experienced with the success Lauren and I had achieved in Bangladesh, personified in the miraculous resurrection and survival of frail little Aniha, certainly contributed to that trust in cosmic order. Smiling up into my eyes from her hospital bed the day I left, Aniha was much recovered. She clasped my hand tightly, pressed her lips to my fingers. She and I both had happy tears.

I felt there would simply be no cosmic logic in the destruction of civilization just as it might be on the brink of some new beginning. So I had put my heart out to Nature and Nature's God, and I dared to hope.

I felt certain that I wasn't alone; that there must be multitudes who shared the same hopefulness as we approached the final days before the comet's arrival.

—⁊⁊⁊—

BEGIN TRANSMISSION

SUBJECT: LAUNCH PROTOCOLS—HR DOC #LP0036A-7714095**021418

DATE: 06/30/20 07:05:34 ZULU

FROM: HOME RUN HOUSTON CCLD [Chief Coordinating Launch Director]

TO: SLD [Site Launch Directors] Baikonur, Jiuquan, Hainan, Kennedy, Guiana

CC: NASA-HOUSTON-HR CCO [Chief of Combined Operations, Alexandra Willis] UNSG, POTUS, SECDOD, CSAF

***Reconfirming agreement: as with established international air traffic control protocol, all communication regarding Operation Home Run shall be conducted in English. ***

This transmission is for <u>Home Run interdepartments only</u>. The Public Information Office will supply formal press release at news conference this day at 16:00:00 ZULU.

Due to the trajectory of Comet Avery dictating different times-to-interception/detonation for individual rockets from each launch facility, it has been determined by the Home Run Astrophysical Computation & Targeting Group that the sequencing of the mission is REQUIRED to be as follows:

T - Represents time of target interception-detonation

T -1:39:18   Baikonur launches

T -1:21:59   Jiuquan launches

T -1:15:07   Hainan launches

T -0:58:22   Kennedy launches

T -0:46:16   Guiana launches

Calibrate all local launch countdowns to this PRECISE TIMETABLE in sync with MASTER GPS time code. Follow all pre-launch com protocols with CCLD-HOUSTON per previous HR DOC #LP0013C-7714095**021418

CONFIRM RECEIPT

END TRANSMISSION

Courtesy NASA, Home Run

Lisa McLane...

Almost seven months after Charley and I stood together on that magical moonlit night when we realized and declared our abiding love, each for the other, only to learn about the horrible, life-stealing comet coming to claim us, we had once again retreated to our forested hideaway.

We were lying amid a profusion of daisies, lavender, and other wild-flowers beneath the broad leaves of the spreading sycamore tree. It was right beside the large pond that had been our swimming hole since child-hood. Nicely situated in a wooded area of long-abandoned McAlistair farm near our small hometown of Ashton, Georgia. Many long years pre-vious, when we were but children, this had become our "Special Place." And now Avery's fiery comet of death was invading it. Even now we could see it closing in. There were barely two weeks left before what would likely be the end of our precious, beauteous Earth and all of us residing upon it.

I was staring up through the sycamore's broad branches to the half-moon frowning down from the darkening, early evening sky. Though the comet was still far beyond the waning, glowing moon, it was much larger now than when it could first be seen by the naked eye.

"It's just not fair, Charley," I murmured quietly with bitter tears overflowing my eyes. Charley saw, and touched my cheek tenderly.

"Lisa . . . ?" He whispered lovingly.

But I was so very aggrieved that I could barely speak. "I wanted us to marry, Charley. Have three kids . . . two girls and a boy . . . a little Charley, junior . . ." My throat tightened, my words became almost inaudible. "Not end like this."

"C'mon, Lise, it's gonna be okay." He put his strong, comforting arm around my shoulder. Charley was so endearing, so genuine, trying to be as manly as a seventeen-year-old could muster. "I really think it will be." I leaned into the warmth of his loving embrace, his soothing counsel, want-ing to believe. He didn't know that I had glanced up at him and beheld his frown as he gazed up at the lowering sky and our impending destiny.

I saw that he, too, was equally as worried, heartsick, and frightened as was I.

Concetta Cordaro...

Looking out across the mountainous Puerto Rican jungle that was skimming past only a few hundred feet beneath our BLACK HAWK, I spotted the gigantic thousand-foot dish of the Arecibo radio telescope nestled into the distant greenery. Until 2016 when the Chinese created a similar sixteen-hundred-foot dish, Arecibo was the largest in the world. Neither of those scientific wonders, however, would be of any help to our current crisis. But I was on my way to something that might be.

It was July 8, barely two days before intercept. I was appropriately red-eyed from my late-night flight from Boston to SJU, San Juan's Luis Muñoz Marin International. Less than ten hours earlier I'd fallen asleep in my office at MIT only to be awakened immediately by my cell. It was the chief administrator of NASA's Planetary Defense Coordination Office in Washington, on a conference line with Alexandra Willis at Home Run, Houston. They had an offer for me to consider. Which I accepted in a nanosecond.

Since I had been the first one who spotted Avery's Comet en route to earthly disaster, they asked if I'd be interested in being among the *last* to see it up-close.

The beefy BLACK HAWK suddenly pitched nose-up so sharply that I was instantly 120 pounds heavier as I pulled two Gs. Then I went weightless as the aircraft flattened out abruptly for a spot-on, ultrafast landing. *Whoa. Thanks for the warning, guys. Nothing subtle about these combat-trained chopper jocks.*

We had barely touched down when the door slid open, and a thirty-something Asian American air force captain stuck his head in, shouting loudly over the aircraft's noise, "Dr. Cordaro?"

"Connie," I shouted back, smiling. I popped open my four-point seat belt as I glanced at his name tag, a touch bemused. "Captain *O'Hara?*"

He smiled back. "I know. Doesn't fit the profiling. First name helps: Manchu." He extended his hand. "Welcome to Starfire."

Guiding me out beneath the spinning chopper blades, Manchu shouted, "Base camp's down there." He was pointing toward the encampment that was situated a hundred yards below our helipad. A dozen or so air force and civilian people were moving between support equipment, military jeeps, and trucks that surrounded multiple 18-wheeler-size trailers. Several had large dish antennae aimed skyward. The camp was on a jungle mountaintop almost a mile above sea level. Stretching beyond and below the camp was a beautiful vista of the lower mountains surrounding us. Ghostly mists were gliding slowly up one of the green jungle canyons from the blue Caribbean beyond. I also noticed a number of armed US Marine guards on alert around the compound. "And up there," the captain said, pointing back across me and up to one side, "is our baby."

I glanced up and got my first look at the Starfire Optical Range. It had been hastily disassembled, moved from New Mexico, and rebuilt atop the rise above us at the highest point of Cerro de Punta on an area about half the size of a football field.

Courtesy AFRL Directed Energy Directorate

There were several other large trailers up on top with air force, marine, and civilian personnel moving in and out. A raised hundred-foot-square section about ten feet high was in the center. Atop that large platform was what looked for all the world like an upside-down cake pan. A fifteen-foot-tall, seventy-foot-wide inverted cake pan. Its polished aluminum surface was so shiny that the sun glinting off it made me squint. But I could see that poking through a thirty-foot hole in the top of it was the Starfire device. It reminded me of the cylindrical, open frame reflecting telescope at Palomar, but only about a third as tall. "My God, Manchu, how did you possibly move all this here so quickly?"

"Because we had to?" His expression was grim and serious. He led me up closer to the giant cake pan. "Have you ever seen those collapsible cups people take camping?"

"You mean cups with sides that nest down into each other so they flatten out for packing away?"

"Yeah." Manchu nodded and raised his eyebrows, indicating toward where we were heading.

I immediately understood what he was talking about. This shiny, giant cake pan was only the outermost of several such giant cake pans nested one inside the next inside the next. So the building could be stretched up taller to the full height of the Starfire Optical Range (SOR). The design was meant to protect SOR from weather with the help of a sliding lid that could cover the central hole. As we entered into the huge cake pan, its walls were only raised up about a third of the way, allowing the top half of the SOR, its telescope and its laser array, to protrude through the opening. We approached its massive circular base. The entire snow-white mechanism loomed thirty feet above us and was framed against the bright blue sky above. The top half was the open frame telescope/laser (LIDAR) unit. It was cradled in a yoke that could pivot the array 180 degrees from one direction, say east, across the zenith directly overhead to the opposite, westerly direction. And that beefy yoke was situated on a turntable that could rotate the entire hefty mechanism 360 degrees on the flat axis. That X-Y axis combination allowed SOR to be aimed at any portion of the sky.

I nodded, admiring the cleverness of the collapsing cake-pan walls around the device. "So to aim it lower in order see toward the horizon you just—"

"Yep. Lower the walls." Manchu responded. "That gives us the maximum capability of acquiring line of sight to the comet at the earliest possible moment, assuming the weather gods keep it cloudless, otherwise . . ." We both knew that cloud cover could render Starfire useless.

Except for its giant collapsing cake-pan housing, the basic design of the X-Y axis telescope was very standard for observational astronomy.

"The main difference, of course," the captain said, "is that the Starfire Optical Range wasn't just built for observing." With a faint grin he added, "I could tell you more, but then I'd have to kill you." I understood. I had been briefed that aspects of the SOR were classified. But they were easy to surmise. With the help of its laser array, SOR could track the movement of any satellite and keep the telescope sharply focused on it. And if that laser array, that LIDAR, was as powerful as I suspected, it could also be used to destroy a satellite. But that was not the mission at hand. I knew the LIDAR itself, despite its unusual power, would not be effective at warding off the mountainous comet. Starfire's job was to "paint" the comet with its laser beam and target Avery for the incoming nuclear missiles. The opportunity I'd been given was to be watching the incoming comet through Starfire's telescope as the missiles intercepted, impacted, and detonated, hopefully deflecting or shattering it.

Or not. Either way I would definitely be one of the last to see it close-up before collision.

BEGIN TRANSMISSION

SUBJECT: WEAPON ARMING PROTOCOL—HR DOC #LP0279-876543-102344

DATE: 07/9/20 18:17:20 ZULU

FROM: NASA-HOUSTON-HR CCO [Chief of Combined Operations] Alexandra Willis

TO: SLD [Site Launch Directors] Baikonur, Jiuquan, Hainan, Kennedy, Guiana

CC: UNSG, POTUS, SECDOD, CSAF

This is final reconfirmation of steps taken to
INSURE PROPER EFFECTIVE DETONATION of all nuclear
warheads targeting Comet Avery.

It is our collective hope that all the missiles
will reach the target at exactly the same moment.
But regardless of whether or not they do, it has
been agreed vital that all the nuclear devices MUST
DETONATE AT THE SAME INSTANT. Any asymmetrical first
detonation could disrupt or incinerate the other
rockets and their nuclear payloads, thereby pre-
venting the maximum explosive effect that must be
achieved by their simultaneous detonation. If one
missile is even milliseconds ahead of the others,
whichever warhead detonates first, it must automatically trigger simultaneous detonation of all others.

Therefore we are confirming that a PRECAUTIONARY
EXECUTE COMMAND (PEC) has been inserted into each
warhead's programming. In the event that there
is any mishap with a missile or a nuclear device
during launch or flight, it has been determined
that the PEC shall not become active until the
missiles are flying on target and within 500 nau-
tical miles of the target.

CONFIRM RECEIPT

END TRANSMISSION

Courtesy NASA, Home Run

Jimmy-Joe Hartman...

My poppa, Joseph, and my always-do-the-right-thing sister, Claire, wuz at church a lot. They wuzn't the only ones. TV showed theys like millions of others who wuz prayin' away like crazy in their churches or temples or them mosques and monasteries and what all. They wuz like nonstop 24/7 services goin' all over the damn world. Everybody wuz beggin' whatever God they wuz into for some sorta dee-vine intervention to stop the damn comet.

I still thought it wuz all a crock. But as the clock wuz tickin' down, I seen some of the boys I hung with gettin' spooked. I even seen my pal, scrawny ol' Scooter, who wuz always chillest o'the chill, I actually seen Scooter duckin' into a church! When I axed him 'bout it, he tried to laugh it off, but I seen his upper lip get kinda sweaty, so I knowed he wuz nervous. Then he got quiet and axed me what did I think it'd be like? How we wuz gonna die. He started talkin' 'bout how'd it feel to die horrible-like. Wuz we just gonna be exploded and feel nothin'? That wudn't be so bad, he said. But how 'bout if we got burned up in a flash of fire, or scorched to death slow, or drownded gaspin' for air under some big-ass tidal wave? And even if we didn't get killed outright, how'd it feel to have that acid rain comin' down on us till our skin got seared off?

"Whoa, whoa, man." I held my hands up, forcin' out a little chuckle. "You forgettin' 'bout them eighteen rockets, man! They gonna blast that sucker to shit."

"Whatchu talkin' eighteen rockets, Jimmy-Joe? Don't you listen to the news? They down to just *thirteen* now."

That gimme a little chill. But I tried not to let on. "Yeah, yeah, 'course I know. But shit man, thirteen nukes'll be plenty 'nuff to take care of—"

"But what if they don't all *get* there?" Scooter said, almost like a whiny little kid. "And even if they do, not all of em's American made, you know? What if they don't do the job?!"

"Aw, man, I'm tellin' ya, ain't nothin' to go on about. They gonna—"

But I seen that Scooter wuz lookin' at me like I ain't never seen him. Scooter always had hisself some sneaky plan to come outta anything on top. But not this time. I seen his eyes had got watery. I seen he was really scared shitless. Deep down. Like we wuz all trapped in a nightmare with no way out. And if fuckin' *Scooter* was scared—

Thas when I started t'get worried.

Dr. Susan Perry...

Reports on CNN and elsewhere grew ever more grave. Across Europe, the Americas, Africa, and Asia, growing numbers of people chose not to wait for the possibly blistering horrific end, but instead took their own lives. As the last days wound down to hours, hope stretched thinner, and no miracle occurred.

Inevitably, inexorably, the day of impact had arrived.

Concetta Cordaro...

We'd run a final full system check of Starfire's LIDAR just before dawn on July 10. The weather gods had kept the sky clear. The thin aluminum walls surrounding SOR were dropped and nested down to their lowest point.

I had of course seen many laser beams in my life, but the widest had been only pencil thin. Consequentially I was quite startled and amazed to see that the powerful beam emanating from LIDAR had a width of one full *meter*. The bright orange beam spiked up through the stratosphere so brightly that I had to squint to look at it. It stretched up into the stratosphere over Puerto Rico and on into the darkness of space.

Courtesy AFRL Directed Energy Directorate

Kenneth Johnson

Once the test was completed, the weighty Starfire laser and telescopic array rotated smoothly on its turntable while tilting down on its yoke until it was aiming toward the eastern horizon. I leaned against the massive, white, circular steel base beneath SOR and gazed off in the direction it was pointing, into the coming dawn. I knew that more than just the sun would soon be rising over the horizon.

Katie McLane, 14, Lisa's younger sister...

My mom, Eileen, had been pretty frazzled ever since Dad left a couple years earlier to live with his girlfriend, Tina, in Atlanta. But that morning Mom was *really* coming unglued. Particularly 'cause Lisa'd gone out before dawn and hadn't come home like she'd promised. I told Mom not to worry. I figured Lisa and Charley had gone out to their "Special Place" on the old McAlistair farm. But Mom kept getting more upset about crazy stuff, like why I hadn't washed my hair that morning. She was always on my case 'cause I had long ringlets that got tangled if I didn't wash 'em.

But Mom, *Today*? *Really!?* I finally got her to come with me up toward Ashton's town square.

Dr. Susan Perry...

At dawn that morning I looked out from our apartment's balcony over Atlanta, normally bustling with street traffic and noise, but today strangely quiet. The sky overhead was equally silent. All aircraft were grounded, worldwide. I felt it must feel essentially the same in every city and village in every country on every continent. Everything had begun to slow: autos, buses, trucks, trains, horse carts, rickshaws, everything everywhere was gradually edging to a standstill. Everyone was pausing, perhaps for the last time, to look up.

Concetta Cordaro...

One of the big, expanded double-wide trailers adjacent to SOR was Starfire's Master Control Room (MCR). There were numerous armed

US Marine guards stationed around it. A tough-as-nails marine sergeant with his automatic rifle slung on his shoulder checked the ID badges hanging around my neck, even radioing inside to double-check. Then the sergeant nodded to two other marines on either side of the entrance. One punched in part of a code on the keypad, which the other door guard completed, and the heavy securing bolts snapped loudly. They opened the door. I was turning to enter when the sergeant said, "Ma'am?"

I turned back to look and saw the sergeant's intense brown eyes staring into mine. Then he raised his iron fist into a solid thumbs-up. Holding his gaze, I drew a long breath, nodded an appreciative, silent thanks, and went inside.

There were two armed marines, one female, stationed just inside the door. A narrow pathway ran down the center of the room between equipment and monitoring consoles on both sides. In front of each console sat mostly US Air Force personnel, each wearing a headset and carefully monitoring their individual responsibilities. At the far end were five large video monitors, two each on either side of the much larger main screen. Three air force officers were seated facing them; in the center chair was Captain Manchu O'Hara. I edged to one side, knowing that I was merely a very privileged observer. But when Manchu saw me, he nodded to an empty chair just over his shoulder. There was a strip of tape on it with the handwritten words, "For Dr. Cordaro." I was touched.

On one of the side screens was an image of the SOR unit with coordinate data, angles of incidence, time codes, and so on, all pulsing or scrolling to one side. The second screen was displaying radar. The third screen showed a view of the blue sky and the eastern horizon line through SOR's 1.5-meter telescope. The larger screen in the middle had the same 1.5-meter view. The fourth screen showed a view through the 3.5-meter scope of only blue sky. I heard two airmen reconfirming the coordinates of right ascension and declination where they expected the comet to rise above the horizon as the earth rotated toward it. Manchu passed me a wireless headset so I could listen in to the ongoing communications between us and Home Run Mission Control in Houston as well as all five launch facilities. The transmission was remarkably clear.

VOCAL COMMUNICATION TRANSCRIPT

OPERATION HOME RUN MISSION CONTROL >> HOUSTON-NASA
Date: 07/10/20

COUNTDOWN TIME TO T = INTERCEPT-DETONATION

TIME	COM
T -02:50:41	Starfire, this is Houston. We show you should acquire target on my mark in fifteen seconds.
T -02:50:32	Houston, Starfire. Copy that. All eyes on the horizon.
T -02:50:27	And . . . mark.

All Comm Transcripts Courtesy NASA, Home Run

Concetta Cordaro...

I heard a small ping, which reminded me of a submarine's sonar pulse, and simultaneously a blip appeared on the radar screen's horizon line. Captain O'Hara spoke into his headset, "Houston, Starfire. We confirm radar acquisition. Refining SOR coordinates."

The screen displaying a live picture of the SOR array showed the huge mechanism rotating and tilting slightly as numbers scrolled on the screen in conjunction. That motion was matched on the 1.5-meter telescope's screens, and the familiar smudge of light came into view just peeking above the horizon. A moment later the longer 3.5-meter scope showed a closer image of it. A clear view of the head of the comet. I heard myself whisper, "Oh my God . . ."

A lieutenant to Manchu's left punched a keyboard as she said, "Got it, sir. Correcting for atmospheric errors real-time . . . and locking."

The airman to his right chimed in, "Lock confirmed, sir."

"Houston, Starfire. We have radar lock on Comet Avery. Stand by." Then O'Hara glanced at the lieutenant. "Okay, Jessica, light it up."

"Activating LIDAR." She typed in several more keys on the keyboard, then with her right hand, she flipped up two yellow safeties on her panel that protected the actual red switches beneath. She flipped one of the underlying red ones and then the second. On the screen showing SOR, I saw the LIDAR beam blast to life, creating a brilliant streak toward the horizon. Even in broad daylight, it was bright orange and incredibly vivid. Simultaneously, on the 3.5-meter telescope screen, I saw a bright orange dot appear on the head of the comet. "LIDAR locked on target, sir."

Manchu nodded tightly. "Way to go, team." Then he touched his com key. "Uh, Houston, this is Starfire. SOR is locked on. The target is painted. Repeat: the target is painted."

VOCAL COMMUNICATION TRANSCRIPT

OPERATION HOME RUN MISSION CONTROL >>HOUSTON-NASA
Date: 07/10/20

T -02:47:40   Copy that, Starfire. Target is painted. Well done, Starfire—Break. Break—All stations, this is Houston, Starfire has laser-painted the target for supplementary laser targeting acquisition by onboard guidance. Confirm.

T -02:47:19   (Russian accent) Baikonur to Houston, confirm laser targeting active.

T -02:47:13   (Chinese accent) Houston, this is Jiuquan, confirm our laser targeting engaged.

T -02:47:06   (Chinese accent) Hainan Launch Control to Houston, we confirm laser targeting set.

T -02:46:57   Houston, this is Kennedy, confirm laser targeting up and running.

T -02:46:49   (French accent) Guiana Launch to Houston, we confirm onboard systems to laser targeting.

T -02:46:40   This is Houston to all stations. We copy all laser guidance systems confirmed. Stand by to release all countdown holds on Home Run master GPS sync pulse in approximately thirty seconds at T minus 02:46:00.

T -02:45:32   Houston to all stations. We show all launch pads now locked on master sync—Break. Break—Houston to Baikonur, you're first out of the gate. Stand by for nuclear arming protocol.

T -02:45:15   Roger, Houston. Baikonur standing by for arming protocol.

T -02:44:58   Houston to Baikonur, begin NAP on Home Run launch vehicles one, two, and three: warhead fusing master safeties to on.

T -02:44:01   Baikonur confirms safeties on.

T -02:43:50   Baikonur, Houston: set detonator for contact burst, minus factor Tango 3.

T -02:43:31   Baikonur confirms contact burst, minus Tango 3.

T -02:42:19   Baikonur, Houston: engage primary trigger switch override. Track indicators to maximum deflection.

T -02:41:50   Baikonur confirms PTSO engaged, track indicators to max deflection.

T -02:41:33   Baikonur, Houston: confirm pulse transponders active. Confirm weapon armed and ready.

T -02:41:22   Houston, Baikonur confirming transponders active. Weapon is armed and ready.

T -02:41:12   Baikonur, Houston: continue your countdown protocol for simultaneous launch of HRLV one, two, and three at T minus zero-one, three-niner, one-eight. Stand by for our final authorization at T minus zero-one, four-zero, one-eight to prosecute the target.

T -02:40:53   Copy Houston, Baikonur on launch countdown; standing by for final prosecute authorization.

Katie McLane...

When Mom and I got to the town square, my best pal, Darren Green, was already there. He's my age but with his round baby face and straight black hair, he looked younger. There was a big crowd outside the Ashton Methodist Church. It was townspeople who usually went there plus a whole big bunch of others like us who didn't.

Mom was still really squirrelly, and I couldn't blame her for being freaked. I mean, I couldn't believe it was actually gonna be like the End of the World and all, but at the same time seeing how scared the adults were had my stomach twisting around. One minute I thought for sure the rockets would get that stupid comet. The next minute I felt a sorta nervous wave of panic, like real terror of what'd happen if they didn't.

The minister was on the front steps, leading everybody in singing some hymns about salvation. Mom was twisting a scarf in her hands, trying to sing along with them, but she didn't really know the words. Her face was drawn up real tight. I squeezed her arm some to try to comfort her, but she didn't seem to feel it.

We were standing right by one corner of the old redbrick building. Darren's parents were nearby, and his brother, Tim, who was seventeen and the cool captain of the football team. But Darren was standing closest to me, with his back leaning against the side of the building.

His earbuds were in, and he was busy working his iPhone. "Katie," he whispered. "They're almost ready for the first launches in Russia!"

We looked at each other. Like we were standing on the edge of a superhigh cliff.

VOCAL COMMUNICATION TRANSCRIPT

OPERATION HOME RUN MISSION CONTROL >>HOUSTON-NASA
Date: 07/10/20

T -01:43:28   Houston, Baikonur: on my mark we are at minus four minutes to launch and counting. Mark. Target coded and ready. Checklist complete. Safety checklist complied with. Desired point of impact is loaded. Laser tracking sensors on, checked, and ready. Request FPA.

T -01:42:45   Baikonur, this is Houston. You have final prosecute authorization. Repeat you have final authorization to prosecute the target. You are a go to launch on HRLVs one, two, and three at T minus zero-one, three-niner, one-eight. Confirm.

T -01:42:15   Houston, Baikonur: copy that. Go to launch HRLV one, two, and three at T minus zero-one, three-niner, one-eight. Countdown proceeding.

Dr. Susan Perry...

I had faced many life-threatening scenarios in my CDC work, but the comet had taken on mythical proportions in my mind and probably most everyone's on the planet. It had become more than just a six-mile-wide mass of inanimate rock and ice. The comet had become Death Incarnate. To some I'd seen or spoken to, it was the face of Satan, to others the finger of God. To some it was retribution, to others the supreme example of existential absurdity. Nature's last laugh at our human vanity and hubris.

But virtually all of us knew that whatever else it was, if the missiles failed, it would be the end. And we were about to find out together. CNN was showing the Russian launch complex at Baikonur as the countdown culminated.

VOCAL COMMUNICATION TRANSCRIPT

OPERATION HOME RUN MISSION CONTROL >>HOUSTON-NASA
Date: 07/10/20

T -01:39:25   Houston, Baikonur: we have ignition on HRLV one, two, and three, and . . . liftoff exactly on the mark. Rifle. Rifle. Rifle. Weapons away. Travel time niner-niner minutes, one-five seconds.

Katie McLane...

The Russian launch looked totally *awesome*! Even on Darren's iPhone. It was early evening over there, and the three gigantic rockets all blasting off at exactly the same time was spectacular! Looked like they were about a half mile apart, and the flames from their huge boosters lit up the whole launch complex! Other people in the crowd outside the church heard about it, too, 'cause there were some encouraging cheers and shouts of "Praise God" and stuff.

Clarence Frederick...

Simone, LeBron, and I were out in front of our house. Lots of other neighbors on our street let out a cheer about those first rockets. But I was still nervous, tasted blood in my mouth, saw that my thumbnail was bleeding. Most folks seemed optimistic, but being an accountant-type, I knew the odds. They were very long.

"C'mon, Clarence." Simone nudged me. "Keep a positive attitude now."

Then sure enough about six minutes in there was bad news. After the three rockets separated from their big first-stage boosters, the second-stage engines fired up on two of the rockets, but not the third one. It failed and dropped away toward the Pacific. So now there would only be twelve rockets that would hit the comet. And that was if everything went perfectly from here on. How likely was that?

Katie McLane...

The crowd around the church got quieter, and the young minister read some Bible verses about faith being able to move mountains. I shifted my weight from one foot to the other and nipped at the inside of my cheek while Darren and I watched his cell phone for updates.

Fifteen minutes later the first two Chinese rockets got launched okay from Jiuquan, and *their* second stages worked perfect! Everybody blew out a big puff of relief, and we all felt better again. Six minutes after that we heard that the other two Chinese ones had blasted off from Hainan Island.

That made six on the way! Our hearts were beating faster now.

VOCAL COMMUNICATION TRANSCRIPT

OPERATION HOME RUN MISSION CONTROL >>HOUSTON-NASA
Date: 07/10/20

T -01:09:07   Hainan, this is Houston. We've lost data from both of your launch vehicles HRLV six and HRLV seven. Do you have a transmission relay problem?

T -01:08:45   Hainan, Houston: Do you copy?

T -01:08:20   [static, unintelligible]

T -01:08:01   Hainan, Houston: com check. Do you copy?

T -01:07:52   Houston, this is Hainan. The onboard pitch control in Home Run launch vehicle six malfunctioned. We've experienced a [static, unintelligible]

T -01:07:35   Say again, Hainan. Experienced what?

T -01:07:10   Hainan here. We experienced a catastrophic failure. HRLV six is down.

T -01:06:45   Hainan, Houston: [unintelligible] understood. HRLV six is down. We are very sorry. We still have no data from your HRLV seven. Confirm status.

T -01:06:20   This is Hainan. When HRLV six veered off course it . . . it collided with HRLV seven. Both rockets are destroyed.

T -01:06:01   [static, unintelligible]

T -01:05:45   [static, unintelligible]

T -01:05:18   Hainan, Houston: understood. [static, unintelligible] Thanks for all your hard work, Jiaying. God bless you and your team.

T -01:05:59   And yours, Alex. [static, unintelligible] God help us all.

Katie McLane...

When we heard the news, I got tears in my eyes. Darren did, too. A lot of us did. *God!* Now we were down to only ten rockets at best. And I knew they were like really powerful and nuclear and all, but the damn comet was the size of a mountain! And we had to wait *another* fourteen minutes until we'd hear about the four rockets they were gonna send up from Cape Kennedy. My stomach was turning inside out.

Jimmy-Joe Hartman...

Then I heard how one of them four rockets that wuz s'posed to blast off from Kennedy shut itself down right on the damn launch pad! Never even taked off! I got to feelin' weird and headed toward our house in South Atlanta. I didn't wanna seem like no candy ass, but same time I felt like gettin' on home.

On the way I heard them other three from Florida was goin' okay, though. And so was them last two from French Guinny down in South America. But shit, they started out sayin' we'd have twenty-one o'them nuke missiles, then it kep' gettin' whittled away till we wuz down to *thirteen* nukes, and now we got us just *nine*. My palms wuz really gettin' sweaty.

Concetta Cordaro...

On the main screen from Starfire's 3.5-meter telescope, the image of the comet was noticeably increasing in size. A counter on the bottom of the screen showed the comet's distance from us was spinning downward lightning fast. It was coming at us at over 27.489 kilometers per second—61,491 miles per hour. The bright orange LIDAR beam was still perfectly pinpointing the comet's icy center. On the radar screen the comet's blip was also much larger and now had a small digital tag identifying it as Avery. On the bottom of the screen nine tiny blips had appeared. They represented the Home Run missile fleet proceeding up toward the comet. I realized that both of my hands were clenched so tightly that my fingernails were digging into my palms.

VOCAL COMMUNICATION TRANSCRIPT

OPERATION HOME RUN MISSION CONTROL >>HOUSTON-NASA
Date: 07/10/20

T -00:06:10   All stations, this is Houston. On my mark we are T minus six minutes to target intercept . . . Mark. Release first and second safeties on all weapons. All weapons circuits to green.

T -00:05:58   Houston, Baikonur: we confirm safeties off, weapons to green.

T -00:05:50 Jiuquan to Houston: confirm safeties off, weapons green.

T -00:05:44 This is Kennedy. We are full green, Houston.

T -00:05:28 Houston, this is Guiana. Full green confirmed.

Concetta Cordaro…

I imagined the drama playing out so very far overhead. The nine remaining rockets riding columns of flame thrusting them upward, still accelerating past Mach thirty, over twenty-three thousand miles per hour. Their onboard computers had corrected for variations in the turbulent winds aloft, and those winds were now fifteen thousand miles below them. The hazy arc of our blue-green Earth would be curved beneath them as they roared upward.

Jimmy-Joe Hartman…

I seen my poppa, Joe, standin' out on the sidewalk front of our house on ol' Sylvan Road where I'd growed up. Damned if he didn't have on his janitor uniform like he wuz goin' on to work even if the world ended. Lotsa other folks wuz outside, too. Watchin' the sky.

Claire was near to Poppa, wearin' her light blue nurse's scrubs. I walked up, tryin' not to sound as shaky as I was feelin'. "Yo, sis. Thought it wuz your day off."

She looked at me real level. "Might be *everybody's* day off, James Joseph." I knew she was right, and it made me feel sick kinda. Like the blood wuz all drainin' outta my face. I started to get boiled up at her, to push back, but damn if my lower lip didn't get all trembly, like it always used to when I wuz a little kid tryin' not to cry. Claire seen it and softened up right away, taked my hand into hers, sayin' 'bout her scrubs, "I put 'em on in case the hospital gave me an emergency call. If there's any hospital left, afterward." Then she hugged me and held on real tight. She ain't done that for years. "Oh, Jimmy," she whispered in my ear. I felt her tears on my cheek. "Jimmy, Jimmy, Jimmy."

Lisa McLane...

We two very frightened youths sat so closely together we were almost as one amid the wildflowers at our beloved "Special Place," our scruffy rural swimming pond nestled in the sparse forest on the old McAlistair homestead near Ashton. We knew that the crystal-blue Georgia sky with its wispy morning clouds was arching over us as it had since we were but children. Today, however, we were afraid to look upward.

My dear Charley and I were barely drawing breath as we listened to a radio voice from his cell: "Intercept still predicted on schedule. On my mark, two minutes and counting . . . Mark."

Dr. Susan Perry...

I knew the comet was traveling at such a phenomenal speed that, if the missiles were unsuccessful in intercepting it, collision with Earth would come barely one second after it entered the atmosphere.

I envisioned people in a million villages and cities, Sherpas on their Himalayan mountainsides, members outside Parliament in London and Ottawa, vaqueros by their horses on the Argentine plains, convicts in the prison yard at San Quentin, Buddhist priests in Kyoto gardens, Kenyan women beside dusty stone wells. And so many children everywhere. All waiting. I also knew that many who were cognizant of what was coming were now huddled in dark basements, tunnels, mine shafts or, like our distant ancestors, in caves. Only a very few people in the most remote regions of Earth went about their day or night untroubled, blissfully unaware that the next few breaths they took could well be their last.

I looked in at my sister, Lilly, who was sitting on our couch in her favorite spot, expressionless, reading her iPad peacefully. Lilly was one of those lucky few.

The rest of us stood waiting, facing our destiny.

Across the entire planet, humanity's eyes were on the heavens.

Jimmy-Joe Hartman...

Claire still had her arms round me. Her cheek wuz pressed against mine. Then Poppa put his arms round both of us. Had him his Bible in one hand and was sayin', "'Yea, though I walk through the valley of the shadow of death, I will fear no evil: for thou art with me . . .'"

Katie McLane...

Standing beside me at the church, my mom had tears streaming down her cheeks. I was holding her hand real tight, trying to give her strength. She had bowed her head, like about everybody in the crowd at the church, even Darren. They were being led in prayer by the young minister who was saying, "And we beseech you, heavenly father, that our fair Earth be spared so we might live to rededicate ourselves to thee and thy teachings . . . in the name of him who taught us to pray: Our father, who art in heaven . . ."

I mouthed the words of the prayer, which I was surprised I actually knew. But I didn't bow my head.

No way.

If this was like really going to be IT: then I was determined to face it with my eyes open, looking into the sky.

Dr. Susan Perry...

I had brought Lilly out to stand beside me on our apartment's balcony overlooking Atlanta. She stood patiently with her normal, slightly glazed expression on her gentle and very pretty face. She glanced down at her iPad, which she held like a security blanket. I knew she was eager to continue reading whatever she had been, usually some scientific document that I knew she couldn't really comprehend. But Lilly enjoyed the words themselves, bless her sweet soul.

I was struggling to control my overwhelming sadness at the thought of Aniha whom I'd saved in Bangladesh and of all the children everywhere who might never grow up. My heart had swelled with grief for the unaware, innocents whose lives could be snuffed out in the next few seconds. Emotion had tightened up my throat so that I could barely speak. "I love you, Lilly . . . Here it comes."

"Okay, S-Susie." Lilly's voice was flat. Her face had its regular, unemotional quality.

The echoing TV voice was also nervous now, tremulous: "Here it comes. God be with us all! Ten . . . nine . . . eight . . ."

Concetta Cordaro...

In Starfire's control room all eyes were riveted on the image of Comet Avery that was nearly filling the telescope's screen as the captain said, ". . . three . . . two . . . one. Impact!"

The screen went into a completely silent whiteout.

The silence was prolonged.

And we all held our breath. Then the lieutenant next to Manchu shouted, "The radar! Look at the radar!" We did. And we saw. We saw that the single large blip on the radar screen was now thousands of tiny blips.

Jubilation! Everyone erupted, cheering with joy and peals of laughter! Of greatest, exuberant elation!

Everyone, that is, except Captain Manchu O'Hara and myself. I was fascinated to see that, like me, he also remained completely silent and motionless, even as the cheering, deafening, teary celebration swirled enthusiastically around us. It was as though we were alone, in the silent eye of a hurricane. Even when several patted us on the back and then went to hug someone else, the captain and I sat, unmoving. Over the com link I heard, "Starfire, this is Houston. Status report? . . . Starfire, Houston: Do you read?"

Finally Manchu O'Hara drew a slow breath and pivoted to look back directly into my eyes. It was a moment that I'll remember forever.

Then, still gazing into my eyes, he touched his com key and spoke with quiet, consummate professionalism, "Houston, this is Starfire . . . Mission accomplished."

Katie McLane...

All of us near the church heard a radio newsman's voice echoing across the town square: "Direct hits! On all missiles!" We gasped and hung suspended till we heard, "Radar reports that . . . that . . . *Yes!* The comet has been *shattered!*"

Everybody went *crazy* with shrieks of joy, cheers, and tears! I was a cheerer. My mom was sobbing. She clutched me so tight I could hardly breathe.

Lisa McLane...

By our pond Charley and I were hugging each other while jumping up and down amid the glorious wildflowers like little schoolchildren. Then we shared a heartfelt kiss as tears of happiness flowed bountifully. And we burst out laughing boisterously through our tears.

Charley grabbed my hand manfully, and we rushed off to share the joy we knew would be rampant in town.

Jimmy-Joe Hartman...

Poppa was on his knees in the middle of Sylvan Road, thankin' "God the father Almighty." Claire kneeled down beside him. I hung for a sec, but got to feelin' kinda embarrassed. I just patted their shoulders, said, "Shit, I told y'all it'd be okay." Then I headed off with a springy step to see if ol' Scooter'd survived the 'Pocalypse.

Clarence Frederick...

With a trembling hand I wiped the perspiration off my brow and laughed nervously. Simone was smiling at me through her tortoiseshell glasses with a sweet I-told-you-so look.

LeBron gave his mother a hug. "You know, Mom, maybe the Braves'll win again after all."

Katie McLane...

Darren's big brother Tim was swinging Darren around giddily. Then Darren pointed to the sky, shouting, "Katie! Look! Fireworks!"

In the eastern sky dozens of bright streamers were flaming down. A meteor shower. Another radio voice said, "Radar shows some small fragments of the comet falling through the stratosphere, but experts assure us that most all of them will burn up long before they can reach the surface."

Darren came over beside me. "Cool, huh?"

"Totally," I said quietly. But I remember frowning a little as I gazed into the sky. Something about the sparkling, shooting stars was mesmerizing. Strange, even. All those little pieces of cosmic stuff that had traveled billions of miles from deep space, glittering and sprinkling down.

Dr. Susan Perry...

From our balcony we'd gotten a hint of the nuclear flash low in the eastern sky and heard cheering in the streets and nearby apartments.

I slowly exhaled as I put both arms around Lilly and held her close. A newsman's voice from our TV said, "NASA reports that falling shards of the comet may damage a few weather and communication satellites. The debris field, the area where any small meteorites may actually reach Earth, is surprisingly small, only an ellipse about seventy miles across. It should go from about Valdosta, Georgia, in the south and extend northwest across the tip of Alabama to about Jackson, Tennessee."

I was only vaguely listening. I was feeling thankful to have dear expressionless Lilly leaning her head with its flyaway hair against me.

And knowing that tomorrow we'd have another day.

The Documentarian...

At Lisa and Charley's special place in the forest outside Ashton, there were no security cameras or monitoring devices. But from discoveries made later, we can reconstruct what happened after the comet had been shattered and the teenagers had happily left the area.

At that pastoral hideaway the forest birds would have chirped cheerfully as a breeze ruffled the sycamore leaves.

Then the birds likely grew suddenly quiet, sensing something coming.

In an instant, a high-pitched whistling might have been heard. It would have grown louder until a small, glowing, softball-size object rocketed down through the trees, breaking branches, and impacting explosively into exposed bedrock near the bank of the pond as startled birds scattered frantically.

Then silence returned.

The object would have lay smoking in the small crater it had created. Moisture would have slowly begun appearing from the ice, likely frozen for eons, but which was now thawing. Drops dripped.

They would have looked deceptively harmless.

Dr. Susan Perry...

Lying awake in the darkness that night, I knew I wasn't the only one in the world who was having trouble sleeping after the tumultuous emotions we'd all experienced. It was just after midnight, the new day we might never have seen. The events and outcome of the previous day must have also caused hundreds of millions of us to pause. And think.

I slipped out of bed and looked in on Lilly, who was breathing peacefully. The sleep of the purely innocent.

I felt drawn to go up to the roof of our tall building. A few of us had created a small garden area. Some potted green plants and flowers, some parsley, sage, rosemary, and thyme. The spices of life. I sat on one of the cedar Adirondack chairs, wrapped snugly in my favorite old shawl, looking up at the magnificent dome of stars above me. There was no moon, but some very soft light bathed the rooftop.

I realized it was starlight. Pure starlight. The clean Georgia air allowed me to see the myriad stars and even the soft swath of our Milky Way galaxy above me. I gazed deeply into the heavens. Into the unknowable. Into the infinite mystery. Ever since I was a child that vision had always been a profoundly spiritual experience.

Not unlike the experience of the last twenty-four hours.

Just as Avery's Comet had been about to breach the outermost fringe of Earth's atmosphere, just as it was only one second away from destroying all the very best and very worst of the human race, it had been met head-on by the unified strength of humankind, the international armada of defensive missiles had shattered the comet. We had saved our Earth.

What we didn't know was that we had also opened Pandora's box.

4

AWAKENINGS

Jacob Nichols, 76, Tennessee farmer...

My wife, Lottie, was a good ol' gal. We got together in eighth grade and never looked back. Goin' on perty near fifty-five years. Lottie was a big-boned, ruddy-cheeked farmwoman, come o'German stock. She enjoyed the basics, Lottie did. A well-plowed field, enough rain, the smell of our barn. She liked her coffee black and her TV news programs to the point. She had no patience for that kinda over-jolly, forced cama-raderie y'see on so many o'them local news teams.

So every sunrise she drank her strong coffee in the kitchen of our farm here outside Dayton, Tennessee, and she watched the straight-ahead, no-frills morning news on Channel Six.

She liked the clean-cut young anchorman, Gregg Brantley, par-ticularly because he was a black fella. She'd seen a lotta Gregg's race mistreated while she was growing up on her uncle's farm in the fifties down in Miss-sippi. Oft times she'd sneaked the children among 'em some extra sweets or medicines. She thought it was good to see their people finally gettin' at least a little more o'their fair share.

I remember the mornin' she was watching that Gregg fella doing a recap of the comet story while she was chompin' on her extracrisp wheat toast. He said, "It was one month ago today that we all faced oblivion—and survived." They showed some news clips of that comet comin', gettin' blowed up. Then they showed a farmhouse where a bunch o'scientific guys and gals prowled around a week later with some 'lectronic instruments, goin' into a garage that been damaged by a little piece of that comet comin' through the roof.

Gregg said, "Amazingly, the only problems resulting from the comet were minor." He told how most o'them fragments fell down in less populated areas, a few in Tennessee but mostly 'cross southwestern Georgia. Said civilian and military scientific teams was specially investigatin' a few of them impact sites in certain areas where they found levels of radiation a little higher than it oughta be. Them particular areas got cordoned off till "further study could be done." And they were still waiting to hear results.

Lottie was watchin' it all real intent. She licked her finger to pick up a few toast crumbs on the table by my plate, way she always did. Made me smile. Lottie never wasted a speck o'food. She swallered the last of her coffee while we seen on the news some military-lookin' guys casually takin' stations in front of the "Restricted Area" warning tape. At a coupla different places they showed, I member noticin' this one guy who reminded me o'somebody. He was square-jawed, 'bout forty-five, and clearly the head honcho. His eyes was small, but real concentrated, hawklike. He had this intense look, knitted brow and all. Salt-and-pepper hair trimmed short, military-style.

That's when I 'membered who he called to mind: the hard-assed colonel who'd run my reserve unit. This guy on the TV had that same kinda look: athletic face and body that looked hard from regular, disciplined exercise. He wasn't in uniform, but there warn't no mistakin' that iron kinda bearin'. He was a man accustomed to being at the top of a command structure. He was issuin' orders. We heard one of the uniformed guys respondin' to him, sayin', "Yes sir, Mr. Mitchell."

Then Gregg come back on the screen with that warm voice o'his and finished up the story, sayin' "And very quickly life returned to normal—"

"Yes it did, Gregg," Lottie said as she clicked off the TV. "And we gotta get on with it." She stood and picked up her plate and cup from our old Formica table. She smiled, said t'me, "I cain't wait to see that new knotty-pine table in here."

"Got an email from Walmart this mornin'," I told her. "Deliverin' tomorrow. 'Bout time we dumped this ol' scratched-up thing, huh?"

She leaned down and nipped my ear, sayin', "Long as you don't get any ideers 'bout dumpin' your ol' scratched-up wife."

I swatted at her, playful-like. Then I headed out round back t'finish tunin' up our tractor. I knew Lottie'd be about her normal mornin' chores on the other side.

Few months earlier there'd been some hog stealin' and other mischief hereabouts. We even heard some snoopy sounds at night. So I'd ordered up a coupla them security cameras from Amazon, set 'em up, and natcherly we hadn't seen nothin' unusual since.

Till that day.

That awful day.

I didn't see how the nightmare started that mornin' till way late that night when Lottie's cousin Randy brung me back from the hospital in his deputy sheriff car. He sat with me while I played back the video. TV showed pitchers from both cameras at the same time.

On one side o'the screen I saw myself workin' at the tractor out back o'the house, startin' to rev up the engine. It's a real loud sucker. On the other side I saw Lottie come out carryin' her pail of slop for the hogs and let herself into the pen. Our two sweet ol' hogs was round to the far side o'the trough, back in the shadows. Couldn't hardly see 'em.

But on the video I could hear her callin' to 'em like always, "C'mon, Maribelle. George. Ooooo pig. Souieee."

Then I saw Lottie come to a standstill. Froze in her tracks. Like she was hearin' a sound different'n anything she ever had. I turned up the volume on her half o'the video, and I heard it then: this real deep, ugly growlin'. It was eerie. Made the hairs stand up on the back o'my neck. Musta hit Lottie the same way. I saw her tilt her head toward where the hogs was in the shadows. She said, kinda worried-like, ". . . Maribelle?"

What I seen next on that video made my heart turn inside out.

Lottie barely had time to see them two huge hogs come chargin' toward her, lookin' like I ain't never seen any hogs look: eyes glarin', ears back! She stood there, froze for a split second, then dropped the pail and turned to run, but it was too late. Both o'them 250-pounders was on her. Attackin' her! Vicious! Snappin' at her legs, jumpin' up on her! She cried out, panicked, "No! Oh my God! Jacob! JACOB!"

But I was revvin' the goddamn tractor engine. I didn't hear.

Them monstrous, slatherin' hogs dragged Lottie down into the filth. Their cloven hooves clawed and gouged deep, tearin' her skin. On the video I saw their red eyes gleamin', their lips was curled back, teeth flashin'. I knew the stench of their foul breath musta been hot in Lottie's face while she was tryin' to beat 'em back. And screamin' for me.

But I didn't hear. God a'mighty, it was awful. And there I was right round the corner. But revvin' the goddamn engine. Frustrated that I couldn't get the damn distributor to work smooth.

Then on the video I seen myself look up. I 'membered that moment. Over the engine roar I finally heard Lottie shriekin'. I took off round the corner of the barn.

The rest of it I seen with my own eyes.

I couldn't never thought o'seein' that kinda horror. Them huge hogs had trampled Lottie right down into the thick muck. Their powerful jaws was rippin' ugly gashes in her flesh. Lottie's face was twisted up like a nightmare. Her mouth was open wide screamin', but no sound come out 'cause them monsters had tore open her throat. Blood was spoutin' out like fountains from her severed arteries.

I went bezerk. Bellowin' with rage. I grabbed a shovel, saw Lottie slump unconscious down in the reekin' mire as I leaped into the sty and started tryin' to beat them beasts away. Them crazy-fierce hogs turned right on me. They was fiery eyed, covered with Lottie's blood. Attacked me like wild razorback boars. I never seen such big animals move so fast. So intense. So crazed and blood-hungry.

But I was more crazed than them, by God. I was full o'pure fury. White hot. Didn't even feel their teeth sink in clear to the bones o'my legs. I beat 'em and beat 'em till their blood was splatterin' all over me. I beat 'em frantic till they was bloody and senseless, and finally lay dyin' in the mud, muscles twitchin' in spasms.

I was gaspin' and shakin' all over. I scooped Lottie up. She was limp in my arms. That was when I saw what all they done to her. They'd ripped her whole stomach wide open. Her organs, liver, intestines was all exposed, ruptured open, gorged with blood and muddy manure.

I was blind with tears. Threw my head back and let out a scream so hard and loud that the damn blood vessels in my throat burst.

Dr. Susan Perry...

As I drove along toward my workplace that second week in August, I could hear the leaves of the oaks and yellow poplars rustling loudly, troubled by a disturbing wind. Those old-growth trees thickly line Clifton Road, a pleasant street that curves through a largely residential section on the northeast side of Atlanta. Eventually it reaches a campus-like complex of sparkling, elegant buildings nestled slightly below the street level among the green trees: the headquarters of the Centers for Disease Control and Prevention.

A sprawling federal agency, the CDC operates branch centers in many major cities, but the headquarters in Atlanta was the focal point for all. It coordinated ongoing research efforts against contagious diseases and provided a strike force of trained personnel whenever epidemics broke out anywhere in the country or the world. It was also the acknowledged world leader in the investigation of strange, seemingly unexplainable, biomedical phenomena.

Two crescent-shaped ten-story glass and steel main buildings that faced Clifton Road dominated the campus. Just to the southeast across an inviting, broad green lawn was eleven-story Building 18, which housed several units including VSPB, the Viral Special Pathogens Branch, which I worked for.

Everyone on the campus wore security badges around their necks. Lilly and I used ours to enter through the impressive two-story atrium. We always came in that way because Lilly was fond of the large, papery modern-art chandelier overhead. We walked beneath it. Her hand in mine as usual. Lilly's other hand rested on her beloved iPad in its case hanging from her shoulder. I was in my favorite clothes: white Reeboks, faded jeans, and a powder-blue chambray shirt. Lilly always preferred simple, longish dresses with tiny, intricate pastel prints. She had a favorite thin, coral cardigan sweater, which she frequently wore over her dresses, though it often didn't match. Lilly had little regard for her appearance. A few errant strands of hair always found their way in front of her eyes. She rarely noticed when I'd move them aside. My sweet sister looked particularly pretty in whatever she wore. It always made me smile when people whom she passed noted her admiringly, but Lilly was unaware and kept her eyes down.

As we crossed the atrium, she nodded questioningly toward the women's room. "Okay, honey," I said, "I'll be up in the office." She peeled off as I kept walking with a spring in my step. I was pleased how we'd just beaten back a hepatitis flare in Brazil. En route to my office I detoured past my favorite section, deeper in the building. To me it was the heart of the CDC: the laboratories. I paused to peer through one of the double-thick biosafety windows that looked into BSL-4, the highest security lab, Biosafety Level Four. I knew the vital protocols by heart.

Excerpted from CDC Lab Safety Protocol Link

Why laboratory safety is important

Laboratory safety cannot be achieved by a single set of standards or methods. What is an acceptable workflow in a lower biosafety-level lab may expose workers to risk if used in a higher biosafety-level lab. All levels of biosafety are needed to allow scientists and researchers to work with specimens to identify new health threats, stop outbreaks, and gain new knowledge.

Biosafety—the science of working with risk

CDC has the expertise to operate laboratories at all levels of biosafety. All laboratories require special training and equipment, whether lab staff are working with relatively safe materials or extremely dangerous pathogens. There are four biosafety levels (BSL) of labs at CDC:

BSL-1—these labs handle agents that pose minimal risks and are not known to consistently cause disease in healthy adults

BSL-2—these labs handle agents that pose only moderate risks to lab staff or the environment

BSL-3—these labs handle agents that can cause serious or lethal disease

BSL-4—the highest level of lab safety in the world, these labs handle the deadliest pathogens for which there is no known cure or treatment

Courtesy CDC

Dr. Susan Perry...

I saw a pair of CDC laboratorians working inside the all-white, state-of-the-art chamber that was BSL-4. The two scientists wore bulky, blue isolation suits very similar to space suits. They smiled through their helmets and waved, as pleased to see me as I was them. One gave me a big thumbs-up. I was happy to be back. The CDC had been home to me for the last five years, since I'd completed my postdoc work at Stanford.

I took the elevator up to the third floor and stepped out into a bureaucratic corridor cluttered with stacked file boxes and occasional file cabinets, which had migrated out of overstuffed offices. Approaching me from the opposite direction was Dr. Prashant Sidana, a rail-thin, birdlike Mumbai native with floppy brown hair parted carefully on one side. He was carrying a half-eaten jelly doughnut. I grinned. "What, you didn't bring me one, Prashant?"

He recognized his error as he licked his finger. "Ah. Ah. Most sorry, Susan, but welcome back to you nevertheless." I noticed that his eyes darted nervously around. This was not unusual. Prashant was often stirred by various low-grade paranoias. Today he seemed particularly preoccupied about something, but was determined to get through the appropriate greeting and pleasantries first. "I heard that you bedazzled them down in Sao Paolo," he said in his delightful Marathi accent. "Even more than in Vietnam last month. Or in—"

"Whoa, whoa." I chuckled. "You're much too kind. But that won't get you off the hook for not bringing me a doughnut." While I was certainly very proud of all our recent successes, dear Prashant could often go over the top. "The most important thing is that we stopped the hepatitis."

"Yes, yes indeed. You kicked its buttocks." Prashant often made me smile when he used a catchphrase. Though he'd been in the States for a few years, his grasp of our colloquial linguistics was still a work in progress. He leaned slightly closer. "And the rumor is you are next in line for promotion. Be right up there on Lauren's level."

"Well"—I raised both hands slightly to quell his enthusiasm—"I certainly haven't—"

He snagged my sleeve to interrupt, and I realized he was finally getting to the point of what was disturbing him. He blinked nervously as he leaned closer still, speaking more confidentially, "And speaking of Lauren, *he's here again.*"

I frowned, confused. "Who's here?"

"I've seen him more than once since you've been gone," he whispered as he slowly guided me to rotate with him 180 degrees so that we had switched positions. "Mitchell. I heard his name is Mitchell. Look over my left shoulder. The tall man down there talking to Lauren. See?"

I looked across Prashant's shoulder toward the far end of the cluttered corridor. The man he'd called Mitchell was a hale and hardy sort, over six feet, probably midforties. I sensed a commanding presence and got an immediate impression of power.

Waiting quietly nearby Mitchell and Lauren were two other men, one in a conservative gray suit and tie, the other in more casual clothes with a windbreaker. They were each subtly scanning in different directions. Watchdogs? I noticed that they each had a tiny earplug in one ear with a wire discreetly disappearing into their collars. They lent an added touch of importance and mystery to this Mitchell person. He was conferring with my immediate superior, Dr. Lauren Fletcher, typically elegant and carefully groomed in one of her creamy Donna Karan suits.

Prashant whispered, "I will bet you dollars to a great many doughnuts that he is military intelligence." As I sized up Mitchell and his entourage, Lilly was shuffling past us, engrossed in reading her iPad. Her cardigan was hanging a bit unevenly, as usual. She had that normal vacant look in her downcast blue eyes.

Lilly had overheard Prashant's words about Mitchell. She glanced up absently toward the man, eyed him blankly for an instant, then walked into my nearby office.

I said to Prashant, "Okay. I see him. But why do you think he's military intelligence?"

"Are you kidding? Look at those CIA types with him." I smiled patiently at Prashant's paranoia and followed Lilly into my research office with Prashant right on my heels. "And I am most certain I remember seeing him here three *years* ago. Among some military people. And he definitely has that 'intelligence' look. Surely you must see it, Susan?"

I really liked Prashant. His constant apprehensiveness and OCD attention to detail made him an extremely careful laboratorian. He was exactly the person you wanted by your side when you were in the level four lab, dealing with a hot virus. I drew a breath and turned to him. "Now Prashant," I said, trying to be gentle, "the last time you thought something shady was going on, it turned out to be plumbing repair."

"Yes, yes. I know, but this is different," he urged emphatically.

I tried not to roll my eyes and instead glanced over to our friendly CDC custodian, Joseph Hartman, who smiled back knowingly as he emptied my trash. "Joseph, I think you better do some serious praying for this guy."

"Oh, I do, Dr. Susan. All the time. For all y'all." He tilted his gray head down and gave a pointedly cautionary look over the top of his wire-rimmed glasses. "Particularly when y'all out there in the field." Joseph was a caretaker, in every sense of the word. A gentle, self-effacing white man with thin hair. An Atlanta native, he'd been a fixture at the CDC many years before I came along. We'd often have conversations about his daughter, Claire, who was a respected nurse and "the light of his life." I'd had the pleasure of getting to know Claire when she'd come to several CDC family events. Her natural empathy made it clear to me why patients were so fond of her, as Joseph had told me. Other times a more disheartened Joseph would lean against my lab table and sigh to me with concerns about his prodigal son, James Joseph, who was bent on calling himself Jimmy-Joe and doing everything he could to go down the wrong track.

Joseph was wonderful with Lilly. He was one of the people Lilly was completely comfortable with. That day she was sitting on her tall stool as usual with her iPad resting on her special corner of my lab table. Though most of my office was generally cluttered, Lilly's corner was always organized and neat. Obsessively so. Her head was bent so low over her iPad that when Joseph tried to lean down to catch her eye, he almost had to get on his knees. "S'cuse me, Lilly?" He waited for her millisecond glance of awareness. "Can I get at that trash can, honey?"

Lilly was already intent again on her iPad, but she responded without looking at Joseph, "Uh, okay."

Joseph carefully eased it out past her, then headed to his cart outside my door. He had to dodge around Prashant, who had continued to pace in the central area between my computer desk, bookshelves, lab table, and window. He was gesturing with the last remains of his jelly doughnut. "Susan, surely you remember those rumors about the military pressuring CDC to develop biological weapons. I will bet you that Mitchell is just the type to be at it again."

I sifted through some files, my attention already elsewhere. Prashant got annoyed. He sat on the other stool near Lilly's end of the table and leaned his arm on her neatly organized section, trying to needle me. "I would think you'd worry more about the possibility of biological weapons. After the way BioTeck Industries developed that Agent Orange–type killer stuff out of Chris's DNA research."

His statement sparked exactly the effect he wanted. I glanced sharply at him as I chafed at the memory. Prashant knew very well how deeply I missed Chris Smith. And on much more than just a professional level. My eyes drifted over to a photo pinned on the wall near my desk. It was of Chris and me, laughing and hugging in New Orleans's Lafayette Square two years ago, after we'd finally curtailed that city's West Nile outbreak. Chris was a handsome, midthirties man with thick red hair and multihued, intelligent eyes. *Extremely* intelligent. The photo was taken the day he'd bought me the little opal ring I'd worn ever since. Just three weeks after that day, he went away. Loving memories remained, but so did the sadness. I sighed, acknowledging what Prashant said. My voice was lower. "Of course I care, Prashant."

Lilly glanced from her iPad to her small portion of the table, which Prashant still leaned on. She was uneasy, but spoke flatly to him. "Ooopsie. You m-messed up my pencils."

Prashant stood up from the table, politely understanding his error. "Oh, I'm so sorry, Lilly." He carefully realigned the pencils. "There. All fixed." Lilly stared at them as Prashant went on to me, "Now, Susan, think about it for just—"

"Got j-jelly on one," Lilly interrupted.

Prashant exhaled a puff of irritation. "*Sorry*, Lilly." He wiped the pencil carefully. "There. Okay?"

Lilly stared at the pencil. ". . . But it'll be s-sticky."

Prashant was getting frazzled, his voice took on an edge. "Shall I go and wash them for you?"

"Don't worry, Prashant," I soothed him, "I'll take care of the pencils. But do you have any proof about this Mitchell?"

"Wellll . . ." Clearly he hated to admit it. "Not yet, but—"

I was relieved when a fresh and very healthy-looking new face appeared at my door. "S'cuse me, ma'am. This Epidemiology? Dr. Perry?"

"Yes. Susan. Hi."

"Howdy." The tall visitor reached out a naturally tanned hand. The hairs on his wrist were sun-bleached white. "I'm R.W. Hutcherson. Folks call me Hutch." Of the classic Westerner Butch Cassidy tradition, I registered immediately. With his late-thirties outdoorsman good looks, sun-streaked, light-brown hair, charmingly crooked smile, and seasoned snakeskin boots below his Levi's, the prototype was impossible to miss, and I didn't.

But I also didn't miss a beat as I returned his firm handshake. "Of course. Lauren's been raving to us about you and your work. *Very* unusual for her, believe me."

Given his impressive physical persona, his general attitude was in pleasant counterpoint: he seemed unexpectedly shy. "Mighty glad to hear that, ma'am. I sure paid her enough."

I smiled. "Montana U and Berkeley, right?"

"That'd be right, ma'am."

"Welcome. And that'd be *Susan*," I insisted, as I grinned, privately appreciating his interruption of Prashant's intensity. "*Very* welcome."

Prashant picked up my little barb and smirked, "All right, all right. You are wanting some proof. I will get you some." He glanced toward Hutch, grasping his hand. "Hello, Prashant Sidana." And then before Hutch could respond, Prashant went on to me, "Then perhaps you will listen?"

I looked at Prashant with the patience of a true friend. "Have I ever not?"

Prashant nodded pointedly, making clear how he intended to hold me to it. He started out, but paused, pulled out his cell phone. "Oh, Lilly? 'Lymphocyte Irradiation Studies'?" I saw him click on his cell to record her answer.

Without looking up from obsessively wiping her pencils clean, and *without stuttering*, Lilly rattled off, "Favero, Martin. Article in *The Journal*, 1989, Volume 4, issue 13, page 37. Also Knight, David C., *Microbiological Journal*, 2007, Volume 2, issue 7, page 19, including photomicrographs. Also Locke, Matthew—"

"Yes, yes. That is plenty. Thank you, Lilly," Prashant said as he clicked his recorder off. Then he gave me a last, huffy look and flitted out.

"O-Okay," Lilly said in her monotone, without looking up.

Hutch stared in amazement at Lilly, who was intent on her pencils. I smiled at his incredulity. "My sister, Lilly."

Hutch moved closer to her. He sensed her special needs and offered his warm, Montana-bred smile. "Hi there, Lilly."

Lilly didn't look up from reorganizing her area. She never looked anyone directly in the eye. Her voice was always colorless and level. "Hello."

"How can you remember all that?"

Assessing her pencils, she said, "I'm-m exceptional."

I moved to them and hugged her. "Yes, you are. And here're some fresh ones that haven't been uploaded yet, honey." I carefully laid a handful of new pharmaceutical and medical journals at the edge of her space. Lilly immediately began turning through one, scanning each page in less than two seconds.

Hutch blinked, spoke aside to me, "She's not . . . *reading* those?"

"Yes. Lilly's got an amazing ability for speed-reading and an *exceptionally* dazzling memory." I brushed back an errant lock of her auburn hair. "Because of her autism she doesn't respond much to social stuff. But she's a savant, aren't you, honey?" She nodded without looking up.

"I saw a boy like that on *60 Minutes* a while back"—Hutch looked at Lilly in admiration—"who could play a whole piano concerto after just listening to it."

"Incredible, huh? Autism presents differently in each individual. With that boy it was music. With Lilly it's shapes a little bit—she loves that old Tetris game—but mostly it's words. She's read most of the texts and journals in the CDC library."

Hutch was suitably astonished. "What? Most of—? She understands them?!"

"Oh, not a word." I chuckled. "But she can *recall* every detail." I smiled at his stupefied expression. "Yeah. I know. And what a waste not to use that skill, huh? That's why I brought her to be with me here after our parents died. Never wanted her in a home. Better for her in the real world. She's fairly high functioning. Everybody here loves her."

Hutch laughed charmingly. "Who wouldn't? A living bibliography!" He smiled at Lilly. "And lots prettier than Google. Nice to meet you, Lilly."

Lilly had no reaction. She just went on scanning the dense documents at lightning speed. While Hutch contemplated her, I studied him. I'd immediately noted the wedding ring, of course. Now I considered the healthy tan, the cowboy-handsome face with just enough smile lines to give it character. His jacket was old corduroy, the color of my favorite Cadbury milk chocolate. His shirt was a muted blue-and-brown plaid but with a button-down collar. The jeans were well worn in, as was the broad leather belt, which augmented the wrangler feel. He looked up and almost caught my inspection. He smiled shyly, seeming like he felt uncomfortable about saying, "Listen, Dr. Levering told me to work out of your office for a couple days till mine's ready, but if that's gonna be a bother for you then—"

"Not at all." I smiled.

"Much obliged. He's got me taking over the list of clinical trial subjects for the new AIDS medication."

Really? I was surprised. Curious. "That was Lauren Fletcher's pet project. She must be on something new now . . . or . . ." For a moment I considered Prashant's suspicion about Lauren and Mitchell, then passed it off. "But you're welcome in here. I'll show you how to access—"

"It was r-raining."

I glanced at Lilly. ". . . What honey?"

"October twenty-sixth," she said, while still scanning one of the journals. "Thursday. Three years ago. When that M-Mitchell person was here before. Rained all day."

I was pondering that information when officious-looking, sixtyish Dr. Ernest Levering was passing in the corridor and paused to look in. "Oh good, Hutcherson. You found her." Hutch nodded, and Levering looked at me. "You get the file I forwarded?"

I glanced at my computer screen, tapped at the keyboard. "I saw it come in, but hadn't opened it yet." I did so as he went on.

"About a woman who got attacked by her hogs."

Hutch looked startled. "What?"

"Yeah," Levering continued. "We may have gotten a couple of other similars. Woman was killed this time. Locals are stumped. Sent us a note about it. It's attached. Lauren really wanted to check it out, but she's got enough on her plate, so I gave it to you." As he headed out with his mind on other things, he said, "Let me know if it's anything." And he was gone.

Hutch was bemused, quoted *The Wizard of Oz*, "My, but people come and go so quickly here."

I looked over the file a moment longer, then drew a deep breath. I was puzzling over what Lilly had said. She was still speed-reading her journals. "Lilly, are you certain it was that man Mitchell you saw three years ago?" She nodded without looking up. I explained to Hutch, "Someone Prashant was just talking about. Prashant was suspicious about—"

"He had l-leaves on his shoulders," Lilly added.

Hutch smiled, beginning to dismiss Lilly's recollection. But I knew better. I frowned, prodding, ". . . Mitchell had leaves on his shoulders?" She nodded again. "What kind of leaves?"

"M-maple." Lilly turned a page. "Little gold ones."

Hutch's smile evaporated. "Sounds like an army major."

"Lilly, did Mitchell have a uniform? Like an army man?"

She turned another page, intent on her speed-reading. "Mmm hmm."

Hutch's eyes met mine, shaking his head, confused. "Who *is* this Mitchell guy?"

My frown deepened as I considered that Prashant's suspicions about this man, Mitchell, might possibly have some substance. Finally I said, "That seems to be a very good question."

5

CHANGELINGS

Lisa McLane...

This was an unusual day. To say the very least.

My beloved Charley and I were walking through the woods toward our hideaway on the abandoned farm. It was a very warm and beauteous August afternoon. We hadn't been back in more than a month, since Avery's Comet. Charley pointed ahead toward a butterfly on a fallen tree. He'd told me how they were called "nurse logs" because as they slowly deteriorated, they provided a bounty of nurturing energy for the new growth springing up around and through them. How could I not adore such a philosophical young man?

Charley eased quietly across the loam beneath our feet toward the butterfly. Then he cupped his hands around it, ever so gently. He was very careful not to harm its delicate yellow-and-black wings. He gently held it out to show me. This was one of the primary reasons I loved Charley: he was the manliest of football players, yet he still appreciated a butterfly's fragility. With our foreheads touching, we marveled at the wispy, fairylike creature, then Charley opened his hands and set it free.

We smiled and continued our walk and talk about classes. "History's not a problem. Mr. Castenares is terrific—but biology! God! I hate Navarro, she can be so nasty."

"Hey, I can help you with biology, Lisa," he said as he grabbed me. I squealed gleefully.

"No, Charley! That tickles. And I know what kind of biology *you're* talking about."

He put on his endearing pouty face. "Aww Lise, I thought you liked me."

"Well, I don't!" I said emphatically. Then I pressed my nose to his. ". . . I *love* you, Charley Flinn." Then I kissed him sweetly, and he returned it with tenderness. We had discovered a year earlier the enjoyment of the French style of kissing. Ours was wonderfully intimate, yet always respectful and gentle. We were both on the conservative side when it came to sex. Charley even more than me. The day before the comet arrived had been our first time. Neither of us wanted to die without having made love to each other. We did it safely, of course. It was gentle, sincere, and right.

After our kiss we looked deeply into each other's eyes, seeing so much promise and a long, beguiling future together. Then we walked on through the forest, holding hands.

"I really can help you with biology class," Charley insisted. "If you'll help me with English." He looked down, shaking his head. "Man, I wish Joseph Conrad had stayed in Poland. I mean, like *Apocalypse Now* was a cool movie, I guess—but *Heart of Darkness* is so dense and—"

"Charley . . . ?" My voice sounded very strange even to me. Because of what I had seen.

He glanced at me and saw that I was focused on something ahead of us. Then he saw it, too. And gasped with wonder. "What the *heck* . . . ?"

We were looking toward our special place in complete and utter amazement.

In the month since last we had been there, it had been impossibly transformed. Our ordinary, scruffy Georgia forest hideaway had somehow become *a spectacular rainforest-like garden*! It was truly breathtaking. Beyond belief!

We looked at each other in utter astonishment. Then we walked tentatively closer, slack-jawed, in among the plants. We marveled at many that we barely recognized because they were larger, more lavish, and thriving so thickly we couldn't even see our pond, which we knew was a hundred yards ahead of us. Many plants seemed familiar, but others were like entirely new variations. And they were all incredibly verdant and lush. The dense, explosive growth had formed a gorgeous, jungle-like canopy overtop us. I realized I was breathing more rapidly because I was getting scared. My voice was trembling, whispering, "Charley . . . this is impossible."

"But it's *here*! It's *real*!" Charley's voice was unsteady. He was as nervous as I. And equally bewildered. "This is like totally amazing, Lisa. Look!" He was touching a large plant that reached his shoulder. "This used to be like only a foot tall!" He looked around and above us. "How'd everything get so huge?!"

Then I saw something down lower. "Everything didn't. Look." I touched a plant that was definitely withered. "These have been sorta choked off by all the hardy ones."

"Yeah, but who cares? Look at the rest! How in the heck could this—?"

There was a sudden noise in the undergrowth. I jumped out of my skin! "Ohmigod! What's that?! *What's that?!*"

Charley was startled, too, but he grabbed a heavy stick and disappeared into the thick, green foliage, investigating. I lost sight of him as he shouted back, "I don't see anything, but—Holy *shit*!"

Suddenly there was silence. I waited a moment, my fear growing. There was still no sound. ". . . Charley?" All the birds had gone hushed as well. The silence grew more palpable around me. I felt a cold sweat glossing my skin. "Charley? What's wrong?"

"Lisa!" He shouted from within the undergrowth. "C'mere!"

I moved forward cautiously, spreading the thick, beautiful flora with my trembling hands as I took one guarded step at a time. Then, feeling much relief, I saw him in the midst of the dense greenery.

"Look at these, Lise!" He was lifting one branch of an imposing bush, six feet tall and equally wide. The branches were laden with clumps of knobbly red fruit the size of lemons.

"What are they?" I was completely puzzled by them. "They look a little like wild strawberries, but it's too late in the season . . . ?"

"Yeah, right. But there it is!" He laughed. "And whoever saw any this *big*?!" He picked one off the bush, smelled it, and then opened his mouth.

I grabbed his arm. "No! Charley? Are you crazy?! Put that down! It might be poison!"

"Naw, Lisa. Smell it. Go on."

I did, and blinked. Because it did indeed have a luscious strawberry fragrance. "But still, Charley—"

"C'mon, Lise." He smiled, unworried. "Isn't that like the best strawberry you ever smelled?" He lifted it to his lips.

"Charley! Don't you do it!"

"Take it easy." He opened his mouth.

"*Charley!*"

He bit off a small piece.

"I can't believe that you . . ." I watched closely as he pursed his lips slightly, moving the fruit around in his mouth, tasting thoughtfully, getting a sense of the flavor. The satisfaction I saw growing on his face gave me some small measure of relief. Then he nodded, swallowed it, and took a much larger bite and chewed it eagerly.

"Charley, no. You should wait until you see if—"

He swallowed the larger bite, then he took a long, satisfied breath as I watched him fearfully. He shook his head, gently dismissive, saying, "See. I told you there was—" Suddenly his face contorted grotesquely! He gasped, dropped the fruit, grabbed his throat with both hands!

I panicked, clutched at his shirt. "Charley! Charley! No!"

He was turning beet red, choking. He dropped to his knees, taking me down with him as he emitted a startling, menacing growl.

I was frantic, shaking him, screaming, "Charley! Oh my God! Oh my God!"

He began convulsing on the ground, his arms, legs, whole body, having a seizure! I kept screaming tearfully, "Charley! *Charley!*"

He suddenly stopped. Dead still. Eyes open, unmoving. I stared, terrified, whimpering through my tears, "Charley! No!"

Then he flashed a grin up at me. "That was one great strawberry."

"What!" I slugged his chest very hard, and I fell back, totally furious. "That was *not funny*!" But laughter was bubbling up through my anger. "You scared me to death!"

Charley pushed up onto one elbow among the wildflowers. He scrutinized the strange strawberry. "I have never tasted anything like this in my life. It's absolutely great! Here!" He held it out to me.

I shook my head and pushed his hand away. "There's no way."

Charley took another bite. "Lisa! Do I look like I've been exactly poisoned? Taste it."

"No, Charley."

"Li-sah, we eat 'em all the time. From this same bush!"

I gazed over at the greatly outsize wild strawberry bush. "But it, it's . . . different now."

"Yeah! It's just the best damn strawberry you'll ever have."

I looked carefully at the wild strawberry in his hand. Yes, it was bigger than the ones we always picked and ate here. It did appear perfect, ripe and succulent. I could even smell its delicious, inviting fragrance from where I sat. He held it out again. "It's really okay, Lise. In fact, it's great." It was very tempting. Finally, very tentatively, I took it. I examined all sides of it with utmost care. Smelled it again. Then I looked at Charley. He gave me a little upward nod of encouragement.

I breathed a taut, worrisome sigh. Then I took the tiniest possible mouse bite.

Charley guffawed. "Oh, well careful y'don't choke there, Lisa." Then with a wide-eyed wiggle of his head, he said, "Will you take a serious *bite*?!"

I looked at the strange fruit, screwed up my courage. And then I took a real bite. I chewed it very slowly and warily, my eyes darting around insecurely as my mouth and taste buds worked. Slowly my tension began to ease. I finally admitted, "You're right. It *is* the best strawberry I've ever tasted."

"Hey, would your man lie to ya?" He patted my knee and stood. "I'm getting a couple more." He picked a second strawberry for himself and another for me. We sat among the abundance of flowers, beneath the lush green garden canopy. And together we ate the fruit.

A few minutes later, as was our custom since we'd been but children, Charley had stripped down to nothing and dived into the pond. He swam among the lily pads, which were also strangely large. He held one up. "God! Look at the size of it!"

I shook my head in wonder as I slipped out of my jeans, T-shirt, and underwear. I was proud of my "lithe form," as Charley had immortalized it in his lyrical poem. But even though we used to swim naked together when we were little, I had grown somewhat shy in later years. Charley knew that, and I was aware how he politely confined his glances to moments when I wasn't looking. His poem made clear that he admired my body, but Charley was determined to be a gentleman and not rush me into anything except swimming. He shouted, "C'mon in, Lise, it's great!"

I suddenly lost my balance and swayed a little. "Whoa. I . . . I feel kinda light-headed."

"Must be from seeing my incredible bod," he joked.

I eased my foot into the pond. The chilly water climbed slowly up my tanned calf as Charley snuck a couple more quick glances. I shivered. "Ooo, it's cold."

Charley grinned sweetly. "C'mon over, honey. We'll snuggle."

But suddenly I got very dizzy. I sat down on the bank. "Charley, I am *really* light-headed," I said giggling.

He swam over toward me and suddenly blinked several times himself. "Whoa. Me, too. Feels kinda cool, huh?"

I lay back onto the lush, mossy bank, blinking heavily. "Maybe it's like a sugar rush? Those strawberries were really sweet." I felt exceptionally giddy. Charley pulled up onto the bank and lay beside me, slipping one leg over mine. Our bodies intertwined.

He yawned broadly. "Yeah, yeah, that's probably it. Let's just hang here a minute . . ."

We smiled at each other, feeling very woozy but warm together and extremely content as we drifted into sleep.

When my eyes suddenly snapped open, I saw the sun had set.

The sky was nearly dark. A half-moon was visible through the amazing new canopy of branches interlaced together up above me. At first I thought I'd dreamt it all. But looking very slowly and carefully around me, I perceived that it was undeniably real. That our childhood hideaway really had metamorphosed into this macabre jungle-rainforest.

And it was unnaturally quiet. In the gathering darkness with only the moonlight filtering down, all the plants that had grown so huge and dense, that had seemed so ominous before, no longer troubled me at all. I wasn't frightened in the least now. In fact it was exactly the opposite: I felt completely at home in this new environment. I somehow understood that this remarkably transformed realm was my personal domain. That I was its empress. I slowly realized that part of the miraculous strangeness of my new surroundings was not in *what* I was observing. It was *how*. I understood that, as unearthly as my surroundings had become, an equally strange and powerful transformation had taken place in me. Everything seemed—I searched for a word—*keener*? Yes. Sharper. Darker.

I slowly turned to look at Charley. I wasn't at all surprised to see his eyes already riveted on mine.

Charley Flinn, 17...

Lisa's eyes had a glint like nothing I'd ever seen. She had this dark, superconfident, almost scary smile. She was focused, intense. Like a spring coiled up really, really tight. Or a panther about to pounce. And I realized that I felt exactly the same.

Lisa McLane...

My formerly sweet, mild Charley now looked positively predatory. His normally warm brown eyes now had a sinister, dangerously sexual gleam in them. I sensed that my own looked similar.

I also noted how I wasn't in the least intimidated by him. I instinctively knew that I was more than a match for him. Or anyone. I felt a new razor-edge on my entire personality. On my entire *being*. It was inexplicable. And exhilarating. Regal.

We stared hard at each other. Studying. Taking measure how much the other felt it. It was like we had gone to sleep as infants, awakening as more than mature, experience-hardened adults.

I was suddenly a me I couldn't have even imagined a few hours earlier. And I saw that he was, too.

It was like my brain had jump-started. Had flashed alive with a flurry of sparks. I felt possessed of fresh, raw, extreme *native intelligence*. My mind felt electrified with millions of fiery new neural connections. Ideas, possibilities, schemes, all buzzed around in my head like myriad electrons at the speed of light. Anything and everything seemed within my grasp. It was brilliant. The feeling of pure superiority was tangible and potent.

Charley Flinn...

Lisa and I lay there riveted on each other like two alpha tigers meeting in this strange rainforest. Like we were circling, checking out the opponent's strength and determination. Eager to test ourselves. Each confident of victory. Each assured of achieving domination. Our breathing was deep. Measured. And there was rising sexual tension. Powerful. Visceral. Growing stronger every second. I could literally taste it. I knew she could, too.

I saw the tip of her tongue put a little shine on her upper lip. Then she whispered a command, "I want you."

Lisa McLane...

Charley's whispered reply was equally confident, cocky, heated. "Lucky you."

We leapt into it. Nearly tearing each other apart as each of us tried to dominate the sexuality. It was like nothing we'd ever experienced before. I might have been frightened if I wasn't so entirely consumed by it. And by total self-confidence. In addition to new mental acuity, my physical agility had also increased. My muscles and nerves positively tingled. Clearly his did, too. We rolled back and forth, grasping, kneading, struggling. Our tongues probed deep. Insistently. We were insatiable. Our faces, bodies, were damp with elevating passion.

Charley had never been so hot and hard bodied. My hand squeezed him tighter than ever. I rolled atop him and rode him strenuously. He cupped my breasts in his hands. Pulled me down and took them into his mouth.

I gasped from the erotica. He tried to roll me off, to take command. But my dexterity and determination topped his greater strength. I maintained control. I pressed down harder and harder onto him.

Charley Flinn...

I kept shifting my hips back and forth so I could catch all of her. Catch her good. Meet her halfway. Go deep. It was goddamn electrifying.

Lisa McLane...

And we built up to a final peak that was like nothing I'd ever known or even imagined: so spectacular, high-voltage, primal that I *shrieked/ laughed*! And again. And a third time.

Then we collapsed together, sucking in great gulps of air. Our bodies' pulsations and shivers continued boiling and churning furiously.

As the crest passed and the intensity very gradually ebbed, we remained locked in a tight embrace. Our bodies kept twitching, quivering from the exertion of the encounter.

Charley Flinn...

We'd fuckin' amazed ourselves. We couldn't even move for a long time. Then slowly began to uncoil. Lisa laid herself forward, down on me, but still coupled and breathing hard. Still ready for more, just like I was. Totally psyched. Physically and mentally.

Lisa McLane...

My eyes scanned across the luxuriant, mystical rainforest garden surrounding us. Across all the marvelously large and virile plant life that had magically evolved out of nowhere. My gaze came to rest on the wild strawberries. Despite the transformational expansion that had taken place within our brains, I had no idea *what* dark miracle had caused it. Then I looked at Charley. His eyes were locked on mine. They were cold, hard. Different.

Charley Flinn...

Without saying a word we both knew one thing for damn sure: whatever this was, it was only the beginning.

Katie McLane...

That night my frazzled mom was frantically tearing through a stack of papers on our kitchen table as she held the phone angrily against her stomach, snapping at me, "Where did you put it!?"

I looked up for the third time from writing on my laptop, doing my best to stay patient. "Really, Mom, I never saw a yellow Post-it with notes about—"

"Here it is, never mind." She was digging it out of her purse. "I don't know how it got in here."

I sighed to myself. Mom was generally a bit scattered. It was just her way. Like the sheets and towels in our linen closet that she always folded haphazardly. Whenever I opened that closet, I pictured the folds in Mom's poor brain being a little jumbled. I'd offered some subtle guidance a couple times by arranging the linen neatly, but Mom missed the point, and the closet went right back to being a confused mess. Before Dad moved out, I'd heard him complain how he had to take so much care of everything that he felt like Mom was not his wife but one of his daughters. Obviously theirs wasn't a heaven-made match.

Dad was paying the mortgage and child support, but Mom wanted to earn money herself. I saw how on-the-job business training while single parenting was doubly hard for her. Even after a couple years of separation, she was still hoping he might "get over his little fling" and come back before the divorce she'd filed got finalized.

So I tried to cut her some slack. And hold up my end by helping her at home, keeping up my pretty good GPA and all. But I still managed to ride my bike or do flips on Darren's trampoline or play the piano. My favorite was to climb into the huge oak in the backyard of our wonderful sixty-year-old clapboard house. I loved to lounge up in the branches and just let my imagination wander. Or read. Right then we were studying Greek mythology, which I was really into.

"Of course, I can, Mr. Vronski." Mom had gotten back on her call, using her pleasant, unhurried, professional voice despite busily shuffling papers. "A two-column ad in three colors would be four hundred fifty dollars. But the colors are worth it, sir."

Lisa came in the back screen door. She knew Mom hated it when we let it slam, but I noticed how Lisa let it bang good and loud that time. My sister barely glanced at me, but I zeroed in because right away I'd picked up a really weird vibe. Lisa had this sorta edgy smile, and her forehead was tilted down like the way dogs do when they're getting ready to attack. But it was the look in her eyes that was strangest. They were shining with, I don't know, hardness?

Mom waved angrily for Lisa to "stop right there" while keeping up her smooth telephone sales pitch. "Particularly in a section of the paper that's black-and-white and—all right. I'll call you first thing tomorrow. Thanks." She hung up and immediately went at Lisa. "I was worried sick! Do you know what time it is? Where have you been?"

"Out," Lisa said lightly, totally blowing Mom off. Then Lisa turned away, really haughty. Mom saw red, grabbed Lisa's arm, hard.

"Wait just a goddamn minute, young lady. What the hell has gotten into—"

"*Mother.*" Lisa's voice was low, but commanding. Powerful. Threatening even.

Mom blinked and so did I. Neither of us had ever heard this voice before. Never saw this kind of laser intensity from Lisa, who slowly turned and focused on Mom. Lisa's voice stayed low and even. Her face was fearsomely calm. "Please don't grab me like that." It was not a request but a *warning*. There was a really pointed pause as Lisa kept staring at Mom, then finally said, "Okay?" But it wasn't a question. It was a statement.

Mom blinked again. Never the strongest or most collected person anyway, Mom was clearly thrown off, and so was I, by Lisa's startling, almost dangerous attitude. Lisa eased out from underneath Mom's hand and walked off toward her room.

All my antennae were up, trying to figure out what was going on. Mom stood there stunned, like she was trying to decide whether or not to go after Lisa, when the phone rang. Mom glanced at the caller ID and muttered, "Shit." Then she blew out a puff of air, sucked herself into saleswoman mode, and answered cheerily, "Eileen McLane." As she started jabbering to another client, I followed Lisa.

Normally we were pretty okay with each other. On warm summer nights we'd stay up late out on the porch, talking about all kinds of stuff. We'd laughed and cried together. Particularly after Dad had left. Lisa hardly ever acted like she was so much older and more experienced, or stuff like that. We just talked straight with each other. I tried to be there when she needed me to be. And vice versa. I could usually read her pretty well. She'd always been a little, I dunno, softer, more of a romantic than me. That's how come that night was so weird. Lisa was different than I'd ever seen her. Back in fourth grade my teacher, Miss Schmitt, once told me I was an astute observer of human nature. I took that as a real compliment. But whether or not it was true, I was for sure fine-tuned to Lisa.

And she'd had a strange, seriously cocky gleam in her eyes. I knew that something was up.

Lisa McLane...

Alone in my room I was pacing back and forth restlessly, like a caged leopard, eager to break out and . . . and what? I didn't know. But something, goddammit. I wasn't even seeing the posters of boy-toy rock stars on the walls or the high school stuff on my shelves. I was looking right through them. Looking right through the walls. Feeling way beyond all that. Feeling mature beyond anything I'd ever imagined. Mature beyond myself. I was emboldened by the feeling. But struggling to determine exactly what this incredible buzz *was*.

Katie knocked and stuck her head in. "Lise? . . . You okay?"

"Definitely." I turned away from her, smiling privately to myself. I didn't trust myself to look at her, felt like my eyes must be dancing darkly.

I could feel Katie watching me like a bug under a magnifying glass. She was no fool. She knew something was going on. And trying to fathom it. *You have no idea, little girl,* I thought. And in fact neither did I. But I tried to toss a casual answer over my shoulder. "I'm fine, honey. Just need some private time to—"

"Y'sure, Lise? 'Cause *I'm* feeling like maybe there's—"

"Katie." I wanted her gone. My voice had an edge. "It's not about what *you're* feeling, okay?"

"Sure, Lise, but I just want to—"

"*No!*" I snapped around so quickly it startled her. And me, too. But it also gave me a pleasurable rush. I stared hard at her, forcing a smile that might have looked a bit deadly, but I couldn't help it. And moreover, I didn't care. I said with complete, quiet finality, "Not. Right. Now. Huh, Katie?"

She studied my eyes for a moment. Then she nodded, backed off, and closed the door.

Katie McLane...

I stood silently outside Lisa's door. Frowning. Trying to process what just happened. This was way beyond "something wrong." This was a Lisa I'd never known. The same on the outside maybe. But different inside.

The word *changeling* popped into my head. But I scoffed. That was crazy. I mean, I'd read legends about fairies stealing children and replacing them with identical, and dangerous, fairy children. Changelings, they were called. But I shook my head to get rid of that ridiculous notion. I knew those were fantasy stories. I didn't believe that Lisa wasn't still Lisa.

But what then? I stood there twisting one of my ringlets around my finger, pondering what was going on with my sister. And then I found myself thinking about her eyes. About that peculiar shine in them.

Lisa McLane...

I knew she was still outside my door. And concerned, cogitating while doubtlessly twisting one of her long ringlets around her finger.

110

But in less than half a second, I forgot about her and was back to *me*. The night was all about *me*.

I reached behind the stuffed polar bear I'd gotten for Christmas when I was six and named Frozy. I pulled out my hidden bag of chocolate chip cookies. Frozy fell onto my laptop keyboard, but I pushed her out of the way onto the floor as I sat down to the computer, wolfing a cookie down. This astounding kinetic energy was flowing in me, driving me.

I used the password to open this diary. I started rereading some of the previous entries. I immediately realized that I was reading *really quickly*. Much faster than I'd ever been able to. It gave me another wonderful rush of newly discovered capability. Of skills so far superior they made me laugh out loud. And reading what I'd written in the diary before made me smirk. What a lot of childish drivel. What florid gibberish. I was cynically castigating myself for writing such maudlin, sentimental—

Suddenly I stopped. *Florid gibberish? Cynically castigating? Maudlin? Where the hell*, I wondered, *were those extremely un-Lisa words coming from?* I mean, I knew that some momentous reaction, some stupefying, cataclysmic wonderment had taken place inside my brain. Somehow those wild strawberries had *expanded* my basic intelligence.

But even so, how could my *vocabulary* have instantly undergone such a voluminous download? From where had this capacious—*capacious?!*—glut of new words and phrases magically descended, materialized in my head, and come spewing out like a high-pressure volcanic vent?

I leaned back in my chair, and in two seconds I had the answer: because the words must have already *been* in my head. Just tucked away in a million different places. Unconnected. I simply never had the mental agility or capacity necessary to access and organize them. And now I did. So much of what I had ever seen, read, or heard now seemed available at my fingertips.

I began to type all this, then paused, realizing that I was typing at *a breakneck speed*. Typing way more words per minute than I'd ever been capable of.

I sat back in my chair again for a long moment, staring at the keyboard. Then I chuckled low, whispering with amazement, ". . . Fuck. Me."

I looked around into my mirror, at myself. I studied my image. The long, rich brown hair. The deep brown eyes. Everything looked the same on the outside.

But inside, I knew, *inside* something marvelously astounding had transpired and was continuing to. Everything felt different. I felt more clever than ever before. There was sort of a brave new clarity, an arrogant cynicism born of a mind that was flying in the rarefied stratosphere, far above the clouds, a mind that instinctively knew it was superior. That I was queen of all I surveyed.

Yet I still couldn't fathom the nature of it all. I picked up my biology textbook, thinking I might find within it some clues to an answer. I turned the pages one at a time. Focused. Beginning to read. I quickly realized, and became fascinated by the fact, that I could now absorb, mentally organize, and *understand* the difficult material almost instantly. Like it was kindergarten level.

I slowly looked up at my reflection again, and smiled. Looking closer at my eyes, I could see, and I was *proud* to see, how there was a special new and brilliant glow in them.

6

EVIL-UTION

Dr. Susan Perry...

The bright red plastic cooler was medium size. It could've held a couple of six-packs plus a dozen sandwiches and still have some room left over for fruit, if that's what it had been designed for. Instead it was filled with small bottles containing various preservative chemicals, specimen containers in graduated sizes, surgical tools, syringes, bandages, and one Diet Coke I always managed to squeeze in.

The cooler was standard CDC issue to us epidemiologists for gathering samples in the field, or in this case, from the pigsty. The cooler sat just outside the weathered wooden rail fence.

I'd squatted down in the middle of the muck, where the Tennessee farmwoman, Lottie Nichols, had been killed. I wore my tall rubber boots and surgical gloves as I collected a tablespoon-size sample of pig manure and sealed it into one of the specimen dishes.

Bereaved farmer Jacob Nichols stood nearby, leaning on the fence. He looked hollow eyed and undernourished. I paused in my work and spoke gently to him, "I can't imagine how awful it must've been for you."

"No, miss." Jacob shook his head slightly without looking up. "You surely can't."

I did my best to sound encouraging as I stood up. "Well, we'll try to find out what happened, Mr. Nichols. What I'm looking for are pathogens, bad viruses."

"State feller said maybe some weird kinda rabies."

"*Is* it possible your hogs were bitten by some rabid animal?"

"Ain't seen none round here."

"Virus can also be transmitted by food. What'd they eat?"

"Ever'thing."

"Can I see the hogs?"

"Paid my neighbor to cart 'em off and butcher 'em." He swallowed, bitterly. His voice became choked with emotion. "Couldn't stand t'look at 'em."

"Of course not." I sincerely understood his pain and was trying to sound that way. But I also needed data to work with. Sometimes my investigations made me feel like Sherlock Holmes, and I'd quote him like Chris used to, saying, "Data, Watson! I need facts! I can't make bricks without clay." I stepped out through the pigsty gate and carefully peeled my gloves off, leaving them inside out. I disposed of them in my special waste bag for biohazard containments. Then I sealed the bag. "Could you contact the slaughterhouse and have some of the organs sent to Atlanta? We pay for the shipping. It's very important."

"Yeah. Reckon."

I leaned on the top of the fence, avoiding some bird droppings, which I'd also taken samples of, and wrote a name on the back of my card. "Have them sent to the attention of Dr. Lauren Fletcher. She's our chief lab biologist."

The farmer took my card, lifelessly. I was deeply sad for his anguish. "I'm . . . I'm really heartsick for you, Mr. Nichols."

His voice broke slightly. "Yeah." There was a pause. I waited, sensing he wanted to say more. We stood in silence. I really needed to get back on the road, but I saw that remaining with a sympathetic ear was much more important right at that moment. My instincts were correct. Mr. Nichols finally drew a breath. ". . . Woulda been fifty-five years next week. Use t'complain 'bout her yammerin' . . ." He looked into my eyes, then breathed a long, sad sigh. I touched his arm gently.

I carried Jacob Nichols's grief with me as I drove southeast along the meandering, two-lane Route 30. I passed a sign pointing to the right indicating seven miles to Dayton. It struck a chord. My brow knitted, trying to remember. What was it about Dayton, Tennessee? Oh of course: the "monkey trial" back in the twenties. Black-and-white images came into my head of grainy photos I'd seen and also the later play and movie, *Inherit the Wind*: people sitting in that sweltering court-room. It was so hot that some proceedings were moved outside. Many women had those Southern paper fans on sticks; the men had their jackets off and were in their white shirtsleeves, with elastic armbands and suspenders.

At the defendant's table sat lean schoolteacher John Scopes, who had so inflamed the community by daring to teach Darwin's "blasphe-mous" theory of evolution where it was forbidden by Tennessee law to do so: in the Dayton high school. Sitting beside Scopes was his attorney, the fiery, unpredictable "attorney for the damned," Clarence Darrow. He listened with a wry face to every word flowing like the very wrath of God from his Bible-thumping, stentorian, prosecutorial opponent, the Honorable William Jennings Bryan. Twice a presidential candidate, the golden-throated Bryan gave honeyed voice to all things holy, while casting to eternal damnation all that he perceived as the misbegotten fantasies of atheistic scientific theory run amok—particularly Darwin's ungodly concept that many brethren branded as "Evil-ution."

The Bible Belt had been outraged at the notion that humanity could have evolved from apes and monkeys. I smiled at the naïveté, but knew that even now some people condemned the idea of natural selection and survival of the fittest, they simply dismissed the science of evolution. The whole notion that humans had their origins in the primordial slime, that we had arisen from among the bestial lower primates and indeed were continuously evolving, still struck many otherwise intelligent people as damnably sacrilegious.

I also remembered Darrow's startling tactic of calling to the witness stand his opponent Bryan as an expert biblical witness. Darrow spent several brilliantly calculated hours meticulously poking great holes in biblical "facts" versus scientific and historic accuracy. Though Bryan was a dazzling, facile, and clever hostile witness, Darrow craftily edged the forthright, great communicator off his guard. Then with clearheaded logic Darrow proceeded to quietly get Bryan to admit the possibility that Earth and all its life forms including humanity had *not* actually been created in only *six* magical twenty-four-hour days. That it might have taken millions of years.

Checkmate. Or at least it should have been. But all Bryan's testimony was ultimately stricken from the record, and Darrow lost the case. Scopes was forced to pay a fine of a hundred dollars and promise not to teach such inflammatory, heretical concepts in the future. The excesses of Bryan's passions during the trial took their toll on him. Five days after the trial he died in Dayton. In 1930 a Christian college sprang up there to honor Bryan and still proudly bears his name. The anti-evolution statute remained part of Tennessee's law until 1967.

I was pulled back from my reverie by the sight of a number of farmworkers laboring in a field beside the road. I followed the instincts of any thorough investigator and slowed my dusty blue Honda hybrid to a stop on the shoulder. The workers looked up. I was clearly an outsider. Two dirty-faced, very young children idling nearby eyed me warily, then warmed as I smiled. I spoke to their parents, who were very thin with faces deeply lined by too much sun and too many cigarettes. "Excuse me. Hi. I'm checking for some rabid animals around here? Seen anything unusual? Dogs, foxes, any animals behaving oddly or—"

"Naw," the woman said as she stretched her back. "Ain't seen nothin' like that."

Her husband scratched his stubbly chin. "How 'bout them weird birds?"

"Birds?" I cocked my head. *Was this a scent, Watson?* "Weird how? What kind?"

"Ain't sure. Petey, our little 'un there, got hisself pecked on. They wuz nasty suckers."

I looked down at the grungy three-year-old. He'd been playing in the dirt but stopped to eye me very carefully. In addition to the grime and mucus on his face, there were some ugly scratches. I asked the parents' permission, then knelt beside him, speaking gently, "Hi, Petey. Got some scratches, huh?" The child said nothing, but let me examine his face while he watched me with eyes that probed deeply. I glanced at the father. "Were the birds small, large . . . ?"

"Didn't rightly see. It'uz gettin' dark. Mighta been crows."

I pondered this for a moment. "I've got some antiseptic in the car I can give you for Petey." They nodded and I retrieved it, cleansed his scratches with some saline, showed them how to apply the med with cotton, and gave them my card. "I'd sure appreciate it if you'd call me at this free number if you see anything else unusual." I also took their cell number.

Throughout the whole encounter I registered how Petey was gazing at me. His eyes seemed strangely deep. Far more mature and intelligent than I'd ever seen from a three-year-old. They had a sort of knowledge-able glint that was unsettling.

I was mulling that peculiarity as I walked back to my car. I was also fighting my aching inclination to sweep Petey away and give him a better chance at life. According to Lauren, this was my major weakness as a doctor: that I often developed an emotional involvement with my patients. Unlike Lauren, who could remain clinically detached from their pain and suffering.

I couldn't help it. I'd become a natural caretaker. By age twelve I'd realized my parents were unreliable because of their fondness for alcohol, so I had to mature early and take care of myself. My insurance salesman father and real estate agent mother gave me a childhood in suburban Maryland, free from want, but always lived just enough beyond their means to keep a constant high-wire tension in the house. And that was aggravated during my adolescence as their nightly consumption of cocktails increased.

Certainly Lilly's autism affected us all. I was essentially an only child. I couldn't share a secret with Lilly because she'd often inadvertently blurt it out, simply not understanding the social context. Too often I got angry with her but grew to understand Lilly couldn't help it, so I acclimated.

Lilly's special needs also made my parents' lives harder, but primarily it was alcohol that led to their flailing bursts of wrath that usually targeted me. I learned that fighting back only prolonged the attacks, so I survived by countering their tirades with silent acquiescence. I'd let the slings and arrows fly by until they ran out of ammunition and stalked off, smoldering. I would take a deep breath and carry on unharmed. More or less.

The role of caretaker for myself eventually expanded to my assuming full responsibility for Lilly, whom I truly loved. Then eventually, as an epidemiologist, I took on caretaking for the community at large. My former love, CDC colleague Chris Smith, said my childhood made me an ideal candidate for this job.

As I'd done to survive my challenging childhood, I tried to efficiently manage the difficulties of my many adult responsibilities by forcing myself to keep a cool head and calm demeanor. But there were many times when I felt I'd explode if I didn't vent my bottled-up turmoil. I'd hurriedly park in some lonely place and pound furiously on my steering wheel, sometimes sobbing while shouting my lungs out at fate, at Lilly's disability, at my own failures. The last time was when Chris went away.

I had suppressed the anguish, but finally blown. That time I pounded the steering wheel so hard I triggered the airbag to explode in my face.

That made me laugh through my tears. And as the air slowly sagged out of the bag, my fury likewise abated. I wiped my eyes and grew wistful, deciding to face the situation with as much humor and grace as possible. Then I resubmerged myself in the clinical research work that I loved.

As I walked away from the farmworkers, I took a last look back at Petey. I wasn't surprised to see his eyes still locked on me. Those strange eyes. So cold for a child. I wondered if he might have some form of autism. I was almost to my car when I noticed two crows on a fence following me with *their* beady eyes. I paused, staring at them. Their gaze seemed as piercing and strange as Petey's. I caught his parents' attention, silently indicated the crows, questioningly. They shrugged, unsure.

I recalled the bird droppings at the Nichols' hog pen. It wasn't uncommon for pathogens to be spread that way. Had these crows eaten something infected? I took heavy gloves from my trunk and a net on an aluminum pole that could telescope out. I moved slowly toward the large, oily black birds. I could've sworn they took on a crouching, hooded, menacing demeanor as they carefully gauged my approach. And just when I was within striking distance, they burst startlingly into the air, swooping right past my head, flapping and squawking angrily.

I dodged them, then watched with frustration as they flew off, growing smaller and smaller against the clouding sky. It looked as though a storm was building.

Shelly Navarro, 38, Ashton High School science teacher…

I was already annoyed because the day started badly. Coming in from the school parking lot that morning, one of the admin assistants whispered to me that the board had gone with Prentiss for vice principal. *What?* I almost spit. That idiot? He didn't have two brain cells to rub together. I felt my face contort on its own accord into what I once heard a student call my "cynical simpering smirk." Well, so what if it was.

Prentiss. Of course. He was oh-so-chummy with a couple of board members. Yes, he was pop-u-lar, whereas I heard that a couple of the admin types felt I had an "edge," whatever the hell that means. Like maybe I work hard and I'm demanding and I don't suffer fools? And that's *bad*? I was particularly pissed off because it was the second time I'd been passed over. And for someone with a lot less experience at this stupid school. I really thought that my thirteen years in the classroom and being female *and* a Latina should have finally worked in my favor. But no. So much for their "diversity goals." Screw 'em all. If they couldn't appreciate my skill set, my managerial abilities, then they didn't deserve me. Neither did most of my students.

So by third period that day, I was definitely teaching by rote. Grumbling my way through the lesson for the three-hundredth time to thirty-one seniors, most of whom wanted to be anyplace but in biology class. Lisa McLane was definitely one of those. She sat halfway back, gazing out the window as usual, lazily contemplating the leaves beginning to change color on the *Liquidambar styraciflua* trees outside. She was a lightweight romantic ditz.

I was in the midst of saying, "So at that point biology took a quantum leap forward after DNA was discovered . . ." when Lisa's inattention started to particularly annoy me. She was only a middling student, but I knew that she was one of the girls who was pop-u-lar—certainly much more so than I had ever been. Try being a painfully chubby adolescent. So I sniped, "Are you with us, Lisa? You really can't afford not—"

"'So biology took a quantum leap forward after DNA was discovered . . .'" Lisa parroted, continuing to gaze lazily out the window. I was about to go at her when she continued, ". . . in 1953, *supposedly* by Watson and Crick who won the Nobel Prize. But they didn't reveal how Watson had unethically seen the pioneering X-ray photomicrograph taken by Rosalind Franklin, the crystallographer who was actually the very first to prove the correct structure of deoxyribonucleic acid." She inhaled and went on, "DNA is a double helix of polynucleotides containing amino acids adenine, guanine, cytosine, thymine in nitrogenous bases and deoxyribose. It's a constituent of chromosomes in all cell nuclei where it serves to encode genetic data."

I wasn't the only one staring at her in amazement. All her classmates were, too.

Lisa sighed, seemingly bored, as she continued at a mile a minute, "DNA can be attacked by retroviruses, which alter the sequence of specific amino chains, thereby changing the individual cell, and ultimately the entire host organism. Such viral infiltration can occur by numerous—"

Charley Flinn...

About that same time I was sitting in Tenzer's English class, lookin' around at some of the others, like I was seeing 'em for the first time. And like from a way different place. Like from a mountaintop way above 'em. Or from the fuckin' stratosphere.

Eric Tenzer was an okay guy. Midthirties, I guess. The girls thought he was sorta handsome. Liked his "wavy brown hair."

I never saw anybody wear suspenders before, but Tenzer wore different ones all the time and made 'em look kinda cool. They were like his trademark. He knew we joked about 'em, but he joked about himself, too. Even the pissiest kids liked him. And when we'd get into some serious *literature* stuff, like Conrad, that was real heavy duty, Tenzer talked about it just being "challenging," but how it'd stretch our minds if we'd let it. Gotta admit I enjoyed his classes, even when it was a struggle. He could kinda draw us out and surprise us about what he called "our potential." Told me once I had lotsa possibilities beyond just football. He had this easygoing way and always seemed to make us feel smart.

But I didn't need his help for that anymore. Not since what happened to Lisa and me the night before.

I was thinking about that and sorta drifted off while Tenzer was sayin', "So Conrad's hero continued his trip up the Congo. Any thoughts?" He glanced around and musta spotted me daydreamin'. He said, encouraging kinda, "Charley? How 'bout it?"

I turned kinda slow to look right at him. "Well," I said, taking a casual breath, "some say it's a metaphor for penetration of a woman's vaginal canal, seeking the pure truth of the womb."

That sorta woke everybody up. The room went dead silent. I really enjoyed the hotshot feeling that gave me. Then I looked at Tenzer with a kinda steely smile. "Although I think the more appropriate orifice would be the *anus*, given the depths of depravity and filth that Kurtz sank to." Another pause. The other kids were like completely dumbfounded. A couple of 'em laughed. "For the most part, I agree with Marcel Reich-Ravanki's assessment that it's a night journey into the savage unconscious darkness of Marlow's own soul and—" I saw that my classmates were incredulous. Tenzer was blown away. And extremely pleased. I ate it up. I said politely, "Oh, I'm sorry . . . Shall I go on?"

Tenzer got this quirky, confused smile and gestured affirmatively, so I continued, "Marlow sees that, removed from customary restraints, even the most disciplined, civilized person like Kurtz could give way to destructive impulses rising from the depths of their own primitive natures: unbridled vanity, greed, feeding an appetite for extreme power, and enjoying domination over others. The desire to play God." Then I just sat calm and cool. Nobody moved. I knew they were all caught up in a major WTF.

I realized how very, *very* much I was enjoying the stunned silence in the room.

Katie McLane...

Between classes I kept an eye out for Lisa. I was still trying to figure out what was up with her. I spotted her coming out of biology with Steph and Jenna hurrying to catch up. I sorta drifted in a little behind them. I always liked Steph the best. She was the softer of the three. She usually wore Goodwill treasures, always had to, 'cause her family seemed to have lots of bad breaks. She wore a small silver cross on a thin chain around her neck. Steph was always fighting to keep her weight down, but had a weakness for SNICKERS and was nibbling one. I heard her call out, "Lise! Wait up!"

The other girl, Jenna, was like straight out of an H&M catalog. She was gushing, "God, I loved Navarro's face! How'd you learn all that shit?!"

"Simple." Lisa sniffed, like she was way too cool to be talking to them.

Steph laughed, "Shuh, right! Yesterday you were sure you were gonna fail."

Lisa barely glanced at her, but she had this private smile. "This is a brand-new day."

"Are we still gonna study together tonight?" Jenna asked, pressing, "I could sure use—"

"I'd like to, Jenna," Lisa said silky smooth, "but honestly I haven't got time. Mind, Steph?" Lisa snagged the rest of Steph's SNICKERS and hungrily gobbled it as she peeled off and left them behind, staring after her. But I kept trailing her.

Farther down the corridor, I saw Lisa catch up with Charley at his locker. They were both staring at each other with these strange smiles, like they had a really powerful secret. It flashed on me, *Oh my God, maybe she's pregnant*. My locker was almost across from them, so I eased up to it, listening to their whispers.

Charley's voice had this kinda edge I'd never heard from him, when he snatched at the candy bar. "Gimme somma that. I'm like fuckin' starved."

Lisa's breathing seemed fast. Her voice sounded amazed-concerned-excited all at once. "What the hell do y'think is going on with us?"

Charley smirked, his expression was a little dark but excited, too. "Dunno, but it's great!"

"Kind of like a rush?" Lisa was nodding. "A high?"

"Yeah." Charley laughed. "Like my brain *expanded*."

"Yes! What was *in* those strawberries, Charley!? Wonder if it'll last?"

"Hope so. I'm kickin' ass! C'mere!"

He pulled her into a custodian closet nearby, closed the door, but not all the way. I'd sneaked some peeks a couple of times before, but never saw anything like that day. They were kissing hot and heavy, groping each other all over, couldn't get enough.

I stood there a second, then turned away so they wouldn't see me. I was frowning, probably twisting one of my ringlets. Puzzling it.

Strawberries?

Charley Flinn...

A few minutes later I was still feeling totally like king o'the world, struttin' toward the boys' gym. I caught sight of my least favorite senior classmate up ahead. My eyes kinda narrowed. Tim Green was the older brother of Darren, Katie's pal. He had those all-American, dark-haired, surfer-dude looks. Tim was a couple inches taller than me, just over six feet. Coach Caruso always said Tim had the agility of a dancer and that made him an excellent quarterback. Gimme a break. But he was Caruso's golden boy. Top guy on our JV and now the senior squad, Tim had beat me out again for QB and head of the team. I decided that morning it was time to change that.

In his locker-room office I cornered Caruso. He was this older Italian former minor-pro dude who still pumped up and took high school ball seriously as the Super Bowl. He was in there fixing a damaged helmet. When I hit him up for QB, he just shook his head. "Sorry, but you're not ready to start, Chuckie."

I zeroed in on him, quiet but intense. "Oh yes I am, Coach."

"No. You're not." Caruso set aside the helmet and looked up at me, friendly but firm. "Listen, Charley, you're not a bad strategist, but you don't got that drive to win like Tim does. He's"—Caruso paused like tryin' to think of the right word—"he's the *natural* quarterback. He starts like usual. I'll try to give you a shot down the road." Caruso walked out. I watched him go, wanted to give *him* a shot. I was feeling cold, hard. But smart. Really smart. I chuckled, thinking, *No second-rate minor-pro has-been is gonna stand in my way.*

Darren Green, 14...

I loved when those Friday-night lights came on for our first game in our home field. They turn 'em on early in August when we first start school, even though the sun hasn't set. Katie and I got there a little late, so I was hurrying into the locker room. Our guys were already suiting up. My brother, Tim, got Coach Caruso to let me be towel boy last year. I was really proud of how all the guys on the team—and everybody in our school—admired Tim. He was tall, strong, had dark hair like me. People always said they could tell we were brothers. Tim was handsomer though and didn't need glasses. He was also more athletic than I'd ever been. Girls thought he was cut and a hottie. Even Katie did. I hoped I could end up as cool as Tim was. And on the field he was amazing. Never got flustered. Always sussing out the defense, changing plays right at the lineup. He had this unruffled, calm way of calling the plays.

When I came skidding in, Tim was standing with a foot up on one of the long, heavy wooden benches that ran between the lockers, untying his sneaker. He grinned, grabbed me, and gave me a little noogie on the head. "Hey, Dare. Glad you could make it." I knew he was teasing. "Keep those towels coming, buddy." He pulled off his jeans to hang in the locker and looked over at Charley, who was nearby. "Yo, Charley. Hope Caruso lets you into the game this time." Tim smiled, then saw a dollar someone musta dropped by his locker, and reached down to pick it up.

That's when it happened.

Charley accidentally bumped the heavy bench, and it smashed down onto the concrete floor and Tim's right hand.

Tim yelled out in pain. And Charley was right there to help, saying, "Aw, no! Shit!" Other players came to look. Tim was leaning against the lockers, cradling the injured hand in his left one. He looked like he was seeing stars from awful pain, trying hard to get on top of it. But it musta hurt bad. Charley was leaning in close. "It's not broken, is it, Tim?" But Tim was in too much pain to talk. Charley shouted at me, "Darren! Get some ice. Hurry up!" As I hurried out, I heard Charley say to Tim, "Shit! I'm really, *really* sorry, man."

That evening Charley started as quarterback.

Charley Flinn...

After the game, Lisa and me went back to our own personal Garden of Eden and jumped each other big-time. It was like fiery. She was really suckin' face hot, and in between was sayin', "Jesus, you were a fantastic quarterback, Charley! God! Passing. Running. Mmm." She was chewin' my lips like she wanted to eat me alive. Kept pullin' my hips hard against her again and again. "Oh yes, like that," she sorta gasped. "And the way you called all those great plays. We woulda won for sure if—yes, ooo, like that!" She was callin' her own plays, and I was all for it. Felt *good*. She was breathin' hard, right in my face. "If the rest of the team was half as good as you—then you really woulda shined even more. Mmmm."

She dived in for another deep kiss. But my eyes were open. I kept pouring all my physical energy into the sex, but I was multitasking: looking off at the wild strawberry plant.

My mind was buzzin' with new possibilities.

Dr. R. W. Hutcherson, 35, epidemiologist...

I'd stopped by Susan's office around noon that Monday. She was off doing some local field research so Lilly was temporarily alone. Prashant, Joseph, and others kept an eye on her when Susan had to be out briefly. I needed some background research references for the AIDS testing. I was scribbling notes faster than a Montana jackrabbit because Lilly was rattling off resources to me a mile a minute, without stuttering, while she worked at a complicated connect-the-dots picture. ". . . And there's *Journal of Applied Physiology,* September, 2009, Drs. Zhang Sun Lee and Noro Saxena, 'Side Effects from HIV Treatment Combinations' . . . Also *Scientific American,* January, 2015, Smith, Christopher. 'Bacteriophage and AIDS.' Also—"

"Hang on, Lilly, wait," I pleaded, laughing. "God, if I had a memory like yours I could *run* this place. You're amazing!"

"'Ex-exceptional,'" she said flatly, politely correcting me. "Susie says 'exceptional.' Of course you shouldn't m-move my pencils."

I realized that I had nudged one pencil a couple of millimeters out of line with the other three that Lilly had meticulously lined up on her desk. "Oh. You're right. I'm so sorry."

"I like to keep them nice and n-neat," she said, adjusting them with studious specificity.

"I'll remember, I promise." I smiled at her, but her pretty blue eyes were downcast, so she didn't notice. Her mention of Christopher Smith prompted me to ask about the photo pinned on Susan's note board. It was her and a guy in rock-climbing gear, smiling at the camera. "Lilly, is that the same Christopher Smith who used to be Susan's . . . friend?"

Lilly didn't look up from her connect the dots. "Yeah."

"Were they . . . a couple, Lilly?" She nodded without looking up. "What happened to him?"

"Chris went a-away. Two years ago. It was a Tuesday. Very w-windy."

"Where did he go?"

"Don't know." She rotated the paper to more easily connect a dot.

"Why did he go away?"

"Susie s-said he 'disagreed.'"

"With her?"

"With everybody." Lilly checked her slightly oversize wristwatch and set her dot work aside to turn on her iPad. She focused on it, and I realized that she had unconsciously tuned me out. Not rudely. Simply because Lilly lived in her own autistic savant cocoon. *A shame,* I thought.

Then a familiar, low-pitched woman's voice said, "Hey cowboy, want to hit the chuck wagon again?"

Dr. Lauren Fletcher was smiling from the doorway. She looked striking, as usual. And I got the sense she usually knew it. And also who was boss. I smiled back. "Always happy to chow down with you, ma'am."

And it always seemed like the politic response.

Dr. Susan Perry...

Fifty-year-old rancher Claude Hickock was one of my least favorite types. He was the condescending sort who spent more time evaluating my breasts than looking into my eyes.

He walked lazily beside his corral with me. His Whitesville cattle ranch was in southwestern Georgia. He drew a baronial breath, spoke with a honeyed Southern drawl. "Well, I don't know 'bout them wackos over in Tennessee, little lady, but I think the reports from here in Jaw-juh got kinda exaggerated."

I was astonished, said pointedly, "But one of your men was *killed*."

He paused, put his right boot up on the corral fence and adjusted his expensive Stetson. I felt as though he was measuring his words carefully as he chewed his tobacco. "Yeah." He paused to turn slightly aside and spit a plug. So attractive. "Yeah, and that'uz real unfortunate. But workin' with steers, accidents can happen. Even to experienced wranglers."

"But from the report we got, the cattle sounded uncharacteristically aggressive."

"Uh-huh." He nodded, looked away, and still seemed to be parsing his words. "Never did figure out what the hell spooked 'em." Then he drew a positive breath and looked back at me as innocently as he could muster, gesturing toward the herd. "But you seen how the rest of 'em are fine."

He smiled and checked my breasts again, which made me all the more resolute and determined. "That may be, but I need to examine the cattle that attacked the men."

"Them animals been destroyed." He spat again. Picked a flake of the vile stuff from his lip.

Now I was angry, but maintained my focus. "Mr. Hickock, I specifically sent word that you needed to keep—"

"You wuz too late I'm afraid, darlin'. Sure sorry I cain't help you more."

You patronizing, sexist, dickhead asshole! I screamed. Internally. In my professional capacity representing the CDC, I had to keep those words bottled up tightly until I could pound on my steering wheel later. Instead I could only glare at him. He merely smiled back.

And there was something in his expression that disturbed me: an almost frightening air of superiority, beyond the usual misogynistic BS. I also felt like I'd seen that peculiar glint in his eyes somewhere before. Yes. It was like the strange look from that farmworker's child who had been attacked by the crows.

That image haunted me as, frowning, I pulled onto old Route 35 that bordered the Hickock property. I was angry at being stonewalled by the jerk. Then I saw something ahead and slowed my car for a more careful look.

It was a chain-link fence. It wouldn't have been an unusual sight somewhere else. But in the country along a pasture? Newly erected. And set just *inside* the wooden split-rail fence, which was the regular fencing for this area. The chain link was six feet tall and paralleled the split rail to the far end of the property, then ran off into the woods beyond.

What had particularly caught my eye was how the shiny new chain link veered off at a very peculiar diagonal across the open field.

I noticed that the pasture on the far side of the fence was much greener than on my side. And it looked even more green as it sloped down toward a peach orchard, which was amazingly thick, lush, and beautiful. I got out of my car for a better look. Even from a distance I could see that the peach trees were heavily laden with golden fruit. But the growing season was nearly over. It was all very odd.

I left the car, stepped through the split rail, and then skirted along the diagonal chain link toward the orchard, trying to get a closer look at the greener field and the peaches. Suddenly I heard a whoop-whoop siren. Looking around, I saw a military-style police jeep roaring up the hillside toward me from the woods near the orchard. The African American driver was uniformed in camouflage fatigues, and wore a matching cap over his regulation buzz cut. His face was shaved so closely that it looked as polished as his boots. He wore reflective sunglasses. He had a half-eaten peach in his hand, as he stepped smartly out of the jeep, saying, "Sorry, ma'am, that area's been cordoned off."

"Why?" I frowned, staring at the annoying reflection of myself in his mirrored glasses. I could barely see his eyes.

"Radiation."

I looked sharply at him and then over at the field. "One of those fragments from the comet? Fell out there?"

"Mebbe. Have to ask you to go back to your car now."

"Are you army or—"

"Private security contractor. Y'have to move along, ma'am. For your own safety." Even through the reflective glasses, I saw that he had fixed a smiling, but decidedly chilly, eye on me. I glanced again at the strangely lush pasture and orchard. Preoccupied, I nodded absently to him and began walking back up toward my car.

Then I paused, looking back at the unusual field, the trees with their unnatural abundance of golden fruit, and the steely security officer. The whole scene combined to create an unsettling, mysterious feeling. He took another bite of his juicy, near-perfect peach and held my gaze. Even from this distance I could sense his elevated arrogance, his demeanor that was eerily similar to rancher Hickock's, as though they shared a much-deeper-than-ordinary secret.

Something was very wrong at Hickock's ranch and on this farmland. I determined to find out what it was.

7

TEAMWORK

Darren Green…

All the guys on the Warriors squad were having a loud brawl in the locker room. They didn't know I was back in the equipment room. I'd come early that Friday to get the football gear ready for our second game. I edged up to the door to see what was happening. I was kinda freaked 'cause it sounded really nasty. They were pissed off, shouting, cussing. Then fists started flying, but I couldn't figure who was on what side. It wasn't like juniors against seniors or racial or anything. It was like they were *all* just fighting with *each other*. And it was ugly.

Coach Caruso suddenly plowed in, jerking some fighters apart, shoving others aside. "Hey. HEY! Break it up! You hear me?" In addition to playing football, Caruso'd been a boxer and still worked out on the machines every night after school. He was not somebody to mess with. And he was fuming. "What the hell is wrong with you guys?!" He glared at them. "Save it for the other team!"

There was sudden, angry silence. "Somebody want to tell me how this started?" He stared at one guy then another. Their faces were dark, mean. The room felt like a big pot of hot water just below the boiling point. "Well, if it starts up again, a lot of you'll be doin' laps or warmin' the damn bench or off this team altogether. Got it?" He gave them all a last deadly look. Then steamed off toward his office.

I peeked back in at the players, real careful. Something was different about 'em. About all of 'em. There was almost like a kinda fire in their eyes. Like I once saw on National Geographic: like a leopard's eyes when it's crouched low, muscles flexed, getting ready to attack. They all had this dark, creepy, new attitude. Like they were tougher. Sharper. Hungry for battle.

I watched as Charley pulled 'em all into a tight group around him. He was different than I'd ever seen him. Like *commanding* their attention. Tim, who'd always led the team before, was hanging back, his head tilted down, menacing-like. He was staring at Charley, who waved the whole bunch even closer.

"Didn't I tell you? Huh?!" Charley hissed at 'em. His voice was low and real intense, but barely louder than a whisper. "Didn't I tell you it'd be like this after you had those strawberries! Now you *all* wanta be top dog, right?" I saw several of them nod angrily. "But remember who *gave* 'em to you. Right?" The others nodded. "Damn right. And don't you fuckin' forget it. Now we gotta work *together*, okay?" Charley went on, "Like a wolf pack."

I was getting really nervous. I could feel a sorta mad-dog drive inside 'em, and Charley kept pumping 'em. "There's plenty of wimp mongrels out there for us to chew up without going after each other. We can accomplish a lot more. As a *pack*. Okay?"

They all growled in agreement. Charley grinned, but his face was almost ugly, and his eyes were flashing, scary. "Right. So let's go, Warriors. Let's rip out their fuckin' guts."

Eric Tenzer, 35, Ashton High School English teacher...

That evening the Ashton High football team was startling. With Charley Flinn as quarterback our team bulldozed over the Carrollton High opposition right from the kickoff. It was like watching Green Bay play a junior high team.

Charley called well-conceived plays that his team executed with dazzling—if very rough—efficiency. I noticed Tony Caruso, who usually bellowed constant orders or chastisement from the sideline, stood stone still, watching in confused astonishment.

The home crowd on the bleachers, however, was going positively wild with delight about their team. The students, teachers, our hefty Carroll County sheriff, Randolph, and even the mild Methodist minister enthusiastically cheered their varsity squad.

Clarence Frederick...

My wife, Simone, left her office in the State Capitol building early so she could come down from Atlanta with me and our boy, LeBron, to see the game. I'd grown up in Ashton, gone to this high school. I loved coming back for a game or two each year. I never *played* football, of course. My extracurricular activity was the Key Club, and after graduation I got heavily involved with the club's patron, the Ashton Kiwanis. Proud to say I was the first black president of both. Great organizations that can help a fellow get connected in business. Case in point: sitting in the bleachers near us was Rupert Green. He'd been in Key Club with me and was now on the board of BioTeck Industries, my plant's parent company.

Rupert was whistling loudly at a gain that the quarterback had just made on the field. "Way to go, Charley! Keep it up, Warriors!" Then Rupert looked back at me, shouting over the noise of the crowd, "Hell of a game, huh, Clarence?"

I shouted back, "Yes sir! But I thought your boy Tim was quarterback."

"He is. Hurt his throwing hand. Caruso made him fullback till it heals."

"Well, they're doin' great!" I leaned to Simone, whispered, "See: I got in a little corporate networking. Aren't y'glad we came?" Simone nodded to me as she watched the action on the field. Simone wasn't a football fan but supported me coming here. I noticed her brow was knitted more than usual, though. "What's the matter, honey?"

133

Simone just shook her head as she stared at the action on the field, frowning.

Simone Frederick, 47, press liaison, Public Information Office, Georgia State government...

I really couldn't put my finger on it. I tolerated the boys' interest in football, but the unusual intensity of this particular game was troubling me.

Then I was distracted when LeBron let out a cheer, and I glanced at him sitting next to Clarence. I saw his green eyes drift lazily off across the crowd, mostly, I knew, to see what girls might be eyeing him. That always worried me. Of course I was proud that LeBron was so damned handsome, but unfortunately he *knew* he was, despite my warnings of shallowness germinating. He was rewarded in that moment by catching a pair of girls ogling him. They giggled, embarrassed, brought their hands up over their mouths and looked quickly away. I sighed and wished they hadn't reacted so.

Then the whole crowd was suddenly on their feet cheering.

Darren Green...

In another really rough free-for-all scramble—almost a fight—that the referees had to break up, our team forced a third fumble, and the crowd roared for 'em.

Coach Caruso was amazed. He patted me on the back a couple times, feeling excited and pleased as he watched his team totally crushing Carrollton. Ol' round-face Randolph, our sheriff, shouted down to him, "Hey, Tony! You finally got yourself some *real* Warriors!"

Caruso nodded and waved back appreciatively. Then he looked toward the field. Kinda swelled up with pride and accomplishment. Like maybe he was a better coach than he'd thought, and somehow it was all coming together tonight. But watching from the sideline, I felt this sorta knot growing in my stomach. I'd never seen our guys play this hard. Or this mean.

Tim's hand was bandaged up from that bench falling on it, so I was keeping an extra eye on him. Tim was playing just as hard as the others. Even nasty. But there was something else. He kept throwing these like laser glances at Charley. It reminded me of a rodeo movie I saw where a Brahman bull was penned in as the rider climbed onto his back. The bull's eyes were glaring straight ahead, his nostrils all flaring out wide with each huff and puff. Like he couldn't wait for the gate to open so he could kill the cowboy who was riding him.

Lisa McLane…

I was in the stands with Jenna and Steph on either side. Steph was stomping her old-fashioned brown-and-white saddle oxfords on the wooden floorboards of the bleachers, cheering along with Jenna, me, and the whole crowd each time the team made yet another amazing play. Charley was doing even better than last week's game. It had been exciting to watch. At first.

But as the game went on, I slowly realized that the whole team was somehow working together like they never had before. Ever. Working harder. Smarter. And way more driven.

I found myself sitting more and more silently as I watched them. A dark suspicion was growing in me. By the third quarter it had festered. Turned to anger.

Katie McLane…

I'd glanced up at Lisa a couple times. She always cheered loudly at every game, but near the end of this one, she was just sitting like a stone-cold statue. Glaring at the team. At Charley.

He was flying high, totally stoked by leading his superior team.

Eric Tenzer…

The Warriors continued grinding forward, with increasing ferocity. I saw fingers from Ashton's team, gouging into rival players' eyes. More than once. Definitely on purpose, with not a shred of mercy. Or fair play. The referees threw a few flags, but once I focused on watching specifically for such grisly details, I realized they were so pervasive that the referees couldn't possibly have caught all the unsportsmanlike conduct.

The crowd seemed to miss, or not care about, such troubling particulars. The enthused spectators saw only the broad, unrelenting action, the triumphs, raising cheer after cheer for their . . . their what? Then I realized where my mind had gone: for their *gladiators*. The raves of the masses confirmed, exonerated, urged, and inspired Charley and his teammates to play even more gruesomely rough.

FBI Office of Digital Forensics, Quantico, VA—Doc # A0686118

Subj: High School Football Game, Ashton, GA, played 8/28/20

To: FBI Atlanta Field Ofc, Georgia State Patrol, et al.

Full 137-page PDF transcript of scene-by-scene analysis is available at:

www.FBI.gov/forensics/digital/sub/AHS729416SA-7452

Summary: In response to the request that this office examine numerous sequences of the aforementioned Ashton HS game, which were initially captured on cell phone and/or by the team's student videographer and other civilian amateurs. Upon up-resolution of original footage to 8K video accompanied by FBI proprietary video enhancement and/or enlargement, and then meticulous frame-by-frame analysis of the resulting video, this office has confirmed that there were sixty-seven (67) clearly visible examples not only of unsportsmanlike conduct, but intentional brutality as has been described by several witnesses (full list in transcript). Twenty-eight (28) of those actions were called as penalties by the referees, the others were not.

There were also a minimum of seventeen (17) other probable incidents that were not totally verifiable. Additional information provided by the Atlanta field office notes that seven (7) of the opposing team from Carrollton High School sustained serious injuries, four (4) required hospitalization and two (2) may have permanent damage.

Courtesy FBI, ODF

Simone Frederick...

My husband, Clarence, shouted, "Yeah! Go Warriors!" as they literally stomped over two Carrollton players to make yet another touchdown. "Wow!" He enthused. "What a rout!"

"And way too violent for high school," I said firmly.

"Well, it's a rough-and-tumble sport, honey," Clarence mansplained. Sometimes I wanted to smack him. Another Carrollton player got carried off the field while many around me shouted jubilantly for the Ashton boys. Clarence went on authoritatively, "But they've got much better equipment now, honey. Those new helmets—"

I stood up and headed for a less hostile environment. I didn't care if he was annoyed.

Katie McLane...

Late in the game when Mom leaned closer to me, she was almost gleeful. "God, Katie! It's been a slaughter!"

". . . Yeah. It has." I was worried. I'd long since stopped cheering. I didn't like what I'd been seeing: how the whole Warriors team seemed to have the same new edge that Charley and Lisa had. Even Tim, who had always been such a good guy. I saw him step on one Carrollton guy's hand and grind his cleats into it. The guy screamed, a ref turned, and Tim instantly switched into Mr. Nice Guy and helped the injured kid up.

Darren glanced at me from the sideline. As concerned as I was.

Lisa McLane…

When the handgun was fired, signaling the end of the game, the home crowd erupted with the loudest, wildest cheer I'd ever heard for their victorious team. But I was totally livid.

Charley got lifted onto the shoulders of his hard-breathing, triumphant teammates and carried toward the sidelines. Families and friends were streaming down onto the field to congratulate the players.

I was moving slower, eyeing each guy carefully. Confirming my suspicions one by one. When Charley finally got set down, I pushed through the adoring crowd and sweating players to confront him up close. My voice was low and furious in his ear, "You gave it to 'em, didn't you?"

Charley turned to me, his face aglow with perspiration and the flush of victory. "What? C'mon, Lise. Did y'see how we ground up those little dickweeds! Wooo-eee!"

Others nearby reached around me to bat at Charley and shout praise. I got even closer to his face. "You gave 'em the strawberries, didn't you, you little shit!?"

"Lisa, lighten up, Jesus!" He shouted off to another player, "Way to go, C.J.! Man, that last play was killer."

I pressed him, seething, "It was *our* secret, Charley! Just for *us*!"

"Hey, c'mon, Lise, you said I ought to give it to the team so—"

"I did *not*!" I flared angrily. "You absolutely should not have—"

"Hey. Lisa?" Charley shrugged dismissively. "Fuck off, huh?" He let himself get pulled away from me by a group of laughing parents and students. I saw his eyes flash with pleasure from his newfound fame as he was swept off by their wave of enthusiasm.

I stood rooted. Beyond mad.

Charley Flinn…

About an hour later, I'd ducked Lisa 'cause I didn't feel like indulgin' her drama. I was startin' my third beer, drivin' on a dark road through pine trees at the edge of Ashton. Me and Tim kinda made it up after the game. We were gonna drop off Steph, then meet some of the guys. We were all feelin' the rush. Steph was in the back seat with Tim all jazzed up about what he and the rest of us did in the game. I adjusted the rearview so I could glance at 'em. Almost drove off the road once. They'd just been kissin', but then Tim started around the bases, and she started fightin' off his busy hands. She was gettin' kinda squirmy, and when Tim's hand slipped under her plaid Goodwill skirt and slid upward on her thigh, she was suddenly all: "No, Tim. Stop it!"

And Tim was all, "Stephie, Stephie, take it easy. Just go with it."

And she said, "No. I don't want to!" When his hand reached her panties, she pushed at him. "*Stop!*"

Tim nuzzled her neck. "It'll be really good."

"No! I mean it!" She was soundin' desperate, now.

"C'mon, Stephie, you know you want it."

"No, I *don't!*" She slapped him, hard in the face.

Tim saw red. Slapped her right back. Hard. "You little *bitch!*"

Whoa. This was gettin' good. I eased to a stop off the side of the road so I could pay attention. He ripped open the top of her dress. He musta been surprised as me to see that her boobs were larger than I thought and blooming out of the top of her bra. I felt a surge of blood rush to harden me up. And ol' Tim was way ahead of me.

"No! Will you *stop it*! *Tim!*" Steph was crying now or maybe fakin' it. You know, wantin' it but not wantin' to say so. Lisa'd told me Steph was a virgin. "Charley!?" Steph shouted at me, "Make him *stop!*" I just held up my hands like, *Hey, it's between you two.*

Tim totally ignored Steph. He pulled her bra down and her skirt up, tearing through her panties. Steph cried out. But he was way stronger and rolled right on into it. She squealed, "No! Please!" And from the way she was gaspin', I wasn't sure if that meant "No, stop" or "Please, go."

Tim plowed on ahead while I watched from the front seat, suckin' my beer as ol' Tim dominated the situation.

Katie McLane...

Around midnight, I was coming down the stairs from my bedroom, wearing my nightshirt. Our Bernese mountain dog, Madison, galumphed along ahead of me, figuring I was headed for the kitchen and ever hopeful of getting a treat. But I slowed down when I heard Steph sobbing about Tim raping her! And then Jenna's voice.

". . . I found her walking along the road. With half her clothes torn off. And that was after C.J. tried to rape *me!*"

Easing down a little more, I pulled at Madison to keep her back and quiet. Then peeked through the partially open door into the kitchen.

Steph was sitting, leaning her disheveled head on our oval oak table, quaking with sobs. Jenna had an arm around her and said, "We'll call the sheriff."

"No!" Steph shouted tearfully. "My father would blame *me!*"

Lisa stood still, not offering comfort but observing Steph's anguish with what seemed like detached anger. Her voice was deadly calm as she finally nodded her head emphatically.

"Okay. If the boys are going to have their little team, then we'll just have to have *ours.*"

Steph looked up, red-eyed, distraught and confused.

Jenna also looked curiously at Lisa. "What do you mean?"

I was wondering that, too. And worried.

8

CONSPIRACY

Dr. Susan Perry...

A week after I'd seen that rude Georgia rancher and that strangely lush, cordoned-off peach orchard, I was reading a file as I walked across the CDC's atrium. I was so engrossed that I was startled when I collided with Lauren.

"Hey. Heads up, girl." She smirked. I felt like a klutz, particularly because of her elegant Bacall-style, haughty demeanor. She'd actually seemed a bit more arrogant and aloof than usual in the last few weeks.

"Oh, sorry," I said, trying to regroup and push back a little. "Hey, have I missed a report, or have you not looked at those hog specimens and bird droppings I sent to you?"

"Sorry, no. I've been swamped with a new project."

"Really? What?"

She barely glanced at me, but I detected a secretive glimmer in her eyes. "I'll call you next week, hon, fill you in." Lauren smiled casually and moved on. I knew a dodge when I heard one.

I watched her walk smoothly across the atrium to the man Prashant had pointed out before: Bradford Mitchell. I scanned the nearby area and noted four of the trim, gray-suited men and women with their tiny earplugs and stony faces. Lauren and Mitchell shared a quiet laugh, then walked out together, preceded and followed by the grays.

I kept watching as they went outside. When I finally turned slowly to move on, I caught a glimpse of my reflection on a lab's window. My brow was furrowed with a suspicious frown.

Heading along the cluttered third-floor hallway, I saw Hutch approaching my office. He had on that faded, brown Montana U sweatshirt I liked because it set off his light-brown hair. But my thoughts were elsewhere. I said, "Did you ask for that info about where the comet fragments fell?"

"Yes, ma'am, and good morning," Hutch said with a slight inclination of his head.

I drew up apologetically. "Sorry, I'm a little preoccupied. Hi."

He smiled. "And with our government's usual efficiency, we may have an answer shortly before we retire." Then he casually moved closer and spoke hesitantly, "Would you maybe like to have dinner while we wait?"

I smiled faintly as I turned into my office. I'd sensed this invitation coming and had decided how best to handle it. "Sure." Adding nonchalantly as I picked up an iPad, "I'd love to meet your wife."

Behind me I heard him say quietly, "Marianne woulda liked you."

I looked back, saw his wistful expression, and my face flushed. "Oh. I'm sorry." Hutch nodded, gracefully accepting my sympathy. "Has it been long?"

"Two years. In Namibia." He looked away and, I sensed, back two years into a dusty village with its grass huts, dung heaps, buzzing insects, stone ovens, and coal-black native children with their huge, gentle, beseeching eyes. I knew it all too well. "We were with MSF." Médicins Sans Frontières was the original French name of Doctors Without Borders. I processed it instantly: MSF, Namibia, two years back. I drew a sharp, fearful breath as he sadly confirmed it. "Ebola."

I had seen that particular horror firsthand. Despite my most intense efforts, I had lost many patients to the fearsome virus, which ate away and destroyed living flesh. Hutch was leaning one hand on my desk. My fingertip touched one of his. It was a moment of sincere professional understanding coupled with a tender personal connection. But we were jarringly interrupted as birdlike Prashant flitted into the room with a file folder clutched to his thin chest and his paranoid eyes narrowed conspiratorially.

"All right. All right," he hissed quietly, casting a furtive glance out into the hall to be certain no gray-suits were hovering within earshot. Then he continued, speaking low, "I did some more homework, Susan. Check out our pal Mitchell." He pulled some news photos from his file. "The guy's a power broker." They were shots of Mitchell in various uniforms. "He *was* a major, see? Army. Then a lieutenant colonel. But reduced back to major again." He pointed to a summary page he'd created on his iPad.

I scrolled through the document as Prashant recited it.

Mitchell, Bradford Howell

Born: November 17, 1971—(Base Hospital) Fort Benning, Georgia

Father: Randolf Kane Mitchell, Army drill instructor, retired as master sergeant

Mother: Ruth Elsworth Howell, political activist, (today would be "alt-right")

Physical: Height: 6'4", Weight: 215, Hair: Brown, Eyes: Brown

Medical: Appendectomy (scar), Rotator cuff R (scar); Knife wound L shoulder (scar)

Meds: Lipitor Allergies: Shellfish Blood: AB- Physical Condition: Excellent

Schooling: Virginia Military Institute, United States Military Academy (West Point)

Collegiate Career: Part of an elite group of cadets known as the "star men."

Captain of championship wrestling team. Captain of track and field team.

One of ten of 1,000 applicants admitted to premedical studies. Later said not really interested in medicine but took the course of study because it was the hardest rock to climb. Graduated first in his class.

Early Military: Joined infantry as Distinguished Cadet. Volunteered for Ranger training. Finished with top honors and legendary status among his teammates.

Command and General Staff College, Ft. Leavenworth, KS: Winner General George C. Marshall Award for top graduate.

Princeton University, School of International Affairs: Masters & Doctorate.

Doctoral Thesis: "Counterinsurgency in Vietnam." Began developing different theories about winning over populace.

Later Military: Baghdad, later Mosul as general staff officer, army intelligence. Emphasis on human intelligence (HUMINT) gathering. Cultivated relationships. Rose swiftly. Promoted to major. Then lt. colonel in Bosnia.

Personal Conflict: His superior officer, Brigadier General Maxwell Torkington, pressed for a "hearts and minds" approach in winning over Mideast adversaries, which Mitchell claimed had been co-opted from the core principal of Mitchell's own doctoral thesis. He insulted Torkington in public, was disciplined by military tribunal, and reduced back to major. He soon quit the army.

Post-Military: Extensive work in private and corporate security. Also involved with NGO intelligence-gathering operations.

Courtesy Dr. Susan Perry

Dr. Susan Perry...

Prashant pointed out a small article he'd scanned from *The New York Times.* "He was so mad at the army he returned his decorations. Then he did private corporate security work, including for some companies in Alabama and Georgia. He also became involved with those NGOs." Prashant went on with quiet intensity, "His work became more difficult to trace. They were involved in dark ops."

Hutch glanced at him. "You mean black ops?"

Prashant nodded vigorously. "Yes, yes. Black ops. Dodgy undercover stuff. Two of the military contractor groups he worked with were accused of many abuses. Torture. Even murders."

I scrolled through some of the additional pages on the iPad. "Is there any actual proof of Mitchell being personally involved in any of that?"

"Not that I have yet found," Prashant said. "I am still digging. But my grandmother in Mumbai always said to me, 'Be careful, Prashant, you are known by the company you keep.'"

I felt the weight of my lobby encounter a few minutes earlier. "I just saw him with Lauren again. And there were a couple of gray-suit types that whisper into their lapels."

Hutch was pondering it all. "Okay. But what's he doing *here?*"

"Exactly," Prashant said. "That is the sixty-dollar question."

I knew he meant sixty-four thousand, he was frequently a little off. And I knew he might be off again regarding Mitchell.

"That's the third time he's been here then," Prashant confirmed. Then he glanced around to be certain that no one other than Lilly could hear as he leaned closer to Hutch and me. "Did Lauren say anything about that porcine tissue you had sent to her?"

"Just that she was busy with—"

"Some new project, right?" Prashant cut me off with an arched eyebrow, as though he had just revealed proof of his suspicions. "Which she is extremely secretive about, logged as CAV."

My brow knitted. "I haven't heard anything about that."

In the hall outside my office, I noticed someone edging slightly closer to the doorway, then I saw it was only Joseph, our gentle custodian, making his usual broom-and-dustpan rounds.

"I am not surprised," Prashant said darkly. "She has put a private entry code on the new files. I have not cracked it yet, but I'm telling you, Lauren is up to something very peculiar."

Only in hindsight did I later recall that Joseph had paused outside my door for a moment, occupied with his dustpan. Had I chanced to observe him more carefully, I might have noted in Joseph's eyes something uncharacteristic of him: that unsettling, superior gaze which I'd detected in the eyes of Petey, the farmworkers' child; the patronizing rancher Hickock; and the steely military policeman. And perhaps also in Lauren's.

Eric Tenzer...

Grading my students' latest essays the afternoon before the next football game, I was intrigued by the higher erudition many of my seniors suddenly exhibited. Charley Flinn's unprecedented analysis of Conrad's novel seemed to have triggered a surge of intellect, particularly odd because it was only among the boys. Then in my other senior class, Lisa McLane had a similarly abrupt increase in scholastic ability. When I asked Lisa about it, she smoothly attributed it to my "stellar abilities as a teacher." Flattering, of course, but their sharp intellectual spike struck me as definitely peculiar.

That it oddly coincided with the football team's new aggressiveness didn't occur to me until the next Friday's game. The Warriors didn't just slam viciously into the boys from Americus High. Led by Charley's sly quarterbacking, the entire Ashton squad played more cleverly as they chewed through Americus, causing many bloody injuries, and repeatedly trouncing them brutally.

Katie McLane...

The game against Americus was even uglier than last week's. But most of the crowd loved that we were winning. I saw Sheriff Randolph happily shove a huge mouthful of hot dog into his round cheeks and nudge Darren's dad beside him. "I tell you, Rupert, these guys are unbeatable!" Then he shouted toward the field, "Go Warriors! *Yeah!*"

Others were cheering, too. Some chanting, "Char-ley, Char-ley." On the field, Charley knew he was the top dog. He was completely unaware that Tim Green—playing fullback again—was seriously glaring at him, mad about Charley getting the crowd's adoration that had always been reserved for Tim.

I wasn't the only one who thought the game was extra brutal. Darren glanced back at me several times from the Ashton bench after some violent action on the field.

I also noticed that Steph and Jenna, who were sitting with Lisa as usual, weren't cheering like they had last week. All three of them were watching with a kind of silent intensity. It was a little weird and creepy. They looked like confident carnivores, patiently waiting for some opportune moment to strike.

After the game, Darren and I were riding our bikes beside each other along a quiet street in Ashton when something he said startled me, prompting me to ask, "What? Jenna invited the whole team to her house? But aren't her parents out of town?"

"Yeah." Darren wiggled his dark eyebrows at me. "I want to see what's up, don't you?"

I definitely did, but I was also worried.

Jenna lived in a large ranch-style house in the best part of Ashton. A six-foot-tall redwood fence ran along the back of the property. Darren and I rode up quietly on the outside. He leaned his bike against the fence and stood, balancing on the seat to peek over the top. He thought it was cool to be spying on them, but I was frowning about it as I climbed up.

We were a little closer than I really wanted to be. The football team was straggling in, fresh from the showers and really cocky. Like rock stars. Or maybe gladiators still tasting the blood of their defeated foes. I saw how they were eyeing the group of girls, Steph, Jenna, Lisa, and a bunch of others, who'd been waiting to greet them. It was easy to tell that the boys' internal juices were heating up. Tim leaned to C.J. Gutierez and said, "Gonna make this an orgy, man! Hey, Steph, how's it goin'?" I looked at Steph and was surprised to see her smiling at Tim. That was really weird considering how distraught she'd been in our kitchen after he'd assaulted her. She was actually giving him a look like she was ready for more. It didn't make sense to me. I looked closer at Steph and realized that her smile was strange. It reminded me of a cobra. And her eyes had that peculiar sorta superiority now. Like I'd first seen in Lisa's.

Darren Green…

Charley and his teammates had grabbed beers from a tub near the dark swimming pool. They were tossing 'em to each other. Some of the guys shook them up and squirted them on others, laughing like goofs.

Lisa called out to them, "Hey, guys. GUYS!" Many of them continued their screwing around. Lisa chuckled to the girls. "What a mature group, huh?" She shouted back at the boys. "*Hell-lo?* Could I have your attention? Before we begin the evening's festivities—"

"Hey, I got your festivity right here, Lisa!" Charley grabbed his crotch and chortled.

Katie McLane...

That is so gross. And stupid. I hate it when guys do that.

But Lisa took it in stride. "I know you do, Charley," she said with that dark twinkle in her eyes. "And you guys are such a great team, we thought it'd be fun to try another sport. We're gonna play a little red rover. But to make it more interesting . . ." The lights in the backyard suddenly went out, making the entire area very dark except for one garden light that was behind the girls, shining toward the boys, who all hooted eagerly. Then Lisa said, "We're gonna do it *skinny dipping*. So strip down, you big tough jocks."

Tim chuckled to his teammates. "Wooo! What'd I tell you, man! Let's do it!" The boys pulled off their clothes. Even in the near darkness I caught glimpses of the guys eyeing the silhouettes of the girls across the pool, who also seemed to be tossing aside their clothes.

Lisa's voice came out of the darkness. "Ready? Get up by the edge on your side." The boys did as instructed, then Lisa said, "Okay, now: check it out."

The pool light suddenly turned on. The guys stood there, buck naked, looking into it, curious. There were dozens of big blocks of ice floating in it. Tim laughed, "Whoa! The world's biggest punch bowl! Awright!"

But Charley saw the girls had only stripped down to bikinis. "Hey! You cheated!"

"Yeah," Lisa said with a leer, "we decided it was time for you guys to chill out."

Then four other girls suddenly rushed side by side from behind the team, holding a twelve-foot-long two-by-four in front of them—which they used to *bulldoze* the boys into the icy pool!

The startled boys surfaced with hoots and hollers, laughing, but also gasping for breath in the freezing cold water. They made for the side of the pool and tried to climb out. But the girls were hard-eyed, and used shorter two-by-fours to poke the boys back in. Again and again.

The boys were laughing at the stupid game, and tried to grab the boards, but their hands slipped off.

"What the hell, man?!" Charley panted, "They greased our end!" The boys' hands kept slipping off as the girls prodded them back in among the floating blocks of ice.

In the frigid water, Charley was laughing nervously, his teeth were chattering. "We're g-gonna get your asses!"

Lisa smiled with supreme confidence. "I don't think so." She prodded him back.

Tim determined to rally the team. "C'mon, Warriors! Let's get these bitches!"

The boys all gave a big rebel yell and made a simultaneous swim for the side. Tim led the charge. Until Jenna swung her two-by-four like a baseball bat, smashing Tim violently on the side of his head. He was knocked back into the pool, dazed, barely conscious. Two boys grabbed and supported him in the water. The others were startled into silence. There was blood in the water now. And fear. Darren and I looked at each other. Scared.

On the side of the pool, Steph watched with mixed emotions. Like she was happy but worried at the same time. She seemed less into the harshness than the other girls. Charley looked from Tim to the girls; his voice was thick with cold, "C'mon Lise, Tim's hurt. And w-we're freezin' our fuckin' nuts off!"

Lisa was matter-of-fact and deadly. "Let me know when your fuckin' nuts get up into your chest, you asshole."

Charley made another rush to get out, but she clubbed him really hard on the shoulder with her board. He yelped loudly with pain, then another girl, Beverly, shoved him back. All the boys were beginning to turn blue, their breaths coming in short gulps.

Charley sputtered, "Lisa, g-godammit!"

"Just a little hypothermia, guys, the water's about forty-five degrees." Lisa calmly checked her watch. "You've got another minute before you lose consciousness. Then the brain damage starts."

"Lisa! For fuck sake!" Charley stammered. Then his clouding eyes saw Jenna moving toward the edge of the pool again.

"Maybe we should let 'em off easy," Jenna said, holding up the outlet end of a heavy electrical cord over the water. The boys' freezing eyes widened. There were shouts of "Jenna! No! You'll *fry us*! Don't!"

Darren Green...

Katie gasped in a big scared breath, and dropped down onto her bike, pulling out her cell. "I'm calling the sheriff."

I caught her sleeve, pulled her back up. "Wait. Look!"

Katie stood back up to see that Steph had put her hand on Jenna's arm, holding her back. Jenna was annoyed. "Hey, this is for you, Steph. And all of us."

"I know," Steph said, looking down at my brother, Tim. She seemed really uncomfortable now.

Tim was all bloody and weak. He raised up a shivering hand, pleading, "St-Steph . . . I'm . . . I'm s-sorry. Okay? I'm sorry."

Steph stared at him as Lisa spoke sternly for all the girls, "It's not just you, Tim. We're *equals*, understand? *All of us.* You're not the only ones who've had strawberries. So don't try any more of your fucking macho Neanderthal bullshit. Or this is only a taste of what you'll get."

Katie McLane...

There were embarrassed murmurs from the numbed, faint boys. Like they were all giving in. "Y-yeah," said Charley, shivering badly. ". . . Yeah. Just . . . please . . ."

Lisa looked down at him, slowly smiling, with clear superiority.

Finally she nodded to Steph, who said, "I'll get the blankets."

Then Lisa, Jenna, and the other girls stepped back, allowing the bedraggled, naked boys to crawl—I think the word is *ignominiously*—and with a lot of difficulty, out of the pool. Several of 'em vomited, others collapsed, gasping. The girls stood over them a moment. Then they took the blankets that Steph brought and threw them on the ground beside the defeated boys.

Behind the fence, I looked at Darren. I could tell his mouth was as dry as mine. We were both barely breathing.

9

ALARMS

Dr. R. W. Hutcherson...

Susan had invited me for a homemade dinner with her and Lilly. Their condo's living room was a pleasant reminder of the friendly, homey comfort I'd felt in Montana. Susan had made it warm and inviting: rich woods, leafy plants, and soft, understated furniture. A well-used mountain bike hung on a wall near the door, and there were photos of Susan with her sister and other friends: some in rustic hospitals, of course, also in scuba gear, on horseback, and a particularly striking one of her rock climbing a precipitous cliff face. I noticed Christopher Smith was in several. That made me uneasy.

Anyone who spent a little time with Susan Perry would naturally want to get to know her better. I sure did. Professionally, of course. And yeah, personally, too. But Christopher Smith was an acknowledged *genius* in our field. And from what I'd heard at the CDC, a pretty good guy as well. How could I think that this bright, attractive, engaging woman who'd been *his* partner might have any personal interest in the likes of me? Compounding my unease: I hadn't even thought about getting involved with anyone since Marianne died. So I quickly determined to tread lightly and make a graceful exit as soon as possible.

After dinner Lilly'd gone to her room, and Susan was cutting me another piece of her warm cherry pie while I looked over her bookshelves. I always joked, badly, that bookshelves spoke volumes about their owners. I was impressed by Susan's eclectic collection, which included science books appropriate to her biomedical specialty, but also authors like Hardy, Dickens, Dostoevsky, Twain, plus a sprinkling of later works by Steinbeck, Huxley, and others. The shelf over the wet bar was also crammed with books. "Obviously you're more concerned about storing literature than liquor."

"Thanks for noticing," she said with a warm smile as she brought over our pie. She sat on the Persian rug in front of the gas fireplace and leaned against the couch. One book by Sinclair Lewis had caught my eye. "I loved his *Arrowsmith*, about doctors like us, but what was *It Can't Happen Here?*"

"He wrote it in 1935," she said, "about a wave of autocratic demagoguery and Fascism suddenly rising up in the United States, like what was happening in Germany and Italy then."

"Ah. So it can't happen here, but it does?"

"Big-time." She seemed more mellow than usual. Maybe because Lilly'd gone to bed, so Susan was off guardian duty. "Lewis makes a disturbing case for how insidious it can be. Starts with a low groundswell and creeps up on a whole society until all of a sudden you find yourself living in an entirely different country." She held up my pie, smiling. "Want to sit down around my faux campfire?"

Dr. Susan Perry...

Hutch slid down onto the floor near me, leaning against the couch and taking his dessert plate. He spilled one big burgundy cherry on the rug and seemed mortified. "No worries." I chuckled. "It's the same color."

He smiled, took a bite of pie, and mumbled approvingly, "Mmmph. So good." Then he refocused on the little contest we'd drifted into after dinner. "So. I think it was your turn, Doctor."

I nodded. "Right, Doctor. Well, *I* got diphtheria while I was treating the epidemic in Detroit."

"Diphtheria in Detroit. Pretty good, and alliterative. I've got one of those," he said proudly. "I caught typhus in Texas!"

"Very impressive," I acknowledged. Then I thought for a moment, cocked an eyebrow, and leaned closer. "But not as exotic as yellow fever in Uruguay."

"No way!"

"Ohhhh yeah!" I nodded with delighted emphasis, having played my ace. I celebrated victory with a bite of pie.

Hutch spoke low, "Well, how about . . ."—he paused, setting up to deliver his coup de grâce—". . . dengue fever in Dominica!"

I shook my head, truly amazed. "Get outta here!"

Hutch raised a three-finger salute. "Scout's honor."

I smiled, leaned my head toward his, teasing, "Probably infected yourself. Sometimes I think you're a little too ambitious."

"No." He chuckled quietly. "Just . . ." He glanced downward and suddenly seemed as shy as that first day we met. "Just probably . . . trying to make up for insecurity."

"What?" I thought he was kidding, but inclining my head lower to study his averted eyes, I realized he was entirely sincere. Confiding a closely guarded secret.

It gave me pause. I was extremely touched by him sharing such a personal vulnerability, felt a tingle of emotion rise in my chest that I hadn't experienced in two long and empty years. It was unexpected, but tangible. We sat silently for a moment. Then I ventured, "Why would you feel insecure, Hutch?"

He shrugged. "Always have. Even among longtime colleagues, and particularly now at the CDC, lemme tell you."

"But you've got a tremendous track record, years of experience, and—"

"I know, I know." He shook his head, looked away, trying to frame it. "But I always feel like I'm a teenager in a roomful of grown-ups. I'm positive that at any moment they're all gonna realize I'm way out of my depth, nowhere close to their levels of competence—particularly yours and—"

My blurted laugh was so loud it shocked him. I waved an immediate apology. "Sorry!" I said, still laughing. "Really. Sorry. It's just that I can't tell you how many times I've felt the same way *exactly*!"

"No." He stared in all seriousness. "No. I don't believe that you—"

"Believe it, Hutch! Particularly when I'm around Lauren. And I've known so many people way more knowledgeable and credentialed than me who've admitted feeling the same way when they're in a group."

He wasn't buying it. "No. You're just trying to—"

"Trying to assure you, Dr. R.W. Hutcherson, that everyone— except maybe Stephen Hawking—has felt that sometimes." Hutch gazed keenly at me, like he would really like to believe me. But I saw that I still had more convincing to do.

Dash-Cam Video, Carroll Co. Sheriff, Unit 712,
Date: 09/04/20 **Time:** 01:49:13

Transcript Analysis by: Halzinger, Renata D., GSP #98432

Suspect Vehicle: 2015 Hyundai coupe, GA BB7519

Registration: Timothy Green

S/bound on Bridger Road, Ashton GA, Mrkr 12

Routine traffic-violation stop. No wants or warrants. One person in vehicle.

Weather: Light rain, wet roadway

Vehicle pulls onto shoulder in response to Code 2 from Carroll Co. Sheriff, Unit 712.

01:49:50 Ofcr Badge #14625. Patton, Brice T., age 20, Deputy, is seen slowly approaching vehicle from north, weapon holstered.

Courtesy Carroll Co. GA Sheriff, FBI

—⁓—

Body-Cam Video/Audio, Carroll Co. Sheriff, Unit 712,
Date: 09/04/20 **Time:** 01:49:52

Ofcr Badge: Carroll Co. Sheriff #14625.

Ofcr: Patton, Brice T., age 20, Deputy Sheriff

Transcript Analysis by: Halzinger, Renata D., GSP #98432

Activation Time: 01:49:52

Video:

Deputy Patton approaches 2015 Hyundai coupe GA BB7519. Driver is white male, dark hair, maroon Ashton High School jacket.

Audio:

Timothy Green: (mutters, sounds like) Fucking son of a bitch.

Ofcr Patton: Yo, Timbo. Rolled right through that ol' stop sign. Pretty dumb for Mr. Big Georgia Tech Football Scholarship.

Timothy Green: (sighs angrily) Aw, give me a fucking break, Brice. You already busted me once for what you and I both know was bullshit.

Ofcr Patton: Nuh uh, man. Shoulda had the old turn signal on that time. Now I seen ya weaving across the centerline, and it sure smells like beer in there, huh? (Ofcr shines flashlight into car, then onto TG's face.)

Timothy Green: Look. I'm sorry, Brice. Had a really bad night, take a look, man. (TG turns, pulls left shirt collar back, angles head away to show badly bruised, bloodied, scraped face, neck, and shoulder. Some fresh blood apparent.)

Ofcr Patton: (chuckles) Whoa. Somebody whomped you a good one upside the head.

Timothy Green: Yeah. It was pretty bad.

Ofcr Patton: So . . . what? Am I s'posed t'get all teary-eyed with sympathy and shit? (Ofcr's hands can be seen opening his citation book.)

Timothy Green: Please, Brice. My old man's gonna ground me if I get another ticket.

Ofcr Patton: This just ain't your night, is it? (Ofcr begins to write citation.)

Timothy Green: Aw, come on, cut me some slack, Brice.

Ofcr Patton: Just doin' my job, ol' buddy. Hey, this is the only job some of us can get, Timbo. Gotta uphold my oath. Protect and serve the public. Make my quota so Sheriff Randolph's a happy camper. And 'sides that, I gotcha good, dickwad.

Timothy Green: Hang on, man. (speaks more quietly) Listen. Maybe we can make a deal here.

Ofcr Patton: You 'tempting t'bribe an officer of the law? Thas great. I'll add that to the charge. (resumes writing)

Timothy Green: Wait, wait, goddammit! (reaches toward passenger seat)

Ofcr Patton: Whoa! Keep them fuckin' hands where I can see 'em! (shines light toward passenger seat)

Timothy Green: Take it easy, man. It's just this. (a gallon-size Ziploc baggie seen)

Ofcr Patton: What the hell are those!?

Timothy Green: Something you will *really* like. (TG looks right into body cam) Turn that thing off, Brice, and I'll tell you all about it.

(Camera jostles slightly; flashlight beam momentarily swings across plastic bag. Several objects inside about the size of lemons. But red. Somewhat resemble, but much too large to actually be, strawberries.)

Body Cam Deactivated 01:51:47

Dash Cam Deactivated via remote: 01:51:58

Courtesy Carroll Co. GA Sheriff, FBI

Dr. Susan Perry…

Two days later I was startled when an alarm blared loudly at the CDC. Red lights pulsated. I ran down the hallway, encountering Hutch, who shouted over the earsplitting whoop. "Is this a drill?!"

"No! BSL-4! Prashant's working in there!"

"Jesus . . . ," he muttered as we ran down the stairs, then reached the laboratory floor and the thick window looking into the highest security biosafety level four laboratory. The CDC's director, Ernest Levering, was already outside it with others who were greatly distressed, looking helplessly through the window.

"What happened?!" Hutch shouted.

"They were working with the NZT nerve toxin," Levering said urgently, "Prashant's suit failed!"

My blood turned to ice water. "Oh my God. He'll be dead in sixty seconds!" I looked in desperately through the double-thick glass and saw bantamweight Prashant, wearing a bulky blue isolation suit, lying on the floor, and convulsing violently, as though being electrocuted. Another laboratorian in an isolation suit was bending over him.

Hutch strained to see as he asked Levering, "Who's in there with him?"

"Lauren."

Hutch and I both drew a breath, our eyes met sharply.

As excruciating as it was for us to witness Prashant's tortured thrashing, I knew that inside the laboratory, his death agonies were beyond imagining. Like liquid fire scalding through his veins. My dear, loveable friend had bloody foam oozing from his thin mouth as he convulsed ever more violently. Even through the fogged visor of his helmet, I could tell he was staring out in wild-eyed terror at Lauren, who bent low over him, safe inside her iso suit. She held his shoulders as though trying to provide supportive human contact until the end.

If I'd had a closer vantage point at the time, I'd likely have seen that the last image Prashant had in his life was not at all empathetic. The expression on Dr. Lauren Fletcher's face would have been cold and impassive. With a darkness in her eyes.

10

CONVERSION

Eric Tenzer...

I was mesmerized by the yellow daisy in my hand, studying its colors, textures, its cheerful yellow starburst blossom fully absorbing the rays from the warm autumn sun. It was one of many we'd planted that was now thriving in the small garden outside our Ashton High faculty lounge. I held its delicate stem lightly between my thumb and forefinger, admiring its beauty, its life, and Dylan Thomas immediately came to mind: "The force that through the green fuse drives the flower / Drives my green age . . ."

Which prompted me to think about my own relatively "green age." I was only thirty-five and concerned, with good reason, about how much longer I might have, when I heard the grating, cynical female voice, "Investigating the *Bellis compositae*?" I knew it was Shelly Navarro, the science teacher. She eased her stocky frame down onto a wooden bench nearby as she lit an e-cigarette.

I smiled. "I prefer to think of it as a daisy."

Shelly Navarro...

I exhaled my first long drag and added, "The Latin. Genus, family."

"Of course." Tenzer offered me his friendly smile. "The word *daisy* comes from Latin, too," he said. "Originally *solis oculus*—sun's eye. Then the Old English made it *daeg eage*. Which literally means 'day's eye.'" He pondered the little flower. "One that's looking at us."

"Well," I chortled cynically, trying to cover my annoyance at being one-upped, "I'd rather be looking back at 'em, than pushing 'em up, huh?"

That phrase seemed to make Tenzer feel slightly uncomfortable. He drew a breath, still looking at the flower, spoke very quietly, "Yeah."

I didn't know what deeper meaning his tone was suggesting, or as Tenzer might have put it, what "nuance of hidden troubles it betrayed." And frankly I really didn't care. I was preoccupied with my own annoyances. I took another long puff from my e-cig and looked dryly toward the school building. "Actually, there's a hell of a lot of things I'd rather be doing."

Tenzer glanced at me. "Like . . . ?"

I flicked an ash, though there wasn't one, of course. "Planned to be working with big pharma somewhere. Instead of"—I scanned the area disdainfully—"here." Then I looked at him with mild astonishment. "But you actually *like* teaching, don't you?"

"I do, Shelly. I love it. Particularly lately. Some of my senior kids suddenly blossomed!"

I glanced at him with surprise. "Actually, some of mine, too. Weird as hell. Jumped into advanced work. I figured they had to be cheating somehow, but I've isolated them in ways they couldn't get around. They just seem smarter all of a sudden." I shook my head, puzzling over it again. "I don't get it."

Tenzer grinned. "Ever thought that maybe it's 'cause you're a good teacher, Shelly?"

I looked at him with an arched eyebrow and my expression of *oh puh-leeze*. Then I took another unfulfilling hit on my e-cigarette.

Katie McLane...

I was at our kitchen table, making my homework about the rise of Vladimir Putin more palatable by taking a mouse bite of oatmeal-raisin cookie each time I wrote an answer. A news anchorwoman droned on the TV in the background, something like, "At the State Capitol today, the governor's new plans to streamline state government were received with less confrontation than usual from his normally hard-line opponents." She went on about how both political parties seemed to have "mellowed slightly and become less engaged in their classical partisan bickering." It was only way later that I realized it had been a distant early warning.

I was distracted when Lisa came in. Her attitude toward me still had that new, chilly sorta edge. Like she was keeping me at arm's length, and all of a sudden was just soooo much more mature than me. Steph followed her in like a puppy dog, wearing a thrift-store skirt I hadn't seen before. I always felt sorry she didn't have many clothes.

Steph was softly pleading, "Lisa, please. I've *got* to win the science fair. Your dad can afford to send you to college, but I *need* that scholarship."

"So? Win," said Lisa, snagging a can of Coke from the fridge. "You had your share of strawberries."

That grabbed my attention, but I looked quickly back at my homework so they wouldn't think I was listening. I'd been wondering if "strawberries" was code for some new drug.

"But you're still better in the orals," Steph went on with gentle sincerity. "Couldn't you hold back just a little?"

Lisa turned away from Steph, but I caught the dark flash of her cynical smile. "Okay, Steph. No problem."

Steph sensed the lie. "Look, Lisa, I'm sorry, but there's just no way I can let you win."

As I watched Steph leave quietly, it seemed like she was feeling sad about Lisa, but also pondering how she could be sure to win. Lisa stared coldly after Steph, then turned toward her room, but caught me gazing at her. She gave me this really challenging glare like a blast of arctic air. "*What?*"

I shrugged, returned to my social studies. I could feel Lisa's eyes really boring into me for a moment, then she left the room. I peeked up, chewing my lip and frowning. Then our mom came in as frazzled as ever, searching through papers on the counter. "Have you seen my price list?"

"It was on the kitchen counter," I said, but my thoughts were elsewhere. "Mom, there's something weird about Lisa."

Mom shuffled papers with increasing frustration. "Where is the damn thing?"

"She's not like she used to be, Mom."

She was pulling out drawers now. "Right: her grades have *improved*, so I'm not asking questions. Dammit, where *is* it?"

"No, Mom, it's more than that, it's—"

"Katie, please! I've got a customer on hold. Do you think it's easy for me to keep everything together since"—I knew what was coming, and I silently mimed the words as she spoke them—"your father ran off with that bimbo?!" Mom found the paper behind the toaster oven and grabbed the kitchen phone. "Hello? Mr. Blake, sorry. Okay, a half-page, two days . . ."

As she went giving her sales pitch, I turned off my tablet, and sighed to our big black-and-white pooch, "Come on, Madison." Our friendly Bernese followed me out, as sad eyed as I felt.

Dr. Susan Perry...

I was frustrated, but trying to remain polite as I spoke on my office phone, "Lauren, all I requested was info on what other areas were cordoned off after the comet."

Upstairs, Lauren was on the other end of the line in her corner office. I could not see it at the time, but security camera archives later verified that CDC's director, Dr. Ernest Levering, looking officious as ever, was seated across from Lauren. Wearing his half-moon reading glasses, he studied the file of a farm where one of the comet fragments had hit. Lauren's tone was friendly on the phone, but I detected the clear air of superiority that she'd enjoyed casually projecting more than ever in the last couple of months. "Don't know what to tell you, hon. It hasn't come through here yet."

"But it shouldn't be taking this long," I said with annoyance.

"Oopsie," Lilly said from where she sat in her corner, frowning down at her iPad. "S-Susie?"

I waved for Lilly to be quiet as I heard Lauren saying, "Just typical bureaucratic bullshit."

Lilly was getting aggravated with her iPad. "Something's wrong."

I tried to ignore Lilly as I pressed Lauren, "And I haven't gotten your report on those hog specimens—"

"Something's definitely wr-wrong," Lilly stuttered fearfully.

I covered the phone and snapped, "Lilly, *please!*" Then said to Lauren, "Those specimens from the aggressive farm animals."

Lauren sighed, seemingly frustrated herself, "I know. Just backed up, Suse. Prashant's death and all." As the memory of her leaning over his convulsing body flashed through my mind, Lauren chided, "Hey. When *you're* finally running this office, I'm sure things'll be more efficient—but look, we had no additional reports like those animals, so there's probably nothing to worry about."

I refused to fold. "I'd still appreciate it if—"

"Soon as I can, hon. Got to step into a meeting." She clicked off.

I slammed my phone down. "Thanks. *Hon.*"

Lilly shook her iPad insistently. "Oopsie!"

I snapped again, "What is the *problem!?*"

"S-something's wrong," Lilly said, greatly concerned. "*The Price Is Right* isn't on."

"A first-world crisis," I grumbled. "Let me see." I took the iPad, flipped on the sound. Her favorite program that Lilly watched religiously, compulsively, was preempted. A TV reporter was saying, ". . . special press conference where the governor has just praised the legislature for their extremely rare bipartisan effort."

"It's some kind of news conference, Lilly," I explained. "Maybe *The Price Is Right* will be on in a—"

Lilly shook her head. "Supposed to be on at e-eleven."

"I *know!*" It came out childishly harsh. Lilly flinched. I hated myself whenever I caused that. I struggled to regain my composure. "Sorry, sweetie. But today there's—"

Hutch entered, interrupting. "I've been through all Prashant's files you gave me. I can't find anything about Lauren's new research. Not even as much as he told us before his accident."

I stared at him a moment, short-tempered about everything. Then I walked brusquely out past him. "There's another file cabinet down the hall where he kept backups and hardcopies."

CDC Sec Cam 3044 Date: 09/07/20 Time: 11:06:01

Ofc Lab 3044 S. Perry.

Transcript Analysis by: ATL PD-Op 20743

Visual Desc: 3044 >>shows Drs. S. Perry & R.W. Hutcherson exiting office, L. Perry sitting at lab table looking at iPad.<<

L. Perry: S-something's definitely wrong.

>>Custodian J. Hartman steps into doorway. Looks down the hall where S. Perry & R.W. Hutcherson had headed, then he quickly enters, goes to L. Perry.<<

J. Hartman: Lilly. I need some information. Viroid pathology, specifically—

L. Perry: (stares at iPad) The Price Is Right sh-should've been on six minutes ago.

J. Hartman: (annoyed) Lilly. Please, focus: viroids. Particularly—

L. Perry: (adjusts iPad) It's never late. I don't—

J. Hartman: Lilly, dammit, will you listen? Viroids. Anything by Christopher Smith on anomalous protein coating and—

L. Perry: (shakes head) Something's wr-wrong.

>>J. Hartman suddenly grabs L. Perry's shoulders angrily, shakes her very hard.<<

J. Hartman: Will you listen to me, you stupid retard!

>>His violent action knocks pencils off the table. L. Perry is startled, visibly upset & tearful. Hands trembling.<<

L. Perry: Oopsie!

>>J. Hartman stops. Also seems startled by his own behavior. He steps back, as though trying to understand his outburst. Appears very embarrassed and uncomfortable.<<

J. Hartman: I'm . . . I'm sorry. Excuse me, Lilly. I'm sorry.

>>J. Hartman turns away slowly. Seems introspective, upset. Looks back at L. Perry, who has gotten to hands & knees, carefully picking up pencils. J. Hartman exits office.<<

L. Perry: (nods) Something's d-definitely wrong.

Courtesy ATL PD, FBI

Dr. Susan Perry...

Moving down the hall and around a corner, I led Hutch to the spot I remembered, but instead of Prashant's file cabinet, there was merely a dusty outline of where it had been. I was puzzled, annoyed. "It used to be right here." I saw the director approaching. "Dr. Levering? Do you know what happened to Prashant's files?"

He shrugged. "Maybe he'd finally finished the digitizing and sent it to deep storage. Or Lauren did." He continued on, leaving me staring at Hutch, then again at the empty space where the file cabinet had been.

I noticed that prior to turning into another corridor, Levering looked back, eyeing us.

Darren Green...

My brother, Tim, was in our garage, changing the oil in our car. I was helping him. Then Charley came walking up, saying, "Got your text, Timbo. What's up?"

"Not much." Then Tim looked at me. "Give us a minute, huh, Dare? Maybe grab a soda." It was clear he wanted me outta there. I nodded. But I didn't go inside. I went around to where I could peek in through the dusty back window.

I heard Tim say, with a smile, "I appreciate you standing in for me as QB, Charley."

Charley shrugged it off, smiled back. "No sweat. My pleasure."

Tim kept smiling when he said, "But *I'm* gonna quarterback from now on."

Charley chuckled. "Hey. You wouldn't be feeling this way if I hadn't given you the strawberries. So why don't you just eat me, huh?" He smiled and winked at Tim.

"You wish," Tim kidded, tussling with him. Charley returned the friendly roughhousing. But a poke became a push, then a shove, and in a flash Charley grabbed Tim and rammed him hard over some paint cans. Tim went apeshit. He grabbed a heavy lug wrench, went for

Charley. Their fight was violent, ugly. Really vicious and dirty. Lotsa cheap shots, groin punches.

And Tim was the worst. Tim! Who'd always been an honest, fair guy. Now it was like he had this killer instinct. He smeared a brush full of grease right across Charley's eyes, blinding him, then kicked his legs out from under him and pushed Charley's face down into the catch pan filled with dirty oil. Tim held him under. Like to drown him.

I was gonna bang on the window to make Tim stop, when he pulled Charley up. Charley was gagging, vomiting. But Tim didn't quit. He grabbed Charley's right hand, bent his fingers back so far that Charley screamed.

Tim was shouting into his ear, "You give, motherfucker?! Huh? *Huh*!?"

"Yeah. Yeah! Jesus!" Charley gasped, almost crying. "Leggo man, you're breaking my fucking fingers!"

But Tim bent them harder, said with a scary grin, "Maybe I oughta! Huh?"

"Dumb move, man," Charley said, breathing hard. "Be pretty hard for me to catch your stupid passes."

"I got other receivers." Tim was still smiling. "And you'd remember who's in charge, huh?!"

There was a pause. They both stood there panting, angry, silent.

And then Tim snapped one of Charley's fingers.

Katie McLane...

"Oh my God!" I said, my jaw hanging in disbelief. "Tim *broke* it?!" Darren had found me crossing through Ashton's town square where I'd picked up some stamps for my mom. I'd stopped dead, stunned.

"Yeah," Darren said. He was still frightened. I could tell his stomach was in a knot, and he was queasy from the violence he'd witnessed. "Tim said just 'cause Charley found the damn strawberries don't make him the *natural* quarterback."

"What strawberries? What are they talking about? Does that mean drugs or . . . ?"

"I dunno." Darren shook his head, totally stumped. "*I dunno!*"

Us two fourteen-year-olds stared at each other, trying to figure it all out. It felt so weird. There we were, standing in the middle of this pleasant, green, well-cared-for park that was the small town square of Ashton. Where we'd both grown up. Birds were chirping in the leafy magnolia trees. A few cars moved along the streets around us. People passed, going about their business routinely, unaware of how troubled Darren and I were by the scary changes that were transforming people in our hometown.

The Documentarian...

One didn't have to travel more than a mile or so outside of Ashton to get into good, rich Georgia farm country. Granny Wells had lived on a small farm most of her life. Her given name was Gertrude, but everyone had called her Granny for years, because she was the quintessential image of grandmotherhood. She was eighty-two and tiny. Gray haired and bright eyed. Barely five feet tall, she'd always been a featherweight and a cheery soul who was beloved of her grandchildren and her children, all of whom well knew and were able to describe her habits, foibles, humorous snappy comebacks, and generous nature. Their later descriptions and testimony, along with family photos and letters, allow us to present this composite picture of Gertrude Wells. She preferred dresses of thin material with tiny checks and usually had an apron on over them because her hobby had always been cooking. Since George, her husband of fifty-seven years, had gone to his reward, Mrs. Wells had spent considerably more time in the kitchen, preparing treats for her family and friends. It kept her happily busy.

In addition to the personal information provided by her family, we also have the forensic evidence later gathered by Dr. Susan Perry. From the combination of those sources, we can presume essentially what transpired on the same afternoon that Katie McLane and Darren Green were worried in the town square.

Mrs. Wells had gone on one of her "expeditions," as she called them. She had traipsed through the rural area bordering her farm, and when she came out through a particular stand of trees, she would have stopped short. Looking ahead, she would likely have blinked through her white-framed bifocals partly because of the bright sunlight and partly because of the astonishing sight she beheld.

It was the spectacular area that had grown up magnificently around Lisa McLane and Charley Flinn's swimming hole.

Mrs. Wells certainly would have marveled at the look of plants she recognized, but which had grown in such a fabulous way, to such a burgeoning size, and with such verdant profusion, as she had never seen in her life. She would've felt as though she had wandered onto a different planet. Or the Garden of Eden.

She would have walked slowly into the huge magical garden, touching some of the extraordinary plants, smelling the sweet fragrance of others. With the eye of a master gardener, she would doubtlessly have noticed that while the strong, hearty, clearly superior plants had prospered majestically, they had also choked out those which had somehow not been blessed with the newfound life force that drove the potently predominant layers of vegetation.

At one point Mrs. Wells would certainly have drawn to a stop once again in amazement. Because she had confronted the huge and proliferating wild strawberries.

We know that she picked one of the ripe, inviting strawberries that was larger than her hand. She likely smelled it and smiled with delight. She did not taste it, however, and never would, but put it into her large basket and then continued picking considerably more of the unprecedented fruit.

11

REVELATION

Katie McLane...

As I came in the back door to our kitchen, my head was spinning. I was still trying to sort through all the strange and violent incidents. Lisa was taking something out of the freezer. She turned around sharply, like somebody might if they wouldn't want to be caught doing something. A freezer bag spilled onto the floor.

Lisa laughed at herself. "Oh, good one, Lise."

I stooped to help her pick up the small, scattered frozen items, then I frowned, very curious. "Shrimp?"

"Guess they're Mom's. I was looking for a juice bar," Lisa explained. "Been really pigging out lately." She continued picking up the shrimp. I looked at Lisa, with the definite feeling that I was being lied to. Lisa must have noticed my expression. "What?"

I decided to go for it. "Are you okay, Lise?"

Lisa screwed up her face like I was crazy. "What do you mean?" I could only stare at her for a moment, then sorta shrugged. Lisa smirked, "Well, that's very articulate, but yes. I am great, little sister. Best I've ever been." She poked my shoulder. As she stood up and left the kitchen, she flashed a grin back at me. But it was as cold as the frozen shrimp.

Eric Tenzer...

It was right after lunch. I ran into the school parking lot, and a knot of students jumped out of the way when the paramedic van came screeching in with its siren screaming. I shouted to the medics as they bailed out, "In here! Quickly! She can't breathe!"

I hurriedly led them into the gym, where the science fair was in progress, and the final oral session had been about to start. The medics rushed through the students' homemade exhibits to where Stephanie Lingebach lay gasping and writhing on the floor, her eyes rolled back to the whites. She looked demonic and possessed. Shelly Navarro, the science teacher, was bending over her as worried students crowded in.

"Everybody back," I said. "Give them room!"

As the paramedics kneeled by her, Shelly told them, "I think it's either grand mal or anaphylactic shock."

One paramedic checked Steph's trachea, and nodded in agreement as he clamped on an oxygen inhaler. "Anaphylaxis. Pharynx is swollen closed." He glanced at his partner. "Thirty-three ccs of sub-q-epi. Stat. Throw on the pulse oximeter and get a Benadryl IV fifty. I'll do a trake." She was already on the case as he snapped on latex gloves and spoke commandingly to me about the students, "Back them up, please." With practiced precision, the first paramedic sterilized Stephanie's throat with Betadine, peeled open a sterile scalpel, and then cut deeply into her throat. Blood flowed out around the incision. Several students who were watching from nearby gasped; one boy gagged and ran toward the restroom.

The paramedic inserted a guide tube into the wound and leaned closer as he slid a narrower tube down inside it. "Okay, I'm in," he said, pleased to hear that air was wheezing into Steph's lungs through the incision. He helped his partner with the IV rig as he glanced up at me. "It's a histaminic—allergic reaction. What's she been eating?"

Jenna Mahoney leaned in over a boy's shoulder, worried. "Just a tuna sandwich at lunch, but she's eaten lots of those. Is she gonna be okay?"

The paramedic pressed Jenna. "Any other known allergies?"

"Uh, uh . . . bees. And mold, I think." Jenna was trying to remember. "Yeah, that and some seafood. Not tuna, but, like crabs, lobster. Shellfish, y'know?"

Katie McLane...

I was standing at the edge of the crowd. My eyes snapped up to Jenna, startled. Then I scanned quickly across the other students and spotted Lisa. She wasn't like all the others watching. They were concerned and worried. Lisa's face had almost zero expression. But her eyes were hard. Cold.

Later that afternoon I came home angry. Our dining table was covered with clippings that Mom was using for reference while designing an ad on her laptop. I told her the story and my suspicions about Lisa. Mom was shocked. "What? Do you actually think your sister would *poison* her best friend?!"

Yes. I was convinced. I felt like a lawyer with a clear-cut case. "Lisa wanted to beat Steph at the science fair, Mom. And now she has."

"And you should be proud of her," Mom said, returning distractedly to her work in progress, "not saying things like—" She was interrupted by the phone ringing. "Oh, I can't talk to anybody right now."

I walked off hotly to the kitchen, muttering, "Gee, what else is new." I grabbed the ringing phone. "She can't talk to anybody!" Then I slammed it back down and stood there, fuming. After a moment I picked up the phone again and punched in a number.

After four rings, which I knew meant it was going to voice mail, a man's voice answered, "Hi, this is Jason McLane. I can't take your call right now . . ."

I nodded bitterly. "What a surprise." I waited for the beep, then said gently, "Hi, it's me, Daddy. Call me when you get back to Atlanta. Bye." I hung the phone up, but stood there looking at it, whispering, ". . . I miss you."

Dr. R. W. Hutcherson...

The beams from our pair of flashlights cut through the gloom in a dark CDC storage room in one of the outbuildings. Susan and I had closed the door behind us and were snooping. I was nervous, felt even more out of my depth than usual, whispering, "I know I'm new in these parts and not that familiar with protocol, but it took me a long time to get this job, Suse. Isn't Levering likely to cut us outta the herd if we get caught in here without authorization? How'd you get the keys anyway?"

"*Borrowed* them from Joseph," she said. "Made copies." Her determination to ferret out the truth was clear. "There it is."

"That doesn't answer my first question."

She didn't respond, but led me down a row of file cabinets to a particular one. I pulled at the drawers. They were locked. "Okay," I said, feeling relief. "At least we tried, but now let's—"

Susan expertly tucked the flashlight under her arm so that its beam lit up the lock as she took out a small cloth pouch and unrolled it, revealing a set of lock picks. I stared in wonderment. "Uh . . . where exactly did you . . . ?"

"My uncle was a locksmith." She worked her way skillfully into the lock. "I used to practice in case college didn't work out," she said with a tight grin.

I chuckled, unconvinced. "Come on, you don't really think that you're gonna—" The lock clicked open.

Susan's blue eyes twinkled at me.

I acknowledged her expertise with a nod. She pulled out the drawer. It was empty.

Dr. Susan Perry...

A few minutes later the two of us were walking across the darkened CDC grounds. I was frustrated, questioning myself. "Okay, maybe I'm just getting as paranoid as Prashant was, but damn it, I feel like Lauren's stonewalling me, too. About that comet impact information."

Hutch was mulling it over. "Maybe I can figure some way to bypass her."

"That'd be great."

"And I do like being in dark rooms with you."

He gave me a shy, affectionate look, and I smiled back, genuinely acknowledging it. "Yeah. I like that, too."

But then he frowned about something ahead and caught my sleeve to stop me from rounding the building's corner. I looked at him questioningly as he whispered, "Paranoia time."

I peered around the corner, looking toward the tree-lined staff parking lot. I saw Lauren and Mitchell chatting amiably as they walked to Mitchell's dark limo. Two gray-suited clones were nearby, being casually protective. Just behind the limo was a large black SUV with its engine idling. Hutch seemed nervous, but followed reluctantly as I slipped up behind a parked CDC van to observe them more closely. Hutch whispered, "He's added more security-types?"

Then someone else caught my eye. Joseph Hartman had come out of the lab building and was hovering deferentially nearby Lauren and Mitchell. "What the hell is *he* doing there?" I whispered. We watched as Joseph exchanged a few words with Lauren. He handed a file packet to Mitchell, then moved off. As Mitchell stepped toward his limo, Lauren grasped his arm. We could just barely make out her words.

"I'm jealous that the capitol building sees more of you than I do," Lauren said to the hawkeyed man.

"Well, I'm jealous of the CDC," he responded with a slight softness out of keeping with his stern, militaristic demeanor. "You're extraordinary. And your work has been amazing."

"It's only the beginning," Lauren said, somewhat coquettishly.

"Yes . . . it is." Their eyes held with a powerful connection. Even from across the parking lot, their intimacy was evident.

I traded a glance with Hutch as we ducked back to avoid the sweeping lights of Mitchell's departing limousine and the black SUV.

Charley Flinn...

When Caruso saw my finger that Tim had busted, he made Tim quarterback again. I played fullback. The game was about three minutes into the first quarter. Tim dropped back to throw a pass, but the rival team from the nearby town of Beaumount steamrolled me and the other linebackers. They sacked Tim decisively, slamming him so hard onto the ground that he musta seen stars. Part of me enjoyed seeing him get crunched. But there was something else going on.

A couple Warriors helped Tim up and into our huddle. He was pissed. "Where the hell were you guys?" We all shook our heads. We were playing just as hard, strong, and smart as we had the last couple games.

"Yeah, what the hell's up?" I said, nursing my bandaged fingers. "Why aren't we rollin' over these wimps?!"

"All right, all right. We will," Tim urged, determined to pull the pack together. "Red dog on three." We all clapped, sounding our war whoop, broke the huddle, and went to the line. Tim glanced at the rival team's defensive line. Then I saw him look more closely at those guys. I did, too.

That harsh, dominant glint all us Warriors had was also in the eyes of the Beaumount guys. I drew a breath, wondering how that was possible. Then Tim bent down to business. "Down. Set. Hut. Hut. Hut."

As Tim took the snap, those Beaumount bastards crashed onto us like an avalanche. Tim got sacked again really hard. One of the tacklers stabbed his stiff fingers into Tim's throat, another dug his cleats into my leg. I realized that these guys were just as hard-assed, cruel, and ferocious as we were. They were roaring like a pack o'lions, popping fists all around for how they'd snowplowed right through us and stomped Tim.

The hometown crowd was startled, too. They'd got used to cheering play after play from our supervictorious team. Ashton wasn't used to *their* boys getting so totally, painfully whupped.

Darren Green...

In our locker room after the game, I was passing out towels to the Warriors, who were like really depressed. They were growling at each other, angry they hadn't won. They just couldn't believe it. Charley slammed a locker. "How did they fucking *tie* us! Damn! Those bastards must've found some strawberries, too! Shit! We could lose the goddamn championship!"

All the other guys were grumbling agreement just as Tim entered with this big grin. "Nothing to worry about, guys. That won't be happening." He snagged a towel from me, and I saw him wipe some black, greasy stuff off his hand.

Charley sneered at him. "Oh, you're so fucking sure?"

"Just got a feeling." Tim kept grinning slyly, in a way that gave me the creeps.

Eric Tenzer...

I was driving home after the game when I came upon the accident. Traffic on the country road had been stopped in both directions. There was quite a jam. Word had apparently gotten out quickly via cells and social media. A deputy sheriff's car with its siren wailing sped past me on the shoulder toward the crash site. I walked up to investigate and saw Deputy Brice Patton get out of his squad car near the ugly accident. I'd had Brice in class for two years. It had been a struggle for both of us. In spite of my best efforts, he was one of those cocky kids who barely scraped by and just didn't care about schoolwork. I'd worried for him then and was happy to hear that he'd at least finally found employment with the county sheriff.

The sheriff's car was already at the accident site, along with a fire truck and several civilian cars whose occupants were standing along the shoulder of the dark road. The people's faces were illuminated by the flashing emergency lights and the fire from the school bus, which was on its side in the gully that paralleled the road. It was engulfed in roaring flames.

Firemen were desperately trying to knock down the blaze and make their way in to seek survivors, but I could see that the outlook was definitely grim. So could Brice. Some adults were screaming, trying to get closer to find their sons who had been aboard the bus, but they were being held back by other parents.

I saw our kindly Sheriff Randolph, his round face smudged and burned, trudging upward from the gully. Brice reached down a hand to help pull him up as he said, "What the hell happened, Sheriff!"

"Bus with the Beaumount team we played tonight." The sheriff was breathing hard. "Looks like the brakes failed. Lotta dead kids. Get down there and help pull 'em out."

Brice swallowed. "Why don't I stay up here and reroute traffic?"

"I said get your ass down there, boy! Who the hell's in charge here?!" The sheriff stormed past. I noticed Brice watching him go for a moment. I saw the police and fire emergency lights reflected off the unusually cold glare that was in Brice's eyes.

Darren Green...

The next morning I told Katie what I'd seen and heard in the locker room.

"*Strawberries* again?" She shook her head, trying to figure it out. She was convinced about her idea. "It *has* to be some new kind of drug.

Something that really gets them hopped up. And mean. You know what those football games looked like."

"Yeah." I swallowed. "And how Tim and Charley got so nasty."

Katie nodded. "And Lisa."

Then I had a thought. "You think maybe it could be some kinda *real* strawberries?"

"C'mon, Darren, whoever heard of anything like that?" Katie said, like it was a totally stupid idea. "And where would they have—" She suddenly stopped dead.

"What?" I was confused. She just stood there. "What're you thinking?"

She shook her head again. "Doesn't make sense. And anyway, it's the wrong time of year."

I leaned closer. "Katie, what are you talking about?"

She kept standing there, thinking. "Sometimes in the summer Lisa would bring home wild strawberries that she and Charley had picked."

"From where?"

She looked up at me. Her face was very frowny and tense.

Katie McLane...

We were blown away. Of course we'd heard fables about the Garden of Eden. I'd even read about the real Hanging Gardens of Babylon, one of the ancient seven wonders of the world. But not in a zillion years did I think I'd ever see anything like what we were looking at. And definitely not in the woods on the old McAlistair farm in Georgia.

But there it was: an area easily three times the size of our school gym had turned into the greenest, lushest place I'd ever seen. The woods around it were just ordinary, normal autumn woods. But it looked like the really rich, new, green vegetation had been working its way outward from the pond, which was practically hidden deep in the middle. Darren and I were stupefied. And a little scared. Neither of us said anything. We just walked real slowly and carefully into the area, like we were walking across a minefield. We kept glancing nervously at each other. It was like we'd wandered into a dreamscape. We were really hesitant about touching the large, beautiful plants as we slowly walked deeper in. Down toward the edge of the pond. We were moving so slowly, so quietly, I was really startled when Darren suddenly grabbed my arm.

"Katie!"

Catching my breath, I saw he was pointing off to one side.

Behind some ferns that used to be one foot tall and were now way over my head, I could see a large green bush. Bearing wild strawberries. But not like any I'd ever seen. The smallest of these were the size of my fist. Barely breathing, we walked very slowly toward it.

There were many new buds. Others were still green. Others were completely ripe. You could smell how full grown, perfect, and inviting they were. Many had been pecked by birds. We could also tell that more than a few had been picked recently.

The Documentarian...

From careful investigation by authorities plus statements of close family and friends who knew her habits well, the following can be deduced. In Granny Gertrude Wells's homey, pine-paneled farm kitchen, which always smelled enticingly of vanilla and almond extract, she would likely have been humming her favorite classic, *I'll Be Seeing You*. It had been "their song," hers and the late George Wells's. As she finished slicing up the many pounds of large strawberries she'd picked in the strangely evolved forest garden, she would have scraped the stems and remnants into her zinc garbage pail, carried it out across the screened back porch, and down the three old wooden steps toward the chicken yard.

"Here, chick, chick, chick," she always called out with her squeaky voice. "Tammy? Garth? Shania? Got some goodies for y'all." She would have dipped her hand into the pail and scattered the scraps on the ground. The chickens would have scurried up and eagerly begun eating the strawberry remnants.

Shelly Navarro...

In my classroom that Monday afternoon, I'd thankfully finished my last class and was watching the annoying tenth graders depart. A very troubled-looking Katie McLane was the last of them. I rarely reached out to any student, preferring the arm's-length rule of teaching. But Katie was one of the few I even slightly liked, so I beckoned to her. "Katie? What's going on with your quiz scores dropping?" Katie paused, her eyes downcast as I continued, "Your attention's seemed off lately."

She looked up, then her gaze drifted across the classroom, but she seemed to be looking somewhere beyond it. Finally I shrugged. "Okay. If you don't want to talk about it. Just take it as a warning, so when the finals come—"

"It's Lisa."

That got my attention, because of the changes I'd noticed first in her older sister and now many other seniors. "What about Lisa?"

"She's . . . different."

"Yes." My eyebrows went up, emphatically. "She's started doing some amazing work. A lot of her classmates, too." I grinned. "Like they took smart pills or something."

Katie glanced up at me. "Yeah. But it's more than that. She's not as, I don't know. *Nice*." Her brow knit deeply. "She's not nice at all. She's done some bad things."

"Well, I don't know about that," I said, straightening the assignments that the class had just turned in. "But another teacher also noticed a steep improvement in their scholastic abilities. Along with a sharper edge to many of them. Is that what you're talking about?"

"Yes." Katie looked up at me. Then hesitantly asked, "Could it be from something they ate?"

I laughed. "Well, I hardly think so." But I saw she was dead serious. "Why? What do you mean?"

Katie gazed at me for a long moment, as though she was carefully weighing how much to reveal to me.

Katie McLane...

It was an hour before sunset, when the late afternoon sunlight takes on those warmest colors and casts a sorta golden glow over everything. That made the spectacular garden at the swimming hole look even more miraculous as I led Ms. Navarro to it. She was as staggered as Darren and I'd been. Her eyes darted from one large thriving plant to the next. She musta known way more than me that something really strange had taken place.

"Lisa and Charley have always come here," I told her. "Me and Darren, too. But it never looked like this. Not a couple months ago, not ever."

Ms. Navarro seemed enthralled. Her voice was very low. "I dare say." She walked slowly and carefully, letting her fingers graze over the fascinating plants. "The trees and plants outside of this radius—"

"Are the same as usual. I know," I said. "That's why it's so weird."

"It seems way beyond that, Kate," she said studying them. "It's like these central plants have all somehow undergone a"—she inspected one very closely—"sort of *hyperadaptation*."

"A what?"

"A major alteration—from their normal state into better, hardier, more prolific versions of themselves. Perhaps even creating new, stronger strains."

"Not all of them." I pointed out some that had withered. "See these over here? Looks like some got choked out by the others."

She knelt, examining the bedraggled, dying plants, nodding, saying quietly, "Survival of the fittest." She looked around and drew an awestruck breath. "Let's see if we can find the center."

I led her to the lushest area of growth. Beside the pond. She nodded. "Yeah. About here, huh?" She scanned around, noticed something, and dug down through the thick foliage. I watched her lift out a black, mottled, deeply pocked stone about the size of a softball.

I leaned in for a closer look. "Is that a meteorite?"

"Might well be." Ms. Navarro hefted it in her hand. "Definitely heavy metal, probably nickel or iron."

"One of those that came down from the comet?"

She turned it over in her hands, then she slowly looked at all the thick, rich vegetation around us. She seemed sorta lost in thought. "I'd say that's a possible hypothesis."

I pondered it all for a moment and whether I should say anymore. Finally I did. "There's something else." I guided her to where the extralarge wild strawberries were growing. There were a couple of crows and other birds pecking at the fruit. They scattered and flapped away as we got closer.

"Good God," Ms. Navarro said, kind of excited, almost laughing. "I have never . . ."

"Be careful. I think that this is what they ate."

"Who?"

"Lisa. Charley. The others."

Ms. Navarro picked one of the deep red berries. "And then they were *smarter*?"

"Seemed like it, yeah. I mean, Lisa was suddenly breezing through her homework at like a thousand miles an hour, but . . ." I was very uncomfortable talking about it. "They were also real different, like I said. Definitely not as nice."

"Nice?" She was sniffing the fragrance of the huge strawberry.

"Yeah. Not being fair, caring about others. Just plain meaner. The football team got really superviolent."

She nodded, thinking. "I heard those games had gotten pretty rough."

"They were a lot worse than rough. And both the boys—and the girls—have really hurt each other. And that bus crash may not have been an accident. It might've been because—"

"Well, Katie, my girl," she interrupted, sort of shutting me down as she looked around again at the surrounding beauty of the amazing garden, and blew out a breath. "This is all pretty hard to fathom, but we're gonna get to the bottom of it. Help me gather some samples."

Then she picked another strawberry.

Ashton High School Security Cam Rm 042, Digital Archive File TC50786RW

Date: 09/14/20 **Time:** 23:09:50 (Median)

Transcript by: C. Davis

Visual Desc: The room is empty except for science teacher Shelly L. Navarro, who can be seen sitting alone at one of the black laboratory tables in the biology classroom #42. A small gooseneck lamp illuminates her work. Several reference books are open on the table as well as her laptop. She uses a binocular microscope to study what appear to be leaves and shoots of some green plant. Nearby on the table is what seems to be a black rock approximately the size of a small grapefruit. There is also a four-liter laboratory vessel containing what appears to be some type of large reddish vegetable or fruit. Navarro remains working in this position for three hours and thirty-seven minutes (3:37).

Courtesy GSP, FBI

Shelly Navarro...

I hadn't felt this energized and enthusiastic about anything in years. I was puzzling over the incredible material, fascinated. Among many details I spoke into my microrecorder was: "So the overall summary would seem to be as follows. While the cellular structure is generally consistent with previously known flora, the cell walls are much more densely organized. The entire organism from root through stem to fruit seems to have become far more efficient than samples I gathered from unaffected plants a hundred yards away. All the affected plants are noticeably improved and apparently vastly advanced in photosynthetic abilities. The meteorite being in central proximity to the expansive growth suggests that some bacteriological or viral variant was brought to Earth in a fragment of the comet and has triggered this bizarre hyper-adaptation of the flora—which seems a parallel to my students whose native intelligence actually appears to have been dramatically boosted after eating the . . ."

My voice trailed off to silence as I looked across the table at the strawberries. I stared at them for the longest time. Speculating.

12

HYPOTHESIS

Dr. R. W. Hutcherson...

I'd brought something to show Susan, but when she opened her condo door that September night, I was startled to see that her eyes were very bloodshot, her light makeup completely washed away because she'd been seriously crying. I felt real awkward. "Oh. I'm sorry. I shoulda called. What's wrong?"

Her voice was choked. "Prashant. Mostly." She was struggling to hold back tears. "He shouldn't have died. He—"

I felt terrible. Took a step back. "Look, this . . . can absolutely wait. I'll just—"

"No." She caught my sleeve. I noticed a near-empty wineglass in her other hand. I'd never seen her touch a drop. We just stood there. Looking into each other's eyes. A tear escaped down her cheek.

I spoke quietly, "You said . . . 'mostly'?"

She nodded, her quiet voice strained. "Prashant's death stirred up . . . other losses, too."

I understood, whispered, "Yeah. I've sure had that happen." I opened my hands a little, offering a hug if she needed one. She did lean in, and we held each other. Her cheek was against my chest. I sighed, thinking of my late wife, and said softly, "I've had it come onto me like a sudden storm sweeps over the prairie. Sometimes it just wells up outta nowhere, huh?" Susan looked up into my eyes, her face very close. We were kindred spirits.

I think that's why the kiss happened. Life seeking life.

Jimmy-Joe Hartman...

Walkin' up toward Poppa's house that night, I seen Claire sittin' there on our old wooden bench swing on the front porch. She wuz still wearin' her nurse's scrubs. I didn't live there with 'em no more. Needed me some private space. Friend o'mine over on Ellsworth had a spare room I wuz usin'. Just till I made a better score and got me some cool-ass place.

The old wood porch creaked a little as Claire swung a coupla inches. That swing always been her "comfort spot" even back 'fore I wuz born. But she didn't look so comfy that night. She wuz frownin', lookin' through the porch winder into the small livin' room.

"Yo, sis," I said. "What's goin' on inside there?"

"That's what I'm trying to figure out, James Joseph," she said. "Take a look."

I seen Poppa inside, still wearin' his janitor uniform. He wuz sittin' at our old dinner table, tappin' away really fast at a *laptop*. "What the hey? When he get hisself one o'them?"

"Himself, not hisself." Claire wuz always tryin' t'fix up my talk. "About three weeks ago."

I watched Poppa a minute. Saw him take off his ol' wire-rimmed glasses and rub the back o'his neck. He was frownin', too. Seemed to be worried, or wrestlin' kinda, with something he was thinkin' about, then he started tappin' away again.

"Well. Good for him," I said, stickin' my hands deep into my baggy gangsta pants, so to look kinda casual. "And hey, good for me, too! I come to tell y'all I got me a coupla hot new prospects. They gonna kick over by Friday. Or next week for sure." I seen her glance at me kinda sideways, like she knew where I wuz headed. "Think y'could lend me twenty till then, sis?"

She shaked her head. "No, but they're lookin' for an orderly down at the hospital."

"Aw c'mon, Claire." I scrunched up my face. "I tol' ya: wipin' up puke and dumpin' bedpans ain't my style."

Claire tried to sound encouragin'. "Gotta start somewhere, James Joseph."

I kept it smooth. "Hey, I'm *gettin'* started. I tol' you, Claire, I got these prospects that—"

"Right, right." She heaved out a sigh. Then said more quietly, "Have you noticed anything kind of off about Pop?"

"Whatchu mean?"

"I don't know exactly." She glanced through the window at him. "He just seems . . . different. Like something's eating at him. And look there. Doing his own bookkeeping? With a computer? He was never good at that stuff, now all of a sudden . . ."

I shrugged it off, had other things to worry 'bout. Like my rent. "Aw, he's cool." I went on in the house. "Hey, Pops! How's my man?"

Poppa looked up at me, like he wuz tryin' not to gimme shit about my clothes. "I'm okay, son."

"Awright!" I gave him a friendly poke on his shoulder, noddin' at his computer. "Finally comin' into the twenty-first century, huh?"

"Yes," Poppa said, keepin' to hisself whatever wuz troublin' him. I didn't wanna get into none o'that anyway. So I pulled up a chair and said, confidential-like, "Listen, Poppa"—I leaned closer, my eyebrows wigglin'—"I hadda tell ya, man. I got these real hot prospects, see?"

I didn't see Claire, but I knew sure as shit she wuz lookin' in at us. Still worryin' herself about Poppa. And me, too, probably. But I kept workin' on him. I really needed that twenty.

Dr. Susan Perry...

Hutch and I lay spooned up, snugly between the sheets in my old four-poster. The tender, quiet encounter had surprised both of us, but at the same time had felt entirely heartfelt, natural, comforting.

His left hand was draped over my shoulder. I noticed his wedding ring was gone, and I looked inquisitively at him. He whispered wistfully, "Put it away a few days ago. Seemed like it was about time."

I appreciated the significance and folded his arm tighter around me. I sighed, thinking of Hutch's loss of his wife, my loss of Chris. I felt equally wistful. "I guess it was time for me, too."

And we lay there quietly. Together.

Dr. R. W. Hutcherson...

A bit later when I walked into the living room, buttoning my shirt, I saw that Lilly, who'd been asleep when I arrived, was sitting on the edge of the couch in her long nightshirt. She was fully engaged with that old Tetris game on the TV. I heard a congratulatory beep as computer-generated fireworks burst across the screen and recognized her triumph. "My God, Lilly! Three hundred thousand points! Three hundred lines! You're an Olympic champion!"

She registered no emotion at her accomplishment. For Lilly, it was just her flat, monotonic business as usual. It often struck me as sad. Given her sister's intelligence and skills, Lilly might have been so similar, so engaged in life, so easily welcomed into the company of others. It was a crying shame she was hidden under the bushel basket of her special needs.

Susan entered behind me, wearing a robe, explaining, "She sometimes wakes up and plays a little. Did she max it out again?"

"Look!" I laughed with amazement. "I knew guys at Montana Med who were aces at Tetris, but I've never seen anybody—"

"Where's m-my connect the dots?" Lilly asked, completely oblivious to me talking.

"Ah." I smiled. "Thought you'd forgotten." I reached into my scuffed, floppy leather briefcase, took out a large manila envelope and a connect-the-dots book about farm animals I'd promised her.

Lilly scanned it, nodding flatly. "Th-this is a brand-new one."

"Yep," I said, leaning closer, pointing out a page. "And some of 'em are very complicated."

"Just like I like," Lilly said, assessing them without a trace of a smile.

"I know that." Some folks mighta been put off by her seeming lack of appreciation. But I'd come to know that this was simply Lilly's way.

Dr. Susan Perry...

I stood near the TV, watching Hutch interact with my exceptional sister. Partly, my fondness for him had increased because of his empathy and caring for Lilly. He never patronized or condescended, but always spoke to her directly, as an equal. This wasn't the first gift he'd brought her. His homegrown Montana warmth touched me.

I turned off the video game, and a newscast took its place, showing the Georgia Supreme Court as a reporter's voice said, ". . . And that brings to five the recent, more conservative rulings by the state supreme court justices who're taking an ever-harder line on crime."

"Whoa," I exclaimed, "I never thought *that* bunch would agree on *anything*."

We paused a moment to listen as the newscaster underlined my assessment, how until last month the nine-member court had been a hotbed of conflict. But in recent weeks two of the five normally liberal judges had swung several times into lockstep with their conservative counterparts. It worried some commentators that the court had become much less balanced and that an archly conservative philosophy was becoming the predominant tone in recent decisions.

Lilly wasn't listening, though. She was holding her new book but was disturbed. "My other c-connect the dots are supposed to be on the table."

"They are, honey," I said soothingly. I picked up the envelope Hutch had set atop Lilly's books. "They were hiding under this. Here you go."

Lilly took the books, and her face relaxed, knowing that all was right with the world.

I opened the envelope. "What is this, anyway?"

Hutch sat on the couch with a shy smile. "What I came to show you. The info you wanted."

The material included a map of the Southeastern United States. Hutch pointed to the place where I'd met the farmer whose wife had been killed by her hogs, and said, "The comet's debris field starts about ten miles northwest of Dayton, Tennessee, catches the tip of Alabama, but it's mostly across western Georgia."

"Yes! I thought that's what I remembered." I pulled a folder from my bag. "Look at my charting of that aggressive animal behavior." I laid my map alongside Hutch's.

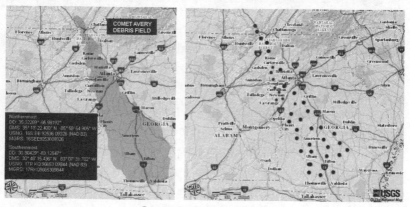

Courtesy Dr. Susan Perry; USGS

He saw it immediately: every animal incident happened along the path of where the comet fragments fell.

We both stared at the matching maps, then Hutch drew a shallow breath. "Should we be getting worried here, Suse?"

Katie McLane...

Ms. Navarro walked away from me around and behind her big lab desk in the sunny biology classroom, saying, "I'll let you know."

I was frustrated that she hadn't made more progress since I'd shown her everything the day before. I wanted answers. "But you said you'd—"

"As soon as I have something *concrete*." She said it in the stinging tone she always used to make it clear there'd be no further discussion.

I did manage to give her an annoyed look before I turned to leave and saw the incoming senior biology class. Lisa, Jenna, and Charley were among 'em. I got the feeling that they were all looking really carefully at Ms. Navarro, like they sensed some kind of trouble. From the doorway I glanced back at the science teacher. She was studying each arriving student like I'd seen her examine specimens under her microscope. Like she was evaluating them carefully. I wasn't sure if it was just me "projecting," like they say, or if that cold, superior gleam I'd noticed in the eyes of Lisa, Charley, and the others was now in Navarro's eyes, too.

Suddenly butterflies fluttered in my stomach. I walked slowly into the hall, where it seemed like all the air conditioners in the world had just been turned on. I was frightened. Didn't know what to do next. Made myself stop. Think. I looked around the hallway that was rapidly emptying as students headed into classrooms. Then I went to the door next to the science classroom. It was a large supply closet that also had a door into Navarro's room. I went in very quietly.

It was dark and smelled of chemicals we used in the class. I eased the hall door closed. Then I walked silently to the inner door to the science room. It was open a crack. I could see Navarro scanning the class carefully as the bell rang and they settled in on their stools around the different lab tables and got quiet. Navarro was standing opposite where I was, up in front of her desk at the far end of the aisle that ran between the two rows of lab tables. She scanned from one student to the next. Examining each one.

The silence went on. I saw Lisa and Charley trade a glance, like they were getting suspicious about what the teacher might be up to. I sure was. Finally Navarro sat against the edge of her desk and dropped the bomb. "Anyone here who hasn't had wild strawberries lately?"

My heart skipped a beat. I saw how most of the students suddenly focused sharply on her. Only four hands went up from quizzical students who must've found the question very odd.

"Okay," Navarro continued smoothly, "I'd like you four to go to the library. Here's a research packet. Get started on it. Then you'll rotate with other students."

The rest of the class watched silently, expectantly, as the four outsiders left. The teacher secured the door behind them, then turned to those remaining. "I assumed they weren't in on it. They were the only four who weren't suddenly doing postgraduate work in here." She strolled back to the front of the classroom. "So. Is this all of us?"

Charley exchanged a glance with Lisa, but Tim took the lead, saying, "There's a few others."

In the closet, I drew a silent breath. My stomach was queasy.

"It's rather amazing," Navarro said, eyeing the class. "I'd been wondering how you turned into geniuses overnight." Her lips curled into her typically cynical smile, which looked uglier than ever. "I knew I wasn't that good a teacher." She drew a long breath. "I wouldn't have thought it possible if I hadn't experienced it myself."

I felt like I'd fallen out of an airplane. With no parachute.

"Yesterday I had an IQ of one hundred nineteen," Navarro was saying. "Not bad. But this morning I took a new test, and I was one hundred forty-four. A huge difference."

In my hiding place, my heart was beating so loud I thought they'd hear it. In the classroom, the students watched the teacher lift one of the large strawberries from the container. "Great to have on cereal, too, I'll bet."

Tim's eyes gleamed with supreme confidence. "Breakfast of Champions."

I saw Lisa eyeing Navarro carefully. "How did you find out?"

"Your sister."

I choked. Lisa stiffened up. Apprehensive. "What!? Has she eaten—?"

"No. But she's very concerned about you. About all of you." Navarro got this peculiar, devious smile on her face. "Although I can't see any reason to worry. Except about gaining weight. I'm so hungry." She picked up a half-eaten Mr. Goodbar, and took a bite.

Charley nodded. "Metabolism's accelerated."

"Yes. But not like my goddamn brain has!" Navarro laughed. "You know, I was positively giddy at first. Like a cannabis high." At their surprise, she said, "Yes, children, teacher has smoked some weed. But *this*." She said expansively. "It's *extraordinary*, isn't it?!"

Most of the students mumbled agreement, but I noticed how they had different levels of intensity or enthusiasm. Lisa, Charley, Tim, and Jenna were among the loudest and most driven. Steph was the least of all. I realized that would make sense: Steph was always the mildest of the bunch. I always admired that she had this kinda moral fiber. The most empathy. Whatever this craving for domination was, this ugly superiority that the others felt, it seemed to be tempered in Steph by her basic nature. By who Steph was deep inside.

Navarro also spotted Steph's softer response. "Does it feel that way to you, Stephanie?"

With what sounded like some misgivings, Steph answered, "Yes."

Navarro walked slowly toward her. "Describe it."

Steph seemed scared that Navarro was testing her. "It's like . . ." Steph swallowed, and it must've hurt. She still had a bandage on her throat from the paramedics. ". . . It's like new channels have opened up."

"Mmm." Navarro nodded as she stopped beside Steph. "I think that's exactly right." The teacher's hand came to rest atop Steph's nervous head. "See that comet fragment on my desk? I found it near the strawberries. I think it carried a microbiological *variant* that accelerates adaptive processes in whatever organism it enters. In flora it makes better plants, bigger strawberries. And in human brains it apparently creates new, unprecedented neurological *interlinking*; amazing new connections that have opened up within every brain in this room. Do you know what that means?"

Lisa said, "It like speeds up evolution? Sped up ours?"

Navarro looked smug. "Well, the more proper scientific term in this case is *hyperadaptation* or the one Darwin used: transmutation. That's what most people mean when they say 'evolution.' But speaking colloquially, yes, Lisa . . ." Her hand still rested atop Steph's head as Navarro's eyes swept around the room like a lighthouse beacon. "You *could* say that what happened in your brains—and mine—represents a significant *step forward in human evolution*!"

Inside the dark chemical supply closet, I was shaky, felt my breathing get shallower as Navarro went on, "Can you comprehend how miraculous, how phenomenal—"

Tim cut her off sharply. "Being older doesn't automatically make you top dog."

Navarro's shining eyes met Tim's. "Ah yes, Timothy. I've felt *that* too. That visceral desire to dominate. To be the top dog. To ignore the rules. Quite compelling. Sure hasn't hurt the football team either, has it?"

Tim held her gaze firmly. "We intend to win—Shelly."

"And Darwin would be proud of you—Timothy. Natural selection. Survival of the fittest, the best adapted. But how have you lot avoided infighting?"

"We agreed to work together," Tim said. He didn't see what I did: how Charley shot a private glare at him.

"Yeah," Lisa chimed in, with a dark, satisfied grin. "We girls threw a little pool party, where *everyone* agreed."

"Excellent," said Navarro, walking among them. "But toward what end?"

I saw several students blink or glance around at each other. It seemed like a question they hadn't considered. Charley shifted on his lab stool. "Well . . . toward winning."

"Football games?" Navarro inclined her head toward him, then flashed a glance at Lisa. "Science fairs?"

Steph glanced sadly at Lisa, who smirked, saying, "It's a start."

Tim, the "natural" quarterback, was looking further ahead. "We could end up running the town."

"Just the town?" Navarro leaned back against her desk, watching them process that. "And there's also the money to be made, of course." Then she drew a breath. "But you realize we're probably not the only ones. That football team from Beaumount looked pretty hot."

Tim raised an eyebrow. "They ended pretty hot, too."

That made me think Darren had been right about Tim causing that awful bus crash.

"Yes. Wasn't that unfortunate." Navarro eyed Tim pointedly, then smirked. "But my point is this." She picked up the meteorite. "Comet fragments just like this fell across half of Georgia."

"So what're you saying?" Charley asked. "There's probably others like us? Over in Beaumount?"

"And elsewhere across southwestern Georgia, maybe even Alabama, Tennessee. We should sniff around to see what—"

"You mean like this?" Jenna said coldly, holding up her cell phone.

Lisa snatched it from her, reading to the others, "Hashtag, get smarter?"

"That's just one," Jenna said. "I was looking this morning. Found a couple new Facebook pages, too. One mentions the comet, and there's an 800 number for free counseling. One's in Beaumount."

The classroom was dead silent as the reality settled upon them. And on me. Navarro spelled it out: "So we *are* just the tip of an iceberg."

Steph was nervous. "I think we should tell the police or—"

"No fucking way!" Tim spouted, and others growled agreement. "We gotta keep it quiet. All to ourselves!"

"Damn right!" Charley said.

Navarro modified the concept. "At least until we've considered the ramifications and how best to use it to our advantage."

"Yeah," Jenna snorted. "I don't want my parents gettin' it, that's for sure!"

Lisa was thinking. "What about Katie?"

"Well," Shelly sighed, "she certainly might spread the word."

Jenna took the lead. "Let's just ram some strawberries down her throat."

"Or shut her up altogether," Tim suggested. Others agreed.

I was getting light-headed as Lisa flared hotly at him. "I don't think so, asshole."

Steph looked at Lisa. "Maybe you could just slip some shrimp into *her* tuna."

Lisa jumped to her feet. "Listen, you little bitch—"

"Wait, wait, wait." Navarro stepped between them. "There's an easier way: Katie trusts me. I'll just tell her there's nothing to worry about. And you all treat her normally. But keep an eye on her"—she glanced again at Tim—"we do have other options."

I took off outta the school like a rocket. Ten minutes later I was whipping along so frantically on my bike that a squirrel barely managed to get out of the way. I skidded to a stop by the front steps of our house and let my bike fall as I bounded up, calling out breathlessly, "Mom!" I slammed open the front door and dashed in, looking around. "Momma! Mom!?"

I heard her giggling from the kitchen. "In here, honey."

I ran in. "Momma! Listen! We've gotta—"

"Whoa, whoa, whoa!" She laughed again, "Easy, honey!"

I had stopped dead, breathing hard, feeling my face go pale. I saw she was giddy, acting weird. ". . . Momma . . . ?"

"Woo!" She laughed. "I'm so light-headed! Old Granny Wells must've spiked her preserves."

I was fearful. "What?"

Mom picked up a Mason jar with a homemade label, saying, "I bought these preserves. Over at the church bake sale. Granny Wells said she'd found these fantastic wild strawberries."

"No!" My heart fluttered wildly. "Oh my God."

"Granny said she never eats strawberries herself." Mom's eyes were sparkling strangely. "But she loves making preserves. Everybody was buying 'em. Here honey, have some!" Light-headed, she held out the preserves.

I was horrified! "No, Mom! We gotta get you to a hospital or—"

"Why, honey? I'm great. I'm—woo," Mom said gleefully, "Granny doesn't know what she's missing! These preserves are really *something else!*"

The Documentarian...

Forensic analysis later confirmed that at about the same time on Gertrude Wells's farm, the kindly old lady had come home from the church bake sale, doubtlessly pleased that she'd sold every last jar. She stuck her gray head into her dusty, shadowy chicken coop. Testimony from those who knew her said she would always call out, "Afternoon, girls. Time for me to steal your eggs again."

A normally passive hen began flapping wildly, pecking at her.

She swatted at the aggressive creature, but the hen only intensified its attack, and was joined by another, and then several more. The frail eighty-two-year-old stumbled awkwardly backward, falling painfully on the rough wooden floor. She hit the back of her head very hard on the edge of a nesting box, likely dazing herself, as a dozen more hens and roosters descended upon her, pecking, clawing, and tearing viciously at her fragile, age-thinned skin.

Gertrude Wells waved her arms in desperate panic, trying to stand, screaming in agony as the birds attacked her hands and face with unbridled, stinging fury.

13

ALLIANCES

Katie McLane...

I raced my bike across Ashton's main street, dodging between cars, and leaned it against the wall outside our small town's sheriff's office, calling out to him as I opened the door, "Sheriff? Sheriff Randolph!?"

The man in the wooden desk chair pivoted toward me. My heart sank. It was not the sheriff. It was that buzz-cut sleazeball Brice Patton, who most people knew was a slacker but somehow ended up as a deputy. He grinned at me. "Whazzup, girlie?"

"Hey, Brice." I tried not to show I was breathing hard. "The sheriff around?"

"I'm afraid not," Brice said with a sadness that sounded phony. "Had hisself a nasty accident."

My antenna went up. "An accident?"

"Yeah." Brice paused, shaking his head unhappily and taking a swig of his Yoo-hoo. "Looked like he'd been cleanin' that old Winchester of his. Damn thing musta went off. I was the one that found him. Real sad. I still cain't hardly believe it." He heaved a long sigh. "But anyways, life goes on, huh?" He set the bottle down and gazed at me. "So I'm in charge now, darlin'. What can I do ya for?"

I tried to cover the fact that I'd recognized Brice's new superior attitude and the telltale glint in his eyes. ". . . Uh. Nothing, Brice. I just wanted to ask him—"

The deputy sensed my hesitation, his suspicion grew. "Ask him what?"

"Um. A question about fireworks for the Fourth next year." I wasn't good at lying and tried to say it lightly.

He didn't move a muscle, but his eyes were penetrating. "What about the fireworks?"

I glanced toward the inner door, which I knew led to the two small jail cells. I didn't want to end up in one. "It's not important, not today," I said, backing casually toward the front door, worried he might leap up and grab me. "I'm really sorry to hear about the sheriff. That's just terrible."

Brice was watching me so closely I got really scared. "Yeah, it's a bitch, ain't it?"

"See you later, Brice," I said, and stepped out onto the sidewalk. I wanted to leap on my bike and race outta there, but I forced myself to casually walk the bike toward the corner. In the window of a parked car, I saw Brice reflected as he stepped into the doorway of the sheriff's office behind me, watching me, and taking another slow hit of Yoo-hoo. I struggled to keep my pace measured, unhurried. The corner was ten feet away, then five. I finally rounded it real slow, then leaped on my bike, and took off like lightning. Pedaling a mile a minute, I remembered that Greek story of how Io fled from the ghost of Argus with his thousand eyes. Now I knew exactly how she felt.

I cut through a back alley that brought me out in front of the Methodist church. I dropped the bike and rushed in through the rectory where the remnants of the bake sale were still on tables. I saw one remaining jar of Granny Wells's preserves. It was open, nearly empty.

Some was spread on crackers, inviting people to taste a sample. I swept the jar and crackers off into a trash can, then heard the minister's voice, "Oh yes, I can hear thee . . ."

It was coming from the chapel. I eased up to the side door and peered in. I saw Pastor Middleton, who I'd always thought was too young and handsome to be a minister. He was lying facedown in front of the altar in a pool of sunlight streaming down through a stained glass window. He was laughing and sorta squirming peculiarly.

"I can hear thy voice within me, heavenly father!" He was rambling. "I can feel thy divine hand opening doors within my unworthy brain. Let it be so, that I might better serve thee!"

I ran out of the church, hyperventilating now, near total panic. I clutched when I heard someone shout, "Katie!"

Darren was rushing toward me across the green grass of the town square, past the Civil War cannon. I ran to meet him. He stumbled and fell near one of the wooden benches just as I got to him. "Darren?! Oh my God, listen. We've gotta—"

I suddenly froze. He had raised his face toward me. He was laughing. But tears were streaming, too. I was confused, scared. "Darren? What is it? What's wrong?"

"Oh God! Katie!" He was trembling, frightened, but with this strange smile flickering across his face. "My mom made this peanut butter sandwich. She used some preserves she bought at church and—"

"Oh no!" My blood chilled. "Your *mom's* got it now?!"

"*Me! I* ate it!"

I stared at him, petrified. I saw that he was getting even more light-headed. "I didn't know, Katie! I didn't mean to!" His tears spilled out. "I tried to throw up, but I couldn't! I—" A wave of emotion passed through him; he laughed. "But you should *feel* it, Katie! God! It's the most wonderful—" His faced twisted from a bizarre smile to an expression of complete agony. Like that classic Greek mask of comedy warping into tragedy. Darren cried out, "Katie! Help me! I'm scared! I don't want this!"

I grabbed him and held him tight. His body was quaking with emotion.

"I don't want to be mean like them!" A weird laugh bubbled out of him. "Oh God! I can *feel* it in me!" He pushed me away. "Run."

"Darren, no, I can't leave you like—"

"*Run*, Katie!" He was crying desperately now. "Don't let 'em get you, too!"

"Darren—"

He shouted at me—part shriek, part laugh. All frightening. "RUUUNNN!"

Terrified, I ran to my bike and pedaled away. I had a last quick glimpse of Darren. My best friend in the world looked simultaneously heartbroken and elated, crazed.

My house was dead silent. I entered the living room real tensely, listening, hearing nothing except my heart pounding. I peeked in the kitchen. Mom was asleep on the floor with a strangely gleeful expression on her face. Madison was resting her sweet head on Mom's leg. The pooch looked up at me with sad, confused eyes.

"Shhh. It's okay, Maddy." I carefully opened Mom's purse and took out all the bills and her Visa card. Then I slipped quietly into the laundry room and stuffed a couple of T-shirts from a laundry basket into my backpack.

I came back into the kitchen really stressed. I looked at my sleeping mother and turned to leave. But I couldn't. I turned back and knelt down beside her. I leaned closer, really cautious, weighing the danger, and gave her a soft kiss on the cheek. Her breathing remained steady and even. I whispered, barely audible, "I love you, Momma."

Then I stood up and headed out—but stopped, had a thought. I went back to the kitchen. Picked up the jar of preserves off the counter. I carefully closed the lid tight and pushed the jar down into my backpack.

Then I looked toward Mom a final time, whispering to Maddy, "Take care of her, Mad."

Then I hurriedly left my home.

Moments later I was on one of the nearby residential streets, pedaling my bike like crazy, when I saw Tim Green's car approaching. Through the reflections swirling across his windshield, our eyes met. He must've sensed instantly that something was off about my look and how fast I was pedaling. As he passed, I glanced back and saw him watching me in his rearview mirror.

Then I heard tires squealing and looked back again. Tim was wheeling the car in a tight U-turn. My heart leaped. "Shit!" I knew he was coming after me. And that I couldn't possibly outrun him.

I swerved my bike off the road, bumping painfully over uneven ground down through a patch of woods. My front tire slid on a root, twisting sharply, threatening disaster. I barely recovered and kept on dodging among the trees at breakneck speed.

I circled back around and into an alley behind our small-town city hall. I locked the bike to a pipe, peeked out to check the street and that Tim or Brice weren't around, then ran across into our one-room Greyhound station. It was empty. My legs were like Jell-O from all the exertion as I rushed up to the ticket window. The agent seemed annoyed at being interrupted in the midst of her crossword.

I pulled some cash from my backpack. "Atlanta, please," I panted, still out of breath, my mouth totally dry. "One way."

The agent glanced up over her half-glasses. Seemed like she noticed the sweat on my face. I looked back, studying her. Was there a gleam in *her* eyes? I wasn't sure if the woman was one of Them or if paranoia was getting the better of me. I tried to act nonchalant as I waited. I wiped the dampness from beneath my long ringlets on the back of my neck. When the ticket agent walked out of sight for a moment, I totally clenched up, but then she returned with some change and a ticket,

205

speaking in a bored voice, "One-way Atlanta. 'Bout to finish boardin' right now. You best get on out there."

I peered out the station's back door to where the bus was revving up. I scanned for Tim or anyone else who might try to stop me. Saw no one suspicious, so I hurried toward the bus.

Then I saw Steph walking across the street. She stopped dead when she spotted me.

I stood completely breathless as we stared at each other. Steph seemed as frozen as me. I sensed that she was considering her options. Finally, Steph sighed, gave me a faint, sad smile, looked away, and walked on. I hurried up to the bus and was about to climb on when a hand came down on my shoulder! I jumped out of my skin and spun around ready to fight or run.

Mr. Tenzer, the English teacher, said, "Oh. Sorry. Didn't mean to startle you."

I had reached my stress limit. I could feel hot tears threatening right behind my eyes. It was a major effort to force a smile. "S'okay, Mr. Tenzer." I stepped quickly up into the bus, but glanced back and saw he was watching me with curiosity. His face looked different than usual. Paler, maybe? That worried me.

I hurried up the aisle of the bus, which was fairly full from its earlier small-town stops. I swung into a seat toward the back and scrunched down, trying to disappear. Through the heads in front of me, I saw Mr. Tenzer approaching with a calm smile. "I'm really sorry, Katie."

I just nodded, afraid to speak for fear of tears spilling out.

"You going alone?" When I nodded, he indicated the seat beside me. "Mind if I . . . ?"

I nodded again. Then turned away. I looked at the window. It was not one of the emergency exits. If he was one of them, I was trapped. I tried to keep watch out the window to see who might be coming after me, but then I thought of Darren, and my vision suddenly got blurry. I rubbed the tears away, angrily trying to make them stop.

Mr. Tenzer offered a Kleenex. I took it without glancing at him, but I nodded thanks. Out of the corner of my eye, I saw him smile gently and pull a paperback out of the inside pocket of his windbreaker.

"You can borrow my Walt Whitman, too, if you want. Kleenex and *Leaves of Grass*. Always good for trips." I nodded again, still keeping my eyes downcast. He absolutely understood, said, "Right. Shut up, Eric. Sorry, Kate."

The bus rumbled to life. The driver closed the door. I heard a hiss of compressed air as he released the brake, slipped the beast into gear, and pulled out—just as I caught sight of Tim's car driving slowly by. I gasped and ducked down lower in the seat. Mr. Tenzer couldn't help but notice. I think he frowned with curiosity, but he smoothed the moment for me, saying, "More comfortable, huh?"

I forced a slight smile, appreciating him. Then I peeked carefully out. Mr. Tenzer pretended to be reading his poetry but had to be aware of my odd behavior.

The bus wheezed along Ashton's main street, slowly headed toward the edge of town. Trying to carefully watch for trouble, I was reeling from the avalanche of frightening circumstances that had swept down on me. And from the unsettling fact that I was running away from the only home I'd ever known. I watched the hometown where I had grown up and been so happy, passing by before my eyes.

"Think you're losing something there," Mr. Tenzer said. The jar of preserves was slipping out of my backpack. He caught it. He turned the jar around in his hands. "Oooh, homemade strawberry preserves. Looks great. Wish I could eat 'em."

"No, you don't!" I blurted, inadvertently. "I mean, they're not very good."

"Well, I couldn't anyway." He handed the jar back to me. "I'm allergic to strawberries. I get hives so big I attract bees."

He smiled, but I wasn't sure I believed him. How could I be sure? He must've seen my extreme tension because he tried to lighten my mood, saying, "Your dad still living in Atlanta?"

"When he's not traveling." I raised up to look out the back window of the bus. I couldn't see any cars following. I knew Mr. Tenzer was sorta studying me sideways. He seemed concerned about my distress, maybe suspected I was a runaway. But he decided not to press any further.

At least not at that moment.

Dr. Susan Perry...

The front door opened into the small apartment, which was dark because the curtains were drawn. I pocketed my lock picks as Hutch followed me inside, speaking quietly with regard to my skills, "I'm definitely getting a dead bolt."

"Much harder," I said, "but not impossible."

Lilly followed in behind us like a baby duck. "It's almost th-three. Time for my walk."

"You'll take it, honey," I promised, soothingly. It was always important to ease her concerns about her schedule.

Lilly looked around. "Isn't this where Prashant l-lived?"

"Yes, honey," I said as Hutch and I began to explore.

"Okay. If he did have info that could help us," Hutch said, "where would he keep it?"

"That's what I'm trying to figure out." I was investigating Prashant's desk.

Lilly just stood, planted, watching and noticing. "Lots neater than usual. Pencils are neat. Everything's n-neat. Very nice."

I paused, looking at Lilly, who was nodding with approval.

"You know, Lilly's right," I said. "Was Prashant ever this neat?"

"Nope." My sister shook her pretty head, emphatically.

"Somebody's already searched here?" Hutch looked around, frustrated.

"Maybe. Doesn't mean they found anything." I prodded him. "C'mon, start looking."

After an hour we'd found nothing, and Lilly was walking back and forth across the room. "'Course it's not the s-same as walking through the park."

"Soon, Lil," I said. "Hutch? Over here." I was holding a framed photo of myself and Prashant, extracting a tiny flash drive taped behind it. With my name on it.

An hour later, after a quick stop at the park for a short walk with Lilly, Hutch and I were in my office, reading Prashant's secreted files on my personal laptop. I didn't want to chance them getting into the CDC system.

"Look." Hutch pointed at the screen. "All your field research on those aggressive animals in the comet's debris field *is* tied into Lauren's new project."

"Whatever the hell that project is. Scroll down." He did and new information appeared. "All about Mitchell."

"Private black ops. Intelligence," Hutch said, adding ironically, "Prashant was prescient. And look: *BioTeck Industries*. Isn't that—"

"The chemical company-slash-defense contractor, yes. The ones who turned Chris's research into a weapon." I sat back in my chair, staring at the screen and then looking at Hutch. "What are we onto here?"

Katie McLane...

I'd turned my cell phone off in case someone was trying to trace my location. I was at one of the few battered pay phones left in the bustling Atlanta bus station. I blew out a frustrated puff as I heard the recorded voice on the other end say, "Hi, this is Jason McLane . . ."

I hung up. Totally unsure where to go. I looked around the terminal. Several people glanced at me in passing. Did some of them have the disturbing look in their eyes, too? Had it reached Atlanta already? Or was I just imagining it? I was frightened. Like the world was closing in on me. Those hot tears were threatening again. I was fighting them down when I heard Mr. Tenzer's voice.

"Katie?" He was sitting on a bench distant enough to respect my space. "Can I help?"

He seemed so friendly, but he definitely looked slightly different: paler than usual. His eyes seemed a little dark and slightly sunken, like my mom's looked when she didn't sleep well. But could I trust him? He had sat there with gentle patience, like he'd wait as long as I needed. I sat down facing him, looking him right in the eye and asked, "What's like the absolute *most* important thing in the whole world to you?"

His brow furrowed. He looked—what's that expression? Nonplussed? He thought for a second. "Well . . . my life, I guess, Katie. Or maybe poetry? What're you . . . ?"

I focused on him, real intense. "Swear to me. On your *life*—that you really *are* allergic to strawberries."

He stared at me, curiously. Then nodded.

Eric Tenzer...

I'd come to Atlanta for a critical, very personal reason of my own; but when Katie told me her story, I realized that where I was headed for an appointment was coincidentally the best place to take her. Twenty minutes later the two of us walked toward the reception desk in the lobby of the CDC. Katie was extremely nervous, glancing at everybody we passed as she whispered, "She's a friend of yours?"

"No, just a doctor I met here. But a very good one, Katie. Maybe she can help." I smiled at the dapper male receptionist who was eyeing the skipper-blue suspenders beneath my jacket. "Hi. Eric Tenzer. Is Dr. Lauren Fletcher in?"

Katie and I took the elevator upstairs and walked along the cluttered third-floor corridor, checking office numbers, until we finally found the one we'd been sent to. I knocked lightly. "Excuse me?"

A woman who was facing away turned to me. She was quite attractive with a friendly smile, but not the doctor I knew. I said, "Hi. Eric Tenzer." She took my hand genially and introduced herself as Dr. Susan Perry. I addressed the outdoorsman-type just behind her, "Dr. Hutcherson?" He nodded, and I said, "I'm a patient of Dr. Fletcher's, but they told me my case had been passed along to you."

"I definitely know your name, Mr. Tenzer. I'm Hutch."

"Eric, please."

Hutch shook my hand firmly, saying, "I've read all your info in the clinical test files, Eric. We deeply appreciate your help. In fact, you're one of the key subjects for the new HIV/AIDS medication."

"So I'm told." I saw Katie blink with surprise. I smiled a bit wistfully at her. "Hope that doesn't change our relationship, Kate."

"'Course not," she said immediately, as though it were a given.

But Hutch was mortified. "Oh God, I'm sorry. I thought you were related. I should never have—"

"No, no, it's okay," I said. "But before we get to me, this is Katie McLane, and she's got a pretty amazing story for you . . ."

Dr. Susan Perry...

Close to an hour had passed, the setting sun could be seen through the trees outside the window behind Lilly. She sat to one side of my office, quietly scanning through journals as usual, absorbing endless information that was meaningless to her but a great resource to all us researchers. Katie'd told us what happened in her small hometown. I found myself looking at the jar of strawberry preserves sitting on my desk, like it was a ticking time bomb.

Eric said, "I'd think it was impossible, too, if I hadn't seen it. In my classroom. On the football field. This huge leap in mental agility, intelligence, coupled with—"

"An intense, aggressive desire to dominate," I said, shaking my head as I tried to process it. "Some sort of remarkable transmutation."

Eric nodded. "Is that how you'd describe it? Seemed to me sort of like evolution on the fast track."

"Well, translating terms for scientific phenomena can be dicey," I said. "I think Darwin described what he called transmutation in 1859 when he published his *Origin of*—"

"Transmutation," Lilly interjected without looking up from her reading and without stuttering, "archaic term for hyperadaptation or evolution, first appears in *Philosophie Zoologique*, Lamarck, Jean Baptiste, 1809, part one, chapter eight, paragraph two."

Eric and Katie stared at Lilly. Hutch and I were once again amazed by her mental storehouse of knowledge. "Well," I chuckled, "there you go. The voice of authority. Thanks, Lil."

She never looked up. "You're w-welcome."

I said to Eric, "So yes, *evolution* might be how the general public would describe it."

Hutch had been mulling everything, spoke low with fearful amazement, "This gets more unnerving all the time."

I nodded to him. "Particularly when you connect it to what we found today about the debris field." I rotated the jar slowly, looking at the contents, then at the teacher and teenager. "Eric, Katie, it's important that you not mention this to anyone else. *Particularly* Lauren Fletcher. We think there's a possibility that she might be infected herself. With whatever this is."

We all pondered that, and what it could mean, for a long moment. Then Hutch picked up the jar like it was radioactive. "I'll set the protocols. It only happened from ingesting, right, Katie?"

"Seems like it, yeah," she confirmed. "Just from eating."

"So it's probably enteric." Hutch nodded.

"Transmitted orally," I translated for Eric and Katie. "That narrows the construct. It also explains how it was likely spread to farm animals through droppings from birds who'd eaten the infected fruit. Those crows that pecked at the migrant child could have gotten it directly into his blood. Get a PCR going, Hutch." I glanced at our new friends. "That's polymerase chain reaction. It creates more samples of the virus so we can study it in various growth media. And Hutch, do it in the level four lab. But don't let Lauren get in there with you."

"Yeah, no shit," he agreed. "Or Joseph."

I shook my head slightly. "That's still a hard one for me to believe."

"Listen." Hutch leaned closer. "Lauren's bumped Joseph up to an *assistant.* I saw him running a plasmid study, for God's sake. Two weeks ago the guy was a career custodian, and now he's—"

"Probably infected, too." I sighed, much aggrieved, "Oh, poor Joseph."

Eric had seemed pensive, then asked, "How could a virus or bacteria have survived in space?"

"Frozen," I explained, "in the comet's ice. A preserved virus can lay dormant forever, just waiting for a host. Then . . . pow."

I knew that Katie must have had images of her mother, sister, and Darren swirling in her head and been afraid to ask, but finally she did, "Can you make the people well?"

I'd been very impressed with the sharp intelligence and obvious courage of this fourteen-year-old. Still, it was a difficult answer to give anyone who had such an enormous personal stake. I sighed. "Katie, I'll be straight with you: of the millions of viruses on Earth, we've only figured out how to treat a very few."

Hutch nodded agreement. "And God only knows where *this* virus came from."

"Yeah, we do," I said, to the surprise of all three. "It came from Ashton, Georgia. And I'm on it." I was already grabbing my coat and giving Lilly a kiss. "Hutch, make sure Lilly gets home, huh? I'll have my friend Justinia meet you there to take over with her." To Eric and Katie, I said, "Let us know where you'll be."

Hutch held up a restraining hand. "Whoa, whoa! Hang on."

"Yeah," Eric added his concern. "It might be kind of dangerous for you in Ashton."

I was resolute. "Hey, whatever is in that jar is dangerous for us *all*." I paused in front of Katie and Eric. "I can't tell you how important it is that you two came here. And Katie, you are one *very* brave young woman." I held her gaze sincerely. Then I squeezed her arm and started out, but Hutch caught me in the doorway. I saw the concern in his eyes and hugged him tightly.

Katie spoke quietly, "Please be careful."

I nodded to her, pressed against Hutch's cheek a final time, and hurried away.

14

CONNECTIONS

Eric Tenzer...

It was early evening when I rang the doorbell of the small, trendy house on a gentrified residential street on Atlanta's Westside. In the gathering darkness I sensed Katie's anxiety. "You don't get to see your dad much since he moved here?"

Katie shook her head. "He travels a lot for this company. Mom says he likes that. She says that he moved out 'cause he 'got bored with us,' but I think their marriage just wasn't—"

She was interrupted when the door was opened by a blonde, bright-eyed, aerobicized, late-twenties woman with a radiant smile, "Katie!? What a surprise! And you're even prettier than your pictures. It's so good to finally meet you." She shook Katie's hand warmly and reached out to me. "Hi. I'm Tina Petroski."

I introduced myself, explaining I was one of Katie's teachers. Katie shifted uncomfortably. "Is my dad back yet?"

"Tomorrow morning. Come in, come in!" She cheerfully ushered us into the living room, which had a spare but modern Ikea feel.

"He's really anxious to see you, Katie," Tina smiled. "And *I'm* so glad to meet you finally. Why the sudden trip?"

On our way there Katie decided not to get too specific with this young woman whom her mother had always blamed for stealing her father. But I reminded Kate that she at least had to have a reasonable story in case her mother called trying to find her.

"My mom's in a pretty bad way with work and some other serious problems," she told Tina. "I really need to talk to Dad about maybe going to a boarding school or living with him."

"Wow," Tina said, seeming impressed with Katie's maturity and presence. "I'm sorry to hear about your mom, but I know he'll be thrilled to have you here. Me, too."

I chimed in, "Katie told me she's a little fearful of her mother knowing that she's come here, at least until she can talk to her dad."

To her credit Tina was concerned about the ethics of subterfuge. "Well, I wouldn't want to lie to your mom if she calls, but—"

"Could you just not answer the phone?" Katie suggested, as we had strategized. "At least for tonight? I get his voice mail practically all the time. It'd seem pretty natural."

Tina considered it and agreed. I told her that I'd come in to work on my doctoral thesis, had run into Katie on the bus, and she'd volunteered to help with some research. It all sounded reasonable to Tina. I looked at Kate. "So, kiddo, I'll call you tomorrow. If you need anything before then . . ." She understood my private meaning.

"Yeah. Thanks for everything." As I turned to leave, Katie caught my sleeve and spoke quietly, "I really hope you'll be okay with . . ." Unsure how to say it, her voice trailed off, but I understood.

I gave her an encouraging wink, nodded again to friendly-faced Tina, and headed out into the twilight.

Dr. Susan Perry...

I arrived in the Ashton area late that night, stayed over in a motel just outside of town till morning. The directions that Katie gave me to Gertrude Wells's farm were easy to follow, though it was well off the main road and isolated. I noticed storm clouds gathering as I got out of my old Honda. There was a distant rumble of thunder as I approached the well-cared-for white wood-frame house, 1940s vintage. I went up onto the porch that had several flowering plants beneath the lightly curtained windows. There were a couple of small throw pillows with floral needlepoint designs on the bench swing. I opened the screen and knocked on the front door's window. No response.

I knocked more insistently. "Hello? . . . Mrs. Wells?" No answer. Frowning, I went down off the front porch and around the side of the house. The west wind gusted a little, creating a small dust devil in the driveway's powdery dirt.

"Hello? Anybody home?" Still nothing. I stood on tiptoes trying to peek in a side window, but the lace curtains prevented me from seeing anything.

I headed on toward the back, rounded the corner, and came face-to-face with a bloody, hollow-eyed skull.

"Jesus!" I yelped, leaping back and gasping.

Gertrude Wells's corpse was bent backward over the four-foot chicken wire fence. Her clothes and what remained of her flesh hung in shreds. The overall sight was ghastly, but her face was the most horrific.

It looked as though she'd been forced backward against the fence, where she'd succumbed to the onslaught of . . . what?

I glanced quickly around and saw the chickens inside the fence. Probably fifteen or twenty of them. And they were nearly motionless, staring at me. I heard a scratching above me and glanced up to see a huge red rooster perched on the eaves of the house, just above where I stood. It lowered its head toward me, menacingly. Very slowly, I backed away, one careful step at a time, for about ten yards. Then I turned and ran to my car, got quickly in, slammed the door closed. My heart was racing, my breath coming in short puffs, as I stared toward the old farmhouse. I started the car and inched it closer so I could photograph the nightmare corpse ensnared in the wire fence, the flock of predatory fowl all standing stock still.

And staring at me.

Dr. R.W. Hutcherson...

I'd brought Lilly in to sit at her usual station in the office that morning. Susan called from the small county hospital that served Ashton to say she was watching paramedics wheel in the gurney carrying the black body bag that contained Gertrude Wells's tortured remains. "What'd you tell them?"

"That I was a friend, just visiting," she said quickly with tension in her voice. "But I think they're suspicious, Hutch. God . . . it's so disconcerting here. I keep glancing at passersby. Some notice I'm a stranger and then seem to watch me closer. I don't know how to tell who has or hasn't eaten the strawberries."

"Yeah," I said, peering down the CDC hallway. "It's dicey here, too. Lauren and Levering stopped talking when I passed by them. I got this unsettling vibe like when it gets too quiet out on the plains and—"

"Watch yourself, okay?" The urgency in her voice was increasing.

"Yeah. I tried some of the entry codes Prashant found and accessed some of Lauren's files. A lot of similars to the tests I'm running, and notes about that new project he told us she was working on called CAV."

"I've been thinking about that. Maybe it's Comet Avery Virus."

"Would make sense. I'm also wondering if—"

"Look, I want to hear about it," she interrupted, "but is Katie still at her dad's?"

"I guess. I haven't talked to her today, but—"

"Because I just called her house to do some sniffing around and found out her mother is headed for Atlanta—to get her."

Katie McLane...

My dad was pacing on the polished hardwood floor of his living room. I'd been totally surprised when I first saw him. He'd dropped about fifteen pounds and looked trimmer than I'd ever seen him. His LASIK surgery musta worked, too, because his glasses were gone. His curly hair, which my ringlets had sprung from, seemed a much richer brown with lots less gray than I remembered. He musta started dyeing it. Maybe those were all symptoms of the "midlife crisis" that Mom thought was part of why he left her.

Dad was shaking his head, looking at me. "And the people at the CDC really think it's *possible*?!"

"Yeah, Daddy, they said there had been all these weird animal attacks and—"

A sharp and insistent rapping at the front door interrupted me. Tina hopped up to answer it as the knocking became pounding. "Whoa! Hang on," she called out cheerfully. But when Tina opened the door, she was startled to find herself facing two uniformed marshals and my mother, who had fire in her eyes.

Mom stepped past the officers, pushed Tina aside, snapping, "Outta my way, bimbo."

Tina flushed with anger. "Excuse me!?"

Mom blew past her into the room and straight to me, grabbing me by the arm. I gasped, "Mom!?" My heart was pounding like when I ran away.

"Get your stuff, Katharine."

"Hey, hey, hey," Dad intervened. "Just hang on, Eileen. You're not gonna—"

"I have custody, a warrant, and these two officers to enforce it." Mom snarled, but with a really scary grin—and that telltale gleam in her eye.

"No!!" I yelled at her and tried to pull away, but she held on tightly as I struggled, until one of the marshals stepped in to subdue me.

"Take it easy, young lady. Nobody wants to—Ow!"

I'd kicked him really hard in the shin. The other marshal, who was beefier and lots gruffer, grabbed my arm like a vise. "Okay, kid, that's it."

Dad snapped at him, "Hey! Don't you hurt her, dammit!" Dad tried to loosen the marshal's grip and quell me at the same time. "Katie, stop it!" But I knew what was up, and I was determined to struggle even though I heard a siren approaching outside.

"I won't go with her!" I shouted, furiously. "I *won't!*"

Tina tried to soothe me. "Katie, honey, why don't you just go along with them until we—"

"Butt out, bitch." Mom glared at Tina, then turned to me. "You're just very confused, Kate. I'm taking you to a very nice hospital for a little while—"

"*No!*" I screamed at her, and Dad also shouted.

"She's not going *anywhere* until—"

Suddenly three more people rushed in through the open front door, startling all of us. They wore one-piece, bright yellow biosafety jumpsuits complete with airtight hoods, goggles, breathing apparatuses, long blue rubber gloves, and boots. All of us living room combatants froze in amazement.

I saw that one of the space-suited people was Hutch. He pointed at me. "There she is! Everybody back! Stand away from her!"

The older, gruff marshal kept one of his meaty hands on me and held up the other, angrily. "Just hang on, pal, who the hell are you?"

Hutch showed his ID. "Centers for Disease Control. This girl is highly contagious." The marshal pulled his hand off me like he'd stuck it into fire.

Dad was stunned. "What?"

Mom was suspicious. "Contagious with what?"

"She was exposed to *Rhus quercifolia* yesterday," Hutch said as he waved the others with him to wrap me up in a Mylar sheet. One of them stuck a breathing mask over my nose and mouth, and handed me a small oxygen bottle to hold. "It's a deadly toxin, and she has to be put into isolation immediately."

Mom's eyes drilled in on him. "No. I'm Eileen McLane, she's my daughter, and I have custody. I'm taking her to—"

Hutch brushed her aside. "Lady, I don't care if she's the *president's* daughter. I have the overriding authority of the US Department of Health to place her in quarantine." He motioned to the other two with him. "Get her into the van, start the IV, five ccs of the vaccine, and sedate her. Stat." Then he looked at the others gravely. "I only hope it's not too late to save her. And that none of you have already contracted it, too." He looked sharply at the other CDC officer. "Rita, get *their* blood samples and contact info. And they can reach her through HQ."

Then the other space-suited man swept me up into his arms and carried me out with Hutch right behind us, leaving behind Dad, Tina, the two marshals, and Mom, who was like totally steaming.

Outside Hutch hustled me into one of two CDC emergency vans. He climbed in behind me and slammed the back door as the other CDC person started the van and peeled out with the siren screaming.

Then Hutch pulled off his headgear and turned off his breather as he smiled at me. "You can take yours off, too." I was staring at him and pretty freaked. "Sorry about that, Katie. Didn't know how else to get you out."

I was scared. "But do I really have—"

"*Rhus quercifolia?* God, I hope not!"

"Why? What is it?!"

"Poison Ivy." Hutch wiggled his eyebrows and gave me a big Montana grin as we went speeding on with the siren wailing.

Dr. Susan Perry...

The storm clouds I'd seen in the west earlier had grown more ominous. Thunder rumbled, and the wind was picking up. I watched from a sidewalk opposite the Ashton Methodist Church. The young minister was loading a couple of charter buses with numerous passengers, including a boy that I recognized from Katie's description as Darren Green, and his dad, Rupert. Then a school bus pulled up with a Warriors banner on the side. I could see the rowdy football team inside.

I drew a tense breath and walked across the street that had grown slightly darker beneath the thickening clouds. I approached the minister and smiled. "Football game?"

The handsome young minister turned to inspect me. And there it was: that same superior attitude and glint in his eye that I had seen in Lauren's and others'. I felt he was looking right into my bone marrow. His smile held zero warmth as he said, "No. It's a church outing."

"Really?" I said brightly. "I'm a member of the First Methodist in Atlanta, may I join you?"

The young minister was polite, but firm. "I'm afraid it's only for a few, very select brethren. Sorry." He nodded goodbye and followed the last of his special flock onto the first bus. I stood back as it departed, looking at the faces inside. I glimpsed girls that might have been Jenna; Katie's sister, Lisa; and the thrift-store girl, Stephanie, who seemed more reluctant than the others to get on a bus. The two charters pulled out, followed by the team school bus. Several boys looked out at me with those haughty, cold eyes.

I watched with all my instincts buzzing. Then hurried to my car and followed the buses.

Katie McLane...

We were sitting in a lab that was part of the CDC's small, new quarantine unit some distance from the main buildings. Leaning over Hutch's shoulder, I saw a strange, grainy image slowly appear on the video screen. I'd seen images of amoebas and other microscopic organisms, but I'd never seen anything like this. "*That's* the virus?"

"The little buggers on the surface of the larger cell. Yeah." Hutch carefully adjusted and fine-tuned the image on the electron microscope. "Magnified eight million times."

I really studied it, trying to understand how something so infinitesimal could have had such impact. "That's what changed them all? Darren and everybody?"

222

"So it would seem," Hutch said as he recorded the image onto the hard drive.

The electron microscope was a supercomplicated piece of equipment that looked like a white desk with a large cylinder thingy coming up four feet from the desktop. It hummed quietly in front of us.

I stared at the image. "Do you know how the virus works, Hutch?"

"Not yet. But I found a bunch of classified reports in Lauren's files about the comet fragments." He brought up data on a nearby monitor:

SUBLOG-839812-3==CAVSTD.fletcher.lauren.prv/encode-262628GT-LF/PW-REQ

DATE/TIME: 08/17/20—14:23:08

LOC: Carrollton, GA

GRID: 33.5801° N, 85.0766° W

ACQ: Holme, Ellen W., SSN 713-358-9683

REP: GSP #782227, Lincoln, Sanford

OBJECT: Diameter 35.45 cm

ACTION: Sequestered for Radiation.

ABSTRACT: Object discovered by Ellen W. Holme in cornfield on her farm, reported to GA State Patrol. Apparent fragment from Comet Avery. Interview verified. Vegetation in cornfield extremely enhanced for a radius of 673 meters. Stalks over three meters tall, cobs larger than others in nearby field by 52%.

Courtesy GSP, Dr. Susan Perry

And there were lots more numbers and words I didn't understand. Hutch was saying, "This is one entry from the teams that investigated fragments across the debris field. They *all* found the same thing: the local vegetation in *each area* was altered spectacularly. As though its adaptive processes had actually been accelerated at warp speed."

"Just like at Ashton," I said.

Hutch nodded yes. "And they sealed off the areas claiming 'radiation hazards.'"

"Because they all got infected. And wanted to keep it secret."

"Sure." Hutch leaned back in his chair with a tense sigh. "You saw what happened in your town, Katie. As soon as each person got a taste of the forbidden fruit, felt their minds expand, they were blown away by the possibilities. For leadership. For domination. In sports, sex, academics. And this could obviously go way beyond small-town conflicts."

"And," I said, "they weren't just smarter, they were really like *devious*. Mean. And violent. A couple girls got raped, my own sister tried to poison her best friend. And Darren was certain his brother, Tim, caused that school bus crash where those kids were killed."

Hutch's expression was grim. "That's exactly the kind of behavior I'm most worried about, Katie." He clicked open a photo of a tough-looking military man. "This is a former military intelligence, black-ops guy, Bradford Mitchell. He'd been seen here a few times recently. Our colleague Prashant Sidana had suspicions—until he was killed in a lab accident."

My eyes got wider. "*Was* it an accident?"

"I don't think so. Lauren was in the lab with him when it happened, but there was no conclusive evidence. Anyway, Prashant's research turned up that Mitchell had private security operations going here in the Southeast. He must've somehow gotten wind of the viral phenomenon and used his connections to clamp the security down tight."

"After he got infected himself," I suggested.

"Sure seems likely, Kate. And my guess is he brought some of the infected vegetation or fruit to Lauren Fletcher and allowed her to infect herself."

I frowned. "Why?"

"Because he needed expert help. Lauren's a brilliant biologist, and a dose of this virus would've clearly boosted her intelligence sky-high. I've been poring over the basic research she did for the last several months, and there's definitely an amazing spike about six weeks back. The level and quality of her work suddenly took such a huge jump that I'm really straining to comprehend it."

I was all the more curious. "But what'd he want her to do?"

"Replicate the virus. Standard protocol to have more study specimens. Susan and I started the same process, but from what I've seen, Lauren's way ahead of us. It looks like she's made quite a bit. And there's another wrinkle that may be worse." Hutch scanned the computer screen through Lauren's file to a new section, full of numbers and complex chemical equations. He highlighted a section. "Lauren seems to be working on modifying the prime CAV into something she's coded CAV-*B*. It may be some kind of *secondary virus*."

I blinked. "Oh my God. What does *that* do?"

Hutch shook his head. "Haven't had time to analyze it, Katie. Or even get a sample. Lauren's notes indicate that she secretly—maybe illegally—moved her research to a chemical plant north of the city that has ties to the CDC. But Prashant found her special access code. I'm going up there."

"With the police?" *The absolute right move,* I thought.

But Hutch threw up his hands questioningly. "Which police? This has obviously been spreading for months. We don't know who may have become involved. I feel just like you did in Ashton, Katie."

I remembered Deputy "Sleazeball" Patton. Understood. "You don't know who to trust."

"Right. I don't even know who else *within* the CDC may be in cahoots with Lauren. Maybe even the director, Levering. I've gotta get the whole picture first." Hutch stood up.

So did I. "Let's go!"

"No, Katie."

"But—"

"Listen, will you?" He put his hands on my shoulders. "This quarantine unit is the only place I can protect you. From your own mother. I've left word out front that you aren't to have visitors. You have to stay in here. Okay?"

No, it was definitely *not* okay, but I knew he was right.

Security-Cam Archive ID: Exterior Atlanta, GA, Sector 186-H
Date: 09/17/20 **Time:** 19:26:12

Lens: Var/14mm **Bearing:** W/SW 252 degrees

Transcript by: ATL PD-Op #52671

Visual Descrpt: Cam shows small, leafy pocket park in recently gentrified neighborhood. Light from streetlamps through trees. Middle-aged cauc. female, med-blonde hair, in raincoat, sits alone on park bench. Seems calm. Middle-aged cauc. male, curly brown hair, tan windbreaker, stands near bench. Shifts weight foot to foot. Seems uneasy.

Courtesy ATL PD, FBI

Eileen McLane, 41, Katie's mother...

A bit of a breeze was increasingly disturbing the leaves in the park. Jason also seemed disturbed. He stood uncomfortably beside the bench where I was sitting. I looked up at the rustling branches. "There's a storm coming, Jason," I said. Then I let my hand rest on the bench seat, invitingly, as my thoughts drifted back to a better time. "Remember how we used to sit on the old bench in the Ashton town square and—"

"Eileen. Please." He was impatient. "If that's why you asked me to meet you, I'm not staying here."

I looked up at him softly, speaking the truth, "I can't help it if I miss you, Jase."

He sighed. I could see that he was trying to push back the guilt that still nagged him. "I'm sorry, Eileen. I really am. Look, I'd better get going."

I caught his sleeve. "You're a very ambitious man, Jase." I looked off in the direction of his house, where I knew Tina waited. "What if I could give you something she couldn't."

"Eileen, we've been through all this. I just don't want to—"

He started to pull away, but I held his sleeve. "Wait. Just listen. What if I could promise you *complete success*. In everything. What if I could guarantee you extraordinary intelligence. Wealth. Power."

I could see he was thinking that I must be having another bout with alcohol. His voice was impatient. "What do you mean?"

I reached into my purse and eased out a jar of Granny Wells's homemade strawberry preserves. Then I looked at him with a penetrating expression I knew he'd never seen on my face before. He frowned. "Eileen, what are you talking about?"

A hint of a smile crept onto my face. I knew my eyes were beaming as I said, "Us."

15

QUARANTINE

Dr. R.W. Hutcherson...

The Everett Biochemical plant was in an industrial park on the north edge of Atlanta. It was a multifaceted division of parent company BioTeck Industries, which produced bulk chemicals for industrial use as well as pharmaceutical medications. Before coming to the plant, I'd left Lilly at her condo in the care of Susan's friend Justinia Marquez.

I'd seen plenty of biochem plants, but to an untrained eye, particularly at night, it'd seem like an impossible confusion of various-sized pipes running from one concrete building to the next. Steam was venting from some junction points.

I had inched my old Durango pickup to a stop some distance from the security gate. I saw an administrator-businessman type, middle-aged black gentleman walk out the office entrance and toward the inner parking lot.

Clarence Frederick...

The pavement was damp from the misty rain that began a few minutes before I came out. I waved to the security guard. "'Night, Sam."

Sam smiled back. He was sixty and close to retirement. Like me, Sam was African American and was pleased that I'd risen to a prominent position as vice president and deputy plant manager. A fact I was proud of, but I tried to never put on airs. I'd also helped Sam's daughter, and quite a few deserving folks of all colors, find entry-level positions with Everett. Sam called out as usual, "You have a good one, Mr. Frederick."

"You, too, Sam. And say hi to Mazie for me."

Dr. R. W. Hutcherson...

My palms were sweating. I felt like the next calf waiting in line to get branded. I'd never been involved in anything remotely clandestine or even sneaky. I knew I was risking some kinda censure for nosing around here, but the startling events of recent days combined with the ominous discoveries that Katie, Susan, and I'd made—and that Prashant had likely died for—made it vital to investigate further.

The plant administrator drove his Prius silently out through the gate and into the drizzly night. Then I drew a tense breath and eased the Durango up to the gate. I heard a baseball game on the guard's radio, tried to sound casual as I handed him my ID. "Hiya, Sam."

The guard squinted. "Evening, sir, do I know you?"

I yawned. "Hutcherson. CDC safety. Usually come during daytime."

As the guard scanned the ID, I watched tensely and waited. And waited.

I finally broke the silence. "What inning?"

"Bottom of the seventh. What's your access code?"

"AA one-oh-seven. Who's winning?"

The guard entered the code. "Damn Yankees." His computer made a strange burping sound, and I clutched. But Sam handed back my ID. "Here y'go. Be sure y'avoid any restricted areas marked with yellow tape."

"Will do, Sam. Thanks." I eased the pickup forward, trying to breathe normally.

I drove past some new construction with several temporary office trailers. All were dark except one with a sign reading "Security." Inside I saw two men uniformed like the gate guard, sitting at a table eating. A pair of gray-suit types were also in there. They didn't notice me passing.

I checked some notes on my phone, parked near the building I thought the likeliest suspect, and went in. Huge stainless steel pipes formed a dropped ceiling. I walked quickly through wafting steam along the concrete corridor. Rounding a corner, I heard someone call out, "Hey! Hang on there." He was a plant custodian the size of an NFL center, wearing a yellow hard hat.

I was turning inside out, but trying not to show it. Felt a drop of sweat from my armpit trace down my side.

The plant worker grabbed a hard hat from a nearby rack and handed it to me with a smile. "Pain in the ass, man, but OSHA says we gotta wear 'em."

"Yeah, I know." I nodded officiously, joking as I put it on. "Just hoping nobody'd catch me."

The worker smiled and moved off. I watched him with my nerves on edge. Then I checked my directions and walked on quickly past several doors with windows revealing chem labs on the other side. I figured the one Lauren was using would be down at the remote end. I knew if they'd started producing that secondary virus already, containers might be in a storage room along here, and I wanted some solid proof.

The hallway opened out wider on one side, forming a dark room about thirty feet square. A floor-to-ceiling chain-link fence cordoned it off. About six feet in front of the fence was a ribbon of yellow tape printed with "Restricted Access—Stay Clear." I ducked under the tape and skirted along the fence past its gate, which had a hefty keypad lock and a sign, "Security Clearance Required." On the other side were stacked some four-foot-tall chemical canisters, all with that ugly bio-hazard warning symbol stenciled on them. One container was close enough to the fence that I could see its postcard-size label. I leaned closer, peering through the chain link, and saw that along with other data imprinted, was: "CAV-B."

I looked through the fence into the dark room. There were similar canisters stacked inside with what appeared to be nearly identical labels.

I saw at least a dozen of them.

Dr. Susan Perry...

In downtown Atlanta the rain had begun in earnest. My Accord glided along the rain-slick street, which reflected neon signs, lamplights, and the red taillights of cars in front of me. I was talking into my Bluetooth, "My God, Hutch . . . why've they made so much? And what the hell is it?"

"Good questions," Hutch responded. I could hear his nervousness. "I'm gonna get some better photos of a label—"

"And then get the hell out of there! We'll go to the police or FBI and get a search warrant."

"No shit, Sherlock," he said. "Where're you?"

"Courtland Street in Atlanta, couple blocks east of Peachtree." I guided my car slowly around one that was parking. "I followed three buses of people from Ashton to the congregational church here." I peered out through my windshield as the wipers swished the rain aside. I could see many people from Ashton moving toward the church, along with dozens from several other buses. "Some kind of gathering. Few hundred. All kinds of people. Heavy security, too."

I spotted numerous gray-suited people with those subtle, secret service–style earplugs, conferring, or speaking into their lapel mikes. They became focused and very attentive to a black SUV escorting a limousine that pulled up in front of the grand old church. Two gray-suits climbed out, one a bulldog of a man with an acne-scarred face and shaved head, then two people I knew.

"Mitchell and Lauren just showed up with an entourage," I told Hutch. I noticed the subservient body language of all the security people. "They're being greeted like royalty by those security types. Something's really up, Hutch."

"Watch yourself, Suse."

"You, too."

Everett Security—Surveillance Archive Stack 1177240AA

Date: 09/17/20 **Time:** 20:12:54 **Cam:** 0127-17-6

Area: 17—Restricted Entry Section 6

Visual Desc: Unidentified cauc. male in hard hat inside yellow warning tape, by security-fenced holding area, using cell phone, then takes flash photos of canisters inside fence.

Action: Duty Sec Ofc activates intrusion alarm. The man reacts. Runs.

Courtesy Everett Biochem, FBI

Katie McLane...

The only hospital-type place I'd ever been in was our small one in Ashton. Once was to the ER when I broke my arm falling out of our oak tree and the other was visiting Darren after his appendicitis operation. Ashton Community had lots of warm earth colors, friendly artwork, and cushy furniture. But the small CDC Isolation Unit was obviously designed to maintain extreme cleanliness easy and fast. The only furniture in my room was a bed, a low stainless steel table, a plastic desk, and a plastic chair. It was all simple and made as comfortable as possible, but the surfaces were all hard so they could be wiped down with disinfectant at the drop of a germ.

The pastel peach-colored walls were the only slight effort to make the place feel less cold and sterile. The lighting helped a little, too, particularly at night when the built-in fluorescents went off, but there were still pools of light from smaller units built into the ceiling. The bed sheet and pillows were covered in plastic. The thin blanket on top was shiny Mylar. There was a robe, hospital gown, and paper slippers, but I was still in my jeans and sweatshirt, hoping Hutch would come back soon and get me outta there. I looked for a magazine or something to distract myself from worrying about my friends. I was still ticked off at being caged up while Susan and Hutch were out on their missions.

Looking out through the double-thick, biosafety glass window to the nurse's station, I saw the outer door open and my dad enter, smiling thanks to the nurse. I thought I wasn't supposed to have any visitors, but seeing Dad felt okay. If it'd been Mom, I definitely would've freaked.

He smiled at me through the glass, giving me his little finger wave like always. Then he spoke with the nice nurse, Mariana, who'd tried to distract me earlier by telling me funny stories about her family in the Philippines. The intercom was off now, so I couldn't hear their voices, but I saw that Dad was being friendly, gesturing toward me as he spoke. Seemed like he was asking to come into where I was. I walked closer to the glass, anxious to hear what had happened between him and Mom after I'd been taken away.

But Mariana politely shook her head as she spoke to Dad, apparently saying no, he couldn't enter my quarantine area. She pointed to a wall phone near the window that communicated with one on my side of the glass. That didn't satisfy Dad.

I watched, sorta amused, as he tried to work his personal magic on the nurse. He could be a very persuasive salesman, but when she kept saying no and pointing to the phone, he slowly got impatient, more insistent. Mariana was sympathetic, but emphatic: he could *not* be allowed in. Dad's smile grew darker in a way that suddenly made me nervous. I'd never seen him act like that. Then he glanced over at me, and the hairs on the back of my neck stood on end. That cold, superior look was now in *his* eyes!

My stomach dropped. I realized, *Oh my God. Mom must've infected him!*

I gasped. Scared. I backed away from the glass as I watched Dad shout at the nurse, then finally slam his hand down on the counter between them. Mariana reached for her phone, but Dad leaned over the counter and grabbed her roughly. She struggled, but he pulled her up close and stuck her with something.

CDC/ATL QIU-3NS Vol: 434368-QIU
Date: 09/17/20 **Time:** 20:25:08

Loc: ATL/Quarantine & Isolation Unit 3

Transcript by: N/A

QIU Nurse Ocampo, Mariana, receives electroshock from hand-held stun gun device, falls to floor apparently unconscious. Male civilian repeatedly tries using keypad to open secure door to ISO chamber. Fails. He scans room. Sees sec cam QIU-3NS. Grabs stool from EEG/EKG monitoring area. Uses it to smash camera.

END RECORDING

Courtesy CDC, ATL PD, FBI

Katie McLane...

Then Dad came back to the air lock door to my isolation chamber. He tried again to open it, but I knew that without punching the correct daily code into the keypad, he wouldn't be able to. Then he paused, chuckled, and smiled at me, very natural and friendly. He beckoned for me to open it from my side and come on out. I shook my head. I was frightened and didn't know the code anyway. He was getting annoyed, but kept his cool and waved more insistently for me to come out. I couldn't hear his words, but I could lip-read enough to know what he said was basically, "I'm your father, and I want you out here right now."

I backed away farther, shaking my head and saying, "No, Daddy."

He tried the door again, and as his frustration increased, he began kicking at it.

I was really getting scared that if he got in, they'd infect me, too. Searching for an escape, I ran to the back of the unit. There was another door near the bathroom. I didn't know where it led, but it didn't matter because it also required a code to exit. I was trapped.

I looked back at the thick security glass window. My eyes got wide when I saw Dad grab the metal stool and begin to smash it against the window. The impact-resistant glass just bounced the chair off. I felt a momentary relief. I looked around for a security camera in my room and saw one high in a corner. I jumped up and down, waving at it and yelling. Trying to get the attention of whoever was supposed to be watching for stuff. No response. Dad swung the stool harder against the glass again and again. Getting more furious.

The fifth time he hit it, I saw a tiny crack appear in the glass.

16

THE FRIENDS

Dr. Susan Perry...

The imposing First Congregational Church on Atlanta's Courtland Street had anchored the neighborhood with a stately Renaissance-style majesty for over a century.

But for me that evening, it also held an unsettling mystery. It rose ominously above me into the dark sky. I tried to blend in among the crowd moving through the rain toward the church entrance. There was a sign: "No Recording Devices." And a metal detector. And before them three tables were set up beneath a temporary awning. On each table was a small suitcase with some sort of biometric monitoring mechanism inside it. People in line ahead of me were required to place the palm of their hand on a sensor panel. Only if it beeped would the security squad allow anyone in. No beep, no admission.

I saw a couple of people get turned away. Obviously neither they nor I had whatever was necessary. I stepped out of the line, pretending to search for something in my rain jacket pockets as I looked around, determined to find a way inside.

A narrow cobblestone alley ran between the church and its rectory. I saw that the responsibility of keeping it secure that evening fell to a gray-suited guard who had taken shelter from the increasing rain inside a back door of the rectory. She had just leaned out to be certain the alley was deserted then ducked back inside, out of the rain. I watched her from behind a dumpster, waiting for a clear moment. Then I quickly climbed up onto the trash bin, very glad I was in jeans. I reached up on tiptoes toward the fire escape ladder. My fingertips could barely touch it. I jumped, grabbed on, and my weight dropped the ladder downward. I scrambled up it as quickly as I could, my hands getting scratched by the wet, rusty surface of the iron rungs.

At the first landing I pressed against the stone wall. Rainwater was running down it. My hair streamed into my face. I pushed it back and carefully peeked in the window, but ducked back into the shadows when I saw a gray-suit passing by just inside. I looked down at the alley, checking to be sure the security woman in the rectory was staying out of the rain. Then I hustled up the fire escape to the third story of the old church.

By the time I reached that landing, I was thoroughly soaked, but encouraged because the window on this level was dark. Droplets of rain were tickling the tip of my nose. I blew them away, took a deep breath, and used the buckle on my purse to partly break the window. I reached through the jagged opening and tripped the lock. I strained to slide the window up just far enough to climb inside.

It took a moment for my eyes to see through the gloom. I was within the dusty rafters of the church. I could hear the muffled sound of the gathering crowd below. I walked carefully through the musty darkness toward the sound and right into a large spider web. I reacted sharply, swiping at it and wiping it away from my wet face.

A sudden bellowing blast of organ music startled me. I was near the huge pipes of the organ at the back of the church. The low, thundering bass notes were absolutely bone rattling as I edged forward, seeking a better vantage point.

Katie McLane...

I desperately tried to jimmy the lock on the quarantine's back door with a fork I'd found. I looked over my shoulder and saw that the double-thick window now had more cracks feathering out as my dad kept smashing that heavy stool against it. He was soaked with sweat, but his anger and determination had gotten stronger.

I realized working the lock was hopeless. "Goddammit!" I threw down the useless fork and looked around the sterile environment as my father continued smashing at the window behind me. I was really scared, but hanging on, trying to stay focused. On the wall just below the ceiling I'd noticed an air vent. It had looked too small. Now it was looking better. I dragged the desk under it, put a chair on top, and climbed up. It was *really* small. Even if I could get in, I'd be like a sardine. And the snap-on vent cover had a warning sign: "Removing This Filter Triggers Alarm." I stared at it for a nanosecond, then said, "Oh, screw it," and pulled it off. An alarm started beeping, but I squirmed up and inside the vent pipe. It was so narrow I had to keep my arms straight out in front of me and could only wriggle along like a snake an inch at a time. I could still hear the crashes of the steel stool against the glass down in the room below me.

Dr. Susan Perry...

In the church rafters, I'd carefully crept closer through the dust so that I could peer out between the organ pipes and into the large neo-Renaissance sanctuary below. It could hold maybe nine hundred but was only half-full. Latecomers were filtering into the pews. They were all ages and ethnicities.

I saw the ones I'd followed from Ashton, but the majority could have come from anywhere. A man in a Beaumount High sweatshirt might have been the coach of that team in the bus accident. Overall the people were a mixture of all classes from well-off to even some street people. Several were in city, county, or state police uniforms. A few military, too. They were a true cross section of Georgia's citizenry.

The majority seemed intense but cautious, studying each other warily. Most seemed to recognize that dominant superior attitude in the body language and eyes of others. I noted that a few seemed more subdued, less into the undercurrent of dark energy the others possessed. Teenage Darren was among those quieter souls. And so was another man who caught my eye: Joseph Hartman, our gentle, religious CDC custodian whom I'd always been so fond of. It saddened me to see him among them, though he seemed uncomfortable.

The organ music stopped. The crowd began to focus their attention toward the front. I adjusted my view and saw Bradford Mitchell, in suit and tie, step forward toward the carved wooden pulpit. He had been sitting on a chair beside Lauren, who was focused on her cell, hastily typing a text message. Dr. Levering and several others were on the raised altar area.

Mitchell squared his strong shoulders and looked out over the gathering as their conversations ceased and they settled in to listen with rapt attention. But the taut faces and stiffness of many suggested a decidedly cynical attitude. I clicked on my cell phone's video recorder.

"Good evening, and welcome." Mitchell's voice was commanding but cordial. I saw that the crowd, however, eyed him very critically.

"We're all here because each of you and I share a common bond that is unique and amazing in history. A bond that raises us above the rest of humanity. And gives us a very special role to play in humanity's future. The role of leadership."

In the midst of the crowd, a woman stood up whom I'd seen in Ashton and who fit Katie's description of her biology teacher, Shelly Navarro. Her voice was strong. "And who put *you* at the top of that leadership?" Several other steely-eyed people around her shouted angry agreement.

I noticed Mitchell's gray-suit security man with the bulldog look and shaved head, standing to one side of the altar, touch his tiny earplug, listening carefully to a radio communication. Then he whispered something into his lapel mike.

Mitchell stared at Navarro a moment. Then he smiled calmly to her and then the crowd. "Very good question. Look up around you."

The assembly did and saw a dozen gray-suited people appear on the clerestory level above them. They wore gas masks, and each held up a gas canister.

Mitchell lifted a gas mask from behind the pulpit. "Without one of these, the nerve gas in those canisters can kill everyone here in less than a minute."

The crowd gasped. I was fumbling with my cell phone to dial 911, but when I saw Mitchell dramatically toss his gas mask aside and hold up a calming hand, I paused.

"There is no nerve gas." Mitchell smiled. "But there could've been. Just making my point: that it would be foolish for you *not* to listen. For us *not* to work together. We want each of you to *share* control of power." His eyes scanned across the faces before him. "In the last few weeks all of us here have been catapulted light-years ahead of most people. Wouldn't you say?" There was definite agreement. "Right," he agreed, focusing on Navarro. "So everyone here deserves to be in a position of leadership."

That brought more positive reaction and a smattering of applause. Navarro sat back down, willing to listen. From my vantage point, though unnerved by the proceedings, I could sense a spectrum of individual reactions. Those who had been naturally more dominant, like Tim Green, whom Katie had called the "natural quarterback," sitting by his brother Darren, had their innate tendencies extremely accentuated by the virus and seemed the most gung ho. Others seemed to have much less personal intensity. Darren and a girl, who I thought might be the Stephanie that Katie'd described, were clearly among those. My colleague Joseph seemed particularly uneasy. I watched the gentle older man look around at the unsettling dark enthusiasm of the majority. Then he rose and quietly headed out a side aisle. He was intercepted momentarily by a gray-suit who seemed to be taking his information, but then Joseph left.

Meanwhile Mitchell continued, "We're going to establish a democratic rotation of leadership among this, our sacred brother- and sisterhood."

There was somewhat more applause. Then my cell phone vibrated in my hand. I jumped, ducked back out of sight, saw who was calling, and whispered into it, "Hutch! Where are you?"

He sounded stressed, breathing hard, "On my way to you. And Suse, I've got some really important new information. Where are you now?"

"Inside the congregational church," I whispered urgently. "Bring the police. No, the FBI! And a news crew! I'll meet you outside at Courtland and Auburn. How long?"

"Twenty minutes. If I'm lucky."

I clicked off and looked back down with growing apprehension at the applauding crowd below me.

Martin Middleton, 34, Pastor, Ashton Methodist Church...

I'd just met this Mitchell person briefly that evening when our Ashton group arrived. Schoolteacher Shelly Navarro had made contact with his people and helped organize our trip.

From the pulpit Mitchell said, "Many of you know the man I'm about to introduce. The pastor of this magnificent church and one of the founders of an important new idea." I didn't know what that idea was, but the man was indeed familiar. "Please welcome," Mitchell continued grandly, "the Reverend Dr. Abraham Brown."

There was respectful applause as the imposing preacher took the pulpit. Brown was a robust African American about sixty with a charismatic, commanding, serious presence. I'd met him at a convention a year prior. He had warmth and charm, but could marshal the intense power of a Dr. King, Jr. He had begun his ministry in an all-black church in rural Appling, Georgia, but Brown's rhetorical ability to capture and invigorate any congregation quickly caught the attention of the Southern Baptist Convention, which moved him to ever larger venues. His services in this multiracial church had been televised each Sunday for years. He had celebrity, but also substantial moral weight.

At six-foot-four, most everyone he met literally looked up to him and was impressed by the grip of his large, firm hand. His physical and intellectual presence could dominate most any gathering.

Dr. Susan Perry...

His face had roundness to it; his skin was very dark and tight. A modest mustache crowned his full upper lip. He looked out over the people, saying modestly, "Thank you." His voice was deep, rich, stentorian. I made sure my cell was still recording.

"My friends, I have been privileged by the grace of God to serve this community for three decades. But as I look around at it and other nearby communities where many of you live, I am saddened by the fact that they are not all they could be. They have not lived up to their promise. But I know now who can change that"—his finger suddenly flashed out arm's length, pointing toward the audience as his voice exploded like a cannon shot—"*YOU!*"

Everyone blinked. His word echoed around the stone walls of the vast church. He had our attention. And he knew it.

From my perch in the loft overhead, I heard a low rolling of thunder outside. The storm was growing as Dr. Brown continued: "The time for a gentle, procrastinating approach to society's problems has passed. What we need is a sharper, smarter one. It's time to shake things up, to *face* the tough challenges." His voice assumed a searing intensity as he made a sweeping gesture with his hand over them. "And I say that *we—we here*—are the ones who know we can do it! Am I right?"

Lisa McLane...

"Yes!" I said with many others. Some applauded. Charley, Tim, and a couple of team guys hooted. Navarro looked like she was dissecting every single one of Brown's words. And approving. As was the crowd. So far.

Dr. Susan Perry...

Even from as high up as I was, I could see that Mitchell's dark eyes were cold, purposeful, imperial, as his spokesman Reverend Brown went on: "All of us here know we've been given a great *gift*. Each of you here has been chosen to be a dominant force in your local communities—in your various areas of expertise. It would be foolish, self-destructive, and just plain stupid to waste our energies working *against* each other. We must set aside distrust. My friend Bradford Mitchell is right: we must all *unite!* To take control of our communities for the good of the masses."

I saw an Ashton deputy sheriff, probably that Brice Patton Katie'd mentioned, and others among the audience murmur approval. They were catching the reverend's flow, except for Darren, Stephanie, and a minority who were silently glancing around or frowning with discomfort. And me. I was outright stunned by the proceedings and the direction the reverend seemed to be heading. I glanced around at the gray-suited men and women who were stationed at strategic points all around the hall. They were cool eyed, watching the crowd carefully, their expressions unreadable.

The reverend lowered his voice and his head slightly, in the manner of a supplicant. "Now, I'll admit something very private to you, my friends: at first I had my doubts." He seemed contrite, ashamed to admit what he was saying. "When this great gift from heaven was visited upon me, I thought selfishly at first: How can I use this to my own advantage? For my own personal benefit? I'm sure that many of you had that same thought. But then I remembered my personal savior, Christ Jesus, walking in the garden of Gethsemane, shaking off the temptations of Satan."

From among the congregation came a few overlapping shouts of "Praise Him!" "Yes!"

"And by the grace of his divine help, I"—the reverend snapped his arms wide apart—"*shook off* the temptations which were coiling around me!"

"Yes!" "Bless you, Brother Brown," came the responses, more enthusiastic now.

"I shook them off!" he reiterated forcefully. "And you must do the same, my dear brethren, with help from *whatever* higher power you believe in. You must also realize that *our* bond—the gift we've each been given—transcends individual religions. You must realize what a *force*—what an *invincible army* we can be. *Together!* Why, the power for good we hold in our hands—and in our amazing *heads*—is *unmatched in human history!*"

Another wave of murmuring agreement swept through those gathered in the sanctuary. I scanned the individuals in the crowd with increasing worry. Most all were smiling, mesmerized. They liked being a part of such a great force.

"This gift of ours is a glorious tool." Reverend Brown held up his large fist as though it grasped the handle of a mighty hammer. "A magnificent tool that a higher power has handed to *us*. It didn't fall on Russia, did it?!"

"Hell no," many responded. "No, it didn't!"

"Did it fall on Japan, or China, or Germany?"

"No!" came the collective, louder shouts.

"No, it did not," the reverend emphasized. "It did not even fall across all of America." His finger pointed up at the heavens. "That comet was a fiery line written in the sky by the omnipotent hand of Almighty God! And his all-powerful finger pointed at *us*. *We* right here are his chosen people!"

The voices of the assemblage were gaining strength. "Yes! Say it, brother! Goddamn right!"

His booming voice dropped low into an urgent whisper, "And you can feel it, can't you, my friends?" There were shouts of affirmation. "Down deep in your soul, can't you feel it!?"

Louder shouts then of, "Yes! We *feel it*!" "Damn right we do!"

"Of course you do. Well, the good and devoted people beside me up here feel it, too." Dr. Brown gestured toward Mitchell and Lauren. "And want you all to join with us to reshape our communities and our great state into a driving force!" The reverend's volume increased, to be heard overtop the crescendo of positive reactions. "To give the masses a good swift kick in the backsides! And get them going!"

The crowd cheered his words. Outside, the thunder rumbled louder.

Then he smoothly changed gears; his tone became very confidential. "But our gifts are a secret—a secret we must guard vigilantly amongst ourselves." There was general affirmation from all. "If we encounter others gifted like ourselves, we must draw them into our special fold so that we can all work together for the greater benefit of our communities as well as *our own secret society*, which we are calling"—he paused dramatically—"The Friends of America."

Most all were smiling, nodding, enjoying their individual and collective specialness.

Dr. Brown added fuel: "Tonight you'll be given access to your private, encrypted server. Communication, coordination, and organization are *vital* if we are to succeed. And something else is equally vital."

He held up a small vial of red liquid. "You've never seen this in its pure form. Its official name is CAV-A. This is the magical elixir that Comet Avery showered upon us from the heavens." He raised it as if in a toast to the gathering. "This is—*the gift*." His audience was entranced.

"When Bradford Mitchell discovered its power and potency, he wisely took it to a very special lady." He gestured toward Lauren, who nodded regally to acknowledge the reverend's attention.

I watched Mitchell eye Lauren like a commanding general surveying his crack troops as thunder rolled closer outside. "She is Dr. Lauren Fletcher of the Centers for Disease Control. She was already one of the leading molecular biologists of our day. But when Bradford Mitchell brought the comet's mind-enlarging gift to her, Dr. Fletcher's own mind expanded to new heights of brilliance. And now she has given us a wonderful second gift of her own."

The reverend held up another small vial. Of yellow liquid. He paused dramatically, watched his audience focus on it. "She has developed a *secondary virus*. Designated CAV-*B*. It also increases intelligence and the driving determination we have each felt—but—to only *half* the potency of that with which *we* have been blessed." His shining eyes swept around the old church. "Do you understand what that means, my dear friends?"

I did. I felt myself go pale.

"It means"—the reverend smiled—"that we Friends have the capability of *creating eager followers*. They will share a *half portion* of our passions, our intelligence, and our drive—but—they will respect *our* innate superiority. We'll always need a majority to handle the less desirable grunt work, but we Friends will retain the high command. *We* are the A's. *They*, the B's, will become our foot soldiers"—he chuckled—"our worker B's."

His audience laughed, but I felt a fist tightening around my heart.

"If we do not flaunt our intellectual abilities," he continued, "but use them wisely, subtly, in concert with our special brothers and sisters, there'll be no need for ugly, divisive purges of the elected leadership of our communities. We Friends can be a level of control *behind and above* the elected leaders!"

I saw that the crowd was bedazzled, their individual heads spinning with possibilities. Even young Darren was getting caught up in the enthusiasm of the mob, and one of the gray-suits actually had a trace of a smile. Dr. Brown spoke quietly, drawing them all further into his confidence, "Have you noticed how our local government is running just a bit smoother lately? How the state supreme court justices have slowly been getting in step together on rulings that all of us here would approve of?" His smile became more cagey. "It's not a coincidence."

The crowd was frozen now. Their superior minds were beginning to clearly see the shape of things to come as he continued, "Many in our current local and state government got elected by appealing to the rising tide of populism. But those leaders haven't gone nearly far enough. They need to press harder. To root out all dissenting voices. They need to unify their efforts into one single irresistible force. But to do that they'd need to be *smarter*. And unfortunately *they* can only be so smart. Because *they* are only human."

He raised his thick eyebrows. "Ah, but that's where *we* come in. Since *we* are *extraordinary* humans. Are we not?" His listeners purred positively. "Indeed we are. Those leaders need *our* superior guidance. So it is our charge, our sacred responsibility, my friends, to fan out into our communities with our brilliant intellects and quiet confidence, with insight and infinite subtlety, to quietly . . . take control and guide every aspect of our society with the wisdom of Solomon—which only we possess!"

The crowd applauded, for themselves it seemed, being more and more drawn in. Their minds must have raced with the prospects of holding dominion over others. "We have begun carefully." Dr. Brown went on, "The CAV-B was cautiously administered to certain few elected officials." The reverend doctor smiled. "You could call it the *ultimate campaign contribution*."

Navarro and others grinned with growing amazement, relishing the fact that they were a part of something so enormous and compelling.

"And not just in government," the reverend continued. "We've also begun bringing into the fold leaders in business as well as large sections of the police and militia. And the news media. They're becoming our helpmates, our minions, our worker B's, followers of *you*! Followers who will take whatever effective actions *we direct*!"

Standing among the organ pipes above and behind them, I could barely breathe. I felt dizzy from what I was witnessing.

A grandiose enthusiasm was swelling within the assemblage. Mitchell scanned them with the hawklike eyes of a born predator. I saw in him a creature that could embrace many high crimes in the name of "effective actions."

"And obviously," Dr. Brown said, "in serving our communities we may have many legitimate and appropriate opportunities to secure our own financial futures, but that's just a pleasant side effect. Far more important—I'm sure—will be the rewards we will feel in our hearts and souls."

Charley Flinn...

Folks clapped really hard. So'd I, but thinking, *I'll take it in the wallet, thanks.*

Dr. Susan Perry...

The powerful reverend inhaled deeply. "Everything," he said, building toward his conclusion, "is falling into place and will soon be ready!" Some applause began again. "The die is cast!" A burst of lightning flashed through the tall windows, and the astute reverend instantly co-opted it. "That lightning is us! We, all of us, with our great secret, we, too, shall flash across this city! Across this great state! And beyond. Sunrise tomorrow brings a new day! A glorious *new era*!"

The applause grew louder, many people were on their feet now, creating a huge groundswell, which the reverend rode upon as he brought his message to its grand finale: "And with the divine gift, which destiny has placed into our hands, into *our brains*"—he drew a mighty breath and roared over their joyful noise one powerful word at a time—"*this new era will be OURS!*"

The crowd exploded with electrified acclamation!

Up in the rafters I was staggered. Terrified. On the move. I hurried across the dark attic, out through the third-floor window onto the rainy fire escape. I was so agitated and fearful as I rushed onto the metal steps that I slipped, almost killing myself when my rain jacket got snagged and ripped. I barely grabbed a handhold. Then I was frightened by a metallic clatter in the alley below. *The guard?!* I hugged the wall closely, looked down, but didn't see her. So I scrambled down faster than was safe, finally dropped breathlessly from the ladder onto the wet pavement, and ran to find Hutch.

Jimmy-Joe Hartman...

Poppa tol' me later how he'd gone back to his night shift at the CDC. Said he was troubled in his soul by what he seen in that church. He wuz walkin' down a back hallway when this teenage girl come crashin' down through the ceiling in a shower of dust, landin' right in front of him.

Poppa jumped! "Lord have mercy! What you doin', child!"

Katie McLane...

I was kinda dazed. Exhausted from crawling inch by inch what seemed like a mile. This older man in a janitor uniform helped me up. "Who are you, child? How'd you get up in—"

"I've gotta get out!" I said, breathing hard. "He's after me!"

"Easy now, child." He was picking chunks of plaster from my tangled ringlets. "Who's after you?"

"My father! He's trying to get me! And he's one of *them*! Please let me—" I saw his ID badge, stopped dead. "Joseph?" I looked up to his eyes, scared of what I thought I saw in them. "Oh no . . . not *that* Joseph. Not you, too. Please! Let me go!"

But Joseph held my arm tightly, staring down at me. Then we both heard running footsteps and shouted voices coming our way. One yelled, "Stop right there, mister!"

The other voice was my dad's, much closer, shouting angrily, "Katie, goddammit! Where the hell are you!?"

My eyes riveted onto Joseph's. And suddenly I felt this, I don't know, kind of *rise* inside me. I was still scared to death but strangely calm. Like I knew instinctively what I had to do. It was the most focused I'd ever been in my life. Like somehow I knew he'd understand. "Joseph," I said firmly, one slow word at a time, "you *must* let me go."

The old man stared at me. Yes, that creepy gleam was in his eyes. But it seemed like there was a flicker of something else happening inside him, too. Some wrestling going on way down deep. Like in spite of being infected, being one of them, he understood. Saw the urgent determination on my face. And he knew what was right.

He let go his grip on me.

I stared into his conflicted eyes, and in that instant I knew he saw my appreciation.

"*Katie?!*" My father's furious voice was nearly on top of us.

"Hurry, child," Joseph whispered, shakily pointing the way. "Go."

I did. I dashed down the corridor, around a corner, and out a back door. It was pouring rain. I heard another alarm sounding behind me, but I didn't look back.

I ran as fast as I could, blinking the rain out of my eyes. I made it up to rain-drenched Clifton Road, running across it through passing cars, and rounded another corner, then I sagged against a wall, completely breathless, shaking from exertion. I looked around every which way, feeling danger from every direction. I wasn't sure where to run. Except away.

I hurried from brightly lighted Clifton heading up another side street and deeper into the rainy darkness.

Dr. Susan Perry...

I was running up windswept Courtland through the rain toward Auburn, soaked to the bone, but mindless of it given what I'd just experienced. I looked around nervously for some sign of the cavalry until a hand grabbed me and pulled me into a dark doorway.

I shouted and started to struggle, then saw it was Hutch. The left side of his face was badly bruised. Drops of fresh blood mixed with raindrops traced down from his hairline. I gasped, "Oh my God! What'd they do to you?" He'd been battered, was more of a mess than me. I ran my trembling fingers over his face, checking his bruises and wounds.

He was very calm. "I'm okay. It's not as bad as it looks."

I glanced around quickly. "Are the others on the way? Wait'll they see what I recorded!" I was reaching into my jacket pocket—and realized it was torn open. My phone was gone. I flashed on that metallic clatter in the alley. "No!" I shouted frantically. "Shit! *Shit!* I've gotta go back! It's all on my phone—"

I turned to run, Hutch caught my arm. "Suse, wait. It doesn't matter."

"Of course it does! The police, FBI, have to see what's—"

"I couldn't contact them."

"Couldn't contact—? Why *not?*" My face contorted with anger and confusion.

"Suse, Suse—listen to me. Things have changed."

"Jesus, I know!" I blinked raindrops away, eager to go back. "And I've got the proof if my phone's not totally—"

"I mean things have changed . . . for me."

He was so damnably calm I snapped at him, "What're you talking about, for God's sake?! What's *changed?!*" I stared angrily into his eyes. "What're you trying to—"

Suddenly I understood. Felt icicles in my blood. I could barely speak. "Oh, Hutch. No. My God. *No!*"

Kenneth Johnson

I tried to pull away, but he held me like a vise. "Wait! *Wait, goddammit!*" He glared with harsh dominance. Then caught himself. "Wait. Please." He seemed to be forcing himself to release my arm. He held up both hands, palms facing me, to make the point: he was not threatening me. I could see he was struggling desperately against his new darker nature to make himself speak much more gently. "Listen to me: I feel so lucky that they caught me."

My heart was pounding, my respiration shallow. But even in the rainy darkness, Hutch's face seemed to be glowing like his warm Montana sun. "You can't imagine how fantastic it is, Suse! The intricate correlations you suddenly become capable of. The inconceivable mental gymnastics your mind can instantly perform! Suddenly you're lifted exponentially above the crowd, seeing clearer, further—"

I was unsteady, near tears. "No! I don't want to be like them! I don't want *you* to be like them! Oh, Hutch, my God, no, I—"

An amazed smile lit up his face. "I know, believe me, I know." He was laughing with enthusiasm. Encouragement. "I didn't think I did either. But you *do*! Oh, Suse, you do. We were wrong to be so frightened of it. It's *wonderful*."

"No! Mitchell and his people plan to—"

Hutch shook his head dismissively. "We can deal with them. It doesn't have to be channeled in Mitchell's direction. It can be used for only good, useful, unselfish purposes! You and I can solve biomedical problems we've been struggling with for years. Suddenly I can feel the answers close enough to touch. Cures for diseases. AIDS, cancer. Medications to prolong life!"

I was staring at him, trying to stay objective, but he could sense that I was at least listening, maybe even wavering, as he pressed on, "That's right, Suse, just think of all the people—all the *children*—we can save. Isn't that why you became a doctor? Isn't it?"

"Of course it is, but—"

"Of *course* it is," he encouraged me with incredibly comforting warmth. "They called it a *gift*, Suse. But it's more, it's so far beyond

252

that, it's . . ." He searched for an image brilliant enough to evoke the wonder he felt. "It's like dawn on a Rocky Mountain peak, like a hundred Christmas mornings. All at once. It's joy. Intelligence! Possibilities. Elation!" With a delighted little bubble of laughter, he added, ". . . And it's so remarkably easy . . ."

He showed me a small vial of reddish liquid in his hand. He held it out to me. "It *is* a gift, Suse. The greatest gift you could ever be given. A gift that I'm honored to pass along to you, that'll enable you to change the world in the most wonderful ways imaginable. To save millions of lives."

I stared at the vial in his hand, then a beam of headlights swept across my face. I saw a police car rounding a distant corner, with its red-and-blue strobes flashing.

"Suse . . . don't be afraid"—he touched my arm softly—"we can change the world. Come with me. Join us."

I stared deeply into his eyes. He reached out his other hand, open to me. I was aching, torn. The police car was coming closer, its emergency lights flicking brighter across my face. I looked back at the vial in his hand. And I grasped it. Hutch smiled. Endearingly. Very happy.

Then I said, "I can't, Hutch. I won't."

I broke away and ran hard. Clutching the vial tightly. I heard the police car pick up speed as I dashed around the corner into a dark alley.

Dr. R. W. Hutcherson...

I watched her go with the rain streaming down my face. I gazed off toward the darkness she'd disappeared into as the police car passed me in pursuit. I felt enormous affection and worry for her.

But I also knew my eyes were shining, reflecting the bright possibilities I felt through my whole being for the future. For the vistas that had opened up with this extraordinarily powerful new intelligence.

I remember whispering quietly toward the darkness, with loving confidence, "Yes, you can, Suse . . . And you will."

17

CRISIS MANAGEMENT

Dr. Susan Perry…

I barely dodged the police car and was crouched down behind a hedge, panting hard. To go back to that church alley I knew would be dangerous—not to mention really stupid. Hutch might have alerted them. But I also knew I had to try. I worked my way back circuitously to see the alley from a distance. Cops and gray-suits were prowling. It was hopeless.

My phone and the truth it contained were lost to me.

I hurried to my car on a shadowy side street. Soaked from the rain, shaking from exertion and unadulterated fear, I dug out a backup cell I kept in the glove compartment for emergencies in the field. I called my nurse friend, Justinia, the dear heart who was tending Lilly at our condo. I told her to cram two suitcases with some of our clothes and take Lilly out of there fast. Justinia understood I was in danger and suggested where to meet her. After I clicked off, I stared at the cell in my trembling hand, knew it was traceable. I couldn't use it for long. I was trying to analyze everything at once. Because of what I knew about the dangerous secret society of the Friends, and because Hutch knew I knew, and that I'd work against them and the enormous threat they posed, I was aware that—at least for now—my home, my career at the CDC, my relationship with Hutch, and my entire old life were lost to me.

I called Eric and discovered that Katie had escaped the CDC and connected with him. He was shocked when I gave him *my* headline: that just like Katie, I was on the run. I told him where they could meet me.

I partly covered my license plate with dirt, hoping it might prevent police from spotting me, then hit multiple ATMs, withdrawing as much cash as I dared.

Next I headed to northwest Atlanta and parked in a dark alley near Marietta Square to wait for the others. I arranged an online transfer of the bulk of my local money to be wired to a secure Swiss account I'd set up years ago while working overseas. At the time I'd been amused it'd be an anonymous, numbered account. Now I was grateful. I met Eric, Katie, Lilly, and Justinia at a small house on Lake Street in a working-class neighborhood. It was the home of Justinia's jovial, round-faced cousin Fernando Marquez and his sprite of a wife, Maggie, who weighed about eighty-five pounds but impressed me as a force of nature. They'd had experience finding safe housing for good people needing to avoid authorities. I explained why Katie and I needed to go underground. I described the frightening situation with the virus, the gathering I'd witnessed in the church, how Hutch had been infected and drawn into their circle. Katie also told her story, which Eric corroborated. Justinia and her family were shocked and frightened by it all. But they would help us.

That morning the situation worsened: we saw a TV news bulletin recalling the recent death of Prashant Sidana while working with deadly nerve toxin. It had been thought accidental. But an "internal CDC investigation" had just uncovered new evidence that implicated me— my photo appeared onscreen—and the police were now investigating his death as a homicide which I might have premeditated. Lauren appeared on camera with CDC director Levering, who had obviously become one of the Friends, by her side. She said sadly, "This came as a great shock to us. Dr. Perry was a valued member of our team, but recently had begun showing signs of severe paranoia and even mental instability. We counseled her to get treatment, but she grew angry and has gone missing, perhaps taking toxic materials." The newsman emphasized I was dangerous. Anyone having contact with me should call a special number. I could only be handled safely by CDC's highly trained hazmat personnel.

We all sat stunned. Particularly Fernando and Maggie. Stalwart Justinia looked at her cousins, saying, "I can tell you two things for certain: I have known this woman for nine years, and I know that accusation is total bullshit."

That was all Fernando and Maggie needed to hear. They would stand by us. Maggie quickly located a partly furnished rental house on Rigby Street in her neighborhood. The owner was one of *her* cousins. Seemed there were a lot of "cousins" in this tight-knit community. Most were beneficent, and when Maggie made it a cash deal, the owner definitely asked no questions. He never even saw our faces.

Lilly accepted our new surroundings with her usual stoicism, though she was disappointed there weren't any books. Justinia promised to bring all Lilly might want from the library. I warned Justinia that she'd need a wheelbarrow.

Naturally I wanted to go straight to authorities, tell the whole, true story, but we all understood I wouldn't know who to trust in the local police or FBI. Or even the Atlanta press.

And even if I found a sympathetic ear, my proof had been destroyed. I just had my word.

"And mine," Katie volunteered eagerly. What a great kid. Then she said, "We can show 'em all those amazing plants at the McAlistair farm—"

"Which the Friends at Ashton may have removed or cut down and plowed over," Eric cautioned. "We have no idea how many townspeople are infected by now. Most want to keep it secret—and they're seriously smart."

Justinia asked me, "What about that sample of the virus from Dr. Hutcherson?"

I'd thought of that as proof, but finding a way to demonstrate it still required finding someone who would believe me to begin with.

We all sat silently. Feeling stumped. Then suddenly Eric laughed. We all looked at him. "You know what I'd do?" He focused on me with all seriousness. "Forget the locals. Call *The New York Times*."

I stared at him. And realized I certainly had nothing to lose.

I actually managed to reach a journalist there who listened intently to my story, but when he heard that my phone containing the proof had been lost, he politely suggested I call the *National Enquirer*.

Undaunted, I tried the *Wall Street Journal*, then the *Daily Beast*, CNN, and others, but all treated me like a conspiracy theory nutcase. Finally I realized what was going on: Lauren.

It was indeed confirmed much later that the renowned, respected Dr. Lauren Fletcher, who'd had very deep involvements with top people at virtually all national news outlets over many years and had become "the voice of the CDC," told Director Levering to set up an urgent mass conference call—as they'd often done in the past. On that call the two of them alerted the media that some would likely get a call from "sadly disturbed, delusional Dr. Perry." They should "report it to the CDC, but otherwise dismiss her ravings."

I was frustrated beyond measure. Forced to stay underground, living as a fugitive.

Eric, however, could remain aboveboard and needed to stay in Atlanta for his treatments, so Maggie found him a place on nearby Fort Street. He bravely volunteered to secretly help shelter the runaway, Katie.

Eric was looking unwell; we knew he had to continue the regimen of trial meds at the CDC.

Eric Tenzer...

That meant I'd be face-to-face with Hutch, who was now one of them. I'd have to convince him that my only interest was in saving my own life or at least continuing to teach for as long as I was able. I'd have to casually brush off any suggestion that I was in contact with Susan or Katie.

That was a daunting challenge; I'd never been a very good liar. But Susan pointed out that Hutch *also* had a very strong personal stake in having the speculative HIV treatment prove successful: the unique med was now Hutch's baby. If I was among those cured, it'd be a boon for Hutch, too.

So the next morning I took a deep breath and went to Hutch's CDC office. To my surprise he seemed very much the same guy, though a bit more energetic. I thought it wise and most natural for *me* to bring up Susan's name and express concern about her. Hutch professed what seemed genuine sadness and hoped her situation would resolve positively. But he was entirely focused on shepherding the clinical trial to a successful, lifesaving conclusion. With an enigmatic smile Hutch said, "In the last twenty-four hours I've had what might be a breakthrough insight, Eric." I knew that was probably because his brainpower had been amplified by the comet's virus. Hutch added, "I've further modified the medication. Let's get you going, man!"

I took that newest treatment, thanked him, then left the CDC, aware that I was walking a very dangerous tightrope. Yet the first thing I did was find a pay phone and call the throwaway cell Fernando had given to Susan. I knew she and Katie were worried about me.

Katie McLane...

I don't know what I would've done without Eric, who began home-schooling me around the substitute teaching job his friend in the school district arranged for him.

But having to stay almost entirely inside was hard for me—and for Susan and Lilly, too—but we had to take care that nobody would recognize us. The only time I'd go out was to hurry through a back alley to their place. We also changed our hair colors. Mine went from honey blonde to muddy brown. Because my ringlets were so distinctive, we decided they ought to go. They'd always kinda annoyed me, but when Susan cut them off, and I saw this brunette pixie in the mirror, I got tears in my eyes. Because, like, where was Katie? I didn't recognize myself. Then I said, "Well duh, Kate. Isn't that the idea?" I sucked it up and rubbed my tears away. Still it was weird. I felt a heavy lump inside my chest. Susan gave me a long supportive hug. By the time Maggie bought some brown contact lenses to cover my blue eyes and added some really awful thick-rimmed glasses, I wasn't sure my own parents would recognize me.

My parents. God. Thinking about them made tears well up again and the lump in my chest hotter and heavier. I took a breath and determined to shake the feeling off. But I couldn't quite.

Eric always understood, bless his heart. One evening about two weeks into my hiding at his place, he seemed very sad, and I was able to return his kindness a little. I encouraged him to tell me what was wrong. He sighed.

It was an anniversary: that same night three years earlier he had lost the love of his life to the disease he was now fighting. His longtime partner, Jeremy, had suffered chronic, severe pain from fibromyalgia, and he'd become addicted to opioids. While away on a business trip, the pain became excruciating. Jeremy couldn't get enough prescription meds and resorted to heroin. The needle wasn't clean. He unknowingly contracted HIV and transmitted it to Eric. Jeremy was heartbroken with guilt. Though many with HIV/AIDS were living successfully, using the standard treatments, thousands did still die. Eric and Jeremy had entered the CDC clinical trial together, but Jeremy succumbed. Eric said his own chances didn't seem very good, either. But his far greater sadness was losing his beloved husband.

We sat silently on the couch, holding hands in the growing darkness, leaning on each other.

Dr. Susan Perry...

By early October, a month into our sequestration, we could see that living in hiding was weighing heavily on Katie. Meanwhile I had faced the dangerous challenge of determining whom I could trust and had been reaching out with utmost caution to my very closest scientific colleagues. It was extremely tricky: when explaining the surreal situation, I had to emphasize that yes, the Friends might offer them the tantalizing opportunity to have their intelligence exponentially boosted, but their humanity, compassion, and morality would be correspondingly lessened or lost entirely. I impressed upon them that if we didn't work together—secretly and quickly—to find an antidote to this growing epidemic, then humankind would very likely go into a perilous downward spiral.

Simone Frederick...

My husband, Clarence, hadn't said much about the goings on at his chemical/pharma plant, but by late October the subtle changes I'd noticed in local and state government became more obvious. Working for eighteen years in the capitol building as press liaison in Georgia's Office of Public Information, I'd developed a clear idea of what was "normal." I'd had ample opportunity to observe the current governor and his staff as well as the state senate and house members and the nine justices on Georgia's supreme court. Even if I hadn't always liked every government worker personally, I'd respected each of them as elected officials eager to promote legitimate democracy and inclusiveness.

Governor Stanton was a good man. Though a fellow Democrat, he had been a tad too populist and right of center for my personal taste, and for that of many people across the state and country. But the governor had basic integrity; he was a white male who was committed to diversity and had good intentions, as did his press secretary and his male Hispanic lieutenant governor who was a moderate Republican. Our secretary of state and attorney general were both very popular

black women. The supreme court justices were equally diverse in gender
and ethnicity, but just as contentious as ever. The senate majority and
minority leaders were usually appropriately, sometimes laughingly, at
each other's throats. Up until that late October.

That's when the climate in the capitol chilled unexpectedly. In
retrospect, I'd swear that it started with the governor himself. Over a
couple of weeks he started sliding toward, and then adopting, *intensely*
"Georgia first" ideas. Some of them were very stern. Some even appeared
unethically self-serving. I had no idea why it was happening. Or why
the governor's immediate underlings, usually strongly opinionated,
were suddenly following him like lemmings. Why were these people
in important leadership positions across the strata of our state and
local government, including even our formerly unifying Atlanta police
chief, altering their longtime behavior? Why were so many politicians of
vastly different stripes suddenly *agreeing* to adopt and promote so many
restrictive, authoritarian measures—like almost doubling the size of the
city police force and the Georgia State Patrol?

Watching and analyzing carefully, I began to think it had something to do with the influence of a strong yet understated presence of
someone who seemed to radiate quietly confident power as he moved
through the capitol.

A man named Bradford Howell Mitchell.

Dr. R. W. Hutcherson...

When I was captured at the Everett chemical plant back on that
night in September, they'd texted Lauren at the church about how they
should handle me. She texted back to give me the full-blown CAV-A,
later telling me she'd always planned to do so eventually. She'd already
carefully researched my history and my published articles. She'd assessed
my native intellect and personality during a few long private meals.
She'd concluded I'd be a powerful asset and ally. She later admitted
another factor had been a certain personal attraction. After I was given

"the gift," Lauren often allowed me into her inner circle. I thus had the firsthand, highly educational experience of watching Mitchell work, manipulate, and maneuver. It was downright amazing.

As a military man, he'd labored hard for his country, but rarely received the full commendation or remuneration he felt entitled to. Worse, he'd been busted from lieutenant colonel back to major, angrily quit the service, and got into the private security black-ops business.

Then came his accidental exposure to the virus when his security people came across one of the meteorite areas, and he'd eaten an infected plum. With his brainpower enhanced he'd easily navigated the new roads that opened up before him. He analyzed all his options, then astutely resolved to maximize his command and control of the vast gold mine he'd stumbled upon. Taking the virus to Dr. Lauren Fletcher was a masterstroke. He'd researched her and recognized not only her brilliance as a biologist, but also her vaunted ambition and a drive to conquer that mirrored his own. Once self-infected with CAV-A, she was an ideal compatriot.

She quickly developed the secondary virus, CAV-B, which was the cornerstone of their burgeoning empire. Lauren, in turn, recognized that Mitchell had given her the opportunities to excel and thus achieve her lofty position in the Friends' hierarchy. So in spite of her heady dominance over others, Lauren was always deferential to Mitchell. He expected no less.

I learned that ever since childhood, Mitchell had steeped himself in the study of history, warfare, and particularly subversion. With the CAV-A he gained instantaneous connection to absolutely everything he'd ever read, heard, or seen, which was immense. And he never stopped adding to his knowledge. He continually devoured more histories, essays, journals—not just on warfare but also treatises on human psychology, mob mentality, biographies of leaders and dictators both successful and not. He was steeped in everything pertaining to the assumption and most advantageous uses of *power*.

I saw him quote offhandedly from Machiavelli's *The Prince*, from Sun Tzu's *The Art of War*, or from *Infantry Attacks*, the 1937 book on tank warfare by Field Marshal Rommel, the Desert Fox. Mitchell noted to me with humor how General Patton had been able to defeat Rommel's seemingly invincible panzer tank division in North Africa simply because Patton had read Rommel's book.

Mitchell could also quote poetically from T.E. Lawrence's *Seven Pillars of Wisdom*, which gave insights into Lawrence's brilliance at using the prejudices of one Arabian tribe against another or bending them to unify.

Mitchell spoke knowingly about specific military strategies, such as those employed by Wellington against Napoleon, or Sir Francis Drake sending eight burning ships into the Calais harbor, forcing the Spanish Armada to cut loose their anchors and sail haphazardly into the Channel, where the long guns of the English fleet decimated them. He could quote and draw insights from Churchill's private letters to FDR, employ Lincoln's humorous backwoods storytelling, or intellectually crush someone with the icy calm of a Stalin or a Putin.

Mitchell could dissect with surgical precision the strategies that won great battles. From the Spartans' defeat of the Athenians at Syracuse in 413 BC, to the victory of Henry V's far-outnumbered archers at Agincourt in 1415, to D-day in 1944.

Mitchell could not only dazzle with his ability to recall and quote such a legion of historical figures, but he took maximum advantage of his new brainpower to cherry-pick and utilize all their various techniques. He never slept more than three or four hours a night, never wasted a spare moment, but studied and absorbed every aspect of covert and subversive warfare both physical and mental.

Mitchell also had a remarkable ability to assess his audience astutely, whether they were a thousand or an individual, as though he could see right into their heads, and their minds were books easily opened and read, my own included. And Mitchell had that singular, masterful ability, unique among the most successful diplomats, politicians, and snake-oil salesmen, of making whomever he was talking to feel as though they were absolutely the most important group or person in the world to him. At least at that moment.

While listening to a person one-on-one, Mitchell successfully projected the impression that he was carefully considering every aspect of that person's thought or idea and sincerely appreciated them sharing it with him, even if it was completely idiotic. There were times I could barely keep a straight face as we listened to some imbecile had I not been buttressed by Mitchell's powerfully convincing false sincerity.

All these abilities, this knowledge, this insight, these talents coming together in an individual with unbridled ambition and driven to unimagined heights by the effect of the virus created a perfect storm of dominating ego. Mitchell was neither insane nor maniacal nor delusional. So convinced was he of his own instincts, based upon the vast treasure trove of knowledge he'd amassed on the subject of successful domination, that once he had made a decision or taken a course of action, he rarely wavered but generally doubled down.

Like Reverend Abraham Brown, Mitchell was over six feet and had an imposing presence, dominating the rooms he entered. He believed he had an irresistible magnetic aura, his "magnetismus" as he half jokingly referred to it—noting that the Nazi Rommel described Hitler as possessing that attribute—which drew people in to be snared if Mitchell chose. Which he usually did. In Mitchell's own mind—and with the magnificent assistance of the virus perhaps in truth—Mitchell believed he was simply destined to become everyone's supreme overlord.

He might have become as compelling an orator as Cicero, Mark Antony, Hitler, or our own Dr. Brown, but Mitchell preferred to work far more subtly. He felt his strongest suit was to be the man *behind* the curtain, the puppet master, the power behind the throne, who secretly—and with enjoyment—moved people and events in the pattern of his choosing.

Mitchell was incredibly shrewd in his overall game plan. He started at the top of each pyramid of power, with the upmost echelons of state and local government, so the ball—the CAV-B virus—would roll easily and unquestioningly downhill, working the tendrils of Mitchell's control into the existing societal fabric. He was an extreme populist. Many of the elected officials in Georgia had avowed that same sentiment before the comet's arrival, as had a number of other states and even the nation. Such populist nationalism was also on the rise in Russia, France, Germany, Holland, Austria, and important parts of Asia. But in Mitchell's opinion their notion of populism was only half-baked and not nearly as strident as the worldview he envisioned. He intended to start arranging things more to his liking and began right here in his home state.

It was fascinating to watch Mitchell manipulate government leaders the way my uncle's ranch dog could work a herd of sheep. Mitchell also lassoed media bigwigs like the owner and managing editor of the *Journal-Constitution*, and local captains of various industries like Jefferson Boswell, Angelo Perini, or Murray Grenwald. They all fell right into line after they'd been unknowingly dosed with the CAV-B. Amazed by the increased intelligence they'd been gifted with, the receivers of the CAV-B virus—whom the Friends referred to as the B's—all instinctively understood their status as being secondary and answerable to the secret society of the Friends. They also understood that a goodly portion of their future profits would be tithed, but that was okay because they'd be making multimillions more now. Tantalizing hope was also held out that any of the B's who performed well enough might be elevated to the elite CAV-A status of the Friends.

Mitchell had the usual power broker contingent of aides and security personnel headed by a tough-as-nails former black-ops Ranger master sergeant, a shaved-headed bull of a man, named Elia Dubrovski. But his chief advisor and confidant was Dr. Lauren Fletcher. While she didn't attempt to match Mitchell's manner or charisma and was customarily aloof, she was more than a match for him in potent intelligence. They were an extreme power couple. Their public relationship was exceedingly professional, and whatever personal side there may have been was kept tightly under wraps, although I certainly had suspicions from the get-go. If they were intimately involved, however, it was definitely not exclusive, at least on Lauren's part, I learned. Pleasantly.

In addition to being a compadre to Mitchell and Lauren, my own newfound mental brilliance was enabling me to achieve startling advancements in medicine and epidemiology that would help humankind. It seemed very likely that my first triumph would be the HIV/AIDS protocol that Lauren had handed off to me and to which I made groundbreaking modifications. The clinical trial Eric Tenzer was part of was particularly promising. Obviously, a success might bring deservedly large financial rewards, but I convinced myself that would be merely a collateral gift.

On a personal level, I felt for the first time in my life that I was completely liberated from all past insecurities. I now possessed an unparalleled confidence—that I was not only one of the grown-ups in any room, but one of the very best. Lauren's enhanced IQ might still top mine ever so slightly, but otherwise I was equal to or surpassing in intelligence everyone else I encountered. Even Mitchell. It was a tremendous rush. I reveled in it.

And I felt mighty pleased with myself, how I'd risen to become one of the MVPs on what I then knew was clearly the winning team.

18

PRIVATE LIVES

Dr. Susan Perry...

Lilly was generally very stoic, but she'd been accustomed to us taking a daily afternoon walk and began to feel extreme anxiety being inside all the time. To keep us both from going stir-crazy in our secret hideaway, Lilly and I occasionally ventured carefully outside. I kept us as incognito as possible. Our auburn hair was dyed mouse brown, pulled back under baseball caps, and we wore sunglasses. We usually just walked the neighborhood or sometimes took a bus. I didn't risk driving and being pulled over for even a minor infraction. Lilly, of course, could recite the entire city bus schedule. Each time one wheezed to a stop, Lilly would check her watch and nod. "R-right on time."

Under the tightening influence and surreptitious supervision of the Friends, the state and local government had everything working more efficiently. I knew that was logical: bipartisan efforts happen more often and effectively when people from both parties are on the same secret side. A majority of the public were as approving as Lilly. But others were fearful of where and how our society was being led. By early December I had collected a number of such people. The first were a handful of scientific colleagues who helped me set up a modest chem lab in the family room and kitchen of our funky rental house. Eric was uneasy about it. He was still getting his HIV treatments twice a week and fearful of us all being discovered. But we knew we had to search for a way to stop the cancer-like creep of the Friends' behind-the-scenes domination. With careful vetting of newcomers, we gained more scientific colleagues, and our house became a gathering place for other dissidents as well.

Chunhua Lee, a five-foot-two powerhouse with degrees from Beijing's Tsinghua University and Columbia who'd previously worked at the CDC, was our resident electrical whiz. She'd dismantled a complex Axio Scope.A1 Polarized Light Microscope on the kitchen counter, where she and pale, gangly young Princeton biochemist Alex Farquar were trying to repair it.

Chunhua had brought several sympathizers into our group including her Columbia pal Nate Balfour, a stocky, midforties journalist for the *Journal-Constitution*. Nate wore 1970s-style aviator glasses, had a bushy Afro, a low tolerance for idiots, and machine-gun-fast speech. He was poking through our refrigerator, chattering with disappointment, "Jesus, you guys, this is all bunny food. I just quit smokin'. I need a nummie."

Alex reluctantly opened a lower cabinet, revealing a crumpled bag of peanut butter cookies. Seeing my surprise, Alex shrugged sheepishly. "Forgot I had 'em."

"Oh, sure." I smirked, reaching for one, but Nate intercepted the bag.

"Me first!"

"Whoa," I blurted. "You turning into an A?"

"Lemme tell you something, Suse," Nate said rapid-fire as he pulled out a cookie, "the day I turn into one of those *A*-holes, you can pull the cookie bag over my head and call the firing squad."

Alex, whose manner was mild and precise, asked, "So what exactly did they say at your paper?"

"Okay," Nate said as he chomped the cookie, stepping away from the fridge, which Lilly quietly reopened to restore everything to perfect order. "So the publisher called everybody together today? Smarmy bugger, I didn't like him *before* he sucked the comet, but least back then he left us alone to—"

"Nate, tell us what the hell he said," Chunhua prodded.

"Okay, okay." Nate flopped onto our seedy, threadbare couch. "He was unofficially discouraging any articles about *some people* that might be perceived as overly critical." Nate leered. "The sonuvabitch told us, 'that sort of writing wouldn't be constructive for our changing society.'"

"So they're getting more overt about censorship. Shit." I paced, glancing at Eric, who had an uncomfortable expression while correcting homework in a battered Lincoln rocker. "I'm sorry. This must be awkward for you sometimes."

Eric shook his head. "You know I'm in your corner, Suse."

"But on the other hand, you might not still be *alive* if it wasn't for them."

Eric drew a breath. We all knew that his need for the Friends' experimental medication was tugging against his innate sense of what was right.

"But you can't let 'em off the hook for all the *other* crap they're tryin' to pull, Eric," Nate said, pointing with another cookie. "And if the erosion of the First Amendment at newspapers ain't enough for ya, how about this one: our local NBC station is dropping *Saturday Night Live*."

Jimmy-Joe Hartman…

Right around New Year's I wuz standin' kinda dumbstruck in the dinin' room of Poppa's old cheapo South Atlanta house. I been lookin' at a sciency book with all kinda math e-quations I couldn't make hide nor hair of. It wuz one of a stack that Poppa'd been readin'. My poppa Joseph, who was a damn *janitor* at the CDC. Dumb shit that I wuz, it'd took me almost a couple months to figure out what wuz goin' on with him. I'd heard a buzz on the street 'bout some kinda brain-booster drug come down from that comet, but you hear so much weird-ass conspiracy horseshit, I didn't pay no 'tention. Till it wuz right there in my face! "So this stuff is *real*?" I wuz plenty pissed. "Why the hell didn't you *tell* me, Poppa?!"

He didn't even look up from the thick book he wuz turnin' the pages of, readin' superfast. "Not important, son."

"Not *important*!?" I sputtered, lookin' at my sister, Claire, who'd just come in from her hospital. "Did you know 'bout this?" She didn't say nothin', but her face was a giveaway. "You *did*! How long? Over a month?!" Her face stayed froze. "Thanks, Claire! What a fuckin' family."

"Stop that talk." Poppa looked up, firm-like. "It's not important."

"Not—" I laughed out loud. "What planet you livin' on, ol' man!?"

Claire snapped like a switchblade. "Don't speak to your father like that!"

"You one of them special ones I heard tell about, Pop? On the damn A-team, or whatever, and that ain't *important*?!"

"Not to me, son. Not to Jesus, neither."

I sniveled. "Well, Jesus ain't around t'appreciate all y'can get from it."

"James Joseph," Poppa said religious-like, "it's easier for a camel to pass through the eye of a needle than for a rich man to enter the kingdom of heaven."

"Amen, Poppa," Claire said quietly, pattin' his old shoulder.

I seen I wuzn't makin' no headway, so I switched gears, chillin' back. "Yeah, 'kay. Amen, Poppa." I got all calm-like, set down beside him. "You know what it is, Pop? You wuz raised so po-white that you got used to just takin' the scraps. But you don't have to do that no more." Poppa looked back at his book. "How'd it happen, anyway?"

He let out a sad little sigh. "Wudn't my idea, son."

"Why'd they do it to ya?" No answer. I leaned closer. "What's it feel like?"

He kept readin' his book, shaked his head a mite. "Not good."

"Probably just takes some gettin' used to, huh?" Still no answer, so I said real soft, kinda smilin', "But Poppa, bless your heart, now that you *are* one of 'em, can't you help me to—"

"James Joseph." Poppa closed his book. "Son." He looked in my eyes. "Let it go."

I jumped up. "Don't start in with that 'let go, let God' bullshit!" Claire grabbed at me to stop, but I steamed right on. "I don't want no fuckin' hereafter! I want the here and now! Want my brain boosted! Want the *perks*!"

"What you *want*," Claire said real low and deadly, "is some *humility*. Like your poppa."

I yelled at her, "What I *want*, Miss Goody-Fuckin'-Two-Shoes, is some God damn *respect*!"

"Well," Poppa said quietly, "y'never gonna get it by takin' his name in vain."

"But I'm gonna get it." I wuz hotter'n a pistol. "You'll see!" I bashed the front screen door open and steamed off down the sidewalk.

Dr. Susan Perry…

By early January 2021, our ragtag team had grown to over twenty dedicated scientists, some were still working at their regular jobs while secretly moonlighting here. Others had gone underground full-time like I'd had to. Our fledgling lab facilities had spilled out into the ramshackle two-car garage and now included some more sophisticated pieces of bootlegged equipment. In addition to physical experimentation, we were all convinced the Friends must have some Achilles' heel, so we constantly brainstormed, theorizing on the best biological avenues for exploration that might lead to some viable antidote.

Katie was reading in one corner of our piecemeal living room. Though staying at Eric's small place, she'd started biking quickly through back alleyways to do her studying where she wouldn't be alone so much. I was at a table, doing research by digging into Lilly's magical memory of the CDC library. As usual Lilly poured out information faster than I could write it.

"Wait, wait, not so fast, Lilly," I said, beleaguered. "*What* date?"

She was watching a documentary about dolphins with the sound muted as she rattled off flatly, "August, '92. *Bio-science Journal*, Kristenson, Anna B., 'The proto-incubation period of tested retro viruses was *not* vector related, but *did* correspond to varied sequencing of ASN, PHE, GLY, LEU,' and *Trust the F-Friends*, and there's also—"

"Wait." I blinked. "Stop. What was that?"

Lilly tipped her frizzy head toward the TV. "I saw 'Tr-trust the Friends.'"

"What?"

"Yeah," Lilly said, glancing away. She never looked into anyone's eyes, even mine. I rewound the DVR, then pressed play and watched as a dolphin swam toward the camera.

"There." Lilly pointed. "'Trust the F-Friends.'"

I'd had a frustrating day. My patience was thin. "What're you talking about? I didn't see anything."

Lilly picked up her iPad to start a video game. "It's th-there."

I rewound the DVR again, then clicked it forward frame by frame—and sure enough there came a single frame where "Trust the Friends" was faintly superimposed over the grinning dolphin. I felt a chill, staring at it for a moment. "Lil, you really *are* exceptional."

"Uh-huh," Lilly mumbled, engrossed in her video game.

I stared at the frozen video frame, imagining what other subliminal messages the unaware public was being brainwashed with. It hardened my resolved to fight them.

Then I heard the secret knock announcing a compatriot outside the door.

Through the peephole I saw it was Eric, with a peculiarly profound expression on his face. I opened the door. He was carrying a small bouquet of daisies. His smile seemed forced and his manner subdued. I was immediately concerned, but didn't want to press.

Katie had also spotted the strange expression on his face and worried aloud, "Eric? What's wrong?"

Eric remained silent for a moment. He seemed in a state of combined anxiety and confusion. My first fearful thought was that he had been infected with the CAV-B or had been compromised. Or we all had. He took three daisies from his bouquet and handed one to each of us, smiling wistfully. "You know, daisies have become my favorite flower. So simple." He breathed a very long sigh. "It's too bad more people can't be confronted with the possibility of an early death, because it makes you grasp at life more than ever."

I barely found enough voice to question, "Eric . . . ?"

He went on, "'When a man knows he's to be hanged in a fortnight—'"

Without looking up Lilly flatly completed the quote, "'It concentrates his mind wonderfully.' Dr. Samuel Johnson, London, seventeenth of September, 1777."

Eric swallowed, very emotional. He whispered, "Exactly right, Lilly. As always."

Katie was really concerned. She took his hand. "Eric, is it the AIDS?"

He looked at us, paused with his eyes brimming. He was barely able to speak. "Yes."

Katie and I both drew a breath, fearing the worst. Eric said, "They developed a cure. Hutch. The Friends . . . I'm cured."

We stared at him as his tears spilled over. Katie hugged him tightly. "Oh, Eric!"

Lilly was impassive, but I immediately joined Katie at Eric's side and pressed my cheek against his. "I'm so happy for you." But if Eric had seen my face, he would have seen my very mixed emotions. Of course I was happy for him and for everyone with the horrible disease, but I also knew this new triumph for the Friends would bring an even deeper acceptance of their shadow leadership.

And it did. Only a few weeks later at a special convening of the Nobel Institute in Stockholm, we watched on TV as Bradford Mitchell and the Reverend Dr. Abraham Brown looked on proudly, though Hutch watched stone-faced, while Dr. Lauren Fletcher received the coveted Nobel Prize in Chemistry. In her acceptance she publicly thanked her CDC colleagues, including Dr. R.W. Hutcherson and other . . . friends—she clearly enjoyed using that code word—who had "contributed so meaningfully to her triumphal achievement over this dreadful disease." That brought strong applause. She then announced, "The AIDS cure is already being manufactured in immense quantity by Everett Biochemical, a BioTeck Industries Company, for immediate sale worldwide at a surprisingly low cost and will be supplied to many poverty-stricken third-world countries at absolutely no charge."

That brought the black-tie audience, representing the world community, to its feet. They gave Lauren a thunderous ovation. And though that audience didn't know it, their praise extended to all Lauren's growing number of secret Friends and "worker B's."

Clarence Frederick...

Since Rupert Green was executive secretary of the BioTeck board and moved in loftier circles than I, I'd only encountered him a couple of times in social situations. The last was at that Ashton High football game. At times like that, we only spoke for a moment. Never about company business.

But after the Nobel ceremony his office sent word that he wanted a personal walk-through of the Everett Biochemical plant where I was VP and the HIV/AIDS cure was in production.

My wife, Simone, personally approved my tie that morning, otherwise I was in what she called my uniform: one of my low-key three-piece suits—that day a gray pinstripe—and a pair of wingtips. I liked to think my careful grooming and general demeanor attested to the fact that I was a conservative man. That I was earnestly determined to keep Everett operating smoothly and upper management pleased. My track record at the plant was so solid and reliable that Green and his Friends had not offered me CAV-B, nor did I ask them to do so. My eagerness to serve was already a matter of long record. I felt relatively confident that I could continue along my career path until retirement in another ten years or so. I say "relatively" because I can be a worrier.

I fell squarely in the keep-your-head-down, nose-to-the-grindstone category, as did many middle-class, middle-of-the-road people like myself. I was pleased with the new attention that my plant was receiving and the modest financial bonus I'd been given. My chewed thumbnail was actually healing up.

When Rupert Green arrived in my office with his two assistants on the day of his tour, he found a lightly toasted poppy seed bagel with cream cheese awaiting him. My research had determined his favorite. He was pleased. Of course, I had a small selection of other bagels for his attendants.

I had been showing Mr. Green the new construction designed to increase the plant's output. As we came out from one of the concrete buildings and through a stand of stainless steel pipes, I saw ahead of us two women who had arrived to join the expedition. They were conversing outside one of the noisy heat converter units: three stories of pipes, junctions, and filters. Like ourselves, they were wearing yellow hard hats, which clashed considerably with their clothing. Dr. Lauren Fletcher was typically elegant in a tailored navy blue suit. I didn't know the other woman who was middle-aged, Hispanic, and wore a dress Simone would've liked with a tiny print of pink roses. She stood solidly with a thoroughly professional air, chatting confidently with Dr. Fletcher.

One odd thing that surprised me was how Mr. Green's corporate leadership persona instantly melted away as soon as we caught sight of them. He became subservient, meek, toward Dr. Fletcher. As though he were considerably inferior.

Mr. Green smiled, even bowed slightly, as we approached them. He said to me, "Nobel laureate Dr. Fletcher you know, of course, as does the world." I greeted her. "And this is Shelly Navarro, a brilliant biochemist that we've been lucky enough to lure away from her sterling work with the school district. She's going to oversee production here at Everett."

I'd heard through the grapevine that I might be getting some sort of new supervisor, which was worrisome. I'd quietly enjoyed my position at the top of the Everett organizational chart since our president had just resigned over some hush-hush conflict with the BioTeck board. I'd been hoping to be promoted to his job. Nonetheless I greeted her cordially, "Ms. Navarro."

I was rewarded by a warm handshake and smile. "Oh, Shelly, please." But her intonation expressed that I should always remember she was Ms. Navarro.

Shelly Navarro...

When Clarence Frederick turned his attention back to Lauren, he missed my careful assessment of him. I'd never had much patience for men or interest in personal involvements, but many intriguing new ideas and horizons were opening up to me since I'd eaten the strawberries and achieved some corporate power.

Getting involved with the Friends, which led to this prestigious Everett job and the stock options that accompanied it, had also provided a welcome uptick on my financial future.

VIA BioTeck Industries SEES [Secure Encrypted Email Server]
From: Clarence Frederick [Sr. VP Everett Biochemical Div]
To: Rupert Green [Exec Sec, BA Board], Shelly Navarro [Sr. Everett Prod Mgr]
Date: 02/27/21 09:27PM
Subject: Current Profit Analysis, AIDS Vaccine

Dear Mr. Green and Ms. Navarro,

Again, let me say what a pleasure it was to escort the two of you around Everett last week. Per your request, please see the attached 7-page PDF detailing the most recent P&L status on the HIV/AIDS vaccine. As you will see from the thorough analytical review that I've conducted, the net profit income is nothing short of staggering. The worldwide demand for the vaccine is so overwhelming that—even at the extremely reduced price we decided upon—our profit margin vs R & D costs is an astounding 1,747 percent.

That of course does not include the enormous international public relations value, which has skyrocketed the market value of Everett's and BioTeck Industries' stock through the roof. I'm hoping that our stockholders—particularly the principals, including Dr. Fletcher, Mr. Mitchell, Rev. Brown, and of course yourselves—are pleased.

Personally, I am extraordinarily gratified to have been helpful in this venture, and I assure you that all of us here at Everett will continue to serve BioTeck Industries and our Friends in every way beneficial to our cause.

Respectfully,
Clarence Frederick
SVP Everett Biochemical
A BioTeck Industries Company

Courtesy FBI, Clarence Frederick

Dr. R. W. Hutcherson...

Dominance in sexuality increasingly became a key issue in our personal lives. Some of us A's sought equally dominant mates because of their matching intelligence and common drives. But that also meant that sex between us could take on an aggressive, competitive nature, even pushing pleasure to the very brink of ecstatic pain. Lauren and I ultimately became that kind of pairing, though our relationship took several months to fully mount up.

Lauren later told me how she'd been attracted right off by my "smarts and Montana cowboy looks." *Well shucks, thank you kindly, ma'am.* She admitted how she'd carefully set out to gain my allegiance by moving in measured increments. I'd seen plenty of wolves do that out on the plains. She also knew Susan and I'd had a thing. And that I looked like a shitkicker all right, but I was nobody's fool. She never said it, but I was pretty sure she thought since I'd gotten the gift, my mental chops were right up there, close to rivaling her own.

I felt her vibe from that first night I got dosed, but for quite a spell I held out hopes that Susan would reconsider, come back onto the reservation, take the virus herself, and join me among the Friends. But as weeks went by without Susan returning, my focus slowly shifted. I was plenty aware that the world had changed and so had I. For the far better.

I had diminishing patience with folks who weren't A's. I felt evermore entitled to what Reverend Brown kept repeating was our destiny because of our natural superiority. It was seductive, made a guy pretty heady to know how smart and savvy he was, how he could think circles around most everyone he came across—even a lot of the other A's. Some of 'em were übermoral or religious types who let that inbred superstitious dogma hold 'em back from being all they could've been. But I was wise enough to know there'd always be a bell curve, a spectrum of personalities and of natural drives even among the Friends. All the Friends were leaders, yes; all relatively equal, more or less; but a lucky few of us knew that we were definitely on the *more* side.

Lauren and Mitchell wisely drew me into their highest inner circle, invited my ideas, and received 'em with the gratitude and respect they sure as hell deserved. That's what led to me going a giant step past Lauren's work on the HIV cure and figuring how to make the sucker work.

Okay, so Lauren and me: I'd never been into older women, and she had a good dozen years on me, but I was increasingly flattered by this good-looking, brilliant woman who was also at the top of the power structure. When she carefully orchestrated the timing one night and invited my intimate favors, I readily capitulated.

I was pleased to discover that underneath those stylish duds was a silky, very well-cared-for body. And we were good together. That first time was like a couple of hot kids really getting it on in a barn loft. After that we got into some extremely sophisticated activities. We worked our way slowly and delectably through the entire *Kāma Sutra*. Our sexuality sometimes reminded me of my Montana rodeo days, only this time I was often the bull being ridden.

I realized, like so many others who got the gift, that it wasn't just my brainpower that had ramped way up; my sexual appetite and prowess had been increased exponentially by it also. Even the enjoyment and intensity of Lauren wasn't enough. I frequently sought and relished the pleasure of other women, being careful to keep such hookups from Lauren's attention. I was fairly certain that Lauren was also enjoying intimacy with Bradford Mitchell.

After that annoying Nobel ceremony, Mitchell had flown back to the States, leaving Lauren and me to handle the glad-handing afterward. I played my part, but was plenty ticked off by how she'd sucked up all the accolades for the HIV/AIDS cure. She nurtured the idea it had mostly been her doing and barely mentioned how I was the one who'd made the critical breakthrough. Would've been nice if she'd given me more credit, but totally in character that she hadn't.

When we got back to her suite overlooking the night-lights of Stockholm harbor, she was charged up more than I'd ever seen her and came on strong. She was unquenchable, and we had us one intense night even as my anger kept percolating higher and higher. Our back and forth encounter heated up volcanically to where she actually sank her teeth into my arm so deep that she drew blood. I slapped her. But she slugged me right back with her *fist* so damn hard I saw stars. We grabbed each other's shoulders and dug our fingers in deep and painfully, holding ourselves at arm's length with teeth bared, breathing hard and furious, neither giving an inch, fiery eyes glaring.

Ah, the private lives of our master race.

Security-Cam Video, Private Residential; Case 71743-AB; Date: 03/01/21 Time: 20:37:32

Address: 69 Granville Dr., Atlanta, GA 30318

Loc: Brown Estate Master Bedroom

Cams # 13, 14, 15

Transcript by: ATL PD-#65420

Visual Desc: Low light. Cam 13 shows wide view of master bedroom with Victorian furnishings, framed wall mirrors, small lights on night tables beside king-size four-poster bed. Cams 14, 15 show closer views of bed. On the bed on her back is young Asian American girl (name withheld; see case file), age 14 years, 7 months. A very thin sheet covers her but she is apparently nude beneath. One end of a silk scarf tied to her right wrist, the other end tied loosely to top right bedpost. She appears groggy. Drugs later found on premises: flunitrazepam (Rohypnol), also called roofies; gamma hydroxybutyric acid (GHB), also called liquid ecstasy; and ketamine, also called Special K. Collectively: Date rape drugs. Large nude male enters in silhouette from bathroom to right of bed. He moves into closer range of Cam 14. — Positive ID: Reverend Dr. Abraham Brown.

Courtesy ATL PD, FBI

Katie McLane...

Eric, Susan, and her growing group of scientists and sympathizers had all been wonderful to me. I loved 'em for treating me like family, but it didn't make up for the loss of my own. Or my best friend, Darren. A few times when I was feeling super homesick, I snuck out of Eric's at night and rode his bike through back streets over to the neighborhood where my dad lived with his girlfriend, Tina. I just sat in the tree-shadowed park across the street and looked at their house. Twice I saw him come home and get out of his car. I wanted so bad to go talk to him. I missed the dad he'd been, the dad I used to walk with, holding hands, my stable father who provided the solidity that my frazzled mother never could muster. But because he was infected with the virus now, I knew I couldn't. My eyes got all blurry as he went into the house. Sometimes I heard him shout at Tina, mad about something.

The final time I went was a whole lot scarier.

When I got to the park, I could see him inside through their bedroom window, yelling angrily at Tina. He grabbed at her. She shoved him hard and ran out of sight. Then through the living room window, I saw where he caught up to her really furiously. He ripped her shirt, and when she struggled, he slapped her hard. But Tina came right back at him with a brutal heel-palm to his nose that knocked him backward over a chair as she screamed at him, "What part of 'no' don't you understand?!"

He was dazed and trying to stand up, but she picked up a wine bottle, smashed it against the side of his head. He went down harder as she grabbed her coat and came blowing out the front door and down to her little Chevy Volt parked in front.

That's when I noticed another car farther up the street, behind Tina's back, start to roll forward. It was weird that the car's headlights were off. I watched it bear down the windy street and realized it was heading right toward Tina, who was standing beside her car, struggling with her keys.

I shouted, "Tina! Look out! *Look out!*"

She spun around, saw the danger at the last second, and dived onto the back of her Volt as the speeding car sideswiped the Chevy and sped away.

Tina slid off the back of her damaged car, very shaken, but looked over at me as I said, "Are you okay?"

With my brown pixie hair she didn't recognize me at first. ". . . Katie?"

I motioned her to be quiet, and she hurried over to the shadowy park, whispering, "Oh, honey. I've been so worried about you. Are *you* okay? What're you doing here?"

I glanced at the house to be sure my dad wasn't watching. "I just come to look sometimes."

She gave me a long hug. "Oh sweetheart, I'm so sorry about . . . everything." I knew she wasn't just talking about Dad being one of them, but also about him being with her. "Please tell me you're not living on the street. Do you need anything? Some money or—"

I told her I was all right, but not to tell my dad she'd seen me. She said she wouldn't be living there or even talking to him anymore. But something else was bothering me. "Tina . . . it all happened so fast that I can't be sure, but I thought that the driver of that car might have been—"

"Your mother." She nodded regretfully. "She tried something like this once before."

"Oh my God . . ."

"Yeah. It's awful. All of it. I don't know what the rest of us are gonna do."

"I'm with some really good people who're trying to figure it out."

She had fished out a card with her cell number on it. "Well, tell 'em to call me if I can help. And you for sure. Please. Twenty-four/seven." I nodded thanks and pulled my coat around me as she said, "Can I take you someplace, honey?"

"No, I'm good. But please be careful, Tina."

"You, too. And Katie"—she paused, pressed my hand—". . . thanks."

Our gazes held for a moment, then I headed quickly away across the dark park.

19

ADVANCEMENTS

Dr. Susan Perry...

From the beginning the Friends had been very shrewd. By early March the streets of Atlanta and other Georgia cities hadn't really seemed to change that much. Daffodils bloomed and people went about their daily lives more or less as usual. Like Reverend Brown had counseled, there had been no apparent usurpation of power, no startling Kristallnacht like Germany in 1938. The state government was simply "more unified" than ever in its history. They eased a lot of workplace regulations, so much that industries and manufacturing thrived, new operations came into Georgia. Yes, fewer regulations resulted in several disastrous incidents where tainted food made lots of people dangerously ill. Yes, fewer safety inspections led to workplace fires leaving many badly burned victims, or on-the-job accidents where others were permanently injured or even killed. But such incidents seemed to be dwindling in number—or at least reports of them were. Local news outlets became far more focused on bringing us cheerful, lightweight stories, and the really excellent news about how Georgia was quickly outpacing California and becoming the place to be as far as businesses were concerned.

My friend Nate and other journalists complained we were all facing death by a thousand tweets. It had become the go-to way of getting out anyone's message—whether true or false—with almost no pushback by more knowledgeable sources. Honest truth telling had been undercut by constant barrages of retweets from lawmakers, police, and other authorities. There was such a tsunami of social media blather, untrue "facts," and outright gaslighting that most of the unsuspecting public was completely confused about whom to trust and what exactly to believe. Antigovernment or antipolice messages got quickly scrubbed. Nate said a lie could fly around the whole state—or even the world—before the truth even got its shoes tied.

That was particularly true because some of the higher-ups in usually reliable media sources had secretly been corrupted by the CAV-B virus themselves. The most important dedicated reporters who did hold out and fought back got nasty threats. Many had been forced to leave their jobs, even go underground for their and their families' safety. Nate shared many articles and blogs with us that he and other journalists had put out on clandestine sites in an effort to counteract the generalized whitewashing of truth. But the Friends kept a weather eye out for all such "rogue" voices and often managed to crush them as soon as they were discovered. Worst of all, a few determined investigative reporters like Nate had "accidents." One died from a mysterious toxic substance.

But like the state's promo said: "The grass is greener in Georgia!" I knew that in parts of the state where comet fragments had fallen, the grass was literally greener. But most importantly there were *jobs*. That's what people cared about most. There were many new job opportunities and retraining programs for people who had been left behind the technological curve.

Many of the jobs were sparked by amazing inventions. Beyond the HIV/AIDS cure, Georgians had suddenly parented and patented startling innovations: Murray Grenwald's new hydrogen battery was more reliable than lithium-ion and cheaper; the Perini Compound—a Teflon-type substance—reduced friction to near the vanishing point, allowing the creation of ultra-efficient machinery like frictionless bearings. And those fostered the creation of lightweight turbines, which were set to revolutionize aircraft engines. There were even prototypes of automotive vehicles equipped with Perini turbines to let them go airborne. The Georgia State Patrol had begun equipping special squad cars with the turbines. They were called ARPCs, airborne recon patrol craft. The media also enthusiastically covered a new type of weaponry developed from Jefferson Boswell's startling invention of the JB Capacitor. Trade named El-Stat, it discharged a burst of electrostatic energy the size of a pea that could shock and disable a person. Handheld El-Stats were coming into police use. Larger versions capable of firing golf ball–sized charges that could disable a vehicle were being mounted on some of the GSP's Perini patrol cars.

And in an ever-so-friendly manner, the ranks of law enforcement personnel continued expanding. At first, most people didn't even realize that there were a lot more police around, and if they did, they'd say: "It's a good thing. Look how much calmer the streets are now. If only they'd been here before." Well, now they were. And playing rougher. All across the state.

Jimmy-Joe Hartman...

I seen that they was a lotta new cops, and they wuz crackin' down way harder, bustin' heads big-time ugly—and gettin' away wid it, too. But it didn't bother me none. I wuz street smart and knew how to dance right past them suckers. And I wuz always on the lookout for any cool new dealio that'd line my pockets. The moment I seen a new angle, I quick figured how to make it work fer yours truly.

So this one night I wuz scurryin' through a back alley in this pricey 'hood on the north side with this wiry black kid, Tyrone. We'd met up when we wuz both kids vacationin' in juvie. He liked cool-ass baggy gangsta threads and hoodies just like me. Tyrone sometimes gave me some crystal meth and other shit to resell. But that night we wuz after some waaaay better stuff. I said to him, "You really seen 'em, Ty?"

"Yeah, man!" Tyrone said. Them brown eyes o'his wuz flashin' with dollar signs. "They wuz these like incredible Godzilla tomatoes growin' in this old guy's garden."

"And he's one of the A's, huh?"

"Damn right," Tyrone said as we dodged round some trash cans. "Them tomatoes got the good stuff in 'em, man. C'mon up here." We stood up on a wooden crate to peer over a fence into the backyard of a fine lookin' house.

There wuz a little garden. Growin' in one corner wuz a tomato plant. One look at the gi-normous size o'them tomatoes got my heart hoppin'. Tyrone gimme this told-you-so look.

Five minutes later we wuz comin' round the alley corner on a dead run, breathin' hard, and laughin' our asses off. I grabbed at the tomato Tyrone was eatin'. "Gimme it, man! *Gimme!*" I took me a huge, sloppy bite. The red juice ran down my chin. I took a deep breath. I didn't feel nothin' special right that second, but it wuz the best damn tomato I ever tasted. "Yes! Man, this has gotta be it!"

"Fuckin' A, bubba." Ty took another big bite. I was lookin' into the plastic bag at the half dozen tomatoes we'd stole. I seen a gold mine.

"Gotta dry the seeds, man! We gonna grow our own! *Deal* this shit! You know what people'll pay?!" I wuz like exhil-i-arated. I slapped Ty a huge high-five, and we scurried off onto the dark street, totally stoked.

Simone Frederick...

As a state press liaison I was constantly moving through the halls and offices of our Atlanta capitol building. My suspicions about Bradford Mitchell's influence were increasingly confirmed. Governor Stanton maintained his smooth diplomatic external persona, his warm political smile, but many of us noticed a new aloofness. The governor, and one after another of his closest advisors, had developed an attitude of condescending superiority that was barely disguised behind the bright glow in their eyes. People who hadn't known them long wouldn't notice, but their change was clearly discernable to us who had. The private, often humorously knowing glances they shared between themselves underlined their airy, confident supremacy.

But it was equally clear how *their* superiority fell away abruptly whenever Bradford Mitchell and his entourage swept in. I was often in an office with Governor Stanton or one of his key staff when that happened. It was disturbing to see how they all, governor included, were quick to jump up to greet Mitchell or his inner circle. Of course I'd seen deep pocket contributors get fawned over by politicians seeking campaign cash. But this was different. This was body language from both quarters that bespoke exactly who was where on the totem pole.

Mitchell was square shouldered, imposing. But I noticed how those around him, even the governor, while not exactly bowing, tended to slouch, to make themselves seem slightly less than they really were. They'd lean deferentially toward him. It was clear who was subservient to whom.

Bradford Mitchell never leaned toward anyone.

Clarence Frederick...

Simone had that dark cloud over her head again, unaware that I had troubles of my own. She rambled on, worried that a "shadow government was undermining our democracy, that some kind of 'deep state' was turning our police into a quasi-military force," and so on. I was packing my carry-on while patiently listening.

"A couple of my colleagues tried to leak their impressions about this Mitchell business to the press," Simone said.

"Well, I don't approve of leaks, so—"

"Two days later they were gone. One was reassigned to the basement and the other fired. And not because the public heard about it, Clarence. It happened because the press people who received it *reported it back* to the governor's staff!"

"Well," I sighed, hoping to end her rant, brighten her mood. "Maybe we don't know the whole story. But I can tell you one thing, whatever's going on at the capitol, this state is having one of its most prosperous years ever. The plant's hired a bunch more new people and—"

"That's not the point!"

"It oughta be. Hey, you remember Akiyama, the manager of that Japanese plant like ours, who was strutting around the convention last year? He was back yesterday with his tail between his legs asking for help 'cause *our* stuff's so much better now, and there's no way they can keep up with our technology. I love it. And so does Shelly. She was really—"

"It's *Shelly* now?" Simone quietly sniped, "Thought she preferred 'Ms. Navarro.'"

"She does. And I still know my place, believe me." I snapped my case closed.

"How long will you two be in Columbus?"

"Just overnight."

"This about all that new chemical you're producing?"

"Simone," I sighed patiently, "I've told you how that's all proprietary. And how . . . *Ms. Navarro* made me sign—"

"That nondisclosure agreement. Yeah," she said, tight-lipped, as she walked away, "you're getting pretty good at nondisclosure, Clarence."

I sighed. She was more right than she knew.

Katie McLane...

Back at Ashton High I'd never taken Eric's English class but heard that his students liked and trusted him. He was a teacher who'd be fondly remembered when kids thought back on who'd given them light bulb moments, made 'em think. Now I was one of those lucky kids. First when he was homeschooling me, then—with help from Eric's school district friend plus some suitably official-looking papers created by another of Fernando's "cousins"—Eric registered me under the false name Katie Bartlett at his school so I wouldn't feel so isolated. We had to be reeeeeally careful about the whole deal. I had to stay low key. Never that easy for me.

When Eric's AIDS got cured, he really blossomed. His new smile was brighter than his trademark suspenders. His sense of humor combined with his teaching talents made even the grumpiest sophomore respond. We students found ourselves laughing and learning a lot. But I never laughed as much as the others. It was nice to be out in the world a little, but sitting there with my brown pixie cut, brown contact lenses, goofy glasses, and never being myself made me miss my hometown school and my old life all the more.

Dr. Susan Perry...

On March 28, the last evening before I set out on my near-lethal swamp adventure, Eric was making primavera sauce as I came in from our garage lab. He saw my frown. "Meeting didn't go well, Suse?"

I leaned against the kitchen counter, rubbing my forehead. "Actually it went great. Those people are the most gifted scientists I've ever worked with."

"And dedicated," Eric added. "Working in shifts, pulling all-nighters. You, too."

"Yeah. But it's just not enough. We need something else."

Eric looked toward the door as journalist Nate entered, fidgeting with his Afro. "Uh-oh," Eric warned, "nicotine fit approaching."

Nate nodded grudgingly. "Just hurry up the pasta, huh?" He grabbed a pencil from the table where Lilly was sitting and chewed on it.

Lilly's nervous eyes flitted up from her volume of Spinoza. "Oopsie."

"Nate," I explained gently, "that's one of Lilly's."

"Oh. Sorry, Lilly. Here y'go." He wiped the pencil off and handed it back.

Lilly carefully replaced it in line with others. "'Course it's got t-teeth marks now."

"Hey, Eric," Katie said, entering, "that book, *Animal Farm*? Not in the library."

He looked over sharply. "Was it out or—"

"Unavailable. Yeah. Another one."

"It's worse at the paper, too," Nate said. "Subtle, insidious, low-key censorship."

"How do you deal with it?" Eric asked.

"A few quit and left the state. But most of us have family and deeper roots here. So either you *don't* work—not an option with two kids in school—or," Nate sighed, disgruntled, "you do the best you can to keep the publisher happy while you try not to feel like a damn propagandist."

"In our meeting we just talked about another choice," I said. "We expand what we've started. Keep researching, but also organize coordinated resistance." I saw Eric's eyes drift downward. "I know how you feel, Eric, but—"

"Seems like the only way," he said. "When they start banning Orwell, the handwriting's on the wall."

"Like what you told us about *Animal Farm*," Katie piped up. "How the handwriting on the barn wall said 'All animals are equal—'"

"'But some animals are more equal than others,'" Lilly quoted flatly while still reading her Spinoza. "George Orwell, 1945, chapter ten."

Nate looked at Lilly in amazement. "Jesus, has she read *everything*?"

"Just about!" Katie, Eric, and I said it in unison, surprising ourselves and laughing. God, it felt good to laugh once in a while. Then I went on, "Gwyneth, the geneticist from Edinburgh with that great ginger hair, and Gerald, from Yale, I think . . . today they may have finally hit on a simple test to screen for the CAV in food."

"Whoa! Are you serious?" Nate's eyes flashed to mine. "That's great!"

"Yeah. But it's only a beginning," I cautioned. "That's why we've decided to spread the net. It's dangerous, but we need to gather more researchers, more equipment, get a bigger place to work. Maggie and Fernando know a man whose son got hospitalized because the cops had beaten him so badly for something he didn't do. The man's got a ramshackle warehouse on the west side. Said he'd even help us move over there."

Katie was enthused. "Your own CDC!"

"I wish. They're gonna move our gear tomorrow. But our basic search for an antidote seems really bogged down even with all those great brains we've got."

"What else can you do?" Eric wondered out loud. "Get more powerful computers or—?"

"Chunhua's working on that. But what we really need the most is one of the very best *human* brains who could give us industrial-strength help. We need Christopher Smith."

Eric was puzzled. "But didn't he drop out of sight a couple years back?"

And Katie questioned tentatively, "Weren't you and he sorta like . . . um . . ."

"Yes and yes. But when I mentioned Chris's name a couple days ago, Rachel Weinstein, the Israeli microbiologist, remembered that she'd heard from a scientist who'd heard from *another* one that he'd recognized Chris at a diner down in Folkston two years ago."

Nate's face twisted up. "Wow. And only three degrees of separation. But what the hell was one of the great biomedical minds doing in Folkston?"

"Chris told the guy he was going on a long sabbatical . . . in the Okefenokee." I took a breath. "So I'm gonna go find him."

"Uh, Susan . . ." Katie blinked slowly. "That's kind of a big swamp. How're you ever—"

"Rachel tracked down the guy Chris talked to. I've got an idea where to look. But I'll need you guys to keep an eye on . . ." I glanced toward Lilly, who had moved on to reading Sir Thomas More's *Utopia*. The others nodded, understanding. I went on quietly, "Once our equipment goes to that warehouse tomorrow, our research team will be down there and not here. You've already seen how she's okay being alone for short spells, but maybe between Justinia and . . ." I saw from their loving expressions I didn't have to say any more than "Thanks."

Katie seemed worried, though. "Do you really think you can find him in there?"

"I'll find him, Kate." I said it with complete confidence. Hoping it would turn into a self-fulfilling prophesy.

It turned into a whole lot more than that.

20

DECEPTIONS

Jimmy-Joe Hartman...

I wuz starin' at myself in the mirror, blinkin', still tryin' to get my head around it all. A coupla nights earlier, I'd chowed down on that super tomato. Hoo-weee, *man*! That wuz some amazin' shit. Like fireworks shootin' off in my brain. Like I'd went from bein' a little kid ridin' a trike to bein' a NASCAR superstar blazin' round the track at two hundred miles an hour. Whoosh! And with my blond hair all spiked up like fire, I wuz thinkin' 'bout callin' myself Blaze! All kindsa thoughts wuz zinging every whichaway in my brain, like hundreds of them shiny balls in a pinball machine, bouncin' round like crazy. And it still felt the same lookin' in the mirror at Poppa's house, admirin' that kick-ass glint in my eyes—and the thick gold chain round my neck. Already got me some serious bling.

I seen my sister, Claire, movin' by behind me. She was wearin' her nurse's scrubs with bunnies and decorated eggs on the top 'cause it wuz almost Easter, but when she seen me, she got this disgusted look on her face. I give her a smirk. "You know what it is, doncha? . . . You jealous."

"Sure, James Joseph." She was drillin' me with them laser eyes. "I'm jealous."

"Miss Hot Shot Registered Nurse," I said, feelin' smart. "What you make in that job?"

"Enough."

"Not by a long shot," I laughed. "And you jealous 'cause you cain't feel so suu-perior no more. 'Cause now I got me this king-size brain!"

"Which is just as empty as ever."

I bristled. "Whatchu talkin'? Listen, Claire—"

"No, you listen." She got right in my face but didn't shout. Her voice wuz low, steady. "More intelligent? Yes, brother, you are. That comes with the infection. But *more educated*? Not at all. You're still headed toward the white trash heap."

I turned away, givin' off how that wuz stupid. "Get outta here."

But Claire kept her calm. "Have you ever read more than a comic book in your life, James? Studied or tried to learn anything?"

Funny how I could feel my eyes wuz shinin'. "Don't need that shit when you got *'tude!*" I brushed past her and started out. "Now, if the lecture's over, I got me a 'pointment."

"With your business partner, Tyrone? Now there's another winner."

"Nuh uh." I laughed. "He ain't in it wid me no more."

"Don't tell me he wised up."

"Naw. I did. He wuz comin' on 'bout how, since he found them tomatoes, he wanted more seeds than me, wanted the biggest cut." I laughed again. "I give him a cut, awright: up the side o'his head."

She got worried. "What are you saying?"

"Told him, screw that shit, I wuz gonna take whatever I wanted. So he pulls a blade and comes at me, but I wuz ready. Had me a bigger blade."

She went pale. "Tell me you didn't stab him."

"Naw, just nicked him a little, then kicked the shit outta him, left him lyin' in a heap. Told him stay clear, or next time I pop a cap in his ass."

That's where she lost it. Throwed her hands up, angry. "Do you even know what that gangsta talk means? Do you know what *anything* means?!"

"Fuck yeah, I do!" I dug in my baggy pocket, pulled out a handful of tiny bags the size of a postage stamp. "These mean I'm a winner." I headed on out. "Catch ya later, sista. I gotta go get paid."

I knew she was standin' there all tight-lipped, watchin' me go. But I didn't look back. I didn't give a shit. Later on I wished I hadda.

From: Capt. Brendan DeForrest, FBI, ATL
To: Dr. R.W. Hutcherson
Date: 03/29/21 Time: 17:45:20
Subject: New Update DOJ/FBI FRAID Software

Dear Dr. Hutcherson,

I hope this finds you well, sir. Let me again say what a great honor it was to have you visit our comm center last month. Your comments were tremendously encouraging to our personnel. Per your inquiry about the status of DOJ's new facial recognition analysis and identification software (FRAID) which I pioneered and brought to your attention, we've made considerable progress. As I demonstrated to you, FRAID is able to scan any reasonable fragment of a person's face from life, video, or photo and compare it against DOJ and other photo databases using my FRAID algorithms. Per your challenge for beta testing, we used photos of the two suspects you supplied. We commenced a specific search utilizing both public and private street-view security cameras and those in public transportation vehicles throughout the Atlanta area.

After running over 4,763,977 comparisons over forty-three days, we believe we've had success. We believe the suspects you seek have been spotted, first in the Marietta/Roswell area of NW Atlanta, and further analysis narrowed the field. We believe they may reside on the SE side of Rigby Street NE between Lawrence and Lemon.

FRAID is still at beta level, so we can't claim 100 percent positive ID, but the two female suspects shown in the attached document seem to be the ones you're seeking.

Please advise if I can be of further service. I am very proud to consider you a Friend whom I can continue to serve.

Courtesy FBI

Dr. R. W. Hutcherson...

Soon after I received that info from the eagerly subservient FBI captain, I went for a slow drive along Rigby Street to take a gander. My new ride was a silver Mercedes roadster, purchased with dividend income I was enjoying as one of the topmost Friends. A misty rain was glazing the working-class street in this mostly Hispanic area. Looking over the various house fronts, I was simultaneously trying to work out a recombinant DNA formula in my buzzing head while also recalling a very hot hookup the previous night with a ripe and succulent grad student. That filly'd given me the best romp I'd had since my calf-roping days, and I was eager to take her on again—and hopped up just thinking about it.

The street was pretty dead that rainy afternoon. A few kids were coming home from school and a handful of other folks came or went from their houses. On my third or fourth slow pass, I noticed through my drizzly window a stocky older Latina just going in the front door of a house where I'd seen no activity. Then I caught sight of something that made me rein in. As the woman was closing the door from inside,

I saw behind her a young white woman with frizzy brown hair and downcast eyes.

I parked behind a rusty pickup across the street to watch. After an hour the Latina finally came back out, and I got a quick but clearer glimpse of the other woman inside. That FBI facial recognition software had actually worked.

Once the older woman disappeared around the corner, I went across the street to knock on the door. No answer. Tried again. Nothing. I said softly, "Lilly? Can I talk to you?" Still nothing. "Lilly, it's me, Hutch. Look through the curtains on the side window, you'll see." There was a pause. Then I saw the curtains tremble a little, and I put my face closer. "Good girl. Take a look." She glanced, momentarily. "There y'go. See it's me, Hutch."

"Nobody's s-supposed to come in," she said, quietly. Her eyes were downcast, uneasy, but her face was as pretty as ever.

"What did you say? I can't hear you." Though I could. She tried again, but I shook my head. "Sorry, I can't . . . it's the rain . . . Could you open the door, just a crack so we can talk?" And finally she did. Two inches. I smiled. "Thanks, Lil."

"Nobody's supposed to c-come in," she said, eyes averted.

"I know. And that's right, Lilly. You don't want to let in any strangers."

"No."

"But I'm not a stranger, right? I'm Hutch." I bent lower to find her eyes. "See? You know me. It's okay, honey. I'm so happy to see you again." I was peering past her, listening, but didn't hear anyone else inside.

"H-Hutch . . . ?"

"That's right." I kept my tone easygoing, soothing, "Lilly, honey, it's really wet out here . . . can I . . . just for a second . . ." I nudged the door an inch or so and finally eased it just open enough.

"N-nobody's s-supposed to—"

Kenneth Johnson

"So this is where you girls have been, huh?" I said cheerfully, moving past her gently, like I would have around a skittish little heifer. Despite my calm demeanor, I sensed her growing anxious. I paused and used my most comforting voice. "I'm really glad you wouldn't let in somebody you didn't know, Lilly." I bent down to find her eyes again. "But you know me, huh?" She nodded slightly. "Of course you do." I smiled, glancing around the sparsely furnished place, trying to discover anything that might be useful as I reaffirmed, "You know I'm an old friend."

Lilly blinked. Like I'd struck a chord. "Trust the F-Friends."

I remembered our subliminal media campaign. "That's right, honey," I said smoothly, "so you know that you can trust me. And remember all the connect-the-dots books I brought you?" She nodded vaguely, seemed a mite less edgy. I kept my voice comfortably casual. "So Lil, where's Susie?" I glanced at her sideways, nonconfrontationally. "I've missed you two a lot. Did you miss me, miss your friend?"

"I g-guess."

"I'd sure like to see Susie again. Where I can find her?" Lilly was staring downward, twisting the narrow cotton belt on her thin dress. I spoke quietly, "It's very important, Lil."

Her voice was nearly inaudible. "She's in the s-swamp."

"In the *swamp*?" I was surprised, but several possibilities went flashing through my keenly multifaceted new brain. "The Okefenokee?" Lilly turned away, picked up her iPad, started a game. "Lil? That swamp?" She just nodded. "Why?" I leaned on the edge of the table she stood beside, but she was silent. "How come, honey?"

She answered, preoccupied with her game, "Looking for C-Chris."

"Christopher Smith?" Lilly nodded. I instantly realized the import of Susan's mission and extrapolated in a flash the enormous, potentially negative impact it could have on the Friends and me personally. "When did she go, Lilly?"

298

"Yesterday. M-morning. Six eighteen." She stayed intent on her iPad.

"But people come by to take care of you?" She nodded. I was pleased with all I'd learned and considering how best to turn it to my personal advantage. I drew a breath, moved to the front door, opened it. "Okay. Well. It was really good to see you, Lilly . . ."

But when I looked back at her, I paused. I was quite taken by the image of Lilly standing there, backlit by a window. She was engrossed in her game and unaware how the light clearly outlined her feminine shape through her dress.

I stood for a moment in the doorway, contemplating her comely silhouette. Then I quietly eased the door closed, remaining inside. I locked it and slipped on the chain. I looked again at Lilly. She generally wore loose-fitting clothes, so I'd never gotten a sense of her body beneath them. But in this particularly favorable light, I could see that Lilly had a slender and well-formed figure, very much like her sister's. I'd often recalled the pleasurable sexuality I'd enjoyed with Susan.

Standing before me now was a stunningly similar embodiment of my former lover. Lilly of course had no idea she'd become the focus of my rising libido. I moved closer to her, examining her form, her fine-featured, lightly freckled face, the smoothness of her skin, her chin, lips. "Lilly," I asked offhandedly, "Chris was Susie's boyfriend, wasn't he?" She nodded but remained focused on her tablet. "Have you ever had a friend like that? A boyfriend?"

She shook her head absentmindedly, playing her game. I edged closer, my voice a calming whisper, "I'm a friend you trust, aren't I?"

She nodded without looking. "Trust the F-Friends."

"That's right, honey. Trust your friend . . ." Very tentatively and lightly, I touched her cheek.

Lilly drew a small breath. "Oopsie," she said. "F-fences."

I spoke softly, touching her cheek again, "What, Lil?"

"Susie s-says I can have f-fences." Her eyes were still downcast, but I noticed that her respiration had increased. "That people aren't a-allowed to cross."

I smiled, whispering, "And that's a *very* good idea. But you and I don't need any fences because I'm your friend . . ."

I slowly traced my fingertip down her arm. She inhaled another short breath, and I sought to distract her. "Can you tell me about endotoxins, Lilly?"

I hoped she'd start rattling references, and she didn't disappoint: "*Scientific American*, September, '92, Tilling, Ernst, page 57, 'Bacterial Endotoxins.'"

"Yes," I whispered, my pulse quickening slightly, as I eased behind her. "I'd like to hear a lot more about that, Lilly." I reached around to lightly touch the top button of her dress as I said, "Tell me all the details of that article."

"'These lipopolysaccharides are components of cell walls in an extensive bacterial group . . .'" As she talked on blindly, my hand moved in slow motion and deftly undid the top button. I felt a tiny quiver run through her body. I recalled similar positive responses from my recent grad student conquest and felt encouraged. As Lilly's litany of microbiological details spilled out ever more quickly, I slowly slid my fingertips one inch inside the top of her dress. She drew another quick breath amid her hurried recitation of biomedical minutiae, but as I gradually eased on toward the next phase, she offered no physical resistance.

Katie McLane...

The rain had eased some, but it was still pretty miserable as I rushed up Rigby Street. I'd been held up at school and was really upset about being late to take over from Justinia for my shift with Lilly. Thinking back later, I remembered a late-model Mercedes parked nearby. Very out of place in our less-than-trendy neighborhood.

Fishing out my keys as I got to the door, I gave our usual secret knock. I immediately heard a sudden rustling and bumping noise inside, like a chair being turned over. Then heavy footsteps went running toward the back. There was also a rhythmic pounding noise. I hurried to unlock and push the door open and was startled that it was chained inside. Now I was really worried, shouting, "Lilly? What's going on?"

I strained to peer in, and when I could see only a glimpse of her bare legs behind a corner of the old couch, my heart leaped. "Lilly! What's wrong?!" I started bashing hard against the door. The third time I threw my whole hundred and fourteen pounds against it, and the chain mount tore out of the frame. I rushed over and choked back a scream when I saw Lilly sitting by the wall in a fetal position, rocking back and forth, not crying but mumbling incoherently, and blindly pounding her head against the wall. Her dress was wide open at the top, the bottom pulled up high, revealing her bare thighs. Her underwear was slightly out of place, like someone had been pulling at them.

"Lilly!? Oh my God!" I was breathless, quaking with tears of fear for her and fury at myself for being late.

"Susie said fences," she muttered, "S-Susie said—"

"It's okay, it's okay, honey," I gasped. "I'm here." I hugged her to stop her head banging. "What happened? Was somebody trying to— trying to *hurt* you?!"

"Susie s-said I could always have fences. Hutch said I didn't n-need fences, but—"

"*Hutch* said?" I burst into a cold sweat. "*Hutch did this?!*" I looked around quickly, saw the back door open. My heart was racing.

"He kept c-crossing my fences," Lilly mumbled, with tears welling in her eyes. ". . . Where's S-Susie?"

I knew that beating myself up had to wait. I had to suck it up fast and handle this. "C'mon, Lilly." Shaky as I was, I helped her up, tried to stabilize both of us, holding her shoulders, speaking quickly, "Susie'll be back, I promise. But we've gotta get outta here. Right now! I need you to help me grab some clothes and any important stuff."

I started to turn as Lilly whispered, "Can I bring m-my pencils?"

I stopped dead, looked back at her downcast, confused eyes, as she leaned slightly toward me. I threw my arms around her, holding her tight. I struggled to keep myself together, to keep my voice strong. ". . . Absolutely."

Jimmy-Joe Hartman...

I peeked round the corner into a back alley off Peachtree near Underground Atlanta and seen my mark. He wuz one of them middle-class white dudes with a bad comb-over, in a drab suit and tie. He wuz lookin' round nervous-like and shiftin' from one foot to the other. I let him twist in the wind a minute, then sauntered up the alley toward him like I wuz king shit. The guy seen me and talked all jittery, "I thought you weren't coming or—"

I grinned. "Now what kinda businessman would I be if I didn't keep my 'pointments?"

The man talked fast, wantin' to get it done. "Did you bring it?"

"'Course I did." I yawned. I wuz enjoyin' him bein' all squirmy.

"Good, good," he said, glancing around to be sure no one was watching. "My kid really needs it. He's getting buried in school."

"Well, this gonna turn him around big-time. It's the primo shit."

"It's CAV-A?! You're certain?"

"Guaran-fuckin-teed. Just show me the money, man."

The guy quick pulled an envelope from inside his suit jacket. Held it tight. "Five thousand."

"Five?" I stepped back. "I thought we said ten!" Guy's face went pale. I wuz lovin' it and let him hang till he started to sputter. "Awright, lemme see it."

His hands was shakin' when he opened it. I seen the thick stack of C-notes. Then I pulled out a tiny packet of seeds. I dangled it for a moment, then handed it to him. "Guess I'll give ya a break."

He took the seeds and gived me the cash. I wuz all smilin' and fannin' through them hundreds. Never even seen him pull out the Beretta.

"Up against the wall, motherfucker!" The guy spun me round and slammed me hard against the bricks.

"What the fuck!" I tried to come back at him, but he made this superfast karate move and decked me 'fore I knew what happened. Then he started pistol whippin' me on the back of my head and shoulders. Two cop cars come screechin' in at both ends o'the alley, red lights flashin' and all. And suddenly theys like three more cops on my ass, kickin' and punchin' and wailin' the shit outta me. Just before they knocked me out, I seen one cop up the alley givin' some cash to a kid who had bandages all up one side o'his head. Tyrone. Muthafucker set me up. One cop who wuz beatin' me said, "You have the right to remain silent, dickwad." Then he bashed my head down 'gainst the concrete, and I wuz gone.

21

CRASH

Dr. Susan Perry...

In the southeastern corner of Georgia, just above Florida, runs a stretch of high ground called Trail Ridge. During the Late Pleistocene, about one million years ago, this geologic landmark trapped receding ocean waters in a saucer-shaped basin that stretched thirty-eight miles north-south and twenty-five miles east-west. Plant life thrived, decayed, and covered the sandy bottom with peat. Over the millennia, rainfall slowly freshened the body of water, creating the vast Okefenokee Swamp.

Seen in sunlight, the water was tea colored from the tannic acid constantly being released by the decaying vegetation. At night the water was shiny black, reflecting the full moon and the stars that winked through the canopy created by the uppermost branches of slender pines and broad oaks. But the pale cypress trees rising smoothly from the black water like columns of smoke toward the black sky were the most eerie in the moonlight.

And there were unsettling sounds. The deepest bass was the rhythmic throbbing of huge, puffing bullfrogs and guttural, growling rumbles of fifteen-foot alligators. Also at a low pitch was the mournful hooting of owls as their black saucer eyes scanned the darkness for unsuspecting prey. A chorus of cicadas and crickets chittered in the higher ranges, and the night was occasionally pierced by the soprano scream of a night bird or squirrel as it was attacked and killed by a bobcat. These sounds and the spooky cypress trees twisting up out of the black water created an ambiance of primeval mystery.

Most forbidding though was when the sounds of all the creatures would suddenly go dead silent. When they sensed something threatening approaching. Then they waited, poised, to determine whether to them it meant fight or flight. I knew that feeling. That night I was already in flight mode.

What made the swamp creatures go silent that night was the low, grating whine of the greasy, straining outboard engine at the back of the funky wooden motorboat I was driving. I was windblown, disheveled, but determined. I'd just curved off the main channel of the Suwannee River and was gunning the old boat to its top speed, about twenty-five at best. That sure as hell wouldn't be fast enough to outdistance my pursuers, so I maneuvered over the inky water into a heavily wooded stand of cypress, dodging perilously among the ghostly trees that might give me some cover if it was a helicopter behind me. But I had a sinking feeling—bad choice of words—that it was not; that escape might prove impossible; that I might never ferret out Chris to help us. How they'd found out I was in the swamp, how they'd gotten on my trail, had me even more worried.

The water suddenly exploded right in front of my boat. A geyser of muck showered down on me. I swerved as another blast blew away part of an oak tree, narrowly missing me. I looked back and caught flickering glimpses of the flashing police lights on the pursuing craft knifing through the darkness as it weaved among the trees two hundred yards behind me—and ten feet in the air. As I feared, it was not a chopper.

ARPC GSP Unit 774 (BETA 3) Cockpit Cam A/V - Date: 03/31/21 Time: 23:49:13

Transcript Analysis by: Fields, Vernon, GSP #876254

Suspect Vehicle: Motorboat; **Lic:** N/A; **Bearing:** W/NW 321 degrees.

Suspect: Possibly Perry, Dr. Susan A.; **GSP Most Wanted list, see dossier #473802**.

Weather: Clear, Wind N/NE 9 MPH

ARPC: ALT 11 FT over terrain; AIRSPD: 38 MPH; GRNDSPD: 39 MPH

Dash Cam: Shows condition nominal. Cockpit environ darkened for night viz.

Heads-Up Displays: TRKNG computer functioning. IFR enhancement on. Suspect image intermitt., shows suspect boat traversing W/NW weaving through trees.

Targeting Grid: Active in SCRL DATA mode, GPS & RANGE DATA active, cross-hair on, ARPC maneuvering to acquire target lock for El-Stat weapon.

CKPT REC Active.

Pilot: Schoengarth, John, GSP #767540

Copilot: Miller, Alicia S., GSP #846530

Pilot Schoen.: Ooo-eee, almost got her. You can run, woman, but you cain't hide.

Co-P Miller: Almost don't count, Schoengarth. Get more starboard.

Pilot Schoen.: Just tryin' to miss the trees, sugar.

Co-P Miller: While you're at it, knock off the sugar shit.

Pilot Schoen.: C'mon, Miller, I'm just ribbin' ya.

Co-P Miller: Keep it up, I'll break your fuckin' ribs—Target lock. Rifle, rifle. Fire in the hole.

23:50:01 EL-STAT lock, weapon six burst discharged.

Courtesy GSP, FBI

Dr. Susan Perry…

Hearing the sizzling crack from the El-Stat gun, I swerved sharply again. I glanced back to see the golf ball–sized pulses of electrostatic energy incoming like a half dozen miniature comets. They traveled at near-lightning speed, each leaving a wispy smoke trail and creating a sparkling explosion when they impacted on the cypress I'd just cut around. The ARPC had overshot me the first time, now they were just short. I knew the next one would likely be dead on. Shit. When I heard the damn gun discharge again I knew I had to bail.

I grabbed my small backpack and dived overboard a millisecond before my boat was hit and the gas tank exploded in a ball of flame the size of an SUV. The boat's fiery wreckage smashed into a big cypress root, rupturing my backup tank and triggering a bigger fireball.

I ducked low in the water behind a beaver mound as a water moccasin swam past my face and a loud humming approached. Flashing police lights drew nearer. The ARPC slowly loomed closer through the dark trees. It looked much like a Georgia State Patrol car except that it swept along eight feet over the water. Its two powerful xenon spotlights cut narrow swaths through the smoky haze and ground fog. The searchlights operated independently, like the eyes of a chameleon, swiveling in two different directions. The ARPC was kept aloft by internal Perini air turbines that kicked up a fine spray from the swamp. While airborne, the lower half of the side panels were folded out to become outrigger stabilizers containing smaller guidance turbines. This gave the craft an appearance of a menacing hooded cobra.

It slowed, hovered, and rotated over the flaming wreckage like a dark bird of prey. It pivoted slowly, like it was sensing for my presence, but unable to pinpoint me. Yet. Then I heard an ugly slurping sound behind me. Two twelve-foot-long alligators were sliding off the muddy bank about twenty yards away and gliding in my direction. Their beady eyes were just above the water's surface as they closed in on me.

ARPC GSP Unit 774 (BETA 3) Cockpit Cam A/V - Date: 03/31/21 Time: 23:51:13

Transcript Analysis [Abridged]

Air Speed: Hover, Rotation C/W

Dash Cam: Shows swamp across dash; turbine wash kicking up mist.

Pilot Schoen.: You got anything, Miller?

Co-P Miller: Nada.

Pilot Schoen.: Bump up the hi-con night eyes.

Co-P Miller: Did that.

Pilot Schoen.: Well, kick it higher.

Heads-Up Display: Hi-con switches to level 3. Night Viz: to contrast/enhanced.

Targeting Grid: Crosshair Active. High-contrast image of swamp area brighter but grainy, low-res.

Pilot Schoen.: C'mon, goddammit. Wanta be sure she's toast.

Co-P Miller: Got somethin'! Gimme some left pedal.

Altitude Indicator: ARPC rotates 7 degrees CC/W.

Display: Targeting screen: dark shape moving through reeds at water level.

Co-P Miller: Think I got her! Hit the bow lights! Give her a shout.

Bow Lights: To On.

Pilot Schoen.: [keys PA] You, in the water. Stay where you are!

Targeting screen: Image zooms in closer.

Co-P Miller: Aw shit. Just a coupla goddamn gators.

Targeting screen: Image zooms in closer on alligators. Target crosshair lock. Trigger: active.

Co-P Miller: Dumb fuckers. Fire in the hole. Rifle. Rifle.

El-Stat: Discharged.

Courtesy GSP, FBI

Dr. Susan Perry...

The ARPC guns flashed, firing the golf ball–sized electrical pulses that streaked inches overtop me and blasted the alligators out of the water in a geyser of reptile fragments and blood that showered down on me. Half of an alligator jawbone with its rows of sharp teeth splashed right in front of my face and sank past my wide eyes.

A man's voice shouted. "Holy shit!"

The ARPC crew heard it, too. The craft instantly rotated, and I was surprised to see one of the glaring searchlights flash on to an astonished man, probably midforties, who'd been poling his flatboat through the darkness nearby. He'd probably been handsome once, but now had a long, badly healed scar that zigzagged from above his left eye, across his cheek, to below his ear. He had a three-day beard. His hair was long, straight, black, with a leather headband crossing his forehead. Seemed like he might have been part–Native American. He wore a faded flower-print shirt with sleeves cut off, showing tattooed arms. His denims were also cutoffs. His legs and arms were muscular and deeply tanned. A cigar stub was clenched between his teeth.

He stared wide eyed into the blinding spotlights of the dark, hover-ing craft, like he'd never seen an ARPC. It sounded like he murmured a prayer—or curse—in what sounded like a Muskogean dialect. The craft moved menacingly closer to him, inspecting him very carefully. I was impressed that he faced it boldly, eyes alert, breathing slow.

The craft finally shut off its emergency lights, pivoted, and hummed away, disappearing back among the trees into the darkness of the swamp. The man stared after it for a second in the flickering firelight from the wreckage of my boat, then slowly poled over toward me. He must've had eyes like an owl, because I was well hidden in a thicket of undergrowth with only my eyes above water. "Hey," he called out, "y'in one piece?"

"Yeah. I think so," I said. He came alongside, reached down to me. "Take this first." I handed up the backpack then tried to pull myself up, but discovered my arms were like rubber. He grasped them with strong hands and strained with my nearly deadweight.

"C'mon, work with me, babe."

I pulled my aching body up and flopped over onto the bottom of his old flatboat. I was still stunned from the explosion, but managed to nod thanks.

The man looked off again toward where the ARPC had disappeared. "What the hell *was* that? Martians finally land?"

I was short of breath, fearful that I'd broken a rib. "ARPC." His look was blank. "Airborne patrol craft. You've never seen one on the news?"

"Nope." He was still scanning the darkness, but seeming to take some comfort in the sound of the bullfrogs that had started up their low drone again.

"Been living in here a while, then," I said, looking to see why my side hurt.

"Yeah. Lost count. Name's Carl Wilder. Folks call me Crash."

"Susan. Perry." For extra substance I added, "Doctor." I lifted my bloody shirttail and grimaced from pain and annoyance when I saw my wounded side. I grumbled, "Aw, shit."

Wilder shined a flashlight on it. "Got a ripe one there, Doc. Let's get something on it." From a nearby tree he peeled off a wide strip of bark, handed it to me. "Press it on."

"You're kidding, right?"

"Don't kid about open wounds, honey. It'll keep the infection out. Trust me, it's the real deal." He saw my still-dubious look. "Swamp willow, okay? Loaded with salicylic acid. You heard o'that?" Adding with a barb, "*Doc?*"

"Yeah. Natural aspirin." I nodded thanks and applied the willow bark to my very tender, bloodied side. "You gonna tell me this is an old Indian trick?"

"Nah. Old Honduran trick. Ancient native guy taught me one of the times I ditched a chopper down there."

"*One* of the times?"

"Yeah. I took a few headers."

"Ah. *Crash*," I deadpanned. "Now I get it."

"So what the hell's an ARPC? New kinda cop car?"

I was tying my shirttail to keep the bark strip in place. "One of the nifty new tools they use to keep people scared and in line."

"Who's they?"

"The Friends of America."

He hadn't a clue what I was talking about, but his eyes narrowed slyly at me. "So, what am I dealing with here? Some kind of notorious desperado or . . . ?"

"Ever come across a man named Christopher Smith? I know he lives in here and—"

"And he likes his privacy."

My eyes lit up. "You know him? Is he out near Big Water Lake?"

"Maybe." Wilder chewed slowly on his unlit cigar, eyeing me carefully top to bottom like maybe he was thinking about chewing on me. I eased my hand down to the Bowie knife I always had strapped to my right ankle. "That's back in there quite a ways, babe. Over on the Middle Fork."

He might have been lying, but I had to go for it, trying to sound more confident than I felt. "North of where Bird Wing Run flows into the Middle Fork, yeah."

"Y'gonna need more than a Bowie knife t'get there."

That focused me. "Well. I've also got determination." I pulled a small watertight bag out of my sodden backpack. In it was a GPS locater, which I turned on.

"Whoa, whoa," he cautioned, "better not. Your pals can likely track that."

"Not if it's on less than seven point three seconds. Supposedly." That's what Chunhua'd said when she gave it to me. I took a quick bearing, shut it off, and got to the point. "Can I rent your boat?"

"Listen, I ain't seen Smith in a while. You sure he's even still there?"

"No, but it's the best lead I've got. Can I rent it?"

"You his ol' lady?" He traced a finger down the ugly scar on his cheek. "He run out on ya?"

None of your business, pal. "He ran out on the world, Mr. Wilder. Look, I've got to find him. You can't imagine how important this is."

He chewed his cigar butt with a faint smile. Maybe he was impressed with what Gramma Lula used to call "my grit." Or maybe I was just the first woman he'd seen in a long time. I realized my wet shirt was clinging tightly to my breasts, giving more than a hint of what was underneath it. But I pressed on, trying to be as professional as possible. "Listen, Mr. Wilder, this is a really vital medical mission. I can't pay you much, but—"

"Don't use money, babe," he said with a slow grin, "but maybe we can work us somethin' out."

I ignored the sexual innuendo as I grabbed an oar. "Great. Let's move."

"No, no, no. Lemme do it," he chuckled. "If you're in such a goddamn hurry, I better get us a little more speed." He took an oily tarp off a tiny, ancient outboard. He pulled on the frayed starter cord three times before it finally sputtered limply to life.

Then he gave me another pruriently sloe-eyed grin as he guided the boat deeper into the dark swamp.

The Documentarian...

The GSP/ATL PD Central Command Control Room in Atlanta was 272 miles north of Folkston. It resembled a darkened situation room in the Pentagon basement. To all who entered for the first time, it felt like a mysterious seat of power. Wraparound video display walls plus many desk console screens showed topographical maps and shifting views of the southern Georgia area, including traffic cameras, night-vision, and satellite images. Even of the Okefenokee Swamp. Men and women in Georgia State Patrol or Atlanta PD uniforms were at various stations in the control room or moved through with iPads in hand.

Records from that particular night show that the duty officer was GSP Captain Winona P. Dushku, a sharp young woman whom many of her underlings didn't like. She was well tailored, upwardly mobile, and politically astute. Her shrewd natural talents let her easily leapfrog over others who had more seniority. Anyone who knew what to look for, like Katie McLane or Susan Perry, would have noted the steely-eyed dominance in Captain Dushku's manner as she leaned closer to one monitor showing a digital replay from the ARPC Unit 774 gun camera of Susan Perry's boat exploding into two fireballs.

An adjacent monitor showed the two patrollers who were in a briefing room at Folkston station for the teleconference. They could likewise see Captain Dushku onscreen in Folkston. The following transcript picks up after the officers Schoengarth and Miller had provided their initial description of their actions.

Teleconference #7780963 - Date: 04/01/21 Time: 00:51:49

Participants: GSP/ATL PD CentCom, DO Cpt. Dushku, Winona P.

Folkston, GA GSP Station 372, Sgt. Schoengarth, Ptrl. First Class Miller

Visual: Two-way link [Abridged]

DO Dushku: I'm confused. We trust you with one of the beta tests of our hottest new vehicle in an ideal venue, and this is how you handle the assignment? Why didn't you report in immediately?

Sgt. Schoengarth: Trouble with our high-gain, ma'am.

313

DO Dushku: And you didn't go to sideband because . . . ?

P1stCl Miller: Uh, we were havin' trouble with that one, too, ma'am, it was sorta—

DO Dushku: You're as bad a liar as your partner. Probably just went 10-7 for a doughnut, so cut the bullshit, both of you. Where's her body?

Sgt. Schoengarth: She had to be dead, ma'am.

DO Dushku: Then where the hell is her body?

Sgt. Schoengarth: Wasn't one, ma'am.

P1stCl Miller: With all due respect, ma'am, you can see the size o'that fireball. Nobody coulda—

DO Dushku: With no due respect, patrollers, you're going to get your lazy asses back into that goddamned swamp. I want Perry absolutely verified dead or—much more preferably—captured. And since you each obviously need help finding your ass with both hands, I'm bringing in an ARPC from Ashton with two more skillful patrollers. The moment they arrive, you'll follow them out as their backup. But if I don't get satisfaction, you two will spend the rest of your careers on dog-shit patrol. Do I make myself clear?

Sgt. Schoengarth & P1stCl Miller: Ma'am! Yes, ma'am!

End Teleconference

Courtesy GSP, ATL PD

Dr. Susan Perry...

The moon was low on the horizon directly in front of the flatboat and created a shimmery pathway reaching out to us across the broad expanse of water that locals referred to as a "prairie." It had opened up in front of me and the man called Crash. Fireflies twinkled above the water lilies and floating vegetation that dotted the water like small islands. He steered the old boat between them over the dark water. He'd been listening to my story. "So you been hiding out since that night at the church?"

"Yes. And gathering as many other scientists as possible. Trying to find an antidote to counteract the virus. Organize a Resistance. The last year's been a nightmare."

Crash frowned knowingly. "Bein' on the run can eat y'up pretty bad."

"Speaking from experience?"

He chewed his cigar stub, looking ahead to steer the boat and also back into his past. "Last time I ditched was Honduras. 'Bout three years ago now. During all that coup shit. But to rescue us, Uncle Sam woulda had to admit our Air Cav unit was down there. That wasn't gonna happen."

"How'd you get out?"

"Very fuckin' slow." It was clearly a harsh memory. "Near three months crawlin' through that goddamn jungle. Both sides down there wanted the four of us dead."

I studied his scarred face as he stared off. "How many made it?"

"'I only am escaped alone to tell thee.'" He sat in silence, his lips drawn tight. Then he sucked in a breath. "Finally got home. Ta da!" His words had a bitter bite. "Yeah, right."

I thought I understood. "Vets seem to get a raw deal so often."

"No shit. The Nam guys were all"—he looked at me with a wild-eyed expression—"crazy potheads, doncha know. And lotsa my bunch were PTSD whackos." Then he added, darkly, "After some o'the shit we saw . . . and some we did . . . I guess a few of us really were."

The boat approached the entrance to a narrow channel, more fire-flies winked from among the trees. I looked at the dense swamp surrounding us. "So you went back into the jungle?"

"Well, I sorta had to. Kinda trashed a liquor store."

I prodded gently, "'Sorta,' 'kinda'?"

"Aw, this shitheel punk was givin' a wheelchair bro a hard time. Pissed me off. I didn't hurt nobody. Well, not too much. But it was stupid." He looked around at the black gum trees crowding in from either side of the narrow channel. "I like it in here. And hey, beats jail."

"'Specially nowadays. Cops're cracking down so hard, prisons are overflowing." I studied him. "Does it get lonely in here?"

"The lady alligators do get nervous when they see me." He grinned sideways at me. "Sounds like it's better in here than out there, though. Like you're up against a brand-new master race?"

"Yes. But the Nazis only *believed* they were a master race. *These* people"—I shook my head as I had a thousand times, trying to get my mind around it—"the ones that the virus got into, really seem to have evolved overnight into almost a new species. A smarter one."

"Which'd seem like a good thing on the surface." He steered the boat between some cypresses. "Being smarter's what lifted us up above Neanderthals and all the knuckle draggers."

"Right. But when their upward evolution also brings a massive desire to dominate others emotionally, physically, even brutally or murderously, and at the same time drastically *drops* the levels of empathy and compassion—"

"Y'mean that old-fashioned stuff we call *humanity*?" He chuckled ironically. "Sure begs the question 'bout what really makes a better human being. And leaves us in some deep shit."

"Exactly."

"So Smith's some kinda hotshot scientist who might be able to help y'all out?"

"He's a genius," I said matter-of-factly, "in molecular and viral biology. Maybe the best mind in the world for this kind of theoretical research."

"Humph." Wilder rubbed his scar, musing. "And all this time I thought he just played a sweet clarinet." He glanced ahead through the mist that was beginning to glow with the first light of dawn. "We'll be comin' up on him soon now."

Jimmy-Joe Hartman...

Lookin' out through them barred winders, I seen that it wuz just startin' to get daylight in spite of the gray drizzle of rain. Been three days or so since I got busted. I ain't sure 'zactly, 'cause they kep' up what they called their enhanced interrogation. Nice way of sayin' leavin' me naked in a freezin' ass concrete cell, wakin' me up every time I dozed by hosin' me down, then layin' me out on a board half–upside down and pouring water on my head till I like to drownded. All tryin' t'get more info outta me I didn't have none of. I think they mostly did it all just 'cause they liked doin' it. Then they give me an old worn-out-lookin' lawyer guy who smelled like stale cigarettes and said I had oughta just plead guilty and get on to prison. Claire'd been really mad. Tried to get me a different lawyer, but they said it wuz too late.

They marched 'bout fifty of us out that mornin', all shackled together, leadin' us to the bus. It had "Georgia State Prison" on the side and barred winders, too. I seen Poppa and Claire standin' other side of the chain-link fence with the razor wire on top.

I wuz embarrassed, tryin' to keep up a tough expression, butch it through. But it didn't fool Poppa and Claire. They knew I wuz scared shitless 'bout where I wuz headed. Poppa looked like his whole body wuz achin'. Claire put her arm round him, and he put his hand flat 'gainst the chain link. He could barely speak, but I heard him say, "I'll pray for ya, son."

I could only manage a kinda surly nod, then I climbed onto the bus with my chains rattlin'. Bus smelled like guys over a lotta years had pissed or puked in it. And we wuz jammed in tight. Fuckin' bus wuz way overloaded. Me and a bunch had t'stand. Couldn't hardly breathe. Through the narrow barred winders, I seen Poppa and Claire watchin'. He wuz wipin' tears, but her face wuz tight as a drum. Then the door hissed closed. The bus rumbled alive and rolled down the street, headin' me to what I heard wuz a bad place. It wuz way worse'n that.

Kenneth Johnson

FOLKSTON, GA GSP Station 372 Sec Cam 014 04/01/21 Time: 06:58:49

Transcript Analysis by: Takamoto, Leon J., GSP #664545

Weather: Cloudy, Wind N/NE 12 MPH

ARPC GSP Unit 774: on pad. **Condition:** preflight

Description: Folkston ARPC unit awaiting arrival of inbound Ashton unit for search and recovery mission of Perry, Dr. Susan A. into Okee. Pilot: Schoengarth, John, GSP #767540, black male; Copilot: Miller, Alicia S., GSP #846530, white female; outside craft performing preflight.

Audio:

PA Announce: Ashton 504 is on final. Unit 774 stand by for departure and backup.

Miller: Incoming, Sarge. Half a click out.

Schoengarth: Playin' backup for them suckers. Pisses me off.

Visual Desc: Unit 504 comes in fast, 29 MPH, 27% over regulation speed; pivots 360 directly over 774; severe turbine ground wash; Miller nearly blown down; shouts up at 504.

Miller: Hey, assholes!

Schoengarth: They're just fucking with us. Let's hit it.

Visual Desc: Schoengarth climbs into 774. Miller makes crude gesture at 504, which departs W/NW.

Miller gets into 774, which lifts off, follows on 504's six, heading back into the swamp.

Courtesy GSP, ATL PD

22

HERMITAGE

Dr. Susan Perry...

A snowy-white egret with its long neck like a question mark stood motionless on spindly legs in a patch of the shallow water, staring patiently down. Then its sharp beak shot in like lightning, and it came up with a small, wriggling fish. The egret tossed its head back, swallowed its living breakfast, then turned to look coolly toward us two humans gliding by. At that moment in my life, I identified with the fish.

The sun was fully up, and the high humidity of the swamp was slowly intensifying the heat. I splashed some water on my face and noticed some yellow flowers on the surface. "Bladderwort," Crash said. "Pretty, huh? Also carnivorous. Bugs crawl in, then can't get out. Kinda like folks in the swamp." He gave me a sideways glance. "So, is this Smith guy your main squeeze?"

"No." Then I relented. "Well. A few years ago. We met and worked together at the CDC and in the field. After a year or so we got . . . y'know, involved." I drew a long breath. "But this trip isn't personal. We need him to help find a way to—"

Crash raised a hand to quiet me as he killed the engine and glided our boat onto the bank. Amid the low sounds of the swamp animals and the high-pitched cries of ibis and herons, we could faintly hear a clarinet. It was being played in a low register. The tune was a slow jazz riff on an old melody from the 1940s, "The Nearness of You." It gave me pause.

Crash nodded. "Well, here's your big chance."

A few butterflies fluttered in my stomach as I stepped out of the rickety boat and moved through the foliage toward the soft sound of the woodwind.

The first thing I saw was the top of an old log cabin. Crash had told me that several in the swamp had been abandoned by loggers decades ago. I could see that its roof had been rebuilt and covered with layers of fan-shaped saw palmetto leaves, carefully laid to act as natural shingles. They were also shaped to funnel rainwater down into a barrel for drinking. The chimney had been rebuilt. I approached from the back of the cabin with Crash following. I walked alongside a vegetable and herb garden, well cultivated and thriving. The smell of the freshly turned earth was pleasant, and I saw that cherry tomatoes and cucumbers were nearly ripe. There was a small shed with tools nearby and a stash of several propane bottles near the shoreline.

I reached the corner of the cabin, inhaled a nervous breath, then peered around. In front was a flat area about twenty yards square neatly covered with peat. It extended down to the waterline of the channel that curved through the verdant swamp. A netted hammock was strung between two trees, with a palmetto leaf awning arranged over it. Chris sat near a stone fire pit near the shore with his back to me, but that thick red hair was unmistakable. My heart lifted inside me. I could see his fingers moving expertly on the clarinet's keys, playing an easy, bluesy version of Hoagy Carmichael's old, romantic tune. I stood watching him for a private moment, remembering that sunset beside our small campfire on the beach in Tanzania. The balmy sea breeze had wafted around us. He'd played the same enchanting melody that day.

This time he stopped right in the middle of the final phrase. He'd sensed something behind him. Then he slowly turned to look at me.

His brilliant individualism, that vibe of quiet, confident intelligence, which first had attracted me five years ago, was still instantly apparent. They marked him as a man of depth and substance. At first glance people thought his eyes were gray, but closer inspection, which I had frequently undertaken, revealed them to be fascinatingly multihued, symbolic of his amazingly multifaceted way of thinking. So often stunningly outside the box. He'd grown a full beard as red as his head since I'd last seen him two years ago. His skin was freckled, ruddier. Appealing. My gaze held his as I had quick flashes of memory: rolling rambunctiously in our bed, interlaced and enjoying it; laughing together with village children we'd inoculated outside Katmandu; sitting close together on the old porch swing at his grandmother's; that happy day in New Orleans he gave me the little opal ring I've worn ever after. And the last painful night, arguing hotly in a CDC laboratory. I sensed that he might be remembering similar moments.

I really didn't trust my voice, but finally managed, ". . . Hey."

Chris just nodded back and was the first to look away. I saw that he had decidedly mixed emotions. Crash later told me he'd seen there was still a spark between Chris and me and had personally been a little disappointed.

Chris set his clarinet aside and grumbled, "Out of all the swamps in all the world—"

"I had to walk into yours. Yeah. Sorry to disturb you." I moved toward him. We were both awkwardly uncertain about how to proceed. I decided to reach out and give him a friendly hug and a kiss on his bearded cheek. I thought of all the times we had held each other and lay comfortably side by side. I'd been very unsure what this reconnection might rekindle. Chris clearly didn't want to consider it immediately. He looked at Crash.

"Why the hell did you bring her here?"

Crash was helping himself to a wooden bowl of nuts and shrugged. "It amused me. And by the way, she coulda got here without my help."

A little bell tinkled, Chris stepped over to it and pulled in a fish that had hit one of several lines. I pried my eyes away from him and looked around his homestead. "Pretty nice. Sort of *Swiss Family Robinson Crusoe*. Although they didn't have solar panels." They were on the south side of his roof. "If it wasn't for needing a Diet Coke now and then, I could probably live in a place like this." He glanced at me, and I held up both hands, palms toward him. "Not why I'm here, don't clutch."

"So, why?"

"How long have you been out of touch?"

"Couple years, I guess." He was taking the fish off the hook.

"Then we've got a little catching up to do."

"Uhhh, speakin' of catchin' up," Crash's tone was cautionary as he gestured toward the swamp behind him, "I ain't sure those guys're done with you, Doc."

Chris glanced from his friend to me. "What's wrong? You in trouble?"

"The world is, Chris."

"Yeah, well, I'm not interested in the world." He put the large trout on a cutting board and prepared to splay it. "Except my little corner right here, so if you don't mind—"

"Hey, don't be an asshole," Crash said sharply. "This chick 'bout got her tits blown off gettin' in here. Least you can do is be a gracious goddamn host and listen to her, or I won't bring you any more cigars."

Chris glowered at Crash, then glanced back at me and grudgingly gestured as if to say, "So?"

ARPC GSP Unit 774 Cockpit Cam A/V - Date: 04/01/21 Time: 07:42:18

Transcript Analysis [Abridged] by: Fields, Vernon, GSP #876254

Dash Cam: ARPC Unit 504 seen thru windshield, flying on point thru Okee., bearing 323.

Alt: 15 FT over water level; AIRSPD: 32 MPH

Displays: TRKNG computer heads-up active.

CKPT REC: Active.

Co-P Miller: Whoa! Lookit him cut round them trees. Them Ashton boys're hot.

Pilot Schoen.: Got nothin' on me.

FDR [Flight Data Rec.]: ARPC swerves sharply, takes heavy jolt.

Co-P Miller: Jesus! 'Cept you're tryin' to cut down the goddamn trees!

Pilot Schoen.: Chill out, Miller. Just clipped a knee. [keys his com] Unit five-zero-four, this is seven-seven-four. You read?

Courtesy GSP, FBI

The Documentarian...

Note the names of the Ashton pilot and copilot below: the former Ashton deputy sheriff, Brice Patton, had been co-opted into the Georgia State Patrol. Timothy Green, former Ashton quarterback, had entered Georgia Tech with his football scholarship and new mental acuity, but hadn't improved his self-control. He was quickly suspended for improper behavior and sexual harassment. With help from one of the Friends who was an Ashton county supervisor, both Patton and Green had been accepted for GSP airborne training. This despite documentation showing neither was as qualified as other candidates. They had, however, completed the orientation with the ARPC beta test protocols and had been performing acceptably, if somewhat overaggressively.

ARPC GSP Unit 504 Cockpit Cam A/V - Date: 04/01/21 Time: 07:43:17

Transcript Analysis [Abridged] by: Fields, Vernon, GSP #876254

Dash Cam: Traversing forested swamp.

Displays: TRKNG heads-up active.

CKPT REC: Active. Pilot: Patton, Brice J., GSP #976535; Co-P: Green, Timothy R., GSP #986538

COM: I say again, five-zero-four, this is seven-seven-four. Do you read?

Pilot Patton: [keys his com] Gotcha five by, brother.

COM: How's it lookin' up there, guys? Got anything yet?

Pilot Patton: [keys his com] Oh, yeah. Forgot to tell ya. We caught Dr. Perry 'bout five minutes after we took off. She's got her face planted in my lap right now. [keys off] Dumb-ass yokel.

Co-P Green: Got that right.

Pilot Patton: [keys his com] I promise we'll keep y'all posted back there. Keep taggin' along so y'don't get lost. [keys off] He just cain't stand us flyin' point.

[Tracking alarm sounds. **Heads-Up Display:** Target Acquired. Data scrolls.]

CENTCOM: ARPC five-zero-four, CentCom. Do you copy?

Pilot Patton: Roger that, CentCom, five-zero-four here.

CENTCOM: We got a high-altitude drone sighting from forty-three minutes ago. Two individuals in open boat on suspect's original bearing. Probability factor eighty-five percent. Coordinates just uploaded to your onboard.

Co-P Green: Copy that, upload successful.

Pilot Patton: We'll get on her, CentCom. Five-zero-four out.

Co-P Green: Hot damn, Brice.

Pilot Patton: Fine-tune that little sucker, Timbo. You know how bad the high-ups want this bitch?

Co-P Green: Shit yeah, I do. This is gonna look great on our records, man.

Pilot Patton: [keys his com] Seven-four, stand by to receive tracking data. Stay on our tail. [keys off]

COM: Copy that.

Pilot Patton: Okay, Timbo. Let's bring her to ground.

Flight Data Rec: Notes airspeed increases to 57 MPH. Ground speed 59 MPH.

Courtesy GSP, FBI

Dr. Susan Perry...

We were sitting in the shade of a spreading oak at the dining table Chris had created from the bottom of an old flatboat, using some kegs for legs. Crash had nosed his boat ashore nearby. We'd been eating the trout plus some green beans, okra, and cherry tomatoes. I hadn't realized how hungry I was. While gobbling it all, I gave Chris a quick overview: told him about the comet, the startling discoveries Katie and I had made; also about the arrival of Dr. Hutcherson, though I skipped over the cowboy-handsome part and how the appealing widower and I had become intimate, until he went over to *them*.

Chris was intrigued about how those infected really were intellectually superior.

"But," Crash interjected, relighting his cigar, "with the big-ass downside of losing their *humanity*."

"Yeah well, let me introduce you to the Pentagon," Chris said sourly, sipping on some sassafras tea. "Some things don't change, Susie."

"But this is way worse," I said. "They're using the existing government structure. They infected a lot of elected officials with the CAV-B virus and made them willing accomplices. Nate Balfour, a senior journalist for the *Journal-Constitution*, told me how Mitchell and the Friends move through the State Capitol, telling the governor and legislators what to do. State supreme court justices, too."

"Shadow government." Crash nodded, taking a thoughtful puff. "Like somma that deep state shit in South America."

Chris asked, "If they all want to be top dog, don't they fight among themselves?"

"You bet. There's a lot of scuffling for dominance," I explained, "which can lead to unfortunate *mishaps*. Like Dr. Levering's *unexpected* death."

Chris was shocked. "What happened to Ernest?"

"Hit-and-run two weeks ago. Conveniently creating an opening for Lauren to take over the CDC."

"So how can they coexist?"

"Same as a wolf pack. Always pressing, testing each other. Working together for the overall pack so long as they each get—"

"A nice big chunk of the red meat," Crash concluded.

"And working together they did improve some things," I admitted, "while also getting filthy rich. Their new brainpower led to an AIDS cure and more."

"They got some nifty new cop cars, too, that hover like choppers," Crash chimed in.

"When did *you* see them?" Chris asked with surprise.

"'Bout six hours ago, shootin' zippy little fireballs at your girlfriend."

Chris and I were both uncomfortable with Crash's take on our relationship, but I went on, "So productivity shot way up. People given the CAV-B work smarter, harder, faster, and happier because of being lieutenants in the power structure. The state is running smoother than ever. On the surface, life seems better and most people like it."

"Or go along to get along." Crash smirked.

"Isn't there any pushback?" Chris questioned. "What about the local press?"

"Also infiltrated or intimidated. Plus, leaders in business, technology, military, everything," I said, feeling yet again the huge weight of it all.

Chris processed it. "Does sound like Germany in the thirties. Or China and Russia a couple years back."

"But this is going to be way worse," I said emphatically, "because of their selfishness, lies, lust for money and power—unless we can create an antidote. A way to reverse or at least stop it. I've got a bunch of great scientists working like hell, Chris. But we need your help."

"Yeah, I could hear that coming. Sorry, Susie." He shook his head, picked up our tin plates, and walked away. I stared at his back. Frustrated, angry. But determined. I pursued him.

ARPC GSP Unit 774 Cockpit Cam A/V - Date: 04/01/21 Time: 08:13:45

Transcript Analysis [Abridged] by: Fields, Vernon, GSP #876254

Dash Cam: ARPC Unit 504 seen thru windshield on point ahead traversing Okee. W/SW, Bearing 245.

Displays: TRKNG computer heads-up active.

CKPT REC: Active.

Pilot: Schoengarth, John, GSP #767540; Copilot: Miller, Alicia S., GSP #846530

COM: Seven-four, this is five-zero-four. We're about four clicks out.

Pilot Schoen.: [keys com] Copy that, Ashton, we're ready to rock!

COM: Negative, seven-four, you guys hold at one click out.

Co-P Miller: (to pilot) What!? Is he kidding? This was our collar!

Pilot Schoen.: [keys com] We really want to go in with you, zero four.

COM: Repeat negative, seven-four. We got the con. You are backup at one click.

Pilot Schoen.: [keys com] Copy that. Hold for backup at one click. [keys off]

Co-P Miller: I can't fucking believe it. You gonna put up with that shit?

Pilot Schoen.: Chill, Mill. I ain't gonna let this go down without us.

Courtesy GSP, FBI

Dr. Susan Perry...

Crash kept a wary eye out over the swamp, as though his special-ops instincts plus Muskogean wilderness-wise senses were working overtime. Chris had rinsed off the plates and was rebaiting fishhooks. I paced around him with increasing anger. "Look, Chris, you want to come back here and spend the rest of your life playing castaway, fine. Just help us long enough to find a way to stop them so that—"

"So that what?" Chris said with sharp cynicism. "The *next* set of bad guys can come along and screw everybody?"

"There won't *be* a next set of bad guys like *these*!"

"Oh, c'mon, Susie," Chris smirked. "Where's your history? There's *always* a next set. That's why I got out." He went on baiting his hooks. "I say let 'em kill each other off."

He marched toward his cabin, but I kept pace, getting in his face. "What about all the people that don't deserve that?! People who got infected without a choice?" My rage ramped up. "Can't you see exactly where this domination is headed? They're going to end up destroying *a lot of innocent people!*" Chris stopped dead, looked fiercely at me.

Shit. I hadn't wanted to say it that way. It came out of my mouth before I could stop it. I closed my eyes tightly, gritted my teeth. But it was too late. I wanted to kill myself. Because I knew how he'd react. And he did. Chris's glare was deadly. "*Innocents?*" Then he laughed bitterly. "Well, I sure know a little about that, don't I, Susie? Some of *my* technology destroyed a few innocent people, huh?" He put on a cheery voice, imitating the bureaucrats he hated with a passion, "'Gee, thanks, Dr. Smith, for creating this miraculous recombinant DNA fertilizer. It'll really help the agriculture in developing countries, Dr. Smith.'"

"And it did, Chris!" I said insistently. "You couldn't've known that they'd—"

"'Oh, by the way,'" he continued imitating, "'we know you won't mind if the government of India sells it to Somalia who'll twist it just a little—probably with illegal help from BioTeck—to make chemical weaponry and kill a million people or so. In agony.'"

Crash was stunned and silent. This was Chris's old, deep, unhealed wound. My voice was low, sincere. "Chris, that wasn't your fault." His glance was so sour that as he opened his mouth to ream me, I scrambled mentally to pivot. "All right, I know you're convinced it *was*. It's why you're living here. Alone. But then can't you see this as an opportunity for you to make up for that?"

"Make up for?!" He flared. "I can't fucking *make up* for it! Ever! Those people are *dead*! You don't—!" Though still furious, he suddenly turned icy calm, his face became expressionless, his voice low. "You have no comprehension what it's like living with that. You don't get it."

"Of course I get it, Chris." I was equally furious, but followed his focused-intensity lead. "Who tried to help you through that trauma? Why the hell do you think I came in here through snakes and alligators and patrollers? Because we're trying like hell to save what's left of this poor, pathetic planet. And the people on it. Just like you always were. And only with your help do we have a prayer of doing it. Chris, it's like living in the middle of a tumor out there. The Friends are a cancer growing more out of control every day. And just like cancer, they're gonna consume and destroy their host. Only in this case, Dr. Smith, the host is the earth and all of us on it."

"And what, Dr. Perry? You're trying to lead the little white corpuscles to fight back?"

"*Somebody's* got to! Because the clock is ticking. So far as we know, they've only corrupted people within the state, but it's obvious that Georgia's just an out-of-town tryout."

Crash caught the wave. "Yeah. I been thinkin' about that one: pretty soon they'll try t'go national and then—"

"Yes," I said categorically. "We've got to stop them before it's too late." Then I leaned closer to Chris, speaking in a still lower key. "Look, I was plenty pissed that you just bagged it all and walked away from everything. From *me*. That really hurt. I loved you. I've never stopped missing you. But this is not about you and me." He glanced up. I seized it as encouragement, tried to press it. "We need you out there, Chris. We need your stubborn, opinionated, outside-the-box, one-of-a-kind invaluable brain working with us."

Chris stared at me, still noncommittal. Crash jumped in. "I'll tell ya one thing, man. I think you were a major putz for ever blowin' off this chick." Then he looked at me, his eyes narrowing. "You remind me of my granddad. He fought like a banshee to keep his tribal land. His way of life. I ain't no big-time biologist-type, but if you can use me, lady, I'm game."

I nodded appreciatively. Then looked at Chris. He stared at me, then looked at his cabin, his solitude, his sanctuary from a world gone haywire, from the unintentional, horrific tragedy he'd caused. I could see he was still unconvinced, still on the fence. I touched his arm. "Chris . . ."

"Too late, sucker." Chris and I glanced at Crash, who had suddenly snapped to alert, antenna up, eyes riveted on the swamp. "Decision's been made for ya."

We looked up the channel and heard the turbine whine of an approaching ARPC.

Crash rubbed his scar. "Don't suppose you got a helicopter?"

Chris was angry; glaring at me. "I'll get you for this."

He reached into his cabin, pulled out a bow and fistful of arrows that he held out to Crash, who guffawed. "What the hell am I supposed to do with *that*?! Who you think I am? Fuckin' Geronimo?" Then Crash took command. Pointing at the cabin, he snapped at Chris, "Hide your ass in there and when you get a clean shot, you take it." Then he looked at me. "You stay out in the open. Down by the shoreline so they see you. Don't resist 'em. Go."

"And then what?" My heart was pounding.

"Just *go*!" Crash was bolting toward his boat. I moved quickly to the open space and looked back to see Chris disappear into his cabin just before the ARPC came humming in overtop and zeroed in on me.

An amplified voice blared, "Halt! Down on your knees. Hands on your head. Now!" I complied as the ARPC settled in between me and the cabin, the turbines kicking up prop wash, blowing over Chris's makeshift dining table as the vehicle touched down. One patroller jumped out of the passenger side, his pistol aimed at me, shouting as he approached, "Facedown on the ground! Hands behind you! Do it, bitch!"

I did. The ARPC pilot had opened his door, using it for cover, and aimed his gun over it at me. "Got your six, Timbo!"

The first patroller stopped right over me, holstered his gun, and reached for his cuffs. At that instant an arrow came zinging out of the cabin and buried itself deep in the driver's left thigh. He yelped and spun to the ground, dropping his gun. The cop over me fumbled the cuffs to redraw his gun as Crash rose up from under a tarp on his boat, aiming the biggest rifle I'd ever seen, shouting, "Freeze, guys!" as he fired a warning shot just over their heads.

ARPC GSP Unit 774 Cockpit Cam A/V - Date: 04/01/21 Time: 08:21:32

Transcript Analysis [Abridged] by: Fields, Vernon, GSP #876254

Dash Cam: Swamp seen W/SW, Bearing 245.

Pilot: Schoengarth, John, GSP #767540; **Copilot:** Miller, Alicia S., GSP #846530

Co-P Miller: Was that a shot fired?

Pilot Schoen.: It's a good excuse, either way. Let's take us a peek, Miller.

Flight data rec: From hover to 17 MPH forward.

Courtesy GSP, FBI

Dr. Susan Perry...

Crash commanded the cops, "Don't move a fucking muscle." They did as told. Crash shouted to the one above me, "Reach across with your left hand, remove your weapon with your thumb and forefinger, and drop it in front of the lady." He did so. "Pick it up, Doc," Crash said, "and step away from the gentleman who will now go facedown, hands behind."

Meanwhile Chris, with another hunting arrow notched, drawn, and aimed, had come out swiftly to the downed driver and kicked the fallen gun away. Then Chris glanced over his left shoulder. He'd heard something else.

ARPC GSP Unit 774 Cockpit Cam A/V - Date: 04/01/21 Time: 08:21:40

Transcript Analysis [Abridged]

Dash Cam: Swamp encampment appearing. Unit 504 patrollers appear compromised.

Pilot: Schoengarth, John, GSP #767540; **Copilot:** Miller, Alicia S., GSP #846530

Pilot Schoen.: Ho! The Ashton guys screwed the pooch. This is great. We get t'save their sorry asses!

Co-P Miller: And make the bust. Yes!

Courtesy GSP, FBI

Dr. Susan Perry...

My heart dropped as I saw that second ARPC gliding slowly in. Chris looked back sharply at Crash, who was keeping the patrollers covered while glancing at the approaching ARPC. His voice was dead calm. "Stand your ground. Let 'em come."

The PA voice blared, "Put down your weapons."

I was petrified. "Uh . . . Crash?" I saw a bright laser pinpoint start dancing across his chest.

"We have you targeted," the PA voice insisted. "Put down your weapons."

Crash was confident and assured, saying to us, "Stand still. Let 'em come . . . to right . . . *there*."

He dropped low and fired a shot directly below the incoming ARPC—into Chris's stash of propane tanks. The resulting massive fireball boiled upward, completely engulfing the ARPC momentarily. Flames got sucked into its turbines, which screeched and malfunctioned. It rotated wildly over the channel, finally flipping upside down and crashing into the swamp water a half mile away, where it kept chugging, convulsing, and sputtering.

The three of us quickly stripped our two patrollers of their radios and other gear. Once both were securely restrained, I removed the arrow from the pilot's leg and dressed his wound. Chris angrily packed up his essentials—which I was pleased to note included a photo of me and him working the cholera pandemic in Uganda. I helped Crash trundle the pilot, named Brice Patton, out to the ARPC to get a flying lesson. Patton refused. Crash sighed, asked me, "Doc, borrow your Bowie?" I handed him my big knife, and he said casually, "Hey, Brice, see this scar on my face?" Crash grinned, making it appear particularly gruesome. "Want one?"

Ten minutes later we had the patrollers trussed up only moderately, but definitely without means of communication. We climbed aboard the ARPC. Crash eased it off the ground, but overcorrected, and we skittered sideways toward a disastrous collision with Chris's cabin, which Crash barely avoided. Then he gained altitude, and within a minute it was like he'd been flying the craft for years. He disengaged the transponder, putting us in stealth mode. We cruised low over where the other craft lay inverted, smoking, and mostly under the swamp water.

Its crew of two had just floundered to the nearby shore, disheveled, exhausted, but alive enough to fend off several inquisitive alligators.

As Crash flew us away across the swamp at—or sometimes frighteningly *below*—treetop level, I said to him, "Pretty amazing."

He glanced around the high-tech cockpit of the ARPC. "Yeah. Interesting ride."

"I meant you."

He glanced at me. Then shrugged it off. But I gave him a pat on the knee. He looked down at my hand, managed a tiny smile at it, then focused on flying. I studied him a moment, then looked back at Chris in the back seat. He was gazing out across the swamp with a grim, thousand-yard stare. I knew he didn't want to be here. I decided to try anyway. "Hope you brought your clarinet."

I was sad that he didn't respond. But I hoped that inside his tormented brain might be the answer we needed so desperately.

23

UPRISING

Jimmy-Joe Hartman...

The heavy iron-barred door slammed loud behind me and the other fifty newbies. Now I seen why that awful smellin' bus been so crowded. Fuckin' Reidsville prison was jam-packed. Smelled like piss, too. I looked up at the three-story main cellblock they wuz takin' us into. I tried to hang tough while we wuz goin' past guys inside their cells, but they wuz scary. Buncha beefy-fisted ones hooted and whistled, one shoutin' right at me, "Oooo-eee, fresh white meat!" Others wuz sayin', "See your ass in the showers, cutie! Welcome to Camp Reidsville!"

The guards give out blankets and taked us up to the cells one at a time. This tall, black guard opened the barred door on mine. It wuz 'bout six-by-ten with two bunks. A big hulkin'-ass Latino guy was asleep, facin' the wall on the top one. A wormy little white dude with one eye swollen shut wuz sittin' on the bottom one with his bare legs crossed, girlie-like. The guard shoved me in, slid the door closed. "Hey, hang on," I said, "where the fuck I s'posed to sleep?"

"On the floor, pal, and you better enjoy it. Next week we gonna be stackin' you assholes like cordwood." Then he walked off. I wuz pissed.

"It's not so bad," Wormy said. "Some of these cells have four or five in 'em."

I looked down and growled-like, "I ain't sleepin' on no fuckin' floor. Move."

"You know, I would," he said all whiny-like, "but that'd make my husband angry." He glanced up at the huge guy. "And believe me, you wouldn't like him when he's angry."

Right then a bell rang, and all the cell doors clanged open. A guard waved us out to join the line headed to the big concrete mess hall for lunch. They wuz a few dozen long metal picnic-kinda tables bolted to the floor. I heard it's 'posed t'hold 'bout six hundred, but there wuz over a thousand smelly guys crammin' in, tryin' to get somma the crap food they wuz dishin' out. I wuz standin' in line and seen a lotta guys sizin' me up. One old black guy 'cross the room had wire-frame glasses like Poppa. He kept starin' like he knowed me or somethin'.

I didn't get no food 'cause a guy grabbed my ass. I heard you gotta be tough, so I whipped round and slugged him hard and *bam*—three guys jumped me to the ground, beatin' me up worse'n the cops had. Knocked me plum out.

Simone Frederick...

My concerns continued to increase about the extent that Mitchell's backroom maneuvers were taking our state government in a dark direction. I'd picked up snippets of rumors that there might even be some kind of mysterious drug involved. That sounded like tabloid conspiracy theory nonsense until I also heard it from a few respectable press people like a local NPR reporter plus the *Journal's* Nate Balfour, and a couple others. Even then I didn't pay much attention until I got to thinking about how Clarence was different, too. Meticulous guy that he was, he always told me about his doings at Everett Biochemical, sometimes in excruciating detail. But in the last few months, except for mentioning a couple of nasty chemical spill accidents, he'd gone quiet. I'd been suspicious that he might be having a dalliance with his boss, Shelly Navarro, at Everett, but maybe something even worse was going on over there.

I also worried as a mom. LeBron's grades had been slipping. Then I saw a letter come in for him from some modeling agency. He took it to his room to read. When he never mentioned it, I asked, and he said in his offhand manner that they had offered him some modeling jobs. "Like the girls are always saying I oughta do." He smirked and added, "As if. I've got waaaay better things to do."

But when I dumped some recyclables that night, I spotted the letter in our bin and couldn't resist. Seems that *he* had applied to the agency. And been rejected. I knew he must've been disappointed, but part of me thought it was a good lesson: that he wasn't the only handsome black teen in Atlanta. At the same time I was worried about what was ahead for him.

And for all of us.

Clarence Frederick…

I felt very upbeat as I pulled the Prius into the driveway and saw LeBron coming up the sidewalk. I called out cheerfully, "Hey, son. Help me with the groceries, huh?" He nodded as I opened the trunk. "Got some good news today. Everett's doing so well that Ms. Navarro got me a raise. Hinted she might even be able to get me another small stock option."

"She really likes you, huh?"

"Well, I'm doing my job." I pulled out one of the bags. "Working hard so that—"

"Is it true there's some kinda new drug that makes people smarter?"

I paused, forced a chuckle. "I wish. Where'd you hear something like that?"

"Kid in school—who got suspended next day." He spoke quieter, "And listen, Dad, I can keep a secret, and I could really use something that'd give me a brain boost so—"

"No secret sauce, sorry. I think all you need to do is buckle down. Study harder and—"

"Yeah, yeah, I've been doing all that, Dad." He continued plying, "But if Everett *was* making something that'd help me, and that Navarro woman *likes* you so much," he said with an inappropriate innuendo, "then couldn't you just, like, *use* that to get me some—"

"That's enough!" I saw red. "Now you listen here, boy. I'm making better money than I have in years, and we're getting along fine. I don't have any desire to—"

"Rock the boat," LeBron muttered, turning away. "Yeah, yeah. Thanks a lot, Dad."

One of those new police cars drove by at that moment. Its light bar on top started flashing, then its stabilizer outriggers folded out as the Perini turbines whined to life. The craft lifted smoothly into the air and banked away from us to answer a police call. "Be so cool to fly one of those," LeBron said, mesmerized. "Maybe I'll be a cop." Then he grumbled sourly, "Sure not getting any help around here."

I grabbed the other bag from him and walked angrily toward the house. He called after me, "And don't think you're fooling Mom. She knows you've got something going on the side."

I just kept walking. I had no choice.

Dr. Susan Perry...

We waited till night to approach Atlanta, on the ground, and on less traveled roads. Crash hid the ARPC under a tarp in a junkyard operated by one of his vet pals who loaned us an old car. From his office trailer phone, I called Justinia.

Hearing what Hutch had done to Lilly was like being struck by lightning. I screamed with rage—startling Chris and Crash—as tears gushed from my eyes. I was utterly devastated for the trauma my absence had caused her.

I struggled with my anguish as Crash drove us to where Justinia told me Katie had taken Lilly: an unused spur of the Southern Railway. Pulling into the abandoned industrial area that night, we could see it'd been idle for decades. The rails were rusted, and weeds had long ago taken over the gravel grading and the rotting cottonwood ties. Dilapidated redbrick buildings dating back to the 1800s were grimy, forgotten monuments to a bygone era. We stopped a hundred yards away from one and flashed our headlights as we'd been told: three short and one last long one. I later learned that particular code had been Chunhua's idea: Morse code for the letter *V*, as in "victory." We saw a flashlight blink back to us from the darkness, and we drove up to where young Princeton biochemist Alex was waiting.

I was out of the car before it stopped, shouting to him, "How's Lilly?"

"Basically okay, Susan. Maybe a touch nervous, but—" I was already rushing past as I heard him recognize Chris behind me. "Dr. Smith, a great pleasure. Alex Farquar."

The old building looked dark and abandoned from the outside because all the light leaks had been carefully sealed inside. The barn-size door was open just enough for entering. Hurrying inside I glanced quickly around the funky place. The tin roof was vaulted with wood to about thirty-five feet. A few pigeons fluttered in the rafters. Light came from an assortment of jerry-rigged hanging lamps or bare bulbs.

Eight or nine trucks of varying sizes were all parked inside. Their sides or backs had been opened outward to access equipment and supplies within. I understood: someone had wisely realized we needed mobility for emergency relocation. Then I met that someone. She was hurrying to meet me: a thirtyish, sturdy, muscular woman wearing a tight Atlanta PD T-shirt. She had the richest velvet black skin I'd ever seen, and the ten tight parallel cornrows running front to back on her head made a visual statement as strong as the no-nonsense military respect from her intense eyes. "Dr. Perry. Glad you made it back, ma'am. Dodsworth, Veronica. Ronnie, ma'am."

I nodded, preoccupied. "I need to see—"

"Your sister. Yes, ma'am. This way." I appreciated how quickly Ronnie walked. "We all love Lilly, ma'am. Katie told us to keep her supplied with fresh books, and she's been going through 'em like lightning."

Ronnie led me down the center of the warehouse, quickly explaining how she'd been horrified by growing Fascism in the PD, and joined our cause. Though focused on getting to Lilly, I took note en route of how things had progressed. The couple dozen people we passed were a cross section of race, gender, age, and class. Many were new faces who merely nodded, but those I knew waved, gave a thumbs-up, or pressed my hand. Rachel, the microbiologist from Tel Aviv who'd put me on to Chris, gave me a quick hug, saying, "You actually found him. Amazing."

Ronnie understood my anxiety and led me hurriedly on past two trucks holding foodstuffs. The makeshift kitchen nearby was a compendium of appliance odds and ends. I noted that a Braun espresso maker must have been treasured since it was carefully enshrined to one side.

There was a paramedic van. Another van was clearly our communications center where Chunhua had her hands full, wiring something, but waved eagerly to me.

Along one side of the warehouse's interior were ratty office cubicles that had been pressed into service as living quarters for those who had to remain here in hiding. Through the doors that were open, I could see the rooms had been personalized with some pictures or items to help those people keep in touch with their lives.

The last section contained a few vans with advanced electronic and biomedical equipment that had transformed our fledgling lab into a more extensive one.

At the very end was a slightly raised platform about twenty feet square that was part chemistry research lab, part living area with a couple of cots. Two shipping crates doubled as tables and storage space for the few articles of my clothes that Katie had quickly grabbed and brought.

In the center of the space was a large battered worktable with microscopes and other instruments. There were three mismatched chairs. In one corner, slightly to the side as usual, was a smaller table with a little Tiffany lamp, missing several of its stained glass pieces, but supplying illumination. There were also books and pencils, meticulously arranged.

And sitting beside it was Lilly. The bruise on her forehead brought tears to my eyes.

She didn't see me. She was busy speed-reading a volume of Carl Sandburg. I came up beside her and the stack of books on the floor: some scientific journals, but also an eclectic mix including history, ethics, philosophy, and autobiographies.

I knelt down beside her. Lilly's eyes flitted for only an instant in my direction. But I was rewarded by seeing her shoulders relax slightly. I put my arm around her and leaned my head against hers, determined to hold back more tears that were threatening. I whispered, "How's my exceptional sister?"

". . . O-okay." She said flatly as she turned a page. Then her other hand found mine and grasped it tightly, like a child might. Its warmth and love radiated through my whole soul.

My voice became barely audible. "Good, honey. That's good." I felt a tear escape down my cheek as Lilly simply turned another page.

I saw that the title of the next poem was "Limited."

Dr. R.W. Hutcherson...

Bradford Mitchell was amused by the pleasant coincidence that the posh office which had been arranged for him in Atlanta's city hall building was on the corner of Washington and *Mitchell* Streets. When people joked that he'd had it named after him, he would smile, lower his hawklike eyes, and quietly say, "Not this one." He was confident that numerous streets in the future *would* bear his name.

His expansive office enjoyed a view of the neoclassical, domed State Capitol to the east, so he had easy access to its inner workings. Mitchell was gazing out at it that morning as Dubrovski, the ex-Ranger black-ops guy with a face scarred by acne who was his chief lieutenant, opened the door to admit Reverend Abraham Brown and myself into the mahogany-paneled chamber. I noticed Dr. Brown's eyes fixate on the lovely young intern arranging a coffee service—for one—on Mitchell's side table. When the girl nodded courteously and moved to leave, Brown's eyes casually followed her all the way out the door, which she closed. But he kept looking. It called to mind some dicey rumors I'd heard about the reverend doctor's private preferences.

"Gentlemen," Mitchell said, turning from the window and gesturing us to chairs before his massive Stalinesque desk that made everyone facing it feel small. We sat obediently as he leaned on the high back of his big leather chair, which always reminded me of a throne. "You know what a gadfly is?"

"Sure do, sir," I said, stretching a leg out. "Seen plenty of 'em annoying my uncle's cattle."

"We've got a couple annoying us in Atlanta. And they're slowing down some of our important efforts here, particularly when it comes to law and order."

I nodded. "Abdulla." He was surprised. I was pleased. Homework counts.

"Right, Hutcherson. Ronald Abdulla is trying to move up in the ACLU at our expense. Getting bothersome. Needs to be brought into the fold. Also that senior FBI guy, Clive what's-his-name."

"Clive McWilliams?" Dr. Brown volunteered. "He's a member of my church."

"Is he now?" Mitchell said as if he was unaware, though I knew better. "Well, Reverend, might you invite Agent McWilliams to one of our special meals?"

Dr. Brown nodded. "Be my pleasure, chief."

I smiled. "And I'll buy Abdulla a drink with a twist of CAV-B."

Mitchell nodded and gestured our dismissal with his coffee cup.

Jimmy-Joe Hartman...

I wuz still all swolled up, but they kicked me outta the prison hospital block after three days 'cause it wuz jammed to the rafters already when there'd been a gang rumble, and a shitload more bleeders got brung in.

The main block wuz empty 'cause inmates wuz all out in the yard. I thought this big redneck guard wuz leadin' me there, too, but he stopped by another door, shoved me through and locked it. I turned round and seen I was alone in a room wid lotsa books on shelves. I wuz lookin' round, confused. Then I heard this gravelly voice from behind a bookshelf, "It's called a library."

I cocked right up. "I know what the fuck it's called."

That scrawny, older black inmate with them wire-frame glasses like Poppa's come out holdin' some books. "Hey, you little shithead"—he looked right up in my face—"don't get surly with me or I'll throw yo' candy ass back to the meat grinders. Only reason I pulled you in here's 'cause you kinda remind me o'my own kid."

"Hell-lo: I ain't black."

"No, but you *dense*. First minute you here you pick a fight with Julio the Magnificent?"

"Juli-who?"

The old guy grabbed my balls wid one hand and my collar wid t'other, pulled me down to his nose. "Julio the Mexican heavyweight champ, numbnuts. Now listen up: fuck up with me, you outta here, and it'll be bend-over-and-grab-the-soap time. Got it, punk?"

I nodded, but still hung tough. He chuckled at me. Went to an old wheeled cart stacked with books, "I'm Phil. You gonna be cleanin' up and shit. Restackin' the books on the shelves. I'm sure you know all about the Dewey decimal system, huh?" He seen the blank look I was tryin' to cover. "Riiiight. Get your candy ass over here, and I'll 'splain it."

Dr. Susan Perry...

Having Dr. Christopher Smith suddenly among our group of scientists gave us all a much-needed shot in the arm. Even though Chris mostly frowned under the invisible dark cloud always hovering over him, I could see he was energized by being among us. After two years of solitude, finding himself abruptly back in his element had kick-started Chris's über-resourceful brain. And the challenge facing us also sparked him: how to stop and ideally reverse the effects of the CAV viruses. He took pains to listen carefully and get steeped in every avenue we'd researched and explored, every solution we'd proposed, and so far failed with. As always, Chris wanted maximum input and had convened a meeting of the minds.

I'd broken away from the group session to help position an older-generation electron microscope Chunhua'd just "liberated" from the deep storage annex of the CDC. She used the keys I borrowed from dear old custodian Joseph back when Hutch and I snuck in there a lifetime ago. Crash and athletic ex-cop Ronnie supplied the muscle power to get the unit here. All that remained was for Chunhua to get it working. "Merely that." She grimaced, intimidated. But I knew if anyone could do it, Chunhua could.

Crash started arranging power for the big unit. All our electricity was bootlegged from a power pole a half mile away and was notoriously unreliable when it rained.

En route back to Chris's symposium, Ronnie and I stopped by the kitchen area. I needed some tea and she needed some beef, grabbed a sandwich. Lilly sat in a nearby chair speeding through Plato's *Republic*. Eric was grading essays on a ragged, sagging couch. He showed us a notice on the school letterhead. "The latest additions to the books that'll be *temporarily unavailable*."

I read the list, "*The Catcher in the Rye, Che Guevara: A Revolutionary Life,* and"—my eyes went wide—"*The Cat in the Hat!?*"

"Mmmph. Shit yeah!" Ronnie chuckled through a mouthful of roast beef. "That scoundrel Dr. Seuss! Famous for bein' a radical anarchist."

"I'll teach about 'em anyway," Eric said. "Outside of school. Kids meet me."

Ronnie wiped some mustard off her lower lip and cautioned, "Better watch your ass, Eric. I hear they're offering rewards for informing on people like you. And us."

One of my throwaway cell phones rang. It was Gwyneth, the chemist from Edinburgh who'd been working on a way to screen for CAV. She was distressed, shouting over crowd noise and sirens; her voice was rushed, nervous. "Susan? I'm down on Washington, outside city hall. There's a big protest! I think there's gonna be some real trouble! I—"

"What? Can you hear me? Gwyn?"

Ronnie had read my expression, stopped eating. "Tell me."

"Have you got your bike?"

Ronnie drove her Indian Chief Vintage 111 like a demon Valkyrie weaving through traffic. I held on for dear life. Within fifteen minutes we were on the periphery of the protest. She locked the bike, gave me a do-rag and dark glasses so I wouldn't be easily recognized, and we hurried through people who were running—either away from the city center or, like us, toward it. At one point I heard a low rumble and looked down an alley to the next street parallel where a large armored SWAT vehicle rolled to a stop with its big diesel engine idling.

Then ahead of us Ronnie and I saw an angry mob of college students and others at least five hundred strong marching down Washington past the dome of the State Capitol toward city hall. I couldn't spot Gwyneth. People were waving handmade signs and loudly protesting police brutality, blacklisting, media censorship, and increasingly restrictive policies of the state government.

I heard Ronnie speaking low, "The revolution begins. About fuckin' time."

Just as she said it, we heard a grinding of gears and the roar of powerful engines. We saw three black SWAT vehicles converging on the crowd from different angles to challenge the marchers. An amplified voice echoed off the buildings on Washington Street, "This is an illegal assembly. Disperse immediately."

The spirited crowd shouted defiance. Across the intersection, nervous pedestrians who were not part of the protesters began to hurry away. Among them I thought I saw someone I knew. Yes. It was our gentle CDC custodian, Joseph. I saw him looking back as he ran—then suddenly come to an abrupt stop. Something had caught his attention. I followed his line of sight and saw, a block away from him, a young woman wearing light blue nurse's scrubs some distance ahead of the crowd. She calmly stepped directly in front of one of the advancing armored vehicles, which came to an abrupt stop.

I had a frightening thought and tried to get a better view between the bobbing heads of the people who were rushing past or crowding Ronnie and me. When I got a clear view, it was what I'd feared. "Oh my God, it's Claire!"

Ronnie was startled. "You know her?"

"Yes. She's Joseph Hartman's daughter. He works at the CDC. And he's over there." We saw Joseph call out a warning to Claire, but his voice was lost amid the angry shouts of the protesters and the growl of the SWAT engines. He began shouldering his way toward her through the mass of humanity that was either protesting or trying to get safely away from the intensifying confrontation.

I saw him shout to her again, but there was no way his voice could carry over the din. He was like a salmon swimming against a surging current that he could barely keep his head above. He looked again, hoping to see that she wasn't still standing there.

But she was. Claire stood, with a workaday carpetbag purse on her shoulder that she'd probably carried for years, wearing a thin, peach-colored cardigan over her blue scrubs. She was calm, unmoving, boldly facing off against the massive armored vehicle.

And then a lone ARPC glided in from behind the SWAT vehicle and hovered twenty feet above the back of it. The strange, futuristic craft gave pause to many in the crowd who had never seen one first-hand, never experienced its ominous hooded-cobra appearance. A hush began to spread across the crowd as more people began to realize something important was happening.

The ARPC's humming turbines churned up gusts of wind that ruffled Claire's light sweater and her dark hair. From a block away, Ronnie and I saw Claire look up with a Gandhi-like passivity at the menacing airborne craft. Everyone watching from their different vantage points saw that Claire was not challenging the power of the mechanical might and authority, but rather merely presenting her person and her humanity in silent opposition to its heavily metallic force.

Those of us who witnessed the scene would recall it afterward as a seminal moment in our lives. The hundreds of people in the street had grown entirely quiet, watching. All eyes were focused on the brave young nurse. Aside from the low, menacing rumble of the vehicles, there was complete silence, except for a lone, anguished male voice, still trying to make his way to his beloved daughter, shouting her name with increasing alarm, "Claire!"

ARPC GSP Unit 331 Cockpit Cam A/V - Date: 04/10/21 Time: 16:22:12

Transcript Analysis [Abridged]

Pilot: ▇▇▇▇▇▇▇▇▇ **Copilot:** ▇▇▇▇▇▇▇▇▇

Dash Cam: Shows white female nurse standing in front of SWAT Unit 286.

Heads-Up Displays: Functioning. **Targeting Grid:** Active. Locked.

CKPT REC: Active.

Co-P: Little warning shot?

Pilot: Sure. What the hell.

Courtesy GSP, FBI

Dr. Susan Perry...

Claire breathed slowly, maintaining her calm serenity in the face of the martial strength. For all of us who observed, it was a lesson in simplicity and an affirmation of the power one individual could channel.

Then, almost casually, the El-Stat gun on the patrol craft flashed. Claire took a fiery hit to her chest that blew her to the pavement. Joseph shrieked, "*Claire!! Christ Jesus!!*"

ARPC GSP Unit 331 Cockpit Cam A/V - Date: 04/10/21 Time: 16:22:26

Transcript Analysis [Abridged]

Dash Cam: Shows white female nurse on ground.

Heads-Up Displays: Functioning.

CKPT REC: Active

Co-P: . . . Ooops.

(Laughter)

Courtesy GSP, FBI

Dr. Susan Perry...

Joseph clawed his way through the stunned people toward Claire's quivering body, but before he could get to her, the SWAT vehicle suddenly lurched into gear and rolled forward right over her toward the crowd, who reacted in disbelieving horror. Five hundred people exploded in righteous fury. There was wild pandemonium as they stormed the SWAT units, and suddenly we were in the midst of a full-fledged riot. I was already pushing through the crowd toward Claire, shouting back over my shoulder, "*Ronnie?!*"

"Go, Sue!" she bellowed. "I got your six!"

Across from us a SWAT truck with a water cannon wheeled onto the scene. Helmeted SWAT officers swung the cannon to mow down the enraged protesters with the stinging high-pressure blast. Tear gas canisters exploded amid other struggling people. Bitter, noxious fumes began to swirl in the air. Still the people in the street fought back with whatever meager weapons they could lay hands on. But they were fiercely outgunned.

Joseph reached his daughter before I did and knelt in the street beside her. Her sweater was smoking from the burning blast. On her chest the open wound—larger than Joseph's hand—was blackened and thick with blood. He raised and cradled Claire's scorched, broken body, weeping so uncontrollably that he could barely see through his tears as he rocked her. "No, no, no . . . Sweet Jesus, no . . ."

I got to him, breathing hard, shouting, "Joseph, it's me. Let me check her." I pressed my fingers on Claire's left carotid, but already feared the worst as Ronnie hovered over us protectively, her powerhouse strength shoving aside anyone who needed to be, as the tumult swirled around us.

Joseph cried to me desperately, "Dr. Susan . . . please! . . . Help my girl."

I couldn't find a pulse. "Ronnie—"

She finished my sentence: "We gotta get 'em outta here." With one swift move the heroic woman swept up Claire's fragile, limp body in her strong arms as I helped Joseph to his feet.

Two more ARPCs swept in overhead, red lights flashing, sirens wailing, El-Stats firing electrical pulses at unarmed protesters. A man next to us took a blistering hit that spun him to the gutter. It was all a horrific blur. Somehow Ronnie steered us through frantic people, some trampling others, into a side alley. At the far end we saw two dozen people, hands on their heads, being shoved into a police van. Ronnie detoured into the back doorway of a restaurant's kitchen. She eased Claire down to the floor, whispering to me, "I think she's gone, Sue."

She was right, no pulse. Pupils unresponsive. Joseph was beside his daughter, sobbing. I said, "I can't just leave them!"

Ronnie was clear eyed, firm. "Listen: there is a world of Fascist cops out there who'd be thrilled to get their hands on you and—"

"*I won't leave him like this!* I—"

"Dr. Susan." Joseph grasped my hand, choked with emotion. "You go. Go find a way to stop this . . . madness." He squeezed my hand tightly.

I stared at him, then dug quickly into my pocket and handed him one of the cheap cell phones. "Joseph, press number one on the contacts if you need me."

"We *all* need you, Dr. Susan . . ."

There were intensifying shouts in the alley. Ronnie grabbed my arm, pulled me up and away.

Simone Frederick…

Clarence came home late again that evening. It was getting to be an every-night thing that had intensified my suspicions. But that night something else was far more troubling. He found me staring at the local TV news with my jaw hanging open. The friendly newscaster was saying, "There was a minor disturbance downtown today: a few dozen drunken, rowdy students created a brief nuisance in front of city hall." As he spoke, the TV showed some cell phone video of people shouting and waving signs that were mostly unreadable, then some other angles that completely minimized the size of the crowd and the police's actions. Additional, similar video bites illustrated the story being told. "The Atlanta PD stepped in quickly, quietly, and efficiently to restore order. Police had to take down one female agitator with their new El-Stat weapon. A few vocal dissidents claimed it was a flagrant civil rights violation, but Ronald Abdulla of the watchdog ACLU agreed entirely with police there was no evidence of that. There was, however, evidence that the woman may have been a lone wolf terrorist. Investigators led by senior FBI agent Clive McWilliams recovered the carpetbag purse the agitator had carried and reported it contained seven pounds of C-4 plastic explosive wired with blasting caps. Agent McWilliams pledged a thorough investigation. The governor said his police and FBI had done a tremendous job, giving them all—and himself—an A plus!"

Then the Eiffel Tower appeared onscreen behind the newsman. "Well, it was a beautiful day in the City of Light today as runners assembled for the Paris Marathon and—" I muted it and angrily threw the remote across the room.

"Whoa, Simone," Clarence said in his most patronizing voice. "What's the problem?"

"That broadcast was a lie! And the local station gave that same footage to CNN!" I turned hotly to him. "I was looking out a window at city hall. I *saw* what really happened. There were at least five to six hundred people. Police used water cannons, and those new flying squad cars were firing on unarmed citizens. It was really—"

Clarence tried to spread calm, as usual. "Simone, Simone, take it easy."

"What are they *talking* about? *Minor disturbance!*" I paced, fuming. "My God, Clarence, people were panicked, getting trampled! That young nurse was no terrorist. They shot her down in cold blood! I saw some posts come up on Facebook showing the real thing just like I'd seen it happen—but before I could blink the posts were *deleted*. The same on Instagram. And Twitter. They blame *technical difficulties* but the truth is being censored by the government while they spread their lies!" I headed for the door. "I'm going into the press office and find out just what the hell is—"

"*Simone* . . ." Clarence stopped me firmly, speaking through a very forced smile.

"What!" I snapped. He gestured toward the kitchen, where LeBron was drinking milk straight out of the carton. I hate that. Clarence pulled at my sleeve. "*What!?*" I was bristling with anger. "I can't speak the truth in my own home?"

Clarence edged me to the hallway, then spoke quietly to me so LeBron couldn't hear, "The police and several private organizations are offering large rewards for informing on dissidents."

I was incredulous. "Dissidents? Me? Because I want the truth?!" Clarence nodded portentously. I hissed at him, "You think our son would *inform* on his own mother?!"

Clarence stared at me, whispering now, "Simone. Our son is talking about joining the police."

24

OPPORTUNITIES

Jimmy-Joe Hartman...

The prison kept getting worser. Whole new bunch come in after some big bust at city hall. Place wuz crowded before, but now they wuz waaaay too many. Wuzn't enough food, toilets always plugged up and filthy, and all them two-man cells wuz crammed with at least four. There'd been two riots. Guys killed. Guards, too. Phil paid off this one guard, Wazinski, to let a few of us sleep on the library floor. Phil'd kinda took me under his wing.

Started back that first day when Phil'd been amazed how fast I caught on to that Dewey shit. Me, too. But them decimal numbers made sense to me like none ever done before. Hadda be my new brain. Same thing happened when I opened a book and discovered I could read like superfast. Phil seen that, too. Trouble was I didn't understand lotsa the words. Phil gave me a dictionary fer little kids, with lotsa pictures. I blowed through that in about a minute. But when he axed me questions 'bout it, we wuz both surprised that I knowed most of the answers. So he gave me a grown-up dictionary. Took me longer t'get through that one. Maybe an hour. Then Phil axed me stuff again 'bout words and what they def-i-nitions wuz. Same deal. I 'membered most all. Him and me wuz starin' at each other. Finally Phil said, "You one of *them*, ain't you?" He'd run acrost a couple others inside. He axed how it happened. I told him 'bout them tomatoes. I axed 'bout them other guys.

"One of 'em was a real educated sciency guy. The other was a punk," he said. "They both got done in by Julio types."

I axed how come I reminded Phil of his kid. He shaked his head. Couldn't put his finger on it. Even though I wuz white, he said there wuz somethin' 'bout my expressions or me havin' such a short fuse that almost got Julio to do me in.

"My boy never got his shit together," Phil said, lookin' away, face gettin' sad. "Never did no studyin'. Never took care o'business. 'Cept his drug dealin'. Got killed by a bunch o'cops. A few months back. When all the po-lice started gettin' hard-ass."

I said I wuz sorry. We just sat a minute. Then I told him it wuz weird I put him in mind of his kid, seein' how his glasses remind me of Poppa.

Phil looked at me, teasin' sorta woo-woo, "Why now that's right cosmic, ain't it, boy?"

And boom. I heard myself sayin', "'*Cosmic*, relatin' to the universe or cosmos, in-con-ceiv-ably vast.'" Then I blinked, looked down at the dictionary in my lap.

"Yeah. Thas right, Jimmy-Joe. You got the *shine*. Wish my son had et one of them tomatoes. Had the chance you got." He looked at me real sharp. "You gonna just piss it away, boy? You for sure ain't done much studyin'."

"Naw," I said, grumbly, "I wuzn't no good at it. Seemed like a waste of time."

He drawed in a big breath and stood up, sayin', "Well, time's some-thin' you got *plenty* of now." He looked around at the shelves, pulled a book out, and gimme it. "There's a good one t'start with."

It look like it was some kinda animal book: *Of Mice and Men*.

Dr. Susan Perry...

The people had been gathering for almost an hour. We'd asked them to arrive at intervals in the fewest cars possible and park inside the empty warehouse next door. If any helicopters or ARPCs passed overhead, we wanted to avoid it looking like what it was: a clandestine meeting about underground resistance to the Friends. Ronnie Dodsworth and Crash were the rock-solid gatekeepers. I'd noticed that Crash seemed intrigued by Ronnie's strong persona, sculpted physique, and particularly those parallel cornrows that ran front to back on her beautiful head. We were just finishing an informal briefing about the CAV-A and -B viruses when Eric and Katie were last to scurry in from the rain.

Crash caught Katie's sleeve. "Hey kiddo, we know you and Eric, but there's a lotta new folks here who don't, so it's a rule that everybody gets checked, huh?" He indicated they should put their hands into a battered suitcase-size unit, like the one I'd seen outside the congregational church on that stormy night seven months ago.

Katie was amazed. "What, you stole one of their screening devices? How?"

Ronnie winked. "Got friends in low places." She activated it. "Good news is it works both ways: they use it to keep us out of their groups. We use it—"

Katie nodded. "To keep them from infiltrating *us*." Crash gave her a fist bump.

Eric slid his hand into the device, saying, "Gives a whole new meaning to Underground Atlanta, huh?" The unit beeped.

"Okay," Ronnie confirmed, "you can come to my party."

Katie slipped her hand in, and the beep sounded. "How does it work?"

Chunhua was nearby, studying it. "Trying to figure that out."

Nate Balfour called out to them in his rapid-fire manner from the coffee setup where he was getting a plastic stirrer to chew on. "Pull up a stool, gotta get this going."

"Yes," I said, "we don't want to have this many of us in one place for any longer than necessary."

Katie McLane...

About three dozen people had turned to watch Eric and me come in. They were settling onto benches, boxes, stools, or the concrete floor of the warehouse. Many were scientists I'd seen working with us. The rest were a mixture of people from well-off to poor, late teens to eighties. Some were state or local cops. Crash sat down next to a man and woman in Air Cavalry military fatigues.

Scanning the new faces, I spotted and smiled at my dad's ex-girlfriend, Tina, who waved to me. There was also a black woman with tortoiseshell glasses sitting next to Nate, who looked familiar, maybe from an Ashton football game. Lilly was sitting to one side, scanning through Aristotle's *Poetics*, and Chris was back in the lab area, working quietly with chemistry equipment. He glanced over as Susan sat on a tall stool facing us. She seemed kinda uncomfortable.

Dr. Susan Perry...

I felt awkward running the meeting with my genius colleague/former lover right behind me, but I pressed on and started with a little gallows humor. "Hi. I'm Susan and I'm *not* a Friend."

Crash and others familiar with 12-step meetings responded, "Hi, Susan."

I smiled. "Thanks. Many of us don't really know each other, except that we're all dedicated to fighting back against the Friends." I told about my work at the CDC and what I'd discovered with Katie's help, then invited the group to quickly introduce themselves and tell who they were. Several were scientists, and all were a cross section of worried, determined people whom we'd carefully vetted and reached out to. Many represented their own clandestine groups from different parts of the city. All expressed encouragement at being among like-minded people. "I think the bottom line is we want to find a way to stop the Friends from dominating everything."

"Before they totally trash the planet," Tina chimed in. Others voiced agreement.

An acquaintance of Nate's named Simone Frederick, who worked at the State Capitol, got more specific. "There've already been a couple of ugly chemical spills at the plant where my husband works." She added with annoyance, "Which they quickly hushed up, of course. Just like that *minor disturbance* at city hall I saw myself." Many reacted angrily about that and the bravery of Claire, who'd been killed.

A rugged man named Javier was in an electric wheelchair. He had the upper body of an Olympic swimmer, but no legs. "Friend of mine told me they'd had some radiation problems down at that experimental cold fusion plant, too."

"Why are we not surprised?" Crash said grimly.

Nate quoted the Friends' doctrine, "'Let's rush to be the best, fastest, most profitable—'"

"And damn the consequences," Simone added.

"Right." I nodded. "So we asked you all here to help formulate a cohesive plan of action against them."

Eric moved to make notes on a dry-marker board, but Katie said, "Um, Eric, sometimes your handwriting . . ."

Eric smiled, handed her the marker. "Go for it, Kate."

"Okay," I said. "First, we've got to protect ourselves from getting accidentally infected." Katie wrote "Protect Ourselves."

"Good news on that front," said Gerald, the balding, thirtysomething Yale chemist. From a Nike shoebox he pulled out one of numerous matchstick-size strips. "You should each take a few. Just touch it to any food or drink that seems suspicious."

The willowy Edinburgh grad, Gwyneth, had joined him. "Aye, and if the strip turns yellow, dump the lot of it."

"And make a note of anyone who tries to slip it to you," Gerald added.

"Yes. We should create a database of those infected," Nate advised.

"We've started one," said a middle-aged businessman wearing a yarmulke, as Katie wrote it down. A much older woman said that her group also had one going. They agreed to coordinate their efforts and get us all access to a secret server. One of Crash's Air Cav friends cautioned, "But it's gotta be carefully encrypted." Then she added, "I can help with that."

"Great," Javier said from his wheelchair. "And add: get weapons. The bigger, the better." But that brought very negative reactions, particularly from Crash and Ronnie. They felt we were far too outgunned and untrained. We could never succeed in out-and-out warfare. The majority agreed.

"Okay," Javier acquiesced. "Then how about: widen the Resistance?"

"Yes, that's the most critical thing." Katie wrote it as I added, "Everyone here and in each of your separate groups should contact at least three other people they can trust."

"But reeeeally carefully," Tina cautioned. "Lots of people are resistant to resistance."

"Yeah, I'm married to one," Simone admitted with frustration.

"Me, too," one of the state cops next to Ronnie added. "The world's gotten pretty cushy for lots of folks. Hard to get people off their asses if they've got jobs and are making money."

"There is one aspect I think we all agree on," I said. "Finding an antidote is key." Katie added it, underlined. "A lot of us here have been working on that for months. And now we're blessed to have Dr. Christopher Smith with us." I pointed him out amid the lab equipment. Chris managed a grudging nod. "He's a Nobel-level research biologist. We hope that together we can find a cure."

"But what *kind* of a cure, Susan?" A woman wearing a Muslim head scarf, Barika, said, disturbed. "What if the only *cure* is to destroy all the infected ones?"

One of Crash's army pals said, "Hey, Barika, if they sucked the damn comet—"

"But are people gonna be killed just because they made the mistake of becoming infected?" Tina said with grave concern.

"Pretty big *mistake*, ma'am," Ronnie huffed.

Javier turned to face Barika, agreeing, "A lot of us have lost family because of them."

"Some of us had family turned *into* them," Katie said pointedly.

Simone supported her. "Right, Katie. And what about all the people who were infected *without their permission*? I mean, it's easy to disparage the Friends' inhumanity, but what about our own ethics?" There was a pause as we considered the dilemma.

"It's a very thorny moral issue. No question," said Eric.

"But until we *have* some kind of cure, it's a moot point," I said, cutting to the chase to keep them on track. "I suggest we put it aside for now." The majority nodded uneasy agreement. I noticed Chris watching me with an expression that seemed supportive of my leadership. I drew a breath. "Okay. One other thing we've got to try to do is infiltrate the Friends."

Katie wrote "Infiltrate" as Nate said, "Yeah. Learn their plans. Get ahead of 'em."

Javier raised his eyebrows. "*That* sounds like the most dangerous game of all."

Crash, who'd had experience with covert ops, nodded. "And you'd be exactly right, brother."

Dr. R.W. Hutcherson...

I'd been alerted that the head honcho was on the way that evening, so I was waiting in the CDC lobby as his three black SUVs arrived. Mitchell's gray-suited posse preceded him inside. He was frowning. Abrupt. As usual. "Where's Lauren?"

"In her private lab," I said, moving in lockstep with him across the Building 18 atrium.

"While I was with the governor just now, he took a call from an old friend asking why our Georgia prisons are so overcrowded. Checking if everything's okay down here." Mitchell glanced at me. "It was the president."

"That imbecile?"

Mitchell smirked. "Be nice, Hutcherson. Pretty soon he'll be *our* imbecile." He shrugged off his overcoat and gave it to an aide. "But I don't like what I'm hearing about the pockets of resistance around the state. Particularly biologists looking to interrupt our flow."

"Understood, sir," I emphatically agreed.

"Anything on Susan Perry?"

"One of our ace patrol units is on it, sir. This week got mighty close."

"Only counts in horseshoes and hand grenades." His hawklike eyes riveted on me.

"We'll find them, sir." As we entered a spacious laboratory, Lauren's personal fiefdom, three white-coated assistants including old Joseph Hartman were working quietly with various lab equipment near the entrance to Lauren's personal office. "And I do have good news about handling the overcrowded prisons. Think I've found an answer."

As we entered, Lauren was hanging up the phone, and her eyes locked on Mitchell's with private electricity that Mitchell returned. He knew Lauren and I had hooked up. Another man approaching fifty might have felt concern about his lover also enjoying the attentions of some younger cowboy. But Mitchell was so solidly entrenched in his power—and knew he could have his enforcer Dubrovski take me on a one-way trip instantly—that he seemed to have no insecurity. Plus I served him well and with good ideas, like the one I was about to present.

Lauren nodded toward the phone. "Did you hear the amounts of our latest dividends from Perini, Grenwald, and BioTeck Industries?"

Mitchell nodded. "Still only the beginning." He stayed focused on Lauren as he spoke aside to me, "What answer for the prison overcrowding?"

"I've developed a . . ." I paused, selecting the word carefully, ". . . solution." I noticed Joseph Hartman passing nearby, and I eased the door closed as I continued, "Which we're just about to test up at Reidsville."

CDC Sec Cam 4004 & 4005 Date: 04/17/21 Time: 19:37:37

Lab Cplx 4004 L. Fletcher. research room; 4005 L. Fletcher, private office

Transcript by: ATLPD-Op 12532 (no audio)

Visual Desc: 4004 shows research room: J. Hartman dismisses other assistants, then moves to eavesdrop at door to L. Fletcher's private office. Simultaneously 4005 shows private office: L. Fletcher, B. Mitchell, listening to R. Hutcherson explain something, then Hutcherson shows small sealed lab container with a green substance, followed by similar container with crystal clear substance.

Courtesy ATL PD, FBI

Dr. Susan Perry...

I was prepping some microscope slides in the lab area of our funky headquarters and looked up at Lilly sitting in a ratty, orange vinyl La-Z-Boy recliner someone had rescued from the roadside. She was unconsciously twisting some strands of her frizzy hair with her usual lack of expression as she quietly turned page after page of Christopher Marlowe's *Doctor Faustus*.

Gwyneth set a sandwich down beside her. "Here you go, lass."

Lilly glanced at it with her downcast eyes, "Peanut b-butter?"

"Aye, Lilly. With apricot preserves," Gwyneth said in her irresistible Scottish accent. "Cut into triangles. Just as you like."

Lilly nodded. "Nice and n-neat." She picked up one, took a bite, and returned to her reading as though Gwyn weren't there. Gwyn smiled, glancing at Lilly's other books nearby: Hawking's *A Brief History of Time* lay completed on a crate beside her, along with Pascal's *Pensées*, Dostoevsky's *The Brothers Karamazov*, and *Happiness Is a Warm Puppy* by Charles Schulz. Gwyn shook her ginger head in amazement, then headed back to her research efforts.

The others who shared our warehouse space completely accepted Lilly's stoic presence. They were always kind to her, but unless they needed to draw information from her amazing memory, they moved around her as if she weren't really there. Lilly wasn't affected by their inattention, being constantly absorbed in her reading, iPad, or connect the dots. Katie, Eric, and a few like Gwyneth would talk to Lilly or answer a question she might ask in her halting voice. But the others, knowing that she was autistic, politely avoided much one-on-one contact, mostly out of their own awkward inability to know what to say. I knew this was the way people often dealt with anyone who had special needs. Chris was different. He got to know Lilly's peculiarities well while we were colleagues and then a couple. He was always kind and open with her. Like many other scientists, he would also avail himself of the vast repository of CDC research stored in her exceptional brain. Lilly never disappointed, was always able to spew fountains of accurate data in her characteristic, flat tone.

While finishing up the slides, I saw Crash frustrated with an antiquated electrical junction box as he ran his fingers through his thick black hair. I asked, "Still no more juice?"

"Not yet, Doc. Wiring in this place looks like Aleppo in '17."

"I saw another transformer farther down the block; can you tap that one?"

"Mebbe." I knew he'd been trying to avoid going that far. He headed off to do the dangerous job, and I called out, "Try not to have a shocking experience, huh?"

He paused to look back at me, chewing his cigar stub. "Nice to know you care."

I looked into his dark eyes, making it clear that I certainly did. He nodded with a smile and continued away. I watched him go, appreciating his skills and smarts. When I turned back, I realized Chris had been watching me. He indicated the stack of my data he'd been studying and grudgingly said, "Not bad. Considering the conditions you've been under."

I was slightly chafed. "Gee, almost a compliment. Thanks."

"But you missed some obvious possibilities."

"Naturally, Dr. Smith. That's why I needed you—to spur me on." With an acerbic smile, I added, "At least *I* wasn't off playing a clarinet in some swamp."

He chuckled. "Yeah. You were working. Remarkably, Susie." His look conveyed genuine respect and even a feeling of our old affection. The moment warmed me. Him, too, I think.

Then Chris tapped at his laptop, beginning to restructure a molecule that floated three-dimensionally on the screen. "You ran an agarose gel electrophoresis of course?"

"Duh. Found no plasmids outside the virus's DNA."

Chris leaned back from the keyboard, drummed his fingers on the rickety arm of the old wooden chair he was sitting in. Then suddenly froze.

"What?" I said. "What is it?" No response. ". . . Chris?"

He was totally still. Staring ahead. "What if . . . What if the plasmids weren't *out*side."

I blinked. Was he nuts? "Chris, there's never been a virus with plasmids *in*side."

"Or a virus that rode in on a comet." He raised his eyebrows.

I laughed in spite of myself. "Jesus! That's brilliant! Grumpy, but brilliant." My mind started flipping through how to explore his hypothesis. "We'd need an electron microscope to verify."

"Is Chunhua making any headway with that old junker?"

I jumped up and hurried off across the warehouse. Glancing back, I was rewarded to see that he was watching me appreciatively. Maybe with renewed affection?

Jimmy-Joe Hartman...

Lots more guys wuz sleepin' on the library floor. Seemed like every spot in the whole prison that'd been empty space had been took up. It was smelly and awful, but leastwise I had my books. I ain't been sleepin' more'n three, four hours a night 'cause I'd been readin' lots. I couldn't believe how gettin' down in to a book could just take y'away to places. I wuzn't inside no prison walls—I wuz hangin' on them sea cliffs with that Count Monty Crisco guy, or chargin' at windmills with ol' Don Quicks-Oat, or listenin' to Atticus Finch tellin' Scout what makes a man trashy, or stompin' around in moondust with Buzz Aldrin. Made me feel like I wuz right out there with 'em all.

Phil'd started me out with easier books, but pretty quick we seen my pumped-up brain could understand lotsa stuff my old pea-brain never woulda. Phil said I wasn't just readin' good, I wuz also "beginnin' to recognize important ideas and concepts." Mebbe, but main thing wuz I just liked it. Made me think 'bout Claire always bustin' my balls to pick up a book. Funny how all it took was goin' to stinkin' prison to get me in to 'em. Couldn't wait to tell Claire 'bout how I finally been hooked. She sure wuz gonna be surprised. And happy.

I felt that fer sure on the day I got to the last page of that huge one, *Les Misérables*. I just closed it real slow and sat there dead still. It wuz a hefty fuckin' read. I knew I didn't quite get it all, but wow. That Jean Valjean guy was some kinda hero. His amazin' story stirred up stuff in me I didn't even know wuz there. Deep down. Like, I dunno, in what they call soul-stuff I guess. Felt like I'd come flyin' outta long, dark tunnel, and the world suddenly opened out around me, all spectacular-like.

I sat there lookin' at that old book, amazed how it made me feel. Then I looked round at all the bookshelves, wonderin' how many others had that kinda power. I laid my hand on the book in my lap, like I mighta touched an old friend. Made me think of when I wuz real little and Claire'd put her hand on my shoulder. I sniffed a little, then realized I had a fuckin' tear in my eye. Damn. I blowed out a long breath. Tryin' to get my head round all I wuz feelin'.

"Hey," somebody whispered. I turned and seen it wuz that big guard Wazinski. He come up real close and slipped somethin' in my shirt pocket. "From your ol' man. He says for you to take it. Right away."

"What *is* it?"

"He said tell you 'Exodus nine, fourteen'—and to *take* it." He headed off quick.

I frowned a sec, then went and pulled out a Bible. Searched out Exodus, ninth chapter, fourteenth verse. "'For this time I will send all my . . . plagues . . . '?"

I kept frownin', tryin' to puzzle out WTF. Then I reached in my pocket and pulled out the little packet Wazinski'd gived me. With one green capsule inside.

Dr. Susan Perry...

Lilly sat under that battered Tiffany lamp in one corner of the shadowy lab area of our Resistance warehouse. She was speed-reading *The Gathering Storm*, Churchill's history of events leading up to World War II. Nearby Chris was peering in the viewer of the old electron microscope Chunhua had indeed gotten to work. Gwyneth, Rachel, Alex, and several others were huddled around their own investigations on the other side of the area. I set down two fresh cups of tea, but Chris didn't glance up from the microscope's binocular eyepiece. I also noticed something highly unusual. "Uh . . . that couldn't be the faintest trace of a smile, could it?"

He moved aside from the scope and urged me to it. "Tell me what you see."

I sat and looked at a grainy image of cell structure magnified 7.5 million times. "Filamentous phage. Couple thousand molecules. B protein?"

"Yes. Go on."

"Arranged around one strand of a DNA molecule about, what, two million AMU?"

"Actually, one million point eight. But who's counting? And . . . ?"

I was beginning to get enthused. "Wait. A single *larger* molecule, of what? A protein?"

"Yeah." He was enjoying my discovery.

I studied the image further. "About a hundred thousand AMU at the end of the phage, attaching it to its host?"

"Looks like it. And now, for twenty-five points and the game, what about just below it?"

I adjusted the critical focus and drew a sudden, excited breath, "Oh my God! There *is* a virion! A plasmid ring *inside* the helix! You were right! Oh, Chris!"

Lilly glanced up momentarily from her thick volume, hearing our enthusiasm and seeing we were like two nerdy kids in a molecular candy store. I gushed, "I'll run a new agarose gel. Retarget the sequencing."

"Yeah. I'll start a serologic test." He got to his feet. "If it's capsid coated—"

I beamed, overlapping his words, "Or has a lipid envelope, then it might be susceptible to inactivation by some agent—"

Chris was nodding exuberantly. "As simple as chloroform—"

"Or *ether*, or—"

I was cut off because he kissed me. It took my breath away, but I instantly gave myself up to it. So did he. We were like two who'd been dying of thirst suddenly finding water. It was joyous. We were back to where we once belonged. Feeling the familiar warmth of each other's breath on our cheeks. It was a wonderful loving, lingering kiss, full of hope and promise.

Then in the midst of it, something happened. Like a light switch being shut off. Like the tide suddenly rushing out. Chris cooled, weakened. Like a time-lapse video of a beautiful flower wilting, its petals withering, falling away. Chris sank onto a lab stool and stared at the floor, seemingly right through it, toward the center of the earth.

I was left standing, emotional, breathing hard. I looked down at him and understood. I rested my hands on his shoulder, spoke gently, "It hasn't abated. After all this time."

He shook his head, deeply tormented, voice choked. "How could it *ever*?" He chuckled bitterly. "They never even got an accurate body count. Just 'a million or so.'"

I tried to find a new way to say what I often had before. "But it wasn't your fault. You didn't *create* a biological weapon, Chris . . . Your research was—"

"What enabled them to do it," he said, sounding empty.

I ached for him, knowing this was why he'd left the CDC—and me—two years ago. This was Chris's unrelenting nightmare demon that had melted his exuberance for science and for life into a mass of misery.

I stood beside him, breathing quietly. "Won't you ever let yourself feel a moment of peace?"

"I want to, Susie. God knows you bring me right to the edge of it. But then . . ." He looked away, grieving. "I get this image . . . of all those people . . . seeing that strange dark cloud rolling toward them . . . wondering what it is . . . not knowing it's going to invade their lungs, burst their capillaries . . ."

"Oh, Chris." I cupped my hand tenderly behind his head.

He leaned his face against my side. His voice became a pained whisper, ". . . All those . . . children, Susie. All those little . . ."

He clenched his teeth. The veins on his forehead hardened as he struggled to contain his turbulent emotion. I felt him start to weep. I whispered, "Oh, my dear boy . . ." I rocked him gently as he quaked, silently, against me.

Kenneth Johnson

Eric Tenzer...

At the urban Atlanta high school where I'd gotten Katie in, she and I were always on the lookout for any sign that the Friends might be sniffing around about us. So when I saw Reverend Abraham Brown and his aides walking up the main hall with the principal, I got edgy.

But as they got closer, a TV news crew intercepted the reverend's group, and I realized this was merely a video sound-bite op for the imposing Dr. Brown, not a posse out to arrest any accomplices of the fugitive Dr. Susan Perry.

I heard the reverend's mellifluent voice resounding down the hallway, ". . . But the main thing I intend to focus on at today's school assembly is *co-op-er-a-tion.*" Though he was talking to the principal, a smarmy bureaucrat, Brown's words were clearly for the benefit of the news crew and ultimately the large audience of the local news. Brown's face adopted a grave sincerity. "Many of us are very concerned about misguided radicals trying to form an unhelpful—even illegal—resistance movement against our local government and police forces that could prove dangerous to the general populace." That felt a little too close for comfort, so I watched and listened carefully.

They stood talking outside the school auditorium where students were gathering. Brown was saying, "I am here to urge students to report anyone who's working against the best interests of our society." As he went on with his smooth litany, several tenth graders headed in, and I saw the reverend give a thorough once-over to several girls of fourteen or fifteen. One particularly caught his lascivious eye: she was wearing a formfitting, scoop-neck T-shirt. She had brown hair in a pixie haircut and horn-rimmed glasses.

She was Katie.

25

PASSAGES

Jimmy-Joe Hartman...

In Reidsville's prison yard one of them beefy inmates who'd beat me up was sicker than shit. He had big purple patches under his skin. He was gurglin' and gaspin' and fell against me. I was wide eyed and scared 'cause all round the yard wuz dozens of cons even worse off. Some of 'em wuz lyin' against the walls, squirmin' in pain, chokin' for breath. I knew they wuz dyin'.

The sun was goin' down, but the guards had left most of us in the yard 'cause mosta the cons couldn't even walk. Wazinski, the guard who'd gived me the green pill, and a prison doctor come to the guy longside me. The doctor checked him and was really shook, talkin' fast. "Same here. Severe subcutaneous bleeding, lungs filling with fluid. Like Ebola. He'll be dead in an hour. Like all the others."

Wazinski looked up at the guards in the watchtowers and on top the admin building who wuz lookin' down into the yard. None of them wuz sick. "Why's it only the inmates?"

"I don't know." The doctor started examinin' me, axed, "No symptoms yet?"

I shook my head. "Nuh uh." My voice kinda quivered.

He was amazed. "You got a guardian angel, boy." Me and Wazinski traded a private glance. Then the doctor prodded him. "Go! Make sure they called the CDC! We need major help!"

Wazinski run off toward admin. The concrete walls of that ol' yard was echoin' with the wails and moans of dyin' men. The doctor looked round at the nightmare, then back at me. "If I was you, boy, I'd do me some serious praying."

Then he got to his feet and run on to check another prisoner, leavin' me to starin' round at all the horror—scared shitless.

Katie McLane...

I was mad that night. Couldn't believe it. Pursued Eric from the kitchen into the living room of the small house Maggie found us all those months ago. "But, Eric, me working for him is like the *perfect opportunity!*"

"It's absolutely out of the question, Katie." He was resolute. "You're too young to play Mata Hari to that—that—!"

"Mata who?" I scrunched my face up.

"Google her!" Eric waved me away, picked up homework he had to check.

I choked back anger, tried to reason with him. "C'mon, Eric, you all said how badly we need to get a spy in among *them*. Now that Reverend Brown—one of their important guys—tells us at school he's *inviting* a few teens to be interns for him, so of course I put my name in and—"

"Katie." Eric turned to face me. "There are disturbing rumors about that *reverend* and his unsavory appetite for young girls. I even saw him eyeing you today, like you were a Good & Plenty."

"I know he did. I made sure of it," I said proudly. Eric was stunned, but I kept at him, "C'mon, you know I can take care of myself, so—"

"No. I won't let you do it."

I flared, shouting, "You're not my father, y'know! Not even my legal guardian!"

He suddenly got calm, low key. "No," he said. "I'm just some jerk who took you in and loved you like his own daughter." I opened my mouth to protest, but he held up his hand, looked me in the eye, shook his head, and went into his room.

I stood there glaring and fuming. I felt so hemmed in. By everything.

Then I found myself looking at the shelf where Eric always left his car key.

Jimmy-Joe Hartman...

Whatever disease wuz killin' all the inmates at Reidsville, it wuz awful ugly. After them blisters, blood started runnin' from their ears, noses, eyes—even out their dicks and asses.

The main cellblock had got real quiet. Walkin' through, I seen most of the cons had died or wuz strugglin' down to last breaths, like they wuz drowndin' in they own blood. One of the books I started readin', *A Journal of the Plague Year*, told 'bout an awful disease like this here, but I'd quit readin' 'cause it wuz so grim. Now here I wuz, seein' it ten times worse.

Old Phil was fadin', too. I sat with him on the concrete floor in the library. It wuz spattered with blood from all the dead guys round us. I was cradlin' the head of the old librarian. His face was covered with them purple bruises. I axed him, "Want a little more water or . . . ?" Phil shaked his head. I felt so helpless. "Listen, Phil. Thanks fer savin' my ass, man. Wish to hell I could do more fer *you*."

Phil managed a sad smile and a faint whisper, "You can, son . . . I want you to . . . just keep . . ." The old man's lips quivered, tryin' to form words. I leaned my ear closer to hear, but Phil's body clutched up and with a final rattly breath, he wuz gone.

I stared down at Phil fer a long time. Mighty sad. Aching to know what he woulda said, though I sorta had an idea. Then I looked around at all the bodies. My chest felt tight, but I kept on breathin'. Feelin' what it wuz like bein' the only one in the middle of all this death who kept on livin'.

Katie McLane...

I didn't have a learner's permit, and I'd never driven more than a couple of miles on back roads the few times my sister, Lisa, had let me. So driving over an hour from Atlanta in the dark made my palms sweat and my body feel like a coiled-up spring. But I needed to go home. Back to Ashton.

I parked under a sycamore tree near my house. I thought maybe just seeing it might give me some comfort, make my heart feel less shriveled. But it didn't. I saw Mom's car in the drive, with scratches on the side from when she'd hit Tina's. Beside it was a shiny new Cadillac Escalade.

Our old two-story, white clapboard house with its forest-green shutters and the lights glowing inside looked warm and inviting. I even glimpsed Mom through the eyelet curtains of the front window, but I knew that woman was not the frazzled, endearing mother I remembered. Infected by the damn virus, she was hardened and fired up by that ugly dominant streak that drove her to try running Tina down.

In the warehouse I'd told Tina how Dad had broken into the quarantine unit so violently, trying to get me. Tina said he'd become so different, so darkened by the virus that Mom gave him. Like lots of people whose partners got infected, Tina had tried to hang on out of loyalty, love, hoping things would somehow change back. But she said his brutality that night I was outside made her leave him for good. Tina was sad. She'd truly loved the man he'd been. So had I.

I heard Lisa and Mom shouting inside the house. Then some glass breaking. God! I just wanted to go inside and grab them and shake off everything that had happened. To get our family back. But I knew I couldn't. Nothing might ever change. My heart clutched, and my eyes got all teary. Coming home to Ashton had only made things worse. Suddenly Lisa blew out the front door angrily. I ducked low, watched her get into the Escalade and burn rubber leaving.

I sat back up—and gasped. Darren was looking in at me.

He raised an eyebrow kinda menacingly, said, "Well, hi there." Seven months older than the last time I saw him, he had peach fuzz on his chin. His voice was deeper. And because of the virus, he had that chilly arrogance.

I watched him warily. ". . . Hi."

"Kinda young to be driving alone," he said. I shrugged, trying to hide my nerves and decide whether to just speed outta there. Darren smiled with that damn gleam in his eye. "You don't seem too glad to see me." He seemed to enjoy me feeling uptight. "Makes you nervous, huh?"

I didn't completely trust my voice. "Yeah."

"I understand. Does it help if I say I'm glad to see *you*?"

"A little." Was he telling the truth?

"I've really missed you, Katie." He saw me studying him. "You can't tell if I'm genuine or playing you."

I measured my answer, decided on honesty. "That's right."

He sighed, seemed sad. "It's kinda weird being in college already. Most all the kids are older." A sly grin crossed his face. "Not as intelligent, but older."

I was getting edgy. "I think I better go." I reached for the ignition key, but he grabbed my arm tightly. My nerves zipped to a razor's edge. I stared into his eyes, which were penetrating. But he released his grip, apologetically.

"Sorry. Didn't mean to frighten you, Katie. I just wish you wouldn't leave." He studied my face, also noticed how my figure had developed, finally drew a long breath. "You know, *I* was very frightened. That day I got the gift."

"Yeah. I was, too." My hands were damp again. "For you."

"But once I got all the way across . . ." He shook his head, trying to express the feeling. "It's . . . beyond extraordinary. And you've gotta admit, the Friends have made some remarkably positive changes."

"Yeah, they have," I said, "if you don't mind democracy crumbling or having your teeth kicked in."

"Well." He shrugged. "Some people need a little discipline."

"Darren, we're not talking discipline," I said, gaining focus. "A lot of innocent people have been beaten, raped. With no caring or compassion or the slightest—"

"Hasn't that kind of thing always gone on?" Darren smiled calmly.

"Not like now."

"Katie, nothing's ideal," he said. "But look at the wonders they've accomplished in less than a year! How they've helped humanity. I mean just—"

"But they don't *have* any humanity!" I flared up. "They think they're some kinda master race!"

Darren smiled. ". . . We *are*."

"Not if you lose your *human feelings* in the bargain!"

"Katie, Katie." He looked at me patiently, sincere. "*I* still have feelings. Particularly for you. But at the same time, it's obvious that we are the next logical evolutionary step."

"No! I don't believe people are supposed to be like what my mother or Lisa or—"

"Hey, listen, I don't think the Friends are perfect, Katie." He saw my surprise. "Some of them have made really big mistakes. Been overzealous." I laughed bitterly. "Okay," he acknowledged, "even cruel. But we could work to change that." He touched my arm. "You and me . . . I see how lonely you are. And I've missed you so much." I wanted to deny it, but couldn't. I looked into his eyes, trying desperately to find the old Darren who had been Dale to my Chip. "Stay, Katie. Please. I know right now that must seem frightening. Maybe even wrong. It did to me, too." He warmed to the subject. "But what happens inside your brain is so utterly magnificent!" His hand tightened encouragingly on my forearm. "Once you see what you and I could accomplish, your doubts will all be washed away. And I'll be right there beside you."

Tears were welling in my eyes. I felt an intense longing, but I said, "I can't, Darren. I'm sorry."

Darren was weighing my words when I saw something in my rearview mirror. A low-slung red Ferrari was easing toward us. I dropped down in the seat to hide as it glided to a stop right beside my car. I heard a familiar voice: Lisa's old boyfriend, Charley Flinn. "Yo, Darren, you fixin' to steal that car?"

Darren sized it up. "Not sure it's worth it."

"Want to make yourself some real bucks, grab somma my stock Monday."

"Yeah, I heard you're going public," Darren said. "Congrats. Sounds like that new solar cell you invented'll be great for the environment and—"

"Even greater for my *wallet*! Check out these wheels! Worth twice Lisa's Escalade."

"Where'd *that* come from, anyway?" Darren asked.

"Microsoft bought her and Jenna's start-up for five point seven mill. Y'oughta catch yourself a piece o' *my* action Monday. Hey, whose car is this anyhoo?"

"Actually," Darren started. I held my breath. Then he said, ". . . I dunno, Charley. Must be a friend o' Lisa's mom."

"Well, between us Friends, I heard we really gotta be looking out for Resistance types. They want to nab one, slip 'em some CAV-B, and turn 'em into *spies* for our team. They're offerin' a big reward: stock options in Perini and other stuff."

From where I was lying low with my face pressed to the front seat, I glanced up at Darren. A slow smile grew on his face as he said, "No kidding? . . . Really?"

"Damn straight," urged Charley.

"Well"—Darren looked down right at me—"I'll be vigilant, Charley. See ya."

Charley nodded and drove on. I eased carefully up to watch him go. I looked at Darren, who was staring after the Ferrari, seemingly as puzzled as I was.

"You're wondering why I didn't turn you in," he said. "So am I." He looked down, avoiding my eyes. "You better leave."

I started the car, then looked back at him with longing. "Darren, I—"

"*Leave!*" His eyes never came up. I saw confused emotions churning in him. I gazed at him a final moment, aching.

Then I pulled away. In my rearview I saw him raise his eyes slowly to watch me go.

Clarence Frederick...

The TV was on, and the local news was showing some ghastly video from down at Reidsville prison. A newscaster said that so far no one had any idea what the horrific fatal disease was or how it had spread like wildfire through the prison. I was only half paying attention, occupied as I was with my own personal turmoil.

I finished putting my tie back on as Shelly Navarro came out of the hotel bathroom with a satisfied smile and wearing only a slip over her very full figure. She nuzzled up and hugged me from behind, saying, "I've been looking forward to this for some time, Clarence. As you well know."

Indeed I did. I felt very awkward but made my best attempt at murmuring a positive response.

"And coincidentally," she said, "this is my second encounter today with a Frederick."

I felt a chill but maintained a steady voice. "What do you mean?"

"HR had a Frederick apply for a job who was supposedly related to you, and they wanted my approval. I asked to have a look." She eased around to my front. "And let me tell you, your boy LeBron is a very handsome young man." Then she pinched my bottom. Like she owned it.

Dr. R. W. Hutcherson...

I'd just returned to the CDC from Reidsville that night and was cruising through Lauren's outer lab when I saw video of myself on the local TV news, standing by our EMT vehicles outside the prison. I was pleased that my expression looked suitably austere as I said to the reporter, "Well, naturally, all of us at the CDC are very concerned, and we've launched an immediate investigation. It's particularly strange that the disease only attacked and struck down all the inmates."

The news anchor added, "The Reverend Dr. Abraham Brown had a differing opinion."

The imposing minister was seen before a bouquet of microphones in front of his stately church. "In one sense, yes, it's a tragedy, and our thoughts and prayers go out to the families of those people who died." He appeared appropriately saddened, then looked directly into the news camera. "But in another sense, it may be a powerful message to all of those who would transgress against God's holy commandments and the letter of the law. Just look who the victims were: thieves, murderers, rapists, child molesters. I have long felt that what our country *needs* is a great and sweeping moral cleansing. I think we should definitely take this occurrence as an urgent sign from the Almighty . . ."

As he went on, I scanned across the several lab assistants and noticed Joseph Hartman sitting apart with his elbows on a lab table and his forehead leaning down on his fists. Looked almost like he was praying.

Going into Lauren's inner sanctum, I saw her behind her elegant desk watching the newscast. She raised one of those perfect eyebrows to me clearly indicating, *Well done.*

I plopped onto her Georgian couch, clomping one snakeskin boot on her polished coffee table. "Thanks, I thought so, too." I wasn't looking at her, but idly spun a nearby Earth globe.

She said, "Bradford wants this *disease*—"

"Spread to other prisons." I nodded. "Already in the works. So we solve two problems at once: make room for more inmates and also—"

"Lower the crime rate." She nodded, pleased to interrupt. "It's a powerful deterrent."

I spun the globe again. "Incidentally, what did I hear his lordship telling you about the Chinese and Russians? They getting edgy about the populism ramping up even more over here?"

Lauren's hackles rose. I loved getting to her. "That was a privileged communication, Dr. Hutcherson. And would you please stop spinning that?"

I looked right at her, smiled, and spun the globe again. "Y'know what?" I said casually, standing up. "I'll go have a little powwow with Mitchell myself."

Lauren was annoyed, but relented. "Yes. The Russians and Chinese *are* nervous about the populist agenda and reports of the United States building up militarily."

"Right. And I'm gonna tell Mitchell we gotta get this show on the road. It's time we got busy picking up all the best draft choices so we'll be the ones calling the national shots."

Simone Frederick...

Clarence was just coming in the door that night. I was angry and getting into it with our son. "LeBron, you haven't got time for a job. You need to spend that time studying! What were you thinking?"

"That I'm eighteen and can do what I want." He was so cocksure and surly.

"I oughta smack you. Where is this job? With the police?"

"I tried, they don't have part time. But Everett needed extra security for some big shipment coming up and—"

"Wait: *Everett?*" I turned on Clarence. "Did you know about—?"

"Not till tonight. I didn't like it either." He pointed at LeBron. "And you should *not* have used my name."

"Why not? Got me hired," LeBron said with a strange little smile, "and that Navarro woman was real nice about it."

I was speechless, but Clarence said, "Listen, son, you've got to be very careful, watch out about that woman."

I laughed angrily as I walked out. "Yeah. I'd say we *all* do!"

The Documentarian…

The worn linoleum floor in Joseph Hartman's kitchen was uneven. The thin layer of plywood beneath it had swelled and shrunk many times over the years. Various sections of the small house had the same or similar symptoms. Built in the middle years of the Great Depression, it was constructed with meager, shoddy materials, which Joseph had attempted to repair or replace over the years since he first mortgaged it in 1987.

In spite of its poor quality, Joseph determined to make it the best home he could on his modest salary as a custodian. He was a good handyman who could fix leaky plumbing or frayed wiring. He'd painted and repainted the kitchen to freshen it, and considered it a small triumph when he managed to get the lopsided cabinet doors to actually close evenly. It had been a good home for him. But it had felt sadly lacking since his beloved wife, Nathalie, had died of melanoma eleven years earlier, leaving him to finish raising Claire and James Joseph on his own. Joseph knew he hadn't been a good enough father to the boy. He'd made mistakes that allowed James Joseph on to a bad course. Joseph prayed about it endlessly, but there was still a hole in his heart.

He stood at the chipped sink in his kitchen that night, slowly washing his one dinner dish, staring out the kitchen window at the darkness. He was thinking about Nathalie, Claire, and James Joseph, who had shared this old house with him and once made it a home. And who now were all lost to him.

The old overhead light fixture flickered and went out. He glanced up at it, then in to the small living room beyond, with its threadbare furniture, where the lights had also gone off. He sighed, tiredly. He knew the patchwork fuse box needed repair. He resolved to attend to it tomorrow and sought a candle to get him through the night.

He opened a box of wooden matches and struck one. As its light flared in the darkness, Joseph gasped. He was startled to see a man's horribly bruised and bloodied face staring in from right outside the back window.

We know all this because his son has told us.

Jimmy-Joe Hartman...

Poppa shouted, "Oh Lord, have mercy!" He rushed to open the back door. I staggered in, leaned against him. When them purple bruises on my face got smeared, Poppa seen that they just been painted on with somebody else's blood. I wuz exhausted, pantin'.

"James Joseph, son! Oh Lord God! I thought you wuz dead!" He eased me onto one of them old ladderback kitchen chairs and grabbed a cloth to mop my sweaty brow, confused about the bruises wipin' off.

"What's with the candle, Pop?" I wheezed. "Forget to pay your 'lectric bill?"

"Oh my boy, how'd you get out?"

"I got out 'cause you saved me, Poppa!" I started feelin' real shaky. "But how'd you know it wuz gonna happen?"

He dodged my question, touchin' my shoulders, my cheeks. "Oh son, I thought you was dead for sure!"

"Yeah, me, too, Poppa. I did, too." I wuz tremblin' somethin' fierce now. Poppa'd told me how a lamp'd burn way too bright just before it blew out. That's how I felt. I was burnin' way too bright. I knew Poppa seen it, too. "I thought I wuz gonna die. But I got out." I laughed real loud. "I . . . aw, Jesus God—"

It wuz like a dam suddenly breaked inside me. Tears come explodin' out. All the emotion I been tryin' to hold back so I could excape come floodin' out. I squinted my eyes tight, wailin' loud, "Poppa . . . Poppa . . ." I clawed at his shoulders with my scratched hands all filthy and bloody. I wuz gaspin', "I had to put stuff on my face so's I'd look dead. They dragged me onto a cart wid a buncha others and dumped us onto a pile outside the walls. By this huge old oak tree. Then they started to scoop up all the bloody corpses with a fuckin' skip loader!" I couldn't hardly breathe again, rememberin' it all. "I had to crawl . . . crawl through . . . a pile of dead bodies . . . before guards . . . started to burn 'em in this great big pit . . ."

Poppa held me tight. "Easy, son. It's okay. It's okay."

"*Hundreds!*" Tears wuz streamin' down my bloody, dirty cheeks. "And all them corpses had they eyes open . . . they wuz . . . starin' back at me . . . like axin' 'How come *you* alive, boy?! Huh? How come?'"

Poppa tightened his arms round me even more. "It's okay, son. I got you now."

I wuz sobbin' all uncontrollable. "Like they wuz axin', 'What *you* done . . . to be *worth* bein' alive, boy? Huh?! You ain't worth shit,'" I shouted, near crazy, "Why the fuck *you* alive, boy?!"

"God's got his reasons, son," Poppa said with certainty. "He surely does." He held me close, whisperin' real calm, "'The Lord is my shepherd, I shall not want . . .'"

I kept on achin', sobbin', lookin' round. "Where's Claire, Poppa? Kinda . . . late, ain't it? When'll she . . . be home? I need to . . . see her . . . tell her I'm sorry . . . 'bout so much . . ."

Poppa looked at me, silent for a second. Then he said, "There'll . . . be time for that, son. There's a time for every purpose under heaven." He was rockin' me gentle. Like Momma used t'do. But his voice was strong. "And right now's a time for you and me t'do important stuff. T'not sit idly by no more while the quality of mercy gets diminished."

26

MARTYRDOM

Dr. Susan Perry...

In the three days since Chris's discovery with the electron microscope, he and I had been doing delicate chemistry in shifts 24/7, trying to create the curative formula Chris thought might work. We'd first infected ten mice with the CAV. We saw them all get extraordinarily more adept at negotiating a maze—and also very aggressive.

Throughout the process Chris was frowning and hunched over. I knew how tormented he was internally. A couple of times I'd reached out to touch his back sympathetically, but stopped myself an inch away. I knew even a loving touch might do more harm than good, might rekindle the turmoil he'd barely managed to get back in check.

Once I turned away and caught Crash watching *me*, though he glanced away immediately. I appreciated his caring and was flattered by the mostly unspoken attraction Crash had evidenced for me. He was a very appealing man and certainly turned the heads of other women. I noticed Ronnie in particular eyeing him. I couldn't blame her. His athletic stature, coal-black hair framing a face that was ruggedly handsome in spite of the brutal scar down his cheek, combined with his innate wisdom and dry sense of humor made him much admired.

But once Chris reentered my life, I was entirely fixated on him because of our deep personal history and because of Chris's profound importance to our cause. Crash respected that, but from occasional glances, I sensed that he wished the circumstances were different.

Near midnight of the third day, we'd treated the mice with Chris's formula. There was no immediate effect. I sat on the couch to wait, answered a couple of text messages, and promptly fell asleep. Awakening early the next morning, I saw Chris checking the rack of cages, but before I could investigate, I was distracted by shouts of trouble from inside the main warehouse door.

Jared Doyle, a big Irish former cop friend of Ronnie's, was roughly pushing two men to the floor with the help of Nate and others. Crash and I rushed over.

"I said spread 'em!" Doyle snapped forcefully, pushing the men down face-first onto the concrete. I saw one was Joseph.

"Wait, wait. It's okay," I said.

"No!" Doyle insisted. "The screening unit said they're infected."

Nate, Eric, and Javier all talked at once, "They're infected?!" "Yes!" "See if they're wired."

"*Wait!*" I shouted. "I know them. They texted they'd be coming. I fell asleep, sorry."

Doyle was gruff. "Well, if you don't mind . . ." He pulled Joseph up off the floor and frisked him while Crash checked the younger man.

"Ain't got no fuckin' wire, man!" the youth snarled. Crash confirmed he was clean.

Joseph nodded respectfully. "Dr. Susan. This is my boy, James Joseph. We came to try and help y'all."

Nate chuckled cynically. "Dominant types *don't* help."

Doyle was equally terse. "With Friends like them, who needs enemies?"

Katie stepped forward, pointing at Joseph. "He did help." We looked at her, surprised. "When my dad was after me at the hospital. He had me, but let me go."

Javier turned his wheelchair toward Katie, suspicious, "Why?"

I spoke up, "Maybe because he was about the most religious and *moral* person I ever met—before Lauren infected him. Without him knowing, I imagine."

"That'd be right, Dr. Susan," Joseph said quietly. "Told me after that I was a test case."

"He worked alongside us at the CDC for years." I touched his shoulder sadly. "How're you doing, Joseph?"

"It's been pretty hard, ma'am."

I told the others how his daughter, Claire, was the brave nurse who'd faced off against the SWAT vehicle at city hall and been killed by the ARPC. How the police later planted explosives in her purse to justify it. Joseph nodded sadly, but it stoked Jimmy-Joe's fury, churned up an angry tear in his eye.

"That's why the fuck we come here, but if y'all don't get it, you can just—"

"*Stop it*, son." Joseph meant business.

Doyle was unmoved. "Okay, so the kid's a loose cannon, and even if Joseph was a saint before, it don't mean anything after they suck the comet."

"Maybe it does," Katie said. "It also happened with Darren. I told you how he let me go, too."

Eric looked at her sourly. He still hadn't forgiven her for making that dangerous trip to Ashton. But I was pondering. "So at least a few still hang on to some humanity and compassion." I looked back at Joseph. "Why'd you come?"

"After they killed Claire, they almost killed James up at Reidsville."

Nate stopped chewing his toothpick, looked sharply at the boy, worried. "That plague?"

"Yes," Joseph said, then looked at me. "Dr. Hutcherson caused it."

"Oh God." I closed my eyes, aggrieved, whispering, "Oh, Hutch . . ."

"Wait." Crash frowned at Joseph, trying to get a grasp of the bizarre concept. "Are you saying that Hutcherson created something that killed all those prisoners?"

"Yes, sir, that's exactly right." Joseph nodded.

Nate had stepped back from Jimmy-Joe. "How do we know he hasn't still got it?"

"I never did," Jimmy-Joe grumbled. "Poppa smuggled a pill to me. I figure the warden and them guards musta got pills, too, or somebody put it in their food, 'cause none of them died neither."

"Bugger all," Scottish Gwyneth growled. "Why would Hutch and them do such a dreadful thing?"

Doyle sniffed. "Prisons are overflowing 'cause of all the people the Friends rounded up over the last year."

"Lot of 'em innocent biologists or other scientists," Nate interjected.

"Yeah, that they made us run in on trumped-up charges," Doyle said. "S'why I bailed outta the PD."

"Dr. Susan, they gonna do other state prisons, too. And worse than that," Joseph said. "They gettin' ready to ship a mighty big load of CAV-B outta state to use somewhere else."

Everyone drew a breath. Nate nodded slowly, whispering the Nazi dream, "'. . . Tomorrow the world.'"

"My son and I figured enough's enough," Joseph said. "We come to try to help y'all."

"We heard that." Crash was still sizing them up. "But trusting you is a whole—"

"If you truly want to help," Chris said, joining us, "then I have a challenge for you gentlemen." He indicated the lab area. "Susan and her team did remarkable initial research. Building on that, I had an idea that might be an antidote for the virus."

385

I was startled that he revealed that. We'd kept the possibility quiet so others working on the problem wouldn't slow their own efforts until we had more assurance. Now everyone had strong, positive reactions and a surge of questions.

But Chris waved them down, saying, "Or . . . it might be very debilitating. Short-circuit neurology to the involuntary systems, which could be lethal." He let that sink in. Then gave them the background on our animal studies and finally told them—and me—where we stood as of that morning. "Seven of the ten subject mice we treated last night seem to have reverted to preinfection normalcy."

Gwyneth asked for all of us, "And the other three?"

"Are dead."

Rachel spoke up soberly, "Well, seventy percent is an excellent success rate for starters."

I nodded agreement. "But not high enough. We've got to do more testing—"

"Of course," Chris said. "But the bottom line is that ultimately it'll need to be tested on someone infected with CAV who volunteers." He looked at the father and son.

"Wait a minute." Simone Frederick had been standing on the periphery. "Are we willing to use tactics that we'd condemn the Friends for using?"

Ronnie said, "I hear ya, Simone, but desperate times mean desperate measures."

Simone didn't back down. "And that's exactly why I'm here. But where do we draw the line about the ends justifying the means?"

Joseph said to her quietly, "Ma'am, maybe that decision has to fall to the volunteer. I know they gonna be shipping out a lot of that dangerous stuff real soon. So y'all got time working against you." Then he looked at Chris. "It's sure good to see you again, Dr. Chris. And I'm ready when you are."

"Whoa! No way, Poppa!" Jimmy-Joe grabbed Joseph's sleeve. "You're too important. Why, you can *spy* for these folks right there on the inside!" Then the boy looked at Chris. "Anybody gonna take your cure, man, it's me." Jimmy-Joe saw his father draw a breath, and stonewalled any objection. "Don't start, Pop. I *need* to do it." He was clearly struggling against emotions to keep his voice steady as he looked into his father's eyes. "For you. For what them bastards . . ."—his throat tightened up—"what they done to Claire. For an old guy I knowed in prison." He forced a dark laugh. "And shit, I shoulda been fuckin' dead already." Then Jimmy-Joe looked at Chris, resolved. "You just say when, man."

The time came only four days later on a cloudy afternoon. We had maximized all the intervening hours with teams working around the clock. Simultaneously Ronnie sought info from her cop friends about the impending CAV shipment, which we wanted to intercept and destroy, but she had no luck. It was a closely guarded secret. Chris modified the formula slightly, and we tested almost a hundred more mice. The rate of apparent success edged up to 73 percent. All of us were concerned about proceeding, except Jimmy-Joe. He was determined.

Finally a clear capsule of fine white powder sat in a Petri dish on the makeshift lab table. Jimmy-Joe eyed it nervously, his brow furrowed. He clearly had mixed emotions as the moment neared. The dominant drive from the virus was clearly tugging at his insides to flee and save himself. It seemed far stronger than the call of liquor to an alcoholic or the magnetic pull of narcotics or opioids to an addict. I could see his body stiffen, his muscles tightening into knots. But the person who most understood the burning conflict raging within Jimmy-Joe was his father. Joseph told me how he'd struggled against himself to let Katie go. He knew the extreme mental push-pull his son was experiencing. Jimmy-Joe was well aware that the medication might be the answer we needed. Or might kill him. Joseph put a comforting hand on his boy's shoulder as Jimmy-Joe stared at the capsule, took a breath. "Thas it?"

Chris nodded. Jimmy-Joe forced a smile to us who were watching silently from a respectful distance. "Well, I'm glad it's a pill. I hate shots." He chuckled nervously as I watched a dark shadow of dominant anger flicker across his face like a creature of the night. Jimmy-Joe struggled to suppress it as he looked at Chris beside him. "So. What's gonna happen, Doc?"

"My hope is it'll close off the same neural channels the virus opened," Chris said, "returning the subject to a preinfection state."

Jimmy-Joe blew out a little puff of air. "Well, this here is one subject that's hopin' his ass off right along with ya." I saw his breathing grow shallow as he looked again at the capsule. I recalled once seeing a high diver standing on the tiny platform at the top of a pencil-thin tower, one hundred feet above a small tank of water below. If the diver hit the water in the precisely correct manner, all was well. But if there was the slightest miscalculation, it was like hitting concrete.

Jimmy-Joe seemed to feel his resolve slipping and suddenly knew he had to hurry. He turned quickly to Joseph, who wrapped his arms around his boy. We watched them have a long hug. Simone looked away, her face tight with misgivings.

Then Jimmy-Joe drew another breath and turned from his father to pick up the capsule.

But it was gone. Jimmy-Joe was confused. "Where'd it go?"

Then his head snapped around to see Joseph smiling gently and swallowing.

We were all stunned. "Poppa!?" Jimmy-Joe went ashen. "No, goddammit!" He reached for his father, and Joseph pulled him tightly into a close embrace, holding him like a vise.

"Sorry, son. Just couldn't bear the thought of losing both my children."

Jimmy-Joe exploded with emotion, shaking free of Joseph's grasp and clutching his shoulders. "No!" He glared at Chris. "You gotta stop him! Y'all can't let him do this!"

Chris and I were both unprepared for Joseph's action, but before we could move, Joseph said calmly, "It's okay, James. It's done."

"Goddammit, Pop." Jimmy-Joe was furious, unrelenting. "You're *important*! Who's gonna spy for 'em? *Me?* I don't mean nothin'! I'm just a piece of shit! I ain't gonna let you do it!"

He grabbed Joseph, as though to turn him upside down and shake the pill out of him. But Joseph laughed, stopped him. "James. Son. It's okay. This is the way I want it."

Crash and Ronnie stepped in to restrain Jimmy-Joe. He flung them off, turned back to his father, who smiled gently as he eased down onto a ratty couch. "It'll be fine, son. You'll see. Come sit beside your poppa."

Jimmy-Joe was still furious. "You stupid, stubborn ol'—"

"Hey, hey, hey," Joseph consoled him, "I'm right where I belong, son. Right here in Jesus's hands. Come sit with me." Jimmy-Joe, collapsing internally, sagged to his father's side.

Eric leaned to Chris, whispered, "How long?" Chris shook his head. None of us knew.

It turned out to be just under five hours. Darkness had fallen outside, and a pall pervaded the atmosphere inside the warehouse. Joseph was suffering. I listened to his failing heart with a stethoscope. My eyes carried the grim report to Chris's. He turned away, angry with himself. Then I looked at Joseph. "What can I get you?"

Despite being in obviously great pain, Joseph somehow maintained his peaceful exterior. He was incredibly composed. "I'd greatly appreciate . . . a little more water, Dr. Susan."

Katie appeared instantly with it. Joseph drank, wincing. Jimmy-Joe, standing to one side, saw it and blew up again, slamming his hand against a wall. He rushed at Chris, but watchful Crash intercepted him. He grabbed Jimmy-Joe. Ronnie caught his other arm.

"You son of a bitch!" Jimmy-Joe shouted at Chris. "Lookit what you done! That ol' man never hurt a fly, and lookit what you done to him!" He swung his searing gaze around. "*All y'all!*"

Simone felt the censure very keenly. It was exactly what she'd feared would happen.

"James Joseph," his poppa called weakly, "come here, son. These folks ain't done nothin' but try their best to help us all." The boy gruffly sat beside his dad. "Pull my covers up," Joseph wheezed. "Gettin' a mite cool in here." Jimmy-Joe did so, and Joseph rested his weakening hand on Jimmy-Joe's arm, which was trembling with anger and tension. "You got to keep the faith, son."

"Ain't got none to keep," Jimmy-Joe said, disconsolately.

His father smiled. "Oh yes, you do. You got my blood runnin' in you . . . so you got to have some of my faith, too. Just gotta let yourself own up to it." His breathing was pained. Everyone who was watching felt it, Simone particularly. But Joseph stayed magnificently on top of it. "I want you to . . . help these people. Help everybody. You hear me, son?" Jimmy-Joe forced an angry nod. Joseph smiled again. "You might even try . . . reading your Bible once in a while."

"I did, Poppa. Read lots o' books in prison. That one, too."

The old man met his son's dark eyes. I saw that there was a lovely light in Joseph's as he said with quiet pleasure, "Really?" His weakening voice had become a whisper, "Tell me, boy . . ."

Jimmy-Joe spoke slowly, softly, and with mild embarrassment, ". . . 'Blessed are the merciful, for they shall obtain mercy.'" Joseph nodded at the verse, which he clearly knew very well, as Jimmy-Joe continued, "'Blessed are the peacemakers, for they shall be called the children of God. Blessed are the meek, for they shall inherit the earth.'" Jimmy-Joe looked at his father, "'Blessed are the pure in heart . . . for they . . . shall see God . . . '"

Joseph's eyes were warm and beatific. And unseeing. Carried forth by Jimmy-Joe's words, his soul had departed.

Jimmy-Joe's jaw set. There was silence in the room. Everyone stood motionless. Jimmy-Joe slowly rested his face on Joseph's chest and wept quietly. I gently closed Joseph's eyelids.

Then Katie and I, very moved and saddened, rested our hands on Jimmy-Joe's back.

Chris, supremely frustrated, feeling a heavier layer of guilt and failure now on his shoulders, went deeper into the lab.

Lilly glanced over for a fleeting moment before she looked away. Even she felt the sadness.

I saw that Simone's face was a bitter mask, which then took on a decisive expression as she abruptly turned and left the warehouse with determination.

Everett Security—Surveillance Archive Stack 1187262AA

Date: 04/28/21 **Time:** 13:12:54 **Cam:** 0127-17-6

Area: 17—Restricted Entry Section 6 & 7

Visual Description: Matches communication below.

Security Office (SO): Possible security breach. We have a lookie-loo. Going to yellow alert. We have an unauthorized adult black female, age indeterminate, civilian clothes, no hard hat, seen moving through RES 6 to 7, possibly taking photos of container being loaded. Unit 26, you're closest, do you copy?

Unit 26: Yes, sir, give me a twenty.

SO: She is left of stack section 23K. Should be about your eleven o'clock.

Unit 26: On it. (static) Yeah. Yeah, I see her. Might be shooting photos.

SO: Going to Red. I'm ringing the bell. (alarm starts)

Unit 26: You! Stand where you are. Hands on your head. Do it now, lady!

Everett Security—Surveillance Archive Stack 1187263AA

Date: 04/28/21 **Time:** 13:12:54

Unit 26 Body Cam: Running toward female suspect who has hands on head. U26's gun in frame.

Unit 26: Keep those hands where I can see 'em, lady.

Suspect: LeBron? Is that you?!

Unit 26: Mom? What the hell are you doing here?!

(Woman turns, has Everett visitor name sticker, "Simone Frederick.")

Frederick: I was going to your dad's office. Guess I got a little lost.

Unit 26: Security, this is 26, stand down. I have ID: Simone Frederick, wife of Clarence Frederick.

(Alarm stops, Clarence Frederick, EMP #3897, in hard hat, seen running in.)

Courtesy Everett Biochem, FBI

Clarence Frederick...

I couldn't believe it. "Simone!" I shouted, "What in the name of God are you—"

"I was just telling, LeBron," she said with self-deprecating humor, "somehow I got stupidly turned around. I was coming to your office to surprise you for lunch and—" She saw Shelly walking in quickly behind me with two security guards. Simone smiled a bit too sweetly. "Oh, you must be Ms. Navarro. So nice to finally meet you."

Shelly was harsh. "Not under these circumstances, Mrs. Frederick. This is a highly restricted area." Her fiery eyes swung to LeBron. "What she was doing?" LeBron mumbled something, and Shelly bellowed, "Out with it, boy, if you want to work here tomorrow!"

"She mighta taken a picture or two, but—"

Shelly snapped at a guard, "Call the police. Mrs. Frederick, I'm having you arrested for trespassing and industrial espionage."

Another guard was rifling through Simone's purse, pulled out her cell phone, but I grabbed it out of his hand. "Let me see that." I tapped it and saw a photo of the shipping container being loaded with individual CAV-B canisters, which all had bogus biohazard symbols to keep nosy people away. I shook the phone right in her face. "How could you do this?!" As she opened her mouth to speak, I slapped her. Everyone was startled, Simone most of all. I shoved the phone in my pocket, grabbed her arm roughly. "I'll take her to meet the police myself." I wrenched her away and started toward the front gate with a guard a few steps in front of us and the others behind as I marched her at a good clip.

Simone hissed at me. "I can't believe you hit me."

"So they'd trust me to take you," I muttered. "You're with the Resistance?"

"Yes. I need information about that shipment. Have you been screwing her?"

"I can't believe you'd put us all in—"

"Desperate times, desperate measures. Have. You. Been—"

"One time! Last week. She'd been harassing me for months, Simone. First with bribes, then threats to fire me. I kept saying no."

"But last week you caved."

"She said if I didn't she'd have you *disappeared*." Simone stared at me. "She can do it. They're dangerous. What would you have done in my place?" She was confounded. I said, "Tell me what you need to know. Quickly!" We were almost to the front gate.

"When it's leaving. Who it's going to. What the route is."

"I don't know much. North, I think. They've kept it very—"

"Find out! Push the 'Bakery' contact on my phone. Tell whoever answers: 'I need a baker's dozen.' Then tell them everything you can."

"I've got to get you out of jail first."

"No! Get the info to them first. People have died, Clarence. More will."

Dr. Susan Perry...

A pigeon fluttered in the warehouse rafters, and a dropping fell onto the corner of Chris's makeshift lab table, but he didn't notice. He was angrily stabbing at computer keys. Suddenly his screen winked off along with all the other equipment. Only a trace of afternoon sunlight came through a narrow crack in the roof. A chorus of groans rose from the scientists working in other lab areas as Chris threw up his hands. "Shit! That's great!" He slammed a book to the floor.

Lilly jumped slightly, glancing from her reading toward me. "Chris's not h-happy."

I patted her shoulder. "No, honey, he's not."

"Is he going a-away again?" Lilly said with her eyes downcast.

"I hope not, Lil. I sure don't want him to." I kissed my sister on the forehead, picked up Chris's book, trying to calm his troubled water. "That transformer's old and funky. Javier's working on a backup genny that'll—"

"It hardly matters." He pushed the book aside. "I can't crack this."

I let a moment pass as he rubbed his aching head, then I said softly, "And it's incredibly hard watching volunteers die." I touched his arm.

"I thought we were so close, Susie." He sighed, and ran his hand through his red hair. "But maybe it's a dead end."

I sat on a seedy vinyl barstool beside him, equally tapped out. "You might be right. Maybe they really *are* the next step. Maybe we should just give up and join 'em. If *you* can't figure it out—and you've got the highest IQ in the field—then I don't see how—" Chris suddenly glanced at me. I'd triggered some idea in him. "What?" I recognized that galvanized look his eyes took on when his agile mind was calculating myriad possibilities. "*What*, Chris?"

He focused sharply on me. "Suppose I did join 'em?"

I felt a chill. "What are you saying?"

"Suppose I took the virus."

"No, no, no—don't even think about—"

"My IQ *was* the highest, wasn't it?" His multifaceted mind was whirring. Dangerously.

I hated to confirm it. "Well, yeah, one-fifty-eight on the last tests we took. Almost the same as Hawking, but Chris—"

"And Lauren was kvetching," he chuckled, "because she was just one-thirtysomething." He looked at me brightly. "So if I took the virus, I'd be way ahead of her. Of all of them."

"*If* that's exactly how the virus works, which we don't know, so that's no reason to try such a hazardous experiment." He opened his mouth to argue, but I kept going, "Yes, your intelligence is *exceptional*. Yes, it would certainly be even *more exceptional* if you took the virus—" I noticed Lilly glance up from her Schopenhauer, reacting to my intensity—but I was intent on driving my point home to Chris. "Should I remind you that there are a couple of slightly unpleasant *side effects*!? Yes, you might find a cure—"

"But I might lose whatever shreds of morality I have." Chris was already mulling how he might well become a very different person.

"You've got way more than shreds," I said. "The man who gave up a fortune in patents, went into a swamp rather than see his creations used for evil. Who can't let himself have any personal joy because of the debt he feels to humanity. You're a grand pain in the ass, Christopher Smith, but your heart is in the right place."

He was pondering. "I wonder if that's enough?"

My head was searing with tension. "Oh God, Chris. How can we know?" I searched his eyes. "It seemed to be enough for Joseph and Katie's friend Darren but . . ."

He unlocked a secured cabinet and took out a vial of red liquid labeled 'CAV-A.' He studied it. "Nice poetic justice, though, this stuff bringing about its own defeat? I've got to admit, Susie, I like the symmetry." He unscrewed the cap.

I grasped his arm, frightened. "No, no. Chris, wait. We've got to think about this."

"While more people die? Like Claire and the others?"

I held his arm tightly, scared. "This involves all of us. You can't just do it."

"Like Joseph said, that decision belongs to the volunteer." He pressed his hand firmly on top of mine. "Just promise that if I veer off down a wrong path . . . or whatever . . . you won't let me keep going."

I went pale. "How could I ever promise that?"

"Because we love each other." His eyes looked deeply into mine. "This is the right choice, Susie. For me. And probably our only chance to save everyone from *them*."

I gazed into his determined eyes and also saw his fear underneath. Could I match the incredibly courageous commitment he was making? I wasn't sure I could ever find that strength, but finally, barely breathing, I made myself nod. Then I watched, with my heart in my throat, as Chris poured a few ccs of the reddish liquid into a medicine cup. He held it up in a small, sad toast. "To Joseph. And victory." Then he drank it down.

I put my arms around him. My cheek pressed against his red beard. I whispered, "You are the best and bravest man I have ever known." I held him tightly. "We'd better tell the others." He nodded, but neither of us moved. Over his shoulder I saw Lilly's eyes flit up momentarily to us holding each other, then to the vial of red liquid, then back to the pages of her book.

Our embrace lingered for a full minute. Finally we took a long breath together, then headed to inform the others.

Katie McLane...

I was in biology class when my teacher was told to send me to the office. I was freaked that they'd discovered my name was false. My heart was fluttering when the principal's sour secretary waved me to his inner office. But he wasn't there. Instead a large man in a tailored suit was looking out a window, watching the girl cheerleaders practicing. My heart did a backflip as I realized who it was. He turned, saying in that deep mellow voice, "Ah, Katharine . . . Bartlett? Is it?" I nodded. "I'm the Reverend Dr. Abraham—"

"Brown. Yes, of course." I smiled and shook his large hand, which was unusually warm.

"I'm *very* happy to make your acquaintance, Katharine. Please, sit."

I eased into the captain's chair that faced the desk. Its wooden arms curved around me slightly. Felt a little like I was in the open jaws of a trap. He sat against the front edge of the principal's tidy desk. "As you know, I'm seeking interns to work alongside me. Sound appealing?"

Ohmigod, I thought excitedly, *whether Eric likes it or not, I'd be a spy on the inside!* I tried to stay cool. "Yes, sir, I think it does. What exactly would I be doing?"

He meandered slowly around my chair. "You'd be one of my closest assistants, Katharine, so it's vital that we always be absolutely truthful with each other."

"Of course," I said as he passed behind me. I felt his fingertip touch the back of my hair. "The pixie cut's an interesting choice. But personally I prefer your blond ringlets."

My blood turned icy. "Uh . . . I'm sorry, what?"

He leaned close to my ear, whispering, "I know who you are, Miss McLane. And that you were in Ashton a few nights ago." He went on in a very personable, friendly tone. "One of your old pals gave us the license plate, which we traced." My heart sank, my eyes closed. *Oh, Darren . . . no.* "The trace led to an Eric Tenzer, with whom we've seen you in CDC security video along with the fugitive Dr. Susan Perry. I'm guessing you're still involved with her."

"No," I blurted, "absolutely not, I—" He pressed the tip of his thick, manicured index finger onto my lips.

"Shhh. Truthful, remember?" Then he took out his cell phone, tapping it as he spoke, "I'm sure you have access. I want you to seek out the very latest information about whatever resistance Dr. Perry is up to and deliver it to my home by ten tomorrow night"—he handed me an address card—"so that nothing further happens to this young man." He showed me a video image on his phone: Darren in a small jail cell, moving back and forth, jittery, very frightened. I stopped breathing. His face was bruised. One eye bloodied, swollen shut.

I was scared, but furious, too. "Why would you do that if he reported me!?"

Brown chuckled. "Darren didn't. It was a young patriot named Charley Flinn. Darren has told us nothing. Yet." He let that word sink in. "I've asked my more aggressive associates to hold off until ten tomorrow night. After that . . ." He shrugged. "And there'll be serious consequences for Eric Tenzer, too."

The big bastard saw how shaken, tormented, and angry I was. He smiled warmly, said quietly, "Perhaps I can make it a little easier for you."

He took out of his pocket a small vial of yellow liquid.

Dr. Susan Perry...

A twilight storm was churning over our Atlanta warehouse that evening. Rain was falling, thunder rumbling like a caged tiger. Chris's mood paralleled the threatening weather. He was pacing with angry impatience. "Susan! I need the damned amino-immunologic analysis, and I need it now!"

Even those who didn't know Chris well recognized he had changed since taking the virus. That dominant glint was now in his eye, and his formerly reserved nature had become petulant. But it was also clear to me how he was struggling against the dark seed planted in him. He snapped again, "Susan!? Goddammit!"

I grabbed the last page of a spreadsheet from our scuffed printer and hurried it to him, passing Crash, who was keeping a weather eye on Chris's gathering storm. Crash knew I was exhausted from trying to deal with Chris's new belligerence and demands. We both knew we could only vaguely comprehend the strife boiling in him. The pendulum swinging within him between hope and darkness. I was determined to eat all the crow necessary to support his struggle. "Sorry, Chris. Your instructions were kind of complex. I had a little trouble—"

"They were the *image* of simplicity," he said with a dismissive grin while scanning through the graphs at lightning speed. "Shit!" He tossed the papers aside, scattering them and startling Lilly nearby. "It's all garbage!"

"Chris," I said gently, trying to calm him, but he raged on, more furious with himself than anything.

"No plasmid interassociation, no viroid linkage, no prion receptor connections. Nothing I can use."

"Why don't you take a rest?" I touched his arm, but he snatched it away.

"Why don't *you* take a fucking *hike*!" His stormy eyes swept across the warehouse, the others had grown quiet, looking away from his outburst. "The whole goddamn lot of you!"

Crash, Ronnie, and also Jimmy-Joe eased on to the alert in case Chris began acting out physically. I drew a breath. "Chris, I can't imagine what you must be going through, but—"

"Right." He laughed. "You certainly can't." He shot me an icy glance, then reined himself in slightly, struggling to focus his anger back onto himself. "I think you were right, Susie. There *is* no damn cure." That truly saddened him, but then a bitter chuckle emerged. "Even when the Scarecrow goes to the Emerald City and gets a brain, he can't find the answer. I'm fucking *useless*!" He bashed a chair, sent it clattering. Crash calmly stood up. Ronnie, too.

Chris drew an irate breath. Then went strangely calm. "I've gotta get out of here for a while."

I smiled. "Good idea, I could use a little walk."

His eyes flashed at me. "Alone." I tipped my head, okay. It seemed like he tried to smile, but it morphed into a smirk. "And I don't need your damn permission, Queen Mother."

He strode off past Lilly, who glanced up at him worriedly, her brow knitted with distress. My own aching eyes found Crash. He understood and discreetly trailed after Chris, who had gruffly blown out the big creaking service door.

Jimmy-Joe Hartman...

When Crash went out, he told me to take his shift as gatekeeper and gived me the Bat Phone. That's this special cell any of us could call in a 'mergency. He wuz barely out the door when the phone ringed, and I answered like he told me, "Goldberg's Bagels." The guy callin' said them code words 'bout 'needin' a baker's dozen,' so I knew he wuz legit. It wuz Simone's husband, Clarence. She been arrested, and he wuz worried 'bout them suckers doin' their enhanced interrogation on her before he could get her out. Meantime she wanted him to give us some info. I grabbed a pen.

Dr. R.W. Hutcherson...

I wasn't always invited into Mitchell and Lauren's private meetings. They'd kept the special out-of-state contacts they'd been creating a closely guarded secret. But I knew something was up when they called me into her CDC office that night. I saw two gray-suits plus big Dubrovski with a Friends' palm ID unit on the secretary's desk. I eased through Lauren's inner door.

The night rain spattered against the window behind Lauren, who sat looking across her elegant desk at the disheveled, bearded man opposite her. His back was to me. His hair and shoulders were wet. Lauren's investigative eyes were drilling into him, trying to be certain of his allegiance. "Well, the fact that you've come forward of your own accord stands you in good favor."

Bradford Mitchell was to one side, also addressing the man in the chair. "The bottom line is that you're here, among Friends, where a man of your intellect definitely belongs—and deserves the financial rewards that'll go with it."

I moved to the opposite side where I could see the man's profile, which I couldn't quite place, but I saw by his tense, troubled countenance that he seemed conflicted about being there. Lauren sought to reassure him, saying, "You've made the right decision." Then she gestured toward me. "This is Dr. R.W. Hutcherson. Hutch, Dr. Christopher Smith."

Without looking, Smith barely nodded his head, but nothing more.

Dr. Susan Perry...

"Wake up, little Susie." It was Crash, whispering.

My eyes snapped open. "Oh, shit!" I was angry that I'd dozed off on the seedy couch while struggling unsuccessfully to turn Chris's near-incomprehensibly complex chemical computations into the answer we needed. I looked for his papers, but somebody'd removed them while I slept. I blinked to gather my wits and realized that the power was off again. "What time is it?"

"Little after eleven, and you aren't the only one who burned out." I saw that the monotonous patter of rain on the tin roof and the darkness had lulled most all of my exhausted colleagues to sleep. Only a few candles provided a soft light. Crash's clothes were soaked. I sat up, looked around for Chris. "He ain't here," Crash said, sitting down on a wooden box. He ran his hand through his wet black hair, mortified. "The great Indian tracker lost him."

I sagged, then touched his wet shoulder as I stood up. "Nobody could've done better. And we've got other problems. Simone's been arrested, but her husband gave us some info." I rubbed my tired eyes and noticed Lilly wasn't in her usual spot. I glanced around the candlelit lab area—and what I saw startled me completely awake. "Lilly?"

My sister was sitting with her back to me at a lab table in the candlelight. Chris's notes were beside her. She was mixing some chemicals!

"What're you—?" I choked myself back, not wanting to frighten Lilly into an accident. "Honey, put that down before you hurt yourself." I eased toward her but halted abruptly as Lilly turned to face me. Her usually unkempt hair was pulled tightly back.

And she was looking at me. Steadily. *Right in the eye.*

I drew a breath. "Lilly?" My voice was an anxious whisper, "What's happened?"

My sister smiled strangely. The candlelight made her smile seem even more eerie, chilling. Then Lilly spoke with a clarity that I had never, ever heard from her:

"I took the virus."

27

METAMORPHOSIS

Dr. Susan Perry...

My blood congealed. "Oh, Lilly, no!" My voice caught in my throat. My eyes searched her face, I prayed it wasn't true. But Lilly's completely uncharacteristic, steady gaze verified what she had said.

She spoke softly, with total assurance and no hint of a stutter, "There's nothing to fear, Susie. I'm well."

Crash came closer behind me. Several others nearby had awakened and realized that something very unusual was going on.

"Actually"—Lilly laughed lightly—"I'm *extraordinarily* well, dear sister." She smiled comfortingly, enjoying the huge understatement, as she reached out her hand to me, still gazing directly into my astonished eyes.

Katie McLane...

Eric and I came quietly into our Resistance warehouse, bringing some groceries. My chest felt so tight I could hardly breathe. Reverend Brown's damn voice kept echoing in my head. I *hated* what he was making me do. When he offered me the CAV-B, I actually considered taking it. I knew it would make me smarter, which might help me figure a way out of this horrible dilemma. But I decided to rely on the brain I already had. I didn't want anything clouding my thinking, and for sure not that dangerous crap—though I had absolutely no idea how to deal with my painful predicament: I *loved* all my friends here, but I was really scared for Darren and Eric. I couldn't let them be tortured or killed.

Then I realized something weird was happening in the warehouse. Eric and I saw there was only candlelight and silence. Everyone was moving slowly toward the lab area in the back that was a little higher than the floor level. They were all gazing at Lilly who was—what?!— *Looking Susan right in the eye?!*

Coming closer I touched the sleeve of the Israeli scientist, Rachel, who whispered to me, "Lilly took the virus!"

Dr. Susan Perry...

Lilly grasped my hand lovingly, then smiled out at the others who were moving closer into the glow of the candles; several carried their own. All of us were amazed by Lilly's remarkable transformation. She had a new countenance that was accessible, inviting, insightful. She seemed to embody the soft humanity and innate wisdom of a Zen master. "There is such clarity now," Lilly said to us with pure enjoyment, "like a veil has lifted."

We all stared in wonder. It felt almost like a candlelit religious ceremony. Then Lilly began to speak more quickly, "Let me explain: many people like me—many kept in institutions—apparently have a latent, ribonucleic viroid. It's held dormant by an enzyme *inside* the amino chains of our DNA molecules—just like Chris postulated and," she paused, realizing that we were all blinking incredulously at her. "I'm sorry," Lilly said with a charming giggle as she looked at me, "this is a bit like when you taught me to ride a bike successfully that first time, Susie. I get so elated, I hate to slow down."

I was more amazed than she. I stared at this person who had been affected by a neurodevelopmental disorder all her life. How could this be my childlike sister with the ever-downcast eyes? How could this be the autistic woman who had needed help to brush her hair? I was staggered by what had become of my beloved, challenged older sibling who, from my earliest memory, had always spoken haltingly in a flat monotone. My pulse was racing as I nervously pressed Lilly's hand. "It's . . . okay. Go on, honey . . ."

She said, "The comet's virus connects with pathology like mine in a way that's . . . exceptional."

I inhaled. "You heard me talking about Chris being exceptional. That's why you took the virus?"

"Yes." Lilly nodded, smiling. "'Exceptional' struck a chord because it was *my* word—the way you've always so kindly described me, Susie. And I've discovered that when autistic savants like me are exposed to the virus, it makes us intellectually superior—but far *beyond* any urge to dominate." We reacted in amazement as Lilly went on, "I can see now that in my autistic state, I was *already* at an intelligence level equal to the Friends. But the myelin sheaths around the axons of my brain cells were impaired, and I lacked the vital, neurological *connective channels* that make correlative thinking possible."

We were all trying to keep up as Lilly continued, "So all that vast reading you let me do, Susie, all those thousands of books, journals, articles from the CDC, and everywhere, including specific research about biochemical neural interactions, all that material that I inhaled nonstop, plus what you and Chris just discovered about the CAV structure—all of that was tremendous *input*, but until I took the virus which opened up those connective channels, my poor brain simply couldn't—"

Lilly and I both burst out laughing, saying it together:

"*Connect the dots!*"

"Yes!" She smiled broadly. "And now I *can*. I'm able to connect and correlate all those billions of input bits. That new ability allowed me to easily extrapolate and deduce exactly how CAV operates on human DNA and neurology. So I instantly understood how Lauren had decreased CAV's potency to create the CAV-B."

"Which is why Lauren's CAV-B makes people somewhat more intelligent, but *not* as driven to domination like those infected by the prime CAV-A?"

"Precisely." Lilly nodded gracefully. "And equally important: I've understood that people with my condition *do not have* that drive to dominate. By infecting myself with the virus"—she took a breath, seemed amazed herself by what she was about to say—"I've actually *surpassed* the level of the dominants."

"My God, Lilly!" I saw the light dawning on several others as it had on me. "You've risen to a level *above* the Friends!? You're . . . *the next step beyond them?*" Lilly modestly nodded yes.

Gwyneth excitedly turned the battered dry board toward us, saying, "So Lilly, lass, is it like this then?" She wrote as she spoke. "Let's call us normal folk: Human 1.0; those given CAV-B are made somewhat smarter, with only a bit of the dominant drive, call them: Human 1.5; and people infected with CAV-A, call them: 'Human 2.0.' Much smarter and with the *strong* drive to dominate." Again Lilly nodded and Gwyneth continued, "But when people like *you* are given CAV, they take a leap that makes them the *most* highly evolved. Call it," she wrote as she spoke, "*Human 3.0.*"

Lilly smiled, inhaling deeply. "Yes, Gwyn. It was as though I'd been in a muddled, troubled sleep and suddenly had a grand awakening. Beyond that actually, more like a complete *enlightenment.*" She pressed my hand lovingly. "I've always wanted to help you, Susie. As much as you've helped me all the years since we were little. Now I truly can." She held out a vial of milky liquid. I was puzzled. Lilly explained patiently, "This is the answer you've all been searching for: the correct molecular structure for your antidote."

I could barely speak. "You've found a way to . . . treat all those infected?!"

Lilly nodded.

Nate voiced the concern plaguing many of us, "Does it bring 'em back, Lilly? Or—"

"No." Lilly shook her head. "There's no bringing them back, Nate." Then her freckled face formed the most curious expression yet. "The correct answer is: to push them *forward*." Everyone blinked again. Even the candles seemed to flicker. "Think about it," Lilly explained softly. "The logical and ideal path of evolutionary progression always leads upward, toward an adaptation that's *better*. In humans that means toward a higher, more intelligent plane that's truly altruistic. Unselfish. Compassionate. And most importantly: soulful. It means for human beings to become entirely *humane* beings." She glanced at the vial in her hand. "This formula will carry everyone upward to that level. And it's easy to demonstrate." Her caring, intelligent eyes sought out one among us. "Would you trust me, James?"

Jimmy-Joe looked at her sharply, with that cynical dark glint in his eye.

Jimmy-Joe Hartman...

Buncha times since Poppa died, I still been tempted by that dark side, heard them angry voices start hissin' inside me. But then I'd think of what ol' Phil done for me, of what he'd want me to do, of all that horror at Reidsville, of Claire bein' so brave, and of Poppa. It'd be like warm water floodin' back acrost me, tryin' to put out all them angry, dangerous fires down deep. But I knowed they was still smolderin' down in there.

And when I heard Lilly ax me, that ol' dark side boiled right up scaldin' hot. Said, *No!* Said, *Fight it and run yo' ass outta there!* Screamed it loud inside my head, like to burst my skull open.

But then I looked into Lilly's eyes . . . and it wuz, I dunno . . . she had . . . some kinda magic in her. And it made somethin' shift in me.

Damned if I didn't let her take my hand and lead me to a chair.

Dr. Susan Perry...

As he sat down, very edgy, Lilly asked, "You took the CAV, right?" Jimmy-Joe nodded. "So, what's 378 multiplied by 1,862?"

"That'd be 703,836." His eyes went wide. "Whoa. Didn't know I could do that!"

Lilly smiled. "But how about 703,836 multiplied by 16,784,221?" He stared. "Uh . . . dunno . . ."

"Nor should you." Lilly knelt before him. "Now, there's nothing to be afraid of." Her gentle nature calmed him only slightly. "This will feel a little startling, you might clutch or slump a little, so I'm going to ask Crash to support your shoulders, but I guarantee you'll be okay. You'll still be you, but better than you can imagine. Just like I am." She showed him a transparent inhaler mask with a tube that led to a small squeeze bottle. "I'm going to hold this over your nose and mouth. You good to go? Ready to take the leap?" He paused, looked about to bolt, but finally nodded. His breathing was still shallow. I saw nervous moisture appear on his upper lip as Crash held his shoulders lightly from behind. Then Lilly lifted the mask up into place. "When I tell you, just take one good breath." Lilly sprayed a fine milky mist into the mask as she said, "Now."

He inhaled. And his entire body clutched slightly. His eyes sprang wide open.

Jimmy-Joe Hartman...

A zillion pictures flashed and wuz swirlin' in my head all at once! Like I wuz in the middle of a tornado! I seen Poppa dyin'. The prison. Them cops beatin' the shit outta me. Them damned tomatoes. Our old house. Claire smilin' in her nurse's scrubs. The moon. The stars. My playpen. Claire when she wuz a little kid kissing my head. Momma. Oh God, I saw Momma. A hospital. Delivery room. Me bein' born. Then this brilliant white light rushin' past all around me.

Katie McLane...

I had moved up closer to stand beside Eric. We watched as Jimmy-Joe's head slumped down onto his chest, his body sagged in the chair, then slightly convulsed. Crash held him in place. Gwyneth and others looked concerned as he started panting. Susan said, "He's hyperventilating!"

Lilly was totally calm. "Yes. Next his heart will fibrillate a moment, then his respiration will normalize."

Susan pressed her ear to his chest. "He *is* fibrillating!"

Lilly smiled with quiet confidence. Nate, Javier, and the rest of us watched in amazement as Jimmy-Joe's breathing grew normal.

Then his head shot up, his eyes snapped open, and he blurted out, "Eleven trillion, eight hundred thirteen billion, three hundred thirty-eight million, nine hundred seventy-one thousand, seven hundred fifty-six."

Lilly smiled. "Of course."

"Yow," he said, catching his breath. "How the hell'd I know that?" Then he paused, like trying to regain his balance, as his new mind understood. "Oh. Yeah. I get it." We sensed Jimmy-Joe was very different. His arrogant, angry, superior vibe was like totally wiped away. When he looked at us, his eyes were clear, soft, friendly.

Dr. Susan Perry...

Jimmy-Joe breathed slowly, looking at each of our faces like a person returning from a life-altering, near-death experience. Seeing the world for the first time. His demeanor was miraculously different. Serene like Lilly's. Jimmy-Joe now had the presence of a sage.

He blinked and looked at Lilly in astonishment. She smiled back at him. They seemed to have an almost telepathic communication. He spoke slowly, in quiet wonder, ". . . Everything seems sorta, I dunno . . ." His newly expanded mind searched for a phrase that might encapsulate the magnitude of what he was feeling. Finally he said, "Clear."

Lilly smiled ironically at the understatement. "Yep. Know the feeling."

Then suddenly everyone was talking at once, asking what the spray was, how Lilly could have devised it and accomplished it so incredibly fast.

"Chris and Susie were close, but hadn't interrelated several key elements." Lilly held up the spray bottle. "Basically it's like the opposite of a typical neurotoxin. Instead of bringing death or paralysis by *blocking* synaptic connections between neurons, this specific molecular formula greatly *enhances* the potassium-sodium flux ratio, accelerating and diversifying the neuroelectrical interlinks between the pons cerebri, the pons cerebelli, and the frontal lobes."

"Rrrright . . ." The uncomprehending Javier chuckled from his wheelchair. "Whatever you say, Lil."

Ronnie was confused, too. "But I still don't get it. How were you able to piece all that together?"

"Simple," I said, touching Lilly's arm, "just *memorize* the entire CDC research library—"

"Not to mention hundreds of other books," Eric chimed in, "about history, philosophy, biography, religion, plus several thousand literary classics!"

"Yes," I went on, "*then* develop an astonishing new brain that can associate, theorize, correlate all that data and"—I laughed again—"connect the dots. Hey, piece of cake."

"Aye," Gwyneth mused, "just your basic supreme wisdom, applied with brilliance."

"It's so strange"—Lilly shrugged modestly—"my mind used to be like a muddy puddle, and it suddenly became a crystal clear, limitless ocean."

Jimmy-Joe's face took on a quirky smile. "And y'all know what? It *feels* good, too."

Chunhua's mind had been working. "So we treat all the infected people with this solution and their drive for dominance will be eliminated?"

"It's not a panacea," Lilly cautioned. "A few people with rare RH factors like AB negative blood, will likely not be changed. But for the most part, it can evolve everyone's minds up to a far higher, soulful ideal."

Crash had picked up the vial of white liquid, peering at it. "'The Milk of Human Kindness.' I can dig it."

Rachel had been pondering and said, "My God, leaders would truly deserve to be leaders."

"You realize of course that was the dream of Socrates and Plato," Nate said. "The unselfish, compassionate, superintelligent philosopher-kings. The ideal leaders of the ideal human community."

Our awestruck group stared at my sister, who smiled back at us with gentle humility. In the candlelight she seemed to glow from within with near divinity.

But one thing had snagged me. "Lilly, you said this could evolve *everyone's* minds. You meant everyone who'd been infected with the CAV-A or CAV-B?"

"No, Susie." Lilly's eyes were positively twinkling. "I meant *everyone* everyone."

A hush fell. Then Crash slowly asked the key question, "Do you mean to say . . . that if *any* of us takes a whiff of this . . . ?"

Lilly nodded. "You'll make exactly the same leap that James and I did: to 3.0."

Stunned silence.

Crash stared, almost reverently, at the bottle in his hand and then eloquently articulated our group reaction, whispering, ". . . Ho-lee shit."

We were all breathless.

After a moment I also whispered, "Yeah," while still trying to gather my amazed wits. "Holy shit, indeed." I tried to imagine it. "A world of Human 3.0s? Talk about 'one giant leap for mankind.'"

"And womankind," Ronnie said with a delighted grin.

We all stared at each other, trying to get our Human 1.0 brains around this staggering concept.

Finally I said, very slowly, "Okaaaay . . ." Then I took a big breath, needing to bring us back to necessities that were pressing. "Okay. What Lilly's done is"—I glanced again at Lilly, a smiling archangel—"beyond astounding." I forced myself to focus. "But listen. Right this second we've all got to stay on track. Chris is missing. He may have gone over to their side." The others reacted with appropriate shock. "Simone's been arrested for snooping at the Everett plant where her husband works." Everyone evidenced more concern as I went on, "Yeah. Means we may have to abandon this place, so we have to prepare for that while we also work quickly to create a large quantity of Lilly's cure."

"But there's so many people infected," Eric said. "How do we cure them all?"

"Pump it into ventilation systems? Spray it from helicopters?" Javier suggested.

Gwyneth shook her head. "Sounds pretty impractical, but—"

"Maybe the best way's one at a time," Crash said. "But we gotta start at the top: shit rolls downhill, right?" He held up the bottle. "*Good* shit'll do the same thing."

"Yes," I agreed, energized. "I've seen a snowball get way bigger, rolling down a mountain, spreading out fast, and turning into an avalanche."

Katie McLane...

Eric put his arm around my shoulder, enthused, "God, Katie, maybe we could win this thing after all."

He had no clue how my stomach was twisting in knots. All I could think about was Darren in that cell, what they'd done to him already. I was scared sick about how much worse would happen to him—and Eric—if I didn't do what Brown demanded.

Meanwhile Lilly agreed with Susan, "Yes. The snowball approach would spread it quickly and exponentially. I can create a few liters of the solution right away, but a larger quantity will take time because first we'll need to replicate a large volume of the virus to use as a base for the formula and—"

"Hey," Jimmy-Joe interrupted, "could y'all use somma that CAV-B as a base?" Lilly nodded. Jimmy-Joe grinned. "Great! 'Cause we know 'bout a whole damn truckload!"

"Right," Susan explained, "Simone's husband sent Jimmy-Joe photos of a shipping container of CAV-B canisters. He said it'll travel on backroads to avoid notice, heading north, likely toward Washington—"

"And all the sitting ducks in Congress, the White House!? . . . Jesus." Nate was fearful.

"Clarence doesn't know exactly *when* it'll depart, but soon," Susan said.

"So we *find out* when and grab it," Crash said.

Others agreed, chimed in with suggestions, their eager voices swimming in my spinning, splitting head, their plans taking shape. I knew that Brown wanted to know those plans.

But I also knew that wasn't all he wanted. I'd seen how he'd looked me over.

And suddenly I realized exactly what I had to do.

Security Cam Video, Private Residential; Case 71782-AB; Date: 04/29/21 Time: 20:08:15

Address: 69 Granville Dr., Atlanta, GA 30318

Loc: Brown Estate Foyer, Night

Cam: # 07

Transcript by: ATL PD - #56230

Visual Desc: Front door chime is answered by Edward Baker, 32, black male, in jacket and tie, assistant to owner. He admits Katharine McLane, 15, white female, in dress w/jacket over. Baker escorts her toward the library-study.

Courtesy ATL PD, FBI

Katie McLane...

At eight o'clock the next night, Dr. Abraham Brown's assistant, Mr. Baker, led me into the private study of the grand old Tudor estate. It had serious furnishings that totally reflected the reverend's "substantial" public image. Dark leather chairs and a matching couch were in front of the fire in the huge stone fireplace.

Bookshelves lined the walls, with one of those rolling ladders to reach high shelves about twelve feet above the polished wood floor. There was a massive rolltop desk large enough for a family to live in. It had a couple dozen drawers, cubbies, and pigeonholes that might hold a treasure trove of secret info if a spy could search them.

"Good evening, Miss McLane." I jumped when I heard that oh-so-deep voice, which he was clearly proud of. I took a nervous breath and turned to see the reverend entering through the tall mahogany archway, wearing a silky crimson lounging jacket. "I'm delighted you decided to honor us with your presence." He took my hand, which looked teensy in his large, thick one as he smiled. "And there's no need to be uneasy, I assure you." He held my hand for slightly longer than necessary, then looked around. "What do you think of my little place?"

"Very impressive, Dr. Brown."

"Abraham, please. Would you like to see a bit more?"

"Sure." I was kinda relieved, 'cause I was very worried about having to get down to business. He gave me a tour of his huge living room with historical stuff gathered from various trips to the Holy Land and a boyhood photo of himself in a group with Dr. Martin Luther King, Jr. He showed me his dining room for twenty, his cushy screening room, and the small chapel where he made his "solemn, daily devotions to Christ Jesus."

Security Cam Video, Private Residential; Case 71782-AB;
Date: 04/29/21 Time: 20:17:05

Loc: Brown Estate Foyer, Grand Stairway Landing

414

Cam: # 08

Transcript by: ATL PD - #56230

Visual Desc: Dr. Brown leads Katharine McLane from chapel to base of grand stairway. He gestures toward second floor, she seems nervous but nods, then precedes him up to first landing, where they stop to admire a statue. Assistant Jay Farrell, white, 28, in jacket and tie approaches upstairs behind them.

Courtesy ATL PD, FBI

On the landing he paused to point out a very lifelike marble statue of three naked girls just slightly younger than me. "The Three Graces," he said. ". . . Exquisite, aren't they?"

"Yeah . . . really," I muttered, getting very tense, my breathing shallow. I was startled by a tailored young guy who'd come up silently behind us, holding a tray with two champagne glasses. As he handed me one, the reverend introduced Jay Farrell as his other house assistant. Then as Farrell walked downstairs, Dr. Brown guided me smoothly up to the second floor with his hand in the curved small of my back. My palms were sweating. I knew I had to focus on the difficult business I'd come for and get it over with as soon as I could.

Security Cam Video, Private Residential; Case 71782-AB; Date: 04/29/21 Time: 20:18:14

Loc: Brown Estate Master Bedroom

Cam: # 13, 14, 15

Transcript by: ATL PD - #56230

Visual Desc: Dr. Brown leads Katharine McLane into master bedroom.

Courtesy ATL PD, FBI

My heart started fluttering wildly as I looked around. The bedroom had a high, beamed ceiling, and furniture with old Englishy patterns. There was a small writing desk with antique inkwells, and a fancy fireplace with a tufted velvet love seat nearby. The creamy carpet was plush. I wondered how many young girls had curled their bare toes into its pile. My stomach was turning inside out. I saw a pair of framed, standing mirrors, which would've provided convenient reflections of whatever was happening on the bed. It was an exceedingly large mahogany four-poster with a patchwork comforter and pillows. I swallowed uncomfortably. "Think it's . . . big enough?"

"It usually is," the reverend said, "specially made for me. I'm rather a large man."

That made me really quake. I turned to look out through the lead glass window, set my champagne glass on the sill, feeling very queasy. "Must be . . ."—my voice was failing now—". . . a nice . . . view from here, huh?"

"Not as nice as my view from here . . ."

In a mirror I could see him looking at my legs, then, setting his own glass aside, he began moving toward me . . .

Security Cam Video, Private Residential; Case 71782-AB; Date: 04/29/21 Time: 20:19:01

Loc: Brown Estate Master Bedroom

Cam: # 13, 14, 15

Transcript by: ATL PD - #56230

Visual Desc: Katharine McLane is looking out the master bedroom window. Dr. Brown approaches her slowly from behind. Places his hands on her shoulders. Then he turns her around and is startled when she sprays a white mist directly in his face.

Courtesy ATL PD, FBI

28

MAYDAY

Dr. Susan Perry...

We were really getting worried. We'd been sitting in an old SUV a half block down from Abraham Brown's Tudor mansion, which Katie had disappeared into fifty-six minutes earlier.

"If she's not out in four more . . . ," Eric said.

Ronnie, in her Atlanta PD uniform, checked her pistol. "I'm ready to rock."

"Hey!" Crash blurted from behind his binoculars, "We got movement at the door!"

We all crowded to look out and saw Katie come flying out of Brown's front door and running toward us. It looked like she was crying hysterically. Crash threw the SUV into gear and sped toward her. Ronnie opened the side door just as Katie reached us, and pulled her in, then Crash burned rubber away. Katie was screaming, "Ohmigod! Ohmigod!"

Eric hugged her. "What did they do to you? Katie!?"

Then we realized she was hysterically *laughing*. "Nothing! It's what I did to *them*! It was perfect! Ohmigod, it was soooo *perfect*! Exactly like we planned!"

"Tell us!" I stammered, amazed, relieved.

"Okay, okay!" She was gushing, trying to catch her breath. "First I checked out like who else was there. Only his two assistant guys, Baker and Farrell. Farrell was actually kinda cute, he had—"

"Katie!" Ronnie shouted, "Get to the—"

"Yeah, yeah, okay. Then I got Brown to take me away from them. Upstairs. To his bedroom."

"What!" Eric scolded, "I told you no Mata Hari!"

Katie grinned. "Don't worry, we didn't *dooo* anything. Although he was just about to try when I sprayed him."

Ronnie was loving it. "And . . . ?"

"It was just like we saw with Jimmy-Joe. He clenched up, sorta convulsed, then collapsed in a heap and lay there a minute. But then when he woke up? Oh. My. God."

"Oh my God, what?" Crash shouted as he kept driving fast.

"Exactly that! 'Oh. My. God!' He fell to his knees in front of me, saying it over and over, '*Oh. My. God.*' It was like he suddenly realized what a lying, hypocritical, child-molesting, shitheel he'd been and was facedown at my feet begging forgiveness, sobbing, tearing his hair. He took the Leap big-time. It was like Born Again on steroids—times infinity!"

"So how'd you handle him?"

"Just like we rehearsed it, Suse. I stayed calm, knelt there beside him, explained what had happened and why. His tears kept like pouring out, but he was nodding, understanding like every single word. Eager—*begging*—to make amends for all his many transgressions. I told him exactly how he was going to do that. He called each of his guys in one at a time, and we sprayed them. Same deal, same reaction."

"Three for three. Sonuvabitch," Crash said. "You rock, Katie!"

"Then I told him to call Ashton," Katie went on. "He got Darren released right away."

"Brilliant, Kate." Eric hugged her again. "Perfect."

"Thanks. And he's working on getting Simone out, too. Then I told him the other stuff: to keep all this totally secret, that we'd let him know when to arrange an urgent meeting at his house with Mitchell, Lauren, and Hutch so we can juice them."

Ronnie focused in. "What about that shipment? Did he know when it's—"

"Day after tomorrow: May first," Katie said, "leaving the Everett plant at three o'clock in the afternoon 'cause they want it to arrive in Washington in the middle of the night."

I reached over, cupped the back of her pixie head, and pulled her in for a big kiss on the cheek. "Katie, you are incredible."

"Thanks, Suse . . . And I asked about Chris, too, but Brown hadn't met him or had any contact yet. He offered to try to get some info from Lauren or Hutch, but—"

"That might've made them suspicious and—"

"Exactly what he and I decided. Sorry, Suse. Hopefully we'll get Chris back soon."

"Yeah." I nodded and gave another kiss and hug to the amazing young woman.

But I remained very worried about Chris.

The Documentarian...

On the morning of May first, the day that shipment of CAV-B was going to move, it was very warm. On days like that the Resistance team would let some air into the warehouse by pushing the large barn door outward, swinging it all the way open and folded back against the outside wall. Because of that, the envelope [seen below], which had been attached to the face of the door, wasn't seen that morning. It was not discovered until two days later. It was a note written by Dr. Christopher Smith.

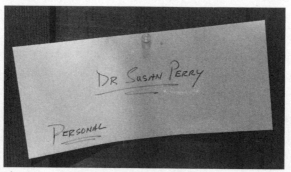

Courtesy Katie McLane

It's important to bear in mind that Dr. Smith had left the ware-house headquarters *before* Lilly had taken her Leap. So he was totally unaware that Lilly had created a cure.

His handwritten letter read:

Dear Susie,

Because of my inability to discover an antidote for the CAV, I decided my best course of action was to let the Friends think I had joined them. Having infected myself, I passed their test to prove I was "one of them." My intention was to work against them from within, somehow incapacitating or perhaps even doing away with Mitchell, Lauren, and the core leaders. But I quickly realized there would always be others driven by their desire to dominate who would immediately move up to take over leadership. I realized it was impossible to swim against such a tide—until a cure can be discovered.

Today I learned that the Friends, having honed their puppet master techniques in Georgia, are planning to move against the national government in DC by infecting many officials with CAV-B. They're about to transport a large shipment of it to Washington. I intend to do my utmost to sabotage and destroy that shipment. I know that will only postpone their efforts, but my hope is that I might at least buy you some time to find a cure.

I'm well aware that my effort will be a one-way trip, Susie. I want you to know I'm content with that. It may also be some small payback for the many lives that were taken by the horrific chemical weapon I was responsible for.

Godspeed, Susie. I have always loved you . . .

Chris

Dr. Smith's letter was not discovered nor read until *after* the following events had taken place.

Esteban Ford, 53, truck driver . . .

We'd got the 18-wheeler rigged and ready there at Everett Biochemical. They'uz just settin' the final ties on the container that'uz sittin' on the flatbed. It'uz just one of them regular containers like y'see on railroad cars or them gigantor container ships. I'uz way more interested in them two ARPCs that'uz gonna be escortin' our truck. I'd been checkin' 'em out. Ain't seen one up close before. Pretty hot. Like t'drive me one, see what it feels like t'be able t'take off and fly right over a traffic jam. That'd be livin' large.

I'uz about t'climb up behind the wheel o'the truck when this red-head guy with a beard come up. He had a security tag round his neck like the rest o'us. Name'uz Smith, Christopher. He said it'uz gonna be a long haul, and he'd like t'take the first leg. Fine by me, but I'uz confused, said, "I thought that big Samuelson guy wuz gonna be goin' with me."

"He's not feelin' so good. Hungover, I think. Told me to do it."

I shrugged, it'uz fine by me. I'd just as soon ride along and snooze. Smith mounted up, I rode shotgun. One of them ARPCs drove around in front o'us, give us a little whoop-whoop signal from his siren, and we headed on out with the second ARPC right behind.

Katie McLane…

The four of us were huddled outside the back entrance to Dr. Brown's library-study. Me, Eric, Gwyneth, and Susan. Through the door we could hear Lauren Fletcher and Hutch in the study talking quietly to Brown. They'd arrived a few minutes earlier and were waiting for Bradford Mitchell.

I was nervous because, just before we left the warehouse, I saw Susan give a flash drive to Lilly and tell her it had all the information we'd uncovered plus an audio journal she'd been recording about everything up till that day. She wanted to make sure Lilly had it "just in case." It was those three words that made me uneasy. Like Susan had a premonition things might not go like we wanted. Like something might happen to her.

But suddenly I couldn't think about it because we heard Mitchell's strong voice coming into the study, saying with annoyance, "This can't take long. The shipment is rolling. The chopper's waiting to take us to DC to get with our people and be ready when the truck rolls in. So why was this meeting so goddamn urgent, Brown?"

We heard Brown's soothing voice, "You'll understand very quickly, sir. I think you know Baker and Farrell here. We have something to show you all."

I imagined his two guys going to Lauren and Hutch while Brown stepped closer to Mitchell. I hoped they couldn't hear my heart pounding. There were a couple of seconds of silence and then *kerthlump*. Like bodies hitting the floor. Then we heard the reverend call out, "Dr. Perry?"

We opened the door and rushed in to see Lauren, Hutch, and Mitchell all on the floor, convulsing slightly. After a minute Hutch and Lauren began to wake up.

Dr. R.W. Hutcherson...

It was . . . beyond imagining. All my thinking, priorities, ethics, were entirely altered, upgraded, enhanced. The mental brilliance I'd received from the Friends' initial gift had been astonishing, but this . . . this reached into the depths of my being.

It was overwhelming, as though I'd gone unconscious as an infant and awakened as Athena, the goddess of wisdom, springing fully formed and mature from the mind of Zeus. This new . . . evolution . . . brought far more than intellect; it brought clarity, understanding, empathy, and a serene soulfulness beyond measure. Tears of joy and gratitude filled my eyes as I tried to catch my breath, to comprehend—

But then I saw Susan and Katie standing over me—and suddenly there came a terrifying backwash; a nightmarish, turbulent tsunami of shame, guilt, and nausea churning catastrophically over me, uprooting my heart, shredding my nerves, ripping the fabric of my being, regurgitating the horrors I'd committed. Bile rose in my throat. I grabbed for a trash can nearby on the floor and shoved my head in, vomiting violently, then dry heaving, trying to expel all the burning malice and cruelty I'd been responsible for. But I couldn't. I was choked, repeatedly, by the faith I'd breached, the trust I'd betrayed, the pain I'd inflicted. The lives I'd taken.

Katie McLane...

Seeing Hutch vomit his guts out over and over again, I can't deny how I felt that was only the smallest taste of what he truly deserved. Yes, I remembered the good guy he'd once been, but the bad had been far too extreme. I stood there watching with my teeth clenched. Glad that we had eliminated him as an adversary.

But feeling absolutely no compassion.

Dr. R. W. Hutcherson...

When I finally came up for air, exhausted and weak from the vomiting, I saw that right beside me on the floor Lauren was undergoing similar convulsive responses to this new awakening. She was gagging, panting, tearfully amazed—yet simultaneously thunderstruck, agonized, distraught, emitting a mournful, "Horrifying . . . !" She painfully clutched fistfuls of her hair, white knuckles jammed against her temples, staring *into* herself wild eyed, rocking in place, her voice high pitched, plaintive. "What have we done . . . ? How could I have . . . ?" Her haughty, biting superiority had vanished. Lauren had become a different woman, staggered as her new consciousness confronted the breadth of the evil her old self had generated. She sobbed, repeating tearfully, "Horrifying . . . *horrifying* . . ."

Then Mitchell began to quiver with emotion as his eyes opened slowly, startled such as I'd never seen him. Of the three of us Mitchell seemed the most shocked and revolted by the monstrous, malevolent immorality he had unleashed. His breaths came in short, powerful growls as he got weakly onto his knees, staring straight ahead, seemingly watching the entire panorama of his wrongdoings play back before his horrorstricken eyes. His nostrils flared with each locomotive grunt, which repeatedly sent massive tremors through his large frame. His normally granite-solid stature quaked again and again apparently from turmoil like my own, roiling deep within. It was like watching the malicious Mr. Hyde transform before my eyes into the humble picture of humility, the ultimately humane Dr. Jekyll.

Eric Tenzer...

Bradford Mitchell had clearly been shaken to the core of his being. He was not tearful like Lauren or Hutch, but I saw his lower lip trembling with emotional stress. Finally, like the old soldier he was, he gritted his teeth, set his jaw hard, and seemed to shoulder the tremendous mountain of his guilt, taking responsibility for the enormity of evil he had caused.

Still on his knees, he looked around at all of us, then bowed his head like a supplicant, speaking with a low, strong voice, "We—I—have to . . . set things right."

It was very clear that Mitchell, Lauren, and Hutch had all taken the Leap. Each had achieved a new birth of humanistic insight. Such extraordinary turnarounds would have been impossible to believe were it not for the similar transformations Katie had triggered in Brown and his assistants, plus Jimmy-Joe's change that we'd witnessed—and of course Lilly's own astonishing metamorphosis.

As they slowly came fully into the moment, we helped them up, explained the situation.

Hutch was still swallowing surging emotions and nausea, but had great concern and said to Mitchell, "But if that CAV-B shipment gets to our Washington people, they'll just take over leadership and continue."

"We know that," Susan said. "Our team is on the way to intercept it."

"You mean *destroy* it, I hope," Mitchell said, with the certainty that it was the only correct choice.

"No." Gwyneth shook her head. "We need that large supply to use as a base so that Lilly can create more of this." She held up one of the spray bottles of white liquid.

Dr. R.W. Hutcherson...

"Lilly?" I choked saying her name, new tears welled in my eyes. *"Lilly created . . . ?"*

Susan and the others nodded, but Mitchell had been processing the situation and was all business, though now completely, uncharacteristically subservient as he spoke softly, "Dr. Perry, there will be a time for . . . the enormous congratulations and gratitude you and your team obviously deserve for this"—he shook his head—"this astounding breakthrough. I appreciate that you have people attempting to capture that shipment, but I have a profound desire to be *certain* they're successful. We absolutely cannot allow that material to reach Washington. May I use the helicopter I have standing by to personally intercept that convoy?" Susan nodded. Mitchell looked to Brown and Lauren. "Will you two come along to help treat anyone with this cure who might need it?" Lauren was shaky, but agreed. "And Dr. Hutcherson," Mitchell said respectfully, "could I ask you to do likewise with our people at the CDC?"

I nodded. As we headed out, Susan said to Mitchell, "I'd like to go with you."

I saw him look into her eyes with admiration and sincerity. "I'd welcome that, Dr. Perry."

Katie McLane...

Outside, Susan, Lauren, and Dr. Brown climbed into the back of Mitchell's stretch limo as he shouted to his bulldog of a driver, "Dubrovski, we've got to get to that chopper as quickly as possible."

The driver snapped a nod. "Sir. Yes, sir." They sped off as Eric got in our SUV's driver's seat while Gwyneth, Hutch, and I climbed aboard. I hated sitting beside Hutch. Wouldn't look at him. I know he felt it.

As we headed for the CDC, Hutch was still very emotional, trying to get his head around it all. "Katie," he asked with a tremble in his throat, "was it really . . . Lilly?"

I stared straight ahead. "Yes. Really Lilly."

"Is she . . . all right?"

"Better than all right. And much better than the way I found her"— I turned, looked him right in the eye—"after you ran away. She survived what you tried to do to her. She might even forgive you. But I can't."

He held my gaze. "I'm"—his voice cracked—"so ashamed."

I stiffened, stared forward again. "Sure. Now."

We rode in silence. Finally he asked quietly how Lilly accomplished it. When Gwyneth told him, he was beyond amazed.

"And it elevates infected people up to 3.0?"

"Not just them," Gwyneth said. "It can elevate *everybody*."

As Hutch processed the concept, his voice became a whisper, "But that could . . . change the world."

"Aye," Gwyneth confirmed, "there is that." Hutch was appropriately stunned.

Then I glanced sharply at him. "'Course it doesn't make up for all the bad things some people have done."

I had to give him credit: he took the punch. Nodded acceptance of guilt.

Gwyneth added, "And Lilly said there is a tiny percentage of people—with AB negative blood—it might not work on."

Hutch pondered it all for a moment. Then suddenly jumped like he'd been struck by lightning.

His face went totally white. Panicked.

Elia Dubrovski, 43, Bradford Mitchell's security chief...

Dr. Perry was in the middle of the back seat. Dr. Fletcher on her left, Brown on her right. Mr. Mitchell was on the rear-facing seat opposite 'em, the back o'his seat was against the back o'mine. They was all real quiet. I knew somethin' big had gone down. Then I heard a cell phone vibrate. Dr. Perry looked surprised. As she was gettin' it out, Mr. Mitchell said, "I'll take that." She looked at him, and we all saw that he'd pulled his Walther PPK outta his jacket. Perry stared a second, then handed him her phone.

The reverend and Dr. Fletcher looked confused, talked at the same time: "What are you doing?" ". . . Bradford?"

Pop. Pop. A clean bullet into each of their heads. Blood across the back window.

I fuckin' freaked, swerved the car. Mitchell put that hot gun muzzle right against my temple and said, icy calm, "Just keep driving, Elia. Get us to that chopper."

"Yes, sir. Yes, sir!"

Dr. Perry was startled when he'd done the others, now she was breathin' shallow, starin' at Mitchell. He looked down at her cell phone in his hand, hefted it. "A bit heavy."

She kept starin' right at him. ". . . Latest model sat phone."

"Ah. And you just got a text from Hutcherson." Mitchell sounded real cagey. "Would you like to guess what it says?"

"Probably that you're AB negative and faking your change."

He was surprised, but in control. "And you and Hutcherson would know that because . . . ?"

"Of the original workup that Prashant Sidana did on you. Rest his soul."

"And I was able to fake it because . . . ?"

She shrugged. "You just watched how Hutch and Lauren reacted, followed their lead."

"Very clever, Dr. Perry."

"Well, I had a little help."

Mitchell kept focused, readin' her, said sarcastically, "You took the great Leap."

I looked at her in my rearview. She nodded at him.

"Think that'll help you dodge a bullet?" he said as he tossed her phone onto the seat beside him.

She drew a breath. "I sure hope so."

I clutched as he raised his pistol—just as her phone rang again. He paused, then picked it up—and suddenly he started shriekin' and convulsin' like he was being electrocuted!

Dr. Perry dived for the floor as Mitchell fired the gun blindly, wildly. I slammed on the brakes, bailed out. Twisted my ankle real bad. Perry scrambled out the back, tried to help me get to the curb, but we didn't make it all the way. Couple bullets hit beside us. We dropped down. That big, tough sonuvabitch had staggered out and fired the last of his clip. Then he stumbled into the driver seat and drove off swervin', fast.

"Shit," she said, breathing hard. "They sprayed you, Elia, right?"

"Yeah, yeah, your Alex guy and that Chinese chick, Choo-Ha—"

"Chunhua."

"Yeah. They gave me the Leap while you guys was all inside. I'm wid you, Doc. But I didn't 'spect him to pull the gun."

"It's okay. S'okay." She was gaspin' kinda.

Then I seen she'd took a bullet on her left side and was bleedin' out bad, gettin' hazy. I was scramblin' to dial 911 while I asked, "What shocked him so bad?"

"My phone." She was breathin' in short puffs. "Because I'd taken the Leap . . . I remembered Mitchell was . . . AB neg . . . wouldn't be affected . . . I had Chunhua rig a Taser . . . into my phone." She showed me an opal ring on her finger. "It also has . . . a couple remotes." I saw two tiny buttons attached on the back. She said one rang the phone, the other fired the Taser.

"The electric charge was . . ." She was really strugglin' t'breathe. ". . . was enough to . . . knock down a mule. But . . . apparently not an asshole." She looked off the way Mitchell'd driven, and one more time muttered, "Shit . . ."

And then she was gone.

Esteban Ford . . .

I'd dozed off while that Chris Smith guy'uz drivin', but I woked up when I felt somethin' sharp stick into my left thigh. I seen that sonuvabitch'd gimme some kinda shot with a needle right through my jeans. "What the hell!" I reached over to swat at him, sayin', "What're you—whoa . . ." All of a sudden my arms and legs didn't feel like they belonged to me. And I got dizzy every time I turned my head.

"It's just a little Nembutal," he said. "Won't kill you, just keep you kind of limp and out of it."

Limp was right, it'uz like I'uz moving through molasses. I could barely get my mouth and tongue to make words. "Whhhy juh hellyoud ooo jhat?"

"So we wouldn't have any disagreements."

I looked out and struggled hard to focus on where we were. Looked like old Route 23, 'bout an hour north of Atlanta past Buford. Small two-lane country road, almost no traffic, just our rig with that container, one ARPC in front, t'other behind. Way farther back'uz a dusty, blue civilian car. But I ain't got no way t'tell the ARPCs what's up.

"So here's the deal, Esteban," Smith says, just as clear-eyed as could be. "In a few miles this truck and everything in it—and on it—is going to come to a very dead end and go blooey. But if you sit there and behave yourself, I'll roll you out just before we get to that last stop. Okay?" It'uz too hard to talk, so I just nodded. He patted my knee. "Atta boy."

GEORGIA AIR NATL GUARD BLACK HAWK BLF 8788 -
Date: 05/01/21 Time: 16:10:13

Transcript Analysis [Abridged] **by:** Evans, DuShawn GA/ANG 8753

Ckpt Cam A/V: Shows condition nominal. Preflight complete.

Heads-Up Displays: functioning. Targeting Grid: inactive.

Engine: At Max Idle.

Description: Pilot and Copilot interact.

Pilot: ANG base, Black Hawk Bravo Lima Foxtrot, request takeoff clearance.

COM: Bravo Lima, stand by.

(Pilot and Copilot react to male voice coming aboard)

Male Voice: I'm in! Get airborne.

Co-P: Is it just you, sir? We were expecting—

Male Voice: It's just me. Get going, goddammit!

Pilot: I need you to strap in, sir, before I can—

(Man sticks his head into frame beside Pilot, ID is Bradford Mitchell)

Mitchell: You get this fucking Black Hawk up now, Lieutenant, or I'll have your balls in a meat grinder.

COM: Bravo Lima Foxtrot, cleared for takeoff.

Pilot: Copy base, Bravo Lima cleared.

Mitchell: Head north up Route 23. We have to catch that shipment convoy. Monitor them on 109.3.

Pilot: Copy that, sir. 109.3. Please hang on.

(Copilot adjusts radio, aircraft ascends.)

Courtesy GA/ANG

Esteban Ford...

We'uz only about five miles farther on when Smith seen somethin' in his side mirror and mumbled, "What the hell? Another one?" Was all I could do t'twist my head t'look into my right mirror. I seen another ARPC comin' in behind. But the new one'uz up in the air.

Veronica (Ronnie) Dodsworth, 33...

Crash was flying the ARPC he'd stolen from the swamp. We'd been barely skimmin' the tops of trees. Then he clipped a couple, givin' us serious jolts, and I wasn't happy. "Uh . . . you wanna come up a touch, partner? Don't feel like you've gotta live up to your name."

Crash smiled, chewing that disgusting unlit cigar stub. "Sorry. Tryin' to stay in their blind spot." He was scoping out the convoy. "Okay, so we got two ARPCs, at twelve and six."

431

"How about that civilian car half a click back there?"

"Shouldn't be a factor. Got that targeting grid on again?"

"Yeah, I think so. You might've given me more than one practice shot."

"Trying t'save ammo, Veronica. Can you see how much charge that El-Stat's got left."

I searched the heads-up targeting display, which I'd only half figured out. "Looks like about seventy-one percent."

"Okay, I'm gonna come in low off the starboard of the trailing vehicle. You shoot for the tires. Try to disable him on the ground and not kill anybody."

I was frazzled by the targeting controls. "Sure. Yeah. Any other requests?"

"Light my cigar?"

I came back with, "Light *this*, mofo."

He laughed and said, "Hang on, Veronica, we're going in." I suddenly went weightless as he made a steep dive toward the rear ARPC. My first shot was short, but my second burst splattered sparks off the right fender, blew out both right tires. Crash shouted, "Whoa! Annie Oakley lives!"

Esteban Ford...

I heard the blowouts and seen in my side mirror the ARPC on our tail swerve onto the right shoulder, where it dug in and rolled over on its top. Smith was startled, lookin' around angry, mutterin', "What the hell? Oh no, no, no! Don't screw this up!"

Then we seen the side turbines on the ARPC in front of us fold out and turn on.

Ronnie Dodsworth...

The front ARPC rose up in the air right in front of us. Crash smiled, saying, "That's it, pally, get on up here." Then to me, "Let him get clear of the truck, Veronica, then give him a kick in the ass."

Esteban Ford...

The front ARPC banked off to the left with the new ARPC right on his tail. Smith was really pissed, shouting, "No, goddammit! I had this!" He pounded the big rig's steering wheel. "Shit!"

GEORGIA AIR NATL GUARD BLACK HAWK BLF 8788 -
Date: 05/01/21 Time: 16:22:43

Transcript Analysis [Abridged] **by:** Evans, DuShawn GA/ANG 8753

Ckpt Cam A/V: Description: Pilot, Copilot interact. Bradford Mitchell's head seen between them.

ARPC Com: Mayday, mayday. This is Everett convoy red leader. We are under attack from rogue ARPC.

Mitchell: Fuck. Contact your base. Call for support. Now!

Pilot: ANG base, Black Hawk Bravo Lima Foxtrot, request backup on authority of Bradford Mitchell. Route 23, north of Buford. Monitor 109.3.

COM: Bravo Lima, stand by.

Mitchell: Put the pedal to the metal, soldier.

Pilot: Copy, sir.

(airspeed increase to 182 MPH)

Courtesy GA/ANG

Ronnie Dodsworth...

The ARPC was trying evasives, banking right and left, but Crash was a top gun. Right on his tail. He'd told me to take out the rear turbine that provided forward thrust, but I hadn't had a clear shot. "Uh . . . anytime there, Veronica."

"Yeah, yeah. Tryin' to get a lock." I fired once, went wide left. Twice, close right. I paused. Inhaled. Held it. Then sent the third burst, which wasn't perfect but caught the inner edge of the rear turbine with a flurry of sparks that shut it down. Crash had to peel off quick to avoid a rear-ender. We looked back and saw the wounded ARPC just hanging there over the woods, rotating dead in the air.

Esteban Ford...

When the ARPCs went off in a dogfight, Smith veered onto a side road and slowed to a stop. "Time to bail, Esteban." I was still really limp. He popped my seat belt, reached across to open my door, then eased me out to where I crumpled down onto the ground. "Take care," he said, then sped off down that side road with the right door flapping.

Ronnie Dodsworth...

We'd banked back toward Route 23 and were surprised to see the CAV truck had gone off on a smaller tree-lined side road. Crash keyed a sat phone, said into it, "Okay, Brenda, showtime!"

I heard a staticky woman's voice respond, "Copy that."

"Brenda?" I shouted, "Who the hell is *Brenda*!?"

Crash just grinned and dived our ARPC down to fly parallel along-side the cab of the 18-wheeler. We were startled to see the driver was Chris Smith!

We started waving and shouting to him to stop. He recognized us but shouted back really furious, "No! I got this. *Back off!*" And he kept on driving, even faster. We couldn't shoot at his tires for fear of wrecking and destroying the CAV-B shipment.

"What the hell is he doing?!" Crash was annoyed, pulled us up steeply to see where Chris was headed, and we both took an *oh shit* breath. About a mile ahead, beyond a chain-link perimeter fence, was a natural gas well, and a gas storage tank the size of a barn. Crash understood. "He's on a kamikaze mission."

At that moment we were startled when our ARPC took a severe hit from behind. We looked back and saw that blue civilian car closing on our tail. It was an unmarked ARPC.

ARPC GSP Unit 494 Cockpit Cam A/V - Date: 05/01/21 Time: 16:32:01

[Abridged]

Dash Cam A/V: Shows Rogue ARPC being pursued, 113 meters ahead.

Targeting Grid: Active, crosshair on, ARPC 494 maneuvering to acquire target lock for El-Stat weapon.

Pilot: Patton, Brice J.

Co-P: Green, Timothy R.

Pilot Patton: Ooo-eee! Almost, Timbo.

Co-P Green: And you thought we were suckin' hind tit back there, Brice.

Pilot Patton: We gonna nail these fuckers.

Courtesy GSP, FBI

Ronnie Dodsworth...

Crash dodged and weaved, but they winged us again. Our ARPC started sounding untrustworthy. And they were closing on us. Crash shouted to me, "I'm gonna try something, Veronica. We'll be looking right at 'em but you'll only have a second to shoot."

I shouted back, "Go!" And Crash spun our ARPC like a plate on a stick into a flat one-eighty. I barely saw them coming at us but fired anyway. The El-Stat burst caught 'em head-on, exploding their cockpit. Crash pulled up just enough for them to pass below us. I saw 'em hit the ground hard, blowing up in a ball of flame.

Crash was already banking around after Chris. We saw his truck smashing right through the perimeter fence, heading straight for the huge gas storage tank. Our ARPC was shaking, listing to one side, losing altitude. "Crash . . . I don't think we're gonna—"

"Hang on, girlfriend!" His eyes were riveted ahead. "May not be the smoothest, but . . ."

We were headed for the storage tank ourselves, angling in from the side to cross Chris's path, when the ARPC shuddered and listed precariously left. Crash had to set us down so hard that we dug in and rolled over once, twice—thank God for seat belts and airbags—and came to a stop right side up by the storage tank, blocking Chris, who slammed on his brakes. The big rig fishtailed but kept roaring right at us till it stopped about six inches from my door, kickin' up a cloud of dust.

Chris jumped out of the truck, hopping mad. "Goddammit! Sonuvabitch! I told you I had this, for Crissake! This load's gotta be destroyed!"

"No! It's gotta be *saved*!" Crash shouted as he helped me crawl out my wrecked window. "We've got a *cure*, man! A fuckin' *cure*! But we need this load as a base to make more. We gotta get this container outta here."

Chris was stunned but still livid. "Oh, really!? And you think more cops aren't on the way? Think nobody's gonna notice us driving it outta here?"

"We ain't driving it anywhere." He keyed his sat phone. "C'mon in, Brenda!" We heard a thundering thump thump thumping, and flying in over the treetops came the most giant-ass chopper I'd ever seen. "Sikorsky CH-53E Super Stallion." Crash grinned at Chris and me. "You saw the pilots at our warehouse meeting. Jose and Brenda. My Air Cav buds." Crash jumped onto the flatbed holding the container. "Let's get this sucker hitched up!"

Within four and a half minutes, the container was secured to cables hanging from the huge chopper hovering overhead. Then it lifted off with Crash, me, and Chris sitting on top of the container, legs dangling over the side, holding on to the cables. Chris was still steaming, looking down at the forest whippin' by underneath us with a couple roads running through it. Chris shouted over the thunder of the chopper, "And you don't think we're pretty easy to spot up here coming into Atlanta?"

"Not where we're headed, pal. Relax," Crash shouted. But he saw Chris was still staring down, fuming. "I know what's going on here, Dr. Christopher Smith. You're pissed 'cause you didn't kill yourself, huh?" Chris looked sharply at him. "Well, you still got that choice, brother." Crash indicated the ground zipping past below, went on shouting, "A header from two hundred feet'll do you. Go ahead." From Chris's expression I thought he was seriously considering it. Then Crash shouted louder at him, "Orrrrr, you could knock off the goddamn pity party and suck it up!" Chris glanced at him. "Stop indulgin' your guilt! Being so damn self-centered! Jesus, man." Crash laughed. "You been given an incredible gift: that big-ass brain in your stubborn head. It was *already* amazing and then it got *supersized* with the virus, and now this cure, this *Leap*, will take you to . . . to another *planet!*" Chris looked slightly inquisitive. "Yeah." Crash nodded. "You won't believe it. Or who found the cure. Lilly!"

Chris was stunned. Crash laughed again. "That's right! Wait'll you meet the all-new and improved Lilly! She'll blow your mind! And speakin' of—lemme tell you somethin'—you got a responsibility, pal. *You've* got one of the most brilliant minds there is, particularly about this biochemical shit. If this situation was reversed, what'd you be telling me to do, Chris? Shoot myself and go tits up in the bay or get out there and use my chops to make the world a little better?"

Chris was pondering the question as Crash's sat phone crackled, and the female pilot's voice said, "We're on final, boss."

We'd been passing low over the small green islands in Lake Lanier and were heading toward a very isolated cove on the remote south side of War Hill Park. We recognized Jimmy-Joe on the shoreline, waving to us along with Tina and Doyle, both in scuba gear, in a Zodiac. Our massive

Super Stallion lowered the container down and right into the water. The three of us hopped into the Zodiac as Doyle supervised the lowering of the container until it was completely hidden below the surface and secure on the lake bottom. Chris understood, of course: the individual canisters of CAV-B would be just fine underwater, and we could take them out in small, less noticeable batches.

Crash and I had climbed onto the shoreline. We sat on a rock and were watching Tina and Doyle free up the cables. Then Crash glanced kinda sideways at me, said, "Nice job out there, Veronica."

"Well, you sure know how to show a girl a good time." I gave him a fist bump.

He kept looking at me, sorta deep, then eyed the cornrows on my head. "I think I finally realized what they make you look like—"

"I know, I know, heard it from couple other wise guys: *a hood ornament.*"

Crash laughed. "Actually I was thinking way more classic than that: a *figurehead*. One of those strong women that sailors carved on the prow of clipper ships to watch out for 'em, keep 'em safe."

I gazed into his eyes, very touched. Then bumped his shoulder shy-like, but appreciative. It all felt kinda good. Kinda special.

We looked out along the cove's shoreline to where Chris was standing alone at the edge of the water a small distance from us, watching as the operation concluded. Crash got to his feet, came to attention, and saluted his smiling pilot buds, who saluted back as they rotated the big chopper away and banked off into the sunset.

And still Chris stood, frowning, weighing all that Crash had laid on him. We saw Jimmy-Joe walk over to stand beside him. Then the boy said a few words to Chris. We couldn't hear what they were, but Chris glanced at Jimmy-Joe, who nodded, like to make a point. Then he touched Chris on the shoulder and walked on.

Leaving Chris thinking.

29

LEAP YEARS

Dr. Susan Perry…

I'd lost a lot of blood, but Elia Dubrovski and the paramedics saved my life.

Mitchell was captured, and convicted of the murders of Lauren Fletcher and Dr. Brown. He realized after his arrest that a dictator without a power base was no longer a dictator. In a plea deal to avoid the death penalty, he gave up all his contacts, including those who'd been waiting in Washington. Belligerent, narcissistic, and egocentric to the end, Mitchell decided if *he* couldn't be the authoritarian leader, then he wanted no one else to be.

One after another, the people who had been infected with the primary or secondary virus, who had been driven to seek selfish power and domination over others, were treated with Lilly's extraordinary formula, and took the Leap. After they inhaled the mist of milky vapor, went to sleep, and awakened to discover their new and exalted mind-set, they were astonished by the transformation within themselves. They gratefully welcomed their startling new consciousness and how they had been soulfully evolved. Each then helped to pass that remarkable change along to others. So the numbers of the 3.0s grew exponentially, like a candle-lighting ceremony.

Dozens, then hundreds, of infected people were treated and looked out through reborn eyes, their intelligence advanced, their compassion, morality, and humanity not merely restored, but amazingly heightened, strengthened, and embraced. Their entire beings had taken a quantum leap forward.

Katie watched as her father, Jason; her mother, Eileen; her sister, Lisa; as well as Charley Flinn and the other townspeople of Ashton were all lifted up to the new, august plateau. Tina and Jason agreed to try again, and Eileen genuinely wished them well.

I witnessed Darren awaken and look up into Katie's waiting, smiling eyes that were brimming with happy tears. Darren instantly realized the splendid new elevation within himself and reached out to Katie, who hugged him tightly.

One by one, members of the police, military, media, business, and government, as well as all the ordinary people who had been infected, were administered the cure. All were not merely cleansed, but took the Leap upward on the wings of Lilly's magnificent discovery.

Some among the top-level cadre of the Friends became the most changed of all. Many sought solace for their crimes in lonely, self-imposed exile, contemplation, and atonement. The greater and the more ill-used that their power had been, the more humble they now sought to be.

There were some, however, when arriving upon this higher plateau, who could not face what they had done, nor blame being under the virus's influence, despite the courts' willingness to be lenient. Some could not forgive themselves and became disconsolate, even suicidal. I accompanied Lilly to visit one who was in that turmoil. Lilly wanted Hutch to hear in person her genuine forgiveness, to encourage him to use his knowledge and abilities for the greater good.

We found him very weak, stretched out on the couch in his Montana-flavored town house, his snakeskin boots on the floor nearby. In a low voice he recounted his guilt for the horrors he had perpetrated, not just upon Lilly, but upon the hundreds who had died agonizing deaths at Reidsville prison because of him. He knew that Chris suffered from a similar guilt, but Chris's had come entirely unintentionally. Hutch knew that his own evil had not. He'd been so swept up by the rush of superiority, power, and entitlement that he'd betrayed the essence of the person he'd always thought he was.

He pointed to a small digital recorder into which he'd dictated his side of the story. He said he'd recorded his final entry after revisiting the prison, standing beneath the huge old oak tree near the mass grave that the piles of dead prisoners had been bulldozed into. All those he had murdered. Hutch said his soul was empty. He apologized for his cowardice about facing the future, for his inability to bear the impossible weight of that guilt. He stared into an abyss. The remorse Hutch felt for the ugly vein of darkness that had emerged from within himself could only be relieved by the massive dose of Dilaudid he was now succumbing to. He turned away and whispered that we should leave him. That he deserved to die alone.

But we remained. The last thing Hutch saw was Lilly's forgiving face.

The several thousand who'd been infected by the viruses became new and far better people than they ever could have imagined: far more intelligent, yes, but most importantly far more empathetic, compassionate, and desirous of treating others the way they would want themselves to be treated. They became truly *humane*.

The most wonderful aspect of Lilly's solution was that it not only transformed virus victims, but transformed *everyone* who breathed it in, including the 1 percent who were AB negative, because Lilly quickly engineered a modification that worked on them. She also formulated a treatment to cure aggressiveness in infected animals.

All of our scientist colleagues and Resistance compatriots, like Gwyneth, Chunhua, Alex, Rachel, and the others who had worked so diligently to help, eagerly stepped up for their breath of fresh consciousness and expanded intelligence. That naturally included Katie; Eric; Nate; Justinia; Fernando and Maggie; Simone, Clarence, and LeBron Frederick—who was thrilled to get his long-wished-for brain boost. It also gave him a jolt of lovely humility that greatly pleased his parents.

True to their independent spirits, Crash and Ronnie, who'd become a couple, were content to stay as they were. At least for now. And it was one of the great joys of my life when Chris asked if I would administer Lilly's formula to him, which I did wholeheartedly.

Naturally we also reached out to many others across the scientific community, notably to Concetta Cordaro, PhD, the astrophysicist who'd first realized that Comet Avery was heading our way. Connie spread it to her colleagues, and they to others, and so on.

It really was like a candle-lighting ceremony—on an epic, global scale. Within only a few years, Lilly's magnificent solution has spread the evolutionary, revolutionary miracle around the world like a balm.

Nate had said it was like Plato's dream of the ideal society come true. But I thought it was even better: it was Sir Francis Bacon's dream. He believed that there would be no gain to humanity if the extension of knowledge brought no gain in benevolence. "Of all virtues and dignities of the mind, goodness is the greatest." Sir Francis had longed for an Age of Reason, a true *Enlightenment*.

Thanks to Lilly's brilliant gift the entire populace of Earth is becoming enlightened: setting aside ignorance for knowledge, discarding superstition for science, facts, and truth. This enlightenment is marrying spiritual altruism with meaningful social action. It is replacing racism, sexism, and bigotry with understanding, empathy, and tolerance.

With America leading, the individual people across our entire planet are evolving for the better. It is certainly not Utopia yet. There are still too many areas of overcrowding, poverty, and potential famine, but thanks to the overwhelming international outpouring of compassionate thinking and concerted, hands-on action, the tide is turning. We've taken the first steps to hammer our swords into plowshares and our spears into pruning hooks, as Isaiah counseled, to ensure that "nation shall not lift up sword against nation, neither shall they learn war any more." We are moving swiftly toward the brightest possible future. Yes, there are still tribes and nations and varying religions, of course; but above all, and transcending all, there has come a new way of living in harmony with our fellow creatures.

A new human *ethic*.

We're no longer facing a dystopian Brave New World, but exactly the opposite: a worthwhile new world. Populated by good people who are properly *human-istic*.

Best of all, we've discovered over recent years that this ethic is passed along to our children, who are being born with this wonderful, pervasive enlightenment built in.

And candle lighting has quickly become a magical way to celebrate our new world.

The Enlightenment is now an annual international celebration on the winter solstices: December 21 in the Northern Hemisphere and June 21 in the Southern, when Earth is tilted farthest away, toward the darkness of space, and beginning its journey back toward the light. People by the hundreds, then the thousands, and now uncountable millions gather before dawn that day on their village commons, small town centers, at sports stadiums, in Times Square, the heart of Jerusalem, Trafalgar Square, Red Square, the shore of Sydney Harbor, the Hollywood Bowl, Rio de Janeiro's Ipanema Beach, China's Forbidden City, the banks of the River Ganges, the mystical mountaintop at Machu Picchu, everywhere there is humankind.

People gather to be a part of the ceremony where one single candle or torch or bright cell phone light in the center slowly begets another, and the lights multiply exponentially, spreading outward until they become an amazing, brilliantly glittering multitude. It is a soul-stirring event to witness.

Even more so to be a part of.

We would very much welcome you to our next celebration which is upcoming.

On the following page is your personal, engraved invitation . . .

Dr. Susan Perry-Smith, Dr. Christopher Perry-Smith

Katharine Olivia McLane, PhD, Darren Joshua Green, Esq.,

& Community Organizer James Joseph Hartman

Representing the Special United Nations Committee

Request the pleasure of your company at

The Seventh Annual International

~~ *Enlightenment Celebration* ~~

on the field and grandstands of

The Atlanta Stadium, 35 Northside Drive NW, Atlanta, Georgia

from four o'clock a.m. until sunrise

On 21 December of this year

Featuring the Atlanta Symphony Orchestra and Chorus

and

Nobel Peace Prize Laureate Lilly Bessie Perry

Attire: warm & comfortable ~~ Breakfast to be served

Please RSVP to www.cdc.gov/enlightenment

Admission is Free

Donations will be gratefully accepted on behalf of

Doctors Without Borders, Amnesty International and many others

~~~~~~

As at all Enlightenment celebrations,

ours will include the singing of its international anthem

composed by John Lennon

Which concludes with the words~

"You may say I'm a dreamer

But I'm not the only one

I hope someday you'll join us

And the world will be as one"

~~~~~~

ACKNOWLEDGMENTS

For their invaluable help in getting this book into your hands, I am greatly indebted to:

My friends at the Johns Hopkins University Applied Physics Laboratory (JHUAPL) including: Uday Shankar & Justin Atchison, for expertly calculating Comet Avery's velocities, complex orbital dynamics, and for providing the astronomical charts and deep-sky photos.

Seneca Bessling, also at JHUAPL, for her biological and biotechnology expertise.

Dr. Lisa Prato at Lowell Observatory for her key suggestion of the star DF Tau.

And particularly Alice Berman, my dear friend at JHUAPL, for her broad-ranging scientific advice and suggestions (including Starfire) and for introducing me to all the brilliant people above—plus inviting me to speak at the APL. It was my honor to do so, to meet them all, and thank them in person.

Gifted artist Damon Freeman for his sterling cover design.

Editor Tegan Tigani, who once again brought her sharp, smart ideas for fixes and enhancements with excellent taste, superlative instincts, and beguiling humor.

Copyeditor Elisabeth Rinaldi for her fine-tooth-combing, thorough fact-checking, and insightful ideas on turning a phrase to improve it immeasurably.

Senior Editor Jason Kirk at Amazon's 47North, who reacted so strongly to my concept and, as he had with *The Man of Legends* before, expertly guided this novel through the entire publishing process.

Italia Gandolfo at Gandolfo, Helin & Fountain Literary Management, for her wisdom, ongoing perspectives, and for introducing me to Jason.

Of course I reserve my deepest personal gratitude to the most solid, humanistic helpmate and moral compass that anyone could hope for, my wise, witty, and wonderful wife, Susie.

And lastly, to the late beloved educator, Susie's sister, Jessie May Appling, without whom there would never have been a Susie.

*Portions of the author's proceeds
from this work go to benefit
Doctors Without Borders,
Amnesty International,
and
The David Sheldrick Wildlife Trust.*

ABOUT THE AUTHOR

Kenneth Johnson has been a successful writer-producer-director of film and television for more than four decades. Creator of the landmark original miniseries *V*, he also produced *The Six Million Dollar Man* and created iconic Emmy-winning shows such as *The Bionic Woman*, *The Incredible Hulk*, and *Alien Nation*. In addition, he directed numerous TV movies as well as the feature films *Short Circuit 2* and *Steel*. Johnson has received multiple Saturn Awards from the Academy of Science Fiction, Fantasy and Horror Films, as well as the Sci-Fi Universe Lifetime Achievement Award and the prestigious Founders Award from the Viewers for Quality Television. He has presented his unique graduate-level seminar, *The Filmmaking Experience*, at UCLA, USC, NYU, Loyola, the New York Film Academy, the National Film and Television School (UK), Moscow State University (Russia), and many others. The author of the recent bestseller *The Man of Legends* and *V: The Second Generation*, Kenneth and his wife, Susan, who have been married forty-one years, live in Los Angeles with their latest two golden retriever rescues. Visit Johnson at kennethjohnson.us and www.facebook.com/KennethJohnsonAuthor.